FOR ALWAYS

FOR ALWAYS

THE INSTANT ALWAYS
book one

a novel by

ari wright

Blue-Eyed Books

This book is a work of fiction. The names, characters and events in this book are the products of the author's imagination or are used fictitiously. Any similarity to real persons living or dead is coincidental and not intended by the author.

For Always: The Instant Always Book One

The cover design and editorial work for this book are entirely the product of the author. Gatekeeper Press did not participate in and is not responsible for any aspect of these elements.

Library of Congress Control Number: 2023935208

ISBN (Paperback): 9781662938429
eISBN: 9781662938078

TO EVERY VICTIM WHO BECAME A SURVIVOR,
WITH THE HOPE THESE WORDS MIGHT
REMIND YOU HOW VERY BRAVE AND BRILLIANT
YOU TRULY ARE.

PLAYLIST

CLAIR DE LUNE—FLIGHT FACILITIES, CHRISTINE HOBERG
GOODBYE—BILLIE EILISH
SORRY HAHA I FELL ASLEEP—EGG
WE FELL IN LOVE IN OCTOBER—GIRL IN RED
TONGUE TIED—GROUPLOVE
LIKE LUST—MOVEMENT
IN THE KITCHEN—RENEÉ RAPP
TECHNICOLOUR BEAT—OH WONDER
NEW YORK, I LOVE YOU BUT YOU'RE BRINGING ME DOWN—
LCD SOUNDSYSTEM
PULSE—IDER
ANSWER—PHANTOGRAM
TURNING PAGE—SYDNEY ROSE
FALLSS—BAYONNE
MAKE YOU FEEL—ALINA BARAZ, GALIMATIAS
LOVE, LOST—DAHLIA SLEEPS
ALL YOUR LOVE—FLIGHT FACILITIES, DUSTIN TEBBUTT
WAR OF HEARTS (ACOUSTIC VERSION)—RUELLE
WINTER IN THE HAMPTONS—JOSH ROUSE
SHAMPOO—CARR
MONSTERS (ACOUSTIC VERSION)—RUELLE
FEELS LIKE—GRACIE ABRAMS
US—JAMES BAY
FALLING DOWN—THÉOS
RECUÉRDAME—NATALIE LAFOURCADE, CARLOS RIVERA
MOON (AND IT WENT LIKE)—KID FRANCESCOLI, JULIA MINKIN

EXTENDED PLAYLIST IS AVAILABLE ON **SPOTIFY**

PROLOGUE

Grayson

I took the subway.

I didn't need to. Or want to. Shouldn't have, some would argue.

Grayson Stryker? Heir to half of Manhattan? On the train? During the busiest time of the day—or the week, really.

What the fuck was I doing?

Hell if I knew. But I waved a taxi off and walked two blocks in the August murk anyway. I descended, diving into a crush of Wall Street's finest. I lingered on the hot platform and bitched internally about the insufferable weather, the putrid smell, my life, generally.

I chose the third car.

"Chose" is probably a strong word. In reality, I didn't think about which car to get on for even a millisecond. But doors squealed open and I stepped forward. Onto a car. *That* car.

Why didn't I get my phone out? Why didn't I find a seat in a corner and close my eyes?

Instead, I stood in the center and held the polished pole. I looked left.

And there she was.

Chapter One

September 2016

Grayson

"Mr. Stryker? You have a call on line four."

I glowered at the intercom. There was always some stupid fucking call on line four. Which I hated for a lot of different reasons, but mostly because it meant there were also stupid fucking calls on lines one, two, and three.

At seven in the goddamn morning.

I pressed the talkback button. "Just take a message, Beth. On all of them. Obviously."

Obviously, I wasn't going to pick up. *Obviously*, I didn't care enough. *Obviously*, I was just a prisoner in this never-ending corporate purgatory.

I shoved back from the smoked-glass expanse of my desk, ramming both hands through my hair. *Damn it.*

I felt bad about snapping at her already. My shit mood wasn't my seventy-year-old secretary's fault. Beth was the best of the best—my father saw to that when he hired her, ensuring I had someone who could keep my clueless ass in line.

An unfortunate necessity.

Tension pulled at my shoulders and traps. I'd worked out too hard all month, trying to burn away excess energy. The two-a-days left me inordinately sore. And they didn't really help, anyway.

I just needed to get laid. Again. More.

But the New York City dating scene was impossible in August, with half the city shut down and every one fucking off to the Hamptons on a weekly basis.

I hated the Hamptons.

Almost as much as I hated dating, generally… but especially in the fall. Women always used the impending holidays to try to turn nothing into something. It didn't help that I also hated the actual holidays themselves, too.

Bored with the thought, frustrated by my own tedium, I spun my chair back to the window. Staring out at the city usually helped me re-center. This time, it just mocked me.

Look at you all high and mighty, my conscious sneered. *Best view in the place.*

When I convinced my father to move Stryker & Sons' headquarters to midtown, I did it almost entirely for the view. We made sure to capitalize on it, of course, sculpting the top two levels of our fifty-story cylindrical monument of concave glass, giving the rounded offices panoramic floor-to-ceiling views.

My half of the executive floor faced southeast—the Chrysler Building and a slice of Grand Central. My father had the northwestern side, with the spire of St. Patrick's Cathedral looming two blocks up.

Other than the world outside my window, there wasn't much else to look at. The firm's decorator insisted on "sparse" furnishing, to give the view priority. Apart from my black desk chair and the two matching Eames pieces facing my desk, everything else was fashioned from smooth, smoked crystal.

Someone passed by my door and I glanced over. The heavy glass always made me do a double take. "GRAYSON STRYKER," the etching bragged, under our new Stryker & Sons logo and above three words that curdled my stomach: "Chief Executive Officer."

I hated that title. Hated that it no longer belonged to its rightful owner, my father. Hated what I had to do to get it. Hated that, despite all my work, there were dozens of more-seasoned, better-qualified employees who had worked for my family for decades—people who deserved that designation way more than I did.

But there it was. There I was.

My iMac pinged, alerting me to the never-ending stream of emails awaiting some response. Sighing, I resigned myself to another day as GRAYSON STRYKER and opened the email app.

The first unread message stopped me cold. A Google alert. One I set up years earlier and then completely forgot, because nothing ever triggered it.

Until now.

Google Alert—Ella Callahan.

Ella

"Good morning, Miss Ella Callahan!" Maggie called as I walked into our living room. She held a printed sheet of paper in one hand, waving it as she quoted, "Author of this fall's 'most anticipated novel'!"

Even though she was lying through her teeth, it was hard not to smile back at her. In her colorful kimono robe, with her cloud of natural hair and perfect ebony skin, she looked like an Aerie ad.

I snatched the page out of her hand on my way to the kitchen, laughing when I saw the heading. "Mags, this is a blog post *you* wrote. Trust me, no one is anticipating the release of my *self-published* novel. There are, like, sixty-thousand titles ahead of it in the Kindle store."

Maggie tossed her head back, lifting her chin to a haughty angle. "Well it's *my* most anticipated novel of the fall," she argued. "And I'm an *influencer*. This is what I do. I teach people to have taste."

I couldn't dispute that. In the two years since we graduated from NYU, Maggie amassed over 500,000 followers, launched a blog lucrative enough to pay her portion of the rent (plus half of mine), and started an Etsy store… which meant that part of our common area functioned as a workshop for "custom pleasure aids."

She made three times more than I did at my nine-to-five as an assistant at an ad agency. It was the only way we afforded our two-bedroom-one-bath walk-up in DUMBO.

I often tried to slip her part of my grocery budget to make up for the higher rent she insisted on paying, but she wouldn't have it. And as much as I disliked letting her pay more than half, I had to admit, DUMBO was a lot more convenient than Bushwick. Or New Jersey.

In true "influencer" fashion, she managed to find an apartment in one of the last truly trendy parts of our neighborhood. We still had street artists, creator-owned galleries, and hole-in-the-wall restaurants. So far, our block had resisted a Whole Foods and one of those "brew-stilleries" owned by Guy Fieri.

Four stories up from the plant shop beneath us, we decorated the space to blend our tastes. Mid-century modern furniture for her; bright, happy colors for me. The blend of "mod" and vintage seemed to work in the tiny place… especially since our kitchen was straight out of the sixties, with light blue Formica counters and tiny enamel appliances.

We split the living space in half, with matching white desks on either side of our TV. Hers was full of her Etsy "work," while mine held my laptop, editing books, assorted yarn for knitting, and whatever work I couldn't finish at the office. She got her way when it came to the too-small, weirdly-shaped end tables; and I got to keep the orange, overstuffed accent chair I used for reading.

I gave my favorite spot a wistful look while pouring coffee into my travel mug. I much preferred staying home with my ugly tangerine chair to hiking all the way over to Midtown. In heels.

"So," Maggie pushed on, sipping her morning tea while she crossed her long legs over the width of our hot pink sofa. "Where are we celebrating tonight? We could go to the High Line! I know you love that. Or Williamsburg. Ugh. It's so *been-there*, but it's close by. Or clubbing! I think there's a rave in the warehouse district!"

I giggled while I grabbed my computer and work files from my desk, loading them into the blush-colored tote bag Mags gave me as gift when I landed my first "big girl" job.

"First, it's literally Tuesday. I can't go to a rave—I have to work tomorrow. And second, I can't do anything tonight. I'm staying late at the office and then I have a therapy appointment."

I click-clacked over to the door as fast as my red Mary-Jane heels allowed, trying unsuccessfully to ignore Maggie's pout. An impossible task, it turned out.

"Okay, okay," I relented, disengaging our deadbolt. "This weekend we can go out to celebrate. Alright? Promise."

Maggie gave me an arch look. "Fine, but we're doing whatever *I* want."

I agreed while I whirled out the door, figuring I had all week to talk her down and no time to argue at the moment. My train left in eleven minutes and it would take me eight minutes to get there in such impractical shoes.

While I tottered down all four flights of stairs, I wondered for the hundredth time where Maggie stashed my favorite clogs when they "accidentally" got lost in our move.

She never did like those. She probably gave them to the lady on the corner who trades origami cranes for cigarettes…

Feeling pleasantly preoccupied, optimistic about the rest of the week, and—*okay*—maybe just a *little* excited about the thought of my book selling a few copies... I was completely unprepared.

But as soon as I stepped out onto our street, it practically slapped me across the face.

A giant sign, ten stories tall, unfurled over the building across from ours. The banner announced the development of exactly what Maggie and I feared. Words like "recreation," "urban living," and "lifestyle" jumped out at me. All code for, "Your rent is about to triple so a bunch of yuppies can feel like cool Brooklyn kids."

That alone probably would have been enough to ruin my morning. But the disingenuous buzzwords were nothing compared to the five-story logo right in the center of the billboard.

Stryker & Sons.

Grayson.

Chapter Two

August 2013

Grayson

I expect there's some mediocre circle of Hell that mimics New York City in August.

One for mundane evil. Insurance executives. Debt collectors. Student loan agents. People who don't quite rise to the level of brutal torture, but still need to languish in mild persecution forever. Like the devil's own white-collar prison.

Sometimes, I wondered if I was in it.

Especially there, underground, in the subway station on Fulton.

My watch stared back up at me, showing the same time it had twenty seconds before. 7:14. The same time my iPhone displayed. I kept checking them, lately, restlessly flicking my attention down to my wrist, mashing my thumb into the button along the side of my phone screen.

It was an odd feeling—always on edge, waiting for nothing. At least there, on the platform, I could convince myself I was anxious for the train to arrive. Just like I told myself I was simply waiting for work to end, waiting for class to start or finish, waiting for whatever takeout delivery.

Just then, with an actual *reason* to feel impatient, I almost believed it.

The tunnel felt like a giant exhaust pipe. No air, just fumes. A herd of small-time Wall Street traders crowded behind me, mouth-breathing. They pushed forward as the wail of the C train approached.

That day, I didn't find them as annoying as I ordinarily did; with their hangdog faces and sweat-stained dress shirts, I felt for the poor bastards. It was clear most of them had a hell of a day.

I knew I had.

We packed ourselves into a car, shuffling to fill available space. I picked a pole in the right side of the crush and glanced around, finding the typical mix of Wall Street pikers and Brooklyn night-shifters, all on their way uptown. Too many people, packed into too little space.

I decided that I hated the damn subway.

I need to talk to Dad about getting a company car. If he insists I haul my ass down here to work every week until graduation, the least he could do is lend me one of Stryker & Sons' drivers.

The caustic bent of my thoughts wasn't fair. Truth was, Dad *did* offer me a company car. All I had to do was call the damn thing.

But something about working under him—as an "intern," no less—turned me back into a petulant teenager. No matter what he said or did, he met my irrational contempt at every turn.

I also, originally, figured that sitting in week-end traffic would take four times longer than riding the train up to the West Side. It only took three stops to realize the time savings wasn't worth it by half. Between the heat and the smell...

Wasn't my future at our family firm torturous enough without the stupid commute? Columbia—and, by extension, my apartment—was on the other side of the damn island.

Most of the Wall Street guys got off in or around SoHo, with a mass exodus at the Canal Street station. Only twelve people remained in the car. For the first time in ten minutes, I managed to take a real breath.

Relieved, my mind spun ahead to my plans for the evening. I committed to meeting some of my business school buddies at a bar in Midtown where I knew I'd wind up paying eighteen-dollars-a-round and nodding along while they rated scantily clad women.

I checked my watch again. 7:25.

Bored, feeling strangely despondent, I turned to look out at the dark tunnel walls.

And that's when I saw her.

Huddled into the corner, but impossible to miss. Not because she dressed like a lunatic—although, she did—or even because her flowing blonde hair was almost as eye-catching as her weird outfit.

But because her hands were… *knitting*. Furiously.

From across the aisle, I couldn't quite tell what she was trying to make with the massive pile of red yarn spilling out of her purse. I thought maybe a hat. I found it hard to focus on the shape of the thing while her long, unpolished fingers *flew*.

I blinked at them, then flicked my gaze up to catch her expression, expecting to find her thin blonde brows folded together, her small round face bent in concentration. Instead, she gazed serenely out the window across the car as if in a trance.

While I watched, she chewed absently on her lower lip and wrinkled her button nose, like she'd thought of something off-putting. When I glanced back down, her needles hadn't so much as paused.

And I suddenly found myself fighting a smile.

As a reflex, my mind catalogued the rest of her appearance to reach its usual verdict: was she someone I would sleep with or not? The answer came immediately.

Without a doubt.

Even under her odd mustardy overalls and mismatched pink tee shirt, I saw she had a great body. Gently curvaceous, with long legs more proportionate to her elegant fingers than her slight frame. While her hands moved to a new row of stitches, she crossed her pale knees, showing off a scuffed pair of green clogs in the process. The ugliest shoes in existence, surely.

My half-smile grew into a grin.

The far-off look on her face left me strangely fascinated. What was she thinking about? Was she worried or irritated or pondering someone she didn't like?

Her head tilted, sending a fluid ripple of wavy blonde over her shoulder. I wished I were close enough to glimpse the color of her eyes without crowding her.

The force of the subway screeching to a halt nearly toppled me. I realized I had no idea how long I spent watching her or what stop we were at.

The girl snapped to at the same moment my gaze flickered up over her head, where the map illuminated W. 4th Street—Washington Square Park.

By the time I glanced back down, her spot sat empty. I pivoted just in time to catch a flutter of gold hair as clunky green clogs stepped off of the car.

***

"Grayson?"

Brunch bustle couldn't sway my focus from a flash of blonde hair. The swishy ponytail bounced into view behind the counter at Sarabeth's. I stared across the restaurant for a long second, caught off guard.

It can't be the subway girl…

And it wasn't.

Of course not. The odds of running to the same stranger twice, in Manhattan, were abysmally low. This was just some other pretty blonde girl. Very pretty, actually… but I found she couldn't hold my interest. My eyes fell to my phone. *11:51.*

"Grayson?"

I tuned back in. My mother regarded me from her place across our table, her dark, sophisticated features somewhere between confusion and amusement. "Am I boring you already? We haven't even discussed the Autumn Gala yet."

I shook my head, trying to empty it out. "Sorry."

Her emerald eyes sparkled while she looked over her shoulder, following my gaze to the waitress who had caught my eye. Wordlessly, she turned back to me, her face expectant.

I shrugged, my attention dropping to my watch reflexively. *11:52.* "Just thought I saw someone."

I didn't tell her "someone" was a literal stranger… and a woman. My mother lived for details on my love life. Even the tiniest crumb would have her salivating for more information.

And there wasn't any.

A guy not much older than me came to take our orders. His eyes widened when they landed on my mom; he didn't so much as glance at me after that.

Years before, a waiter ogling her would have annoyed me. I'd since learned that it happened way too often to get worked up about it every time. Even in her casual Saturday-morning wrap dress, no one ignored Jacqueline Stryker.

I inherited most of my features from her: the black hair, the green eyes, her Mediterranean complexion. On me, the combination fell somewhere just north of ordinary. But not for my mother.

Of all my father's many treasures—and he had quite a few—he often said that she was the most beautiful. The rarest. Luckily, the six-carat Harry Winston on her left hand made her unavailability crystal clear.

Mom took most things in stride, including her husband's possessiveness and her many admirers. Calm and politely indifferent to the waiter's attention, she sat back in her chair, adjusting her white sheath and canting her head at me. "You're distracted today, *mi amor*."

Calm, polite… and perceptive.

It was an irritating combination. She was too relaxed to argue with. Too sure of herself. Too right.

Sometimes I wondered if I'd get away with more if I wasn't an only child. Having her insight targeted on me 24/7 was equal parts exasperating and—if I was honest with myself—comforting.

I sighed, reaching up rub the back of my neck. Checked my watch again. *11:54*.

"I'm fine." Because I was.

She kept her expression smooth, watching me with certainty so complete, I started to doubt myself.

Aren't I fine?

My grades were fine. My apartment was fine. I worked out, went out, didn't do anything addictive with any sort of regularity. My family was fine. Working with Dad at Stryker & Sons was…fine.

Fine?

Boring as fuck. Slightly soul-crushing. But wasn't that just… work? Life? It wasn't like my old man did heel-clicks on his way into the firm every morning. "Loving what you do" was a childish concept.

Impractical. Selfish. Immature.

And there were no rules against doing what I liked on my own time. In the twenty-odd hours I'd have left each week, after my twelve-hour days at the company…

And that was…fine.

"Seriously," I insisted, scratching the back of neck some more and staring down at my dry-fit shirt. "I am."

Mom pursed her lips, her expression an argument in itself. "You just ordered soup."

That made me smirk. "So?"

"So, it's August. And it's breakfast." Her thin black brows curved knowingly. "As I said: distracted."

Caught, I blew out a breath and reached for a familiar excuse. "It's just the usual stuff."

My mother had known about my feelings on the family business for years. She also knew, as I did, that the Stryker name was the golden ticket every parent wanted for their child. And we *both* knew it would literally kill my dad to have me walk away. I didn't like to put her in the middle, pinned between her husband's needs and her son's.

Sympathy softened the lines around her lips. "I am sorry, *mi amor*."

Usually, the subject fired me up. It tended to fill me with some mixture of leftover adolescent sullenness and frustrated indignation. This time, though, I just felt… absent.

Something pulled at my middle, tugging my attention away from our conversation. My eyes skimmed back over the blonde ponytail behind the bar.

"*Dios mio*," my mother huffed, scowling. "*What* is the matter?"

I watched the waitress walk away again, remembering how the girl on the subway breezed by me. The thought of red yarn and green clogs almost made me smile. Some pang of wistful annoyance bounced behind my ribs.

"I wish I knew, Mom. I really do."

I never called about the company car. I told myself it was a waste time, a waste of funds, bad for the environment. I'd begun to notice that I told myself a lot of true things that were also, somehow, complete bullshit.

By the next Friday, when the C train rolled up at 7:14, I had to own up to the truth—I wanted to see the girl again.

Adrenaline coursed through my chest while I waited to step onto the car.

This is dumb, I told myself. *She probably won't even be here. I took this train all week and nothing. She was just a fluke.*

The crowd at Fulton filed into the subway. I scanned the swarm, trying to catch a glimpse of blonde without making myself obvious.

But she wasn't there.

I deflated, blowing out a breath I didn't even know I was holding. *Damn it.*

The weight of my disappoint surprised me. Until I noted her absence—on the same train, at the same time of day, on the same day of the week—I hadn't let myself acknowledge how much I wanted to see her again.

This is getting embarrassing. You saw a literal stranger for ten seconds. That's it. Shake it off.

I wasn't even sure what I had been thinking, anyway. I had a whole life going on. Classes, working with my father, my friends and clubs at Columbia.

I don't have time to chase after some random girl on the subway. This is for the best.

The crowd thinned in SoHo, as per usual. Most of my fellow Wall Street yuppies shuffled off to the bars. Despite all my denial, I did one last rotation, craning my head around to glance behind me.

And found her.

Huddled into the farthest corner—under a clump of fuzzy yellow yarn.

She looked beautiful, once again; but also, just as strange. Tight black pants cropped halfway down her calves and a silky red tunic covered in painted white orchids hung off her shoulder. The shiny crimson material matched the flower-patterned beanie on her head.

And I realized—it was the red hat I watched her make the previous week. Between that and her same green clogs, I smiled before I could help myself.

This time, her project had yet to take any sort of shape, but it seemed larger than the hat. Her fingers looped Big-Bird-hued wool around wooden needles at warp speed while her gaze stared at the spot just past my hip. She seemed distracted, again; chewing on her lip, alternating between the corner of her mouth and the center.

That time, I lingered close enough to really see her.

It didn't help.

God Almighty.

She was gorgeous.

Her smooth and pale skin had a peachy glow to it. The color made her eyes impossible to miss. Blue—a deep, warm indigo with silvery flecks, like sapphires.

On impulse, I shifted right into her line of sight. Automatically, her eyes flashed up from my groin to my face.

For the first time in my life, I worried what someone saw when they looked at me. *Is she noticing the bags under my eyes from the all-nighter I pulled Tuesday? Or the patch of stubble under my chin that my razor missed this morning?*

But she didn't seem to see any of that.

Instead, our gazes settled into one another, like magnetic poles snapping together. She stared and I stared back, transfixed.

A current arched between us. Electric, but soft. Not a bolt of lightning; a slow, building glow. Warmth washed out from my center, trails of heat tingling into my extremities.

The subway stopped abruptly, breaking our spell. She glanced up at the map behind her and stood in a rush, ducking to avoid my gaze.

"Excuse me."

Her soft voice heated my blood as she brushed past me on her way out of the car. I turned my head and opened my mouth, but nothing came out. She disappeared before I could speak, but her sweetness lingered all the way uptown.

Ella

"Did you wax like I told you to?"

I rolled my eyes while I swiped my metro card, shoving my body and my over-stuffed satchel through the turnstile at the High Street station.

"No, Maggie."

On the other end of the phone, my roommate puffed out an exasperated breath. "But what if hot subway guy is on your train again? Now you won't be able to bang him."

I snorted. "Mags, good Lord. I'm not going to hook up with a stranger in a subway station bathroom. Wax or no wax."

I'm not going to hook up with anyone, anywhere.

"All I know is, he had to be seriously fine for you to even mention him because you're basically a nun," she sighed. "C'mon, Elle. You had the driest sophomore year in the history of New York City. In the history of *college*, in general. It should be illegal for someone as hot as you to be celibate this long."

Her confusion was all my fault; I went from being a fairly-normal roommate to a mess of anxious neuroses, literally overnight. Unless I broke down and spilled my guts, she'd never understand why the thought of dating turned my stomach now.

But, every day, I chose not to tell her about that night, the year before last, when we were both just freshmen.

At the time, I figured she'd eventually stop trying to get me to goad me into relationships if I stayed consistent with my rotation of denial and distraction. So far, no such luck.

"Hey, Mags? I'm catching the C so I'm about to lose you. I'll text you when I get to class."

I hung up before she could protest, tucking my phone into the back pocket of my cut-offs. Grimacing down at the rest of my outfit, I shook my head.

No wonder the beautiful man on the subway stared at me last week—a thief at the laundromat left my Goodwill wardrobe in critical condition when they stole my basket, along with half of my summer clothes.

Sometimes, I really hated New York. At least twice a week, I wound up wondering why on Earth I ended up there, of all places. I clearly was not cut out for a city where people stole my laundry and elbowed me into gutters to steal my cabs. Where it was—somehow, impossibly—even hotter underground than it was under direct sunlight. Where I never quite knew if the incredibly handsome stranger next to me would turn out to be a white knight or a criminal.

My anxiety swelled at the thought. As soon as the train doors swung open, I hustled to a spot in the corner and pulled out my knitting needles as quickly as possible. The familiar feeling of the wooden sticks between my fingers soothed some of my tension. I picked up where I'd left off, burning off nervous energy with a hurried pace.

I liked the color, that week; I found the seafoam yarn piled outside one warehouse in the Garment District during an afternoon walk and decided to try to make Maggie a poncho with it. With her statuesque figure, I only barely had enough material to pull it off.

When my fingers got going, my nerves started to settle. Though, I think I may have preferred the panic.

Because as soon as my mind cleared, it started to wander back to the guy I saw the week before.

I kept doing that. In the rare moments when I found my hands suitably occupied and my anxiety at bay, I wondered who he was, where he rode the train to, why he ever looked at *me*…

Why I *liked* it.

I wanted to say it was the *way* he looked at me, and not just the way *he looked*, but that wasn't entirely true. Sure, he and I sort of...connected? But I also knew I'd never seen any other man so effortlessly gorgeous.

It was sort of *obnoxious*, actually. His face just about knocked the wind out of me. A square, solid chin connected to a sharp, slanting jaw that complemented the arch of his cheekbones. A dark layer of barely-there stubble that shaded the golden skin around his sculpted mouth. Eyebrows matching the thick, shiny black hair on his head. He wore it combed slightly off-center, long enough to just barely touch collar of his dress shirt at the nape of his neck.

And, then, of course, his eyes. The bright shocks of green captivated me so completely, I hadn't even realized I was staring until the subway stopped and I had to get off.

That *could not* happen again.

Yet, the closer we got to his stop, the more my foot bounced. My fingers moved faster, like they could somehow outrun my anticipation for me.

I don't know what I'm so worked up about. It's not like I can talk *to him. That would be pointless. And psycho.*

I already looked crazy enough in my mismatched outfit.

No. I decided to do what I usually did—pick an innocuous spot to stare at, and knit. Try to enjoy a little bit of peace before class and work.

I chose a section of the bench across from me and zoned out. As the subway thumped along, the car emptied for those getting off at the first stop in Manhattan, then filled again as we passed near Wall Street.

Without looking up, I heard a group of traders jostle their way on. It was the Friday before Labor Day and clearly these particular brokers made a detour at a bar on their way to the train. The stench of sweat and whiskey filled the whole car immediately.

Two of them dropped down into the bench where I rested my gaze. I'd learned my lesson the last week; this time, I didn't glance up.

Still, in my line of vision, I saw when one elbowed the other, then gesture to the woman holding the rail between us. She'd just gotten on, too. Her black heels and tailored skirt suggested she worked as a young professional, like them.

A minute later, one of the men unlocked his iPhone and fiddled with it. I watched him drop it to the floor of the car—*ew, germs*—and push it with his foot until it sat right between the woman's heels.

The move was odd enough to make my fingers falter. I dropped a stitch, then stopped altogether, trying to puzzle out why he would want his phone *there*. I figured it out—too late—when the screen flickered.

Pictures. He set the phone to take pictures up her skirt.

My stomach dropped while my face heated. The swell of anxiety I rode all afternoon suddenly burst, leaving bright red rage in its place.

My eyes snapped up to glower at the drunken idiots across from me. "Excuse me," I called, not recognizing my own voice. "*What* are you doing?"

They both froze long enough to turn heads. Their victim followed my glare from their ashen faces to the place between her feet. Visibly horrified, she shrieked and stomped her heel into the screen, crushing it like a cockroach.

One of the men bellowed, "What the *fuck*, lady?"

She hurled a string of well-deserved obscenities back at them as the train tumbled to a stop. Then she hurried off, kicking the phone carcass out the car door and down into the chasm under the tracks.

By the time I turned back to the two men, they had lurched to their feet and come to loom over me. "What the hell is your problem?" one of them demanded. At the same time, the other shouted, "That was a $1000 phone, you little bitch!"

My hands started to shake. The wooden knitting needles trembled in my grasp as I scooted as far back into my seat as I possibly could. My brain spun out, trying to remember self-defense or common sense or *anything*. But I couldn't even see their faces through my haze of panic.

"Is there a problem?"

A large, tanned hand pressed into the shoulder of the man on the left, pushing him back. Both men straightened away from me as a familiar figure stepped into their path.

Hot subway guy.

His posture wasn't combative, but, even in stillness, his body was intimidating. The width of his shoulders was enough to send them falling back another pace.

He cocked his head as the car glided to another stop. "Excellent timing. I think this is where you two get off?"

The drunk men roared curse words at him while they staggered out of the car with their tails between their legs. Relief coursed through my body in a heady rush. Before I managed to stop it, a hysterical giggle bubbled out of my lips.

My rescuer turned and gave me a quizzical look, somewhere between amusement and disbelief. "Do you have a death wish?" he asked, "Or were you about to gut them with your knitting needles?"

My knitting needles. The notion to use them for defense never occurred to me while I was panicking.

"Oh," I said out loud. "That would have been smart, actually."

His handsome face broke into a wide, perfect smile. And I swore I might faint.

"Well you also could have garroted them with the yarn," he replied, "But that would have taken more work."

A second nervous laugh tittered out of me. I bit my lower lip, hoping to shut myself up. Our gazes met.

Just that easily, our ordinary moment shifted into something profound. The faint laugh lines around his mouth melted as his eyes became infinitely intense. Some elusive energy charged the air between us.

I thought I imagined it before, but it really was there. The mysterious arc of something intangible. Connection, momentum. The feeling of finding something in a stranger that you thought only existed within yourself.

Dark heat bled into his irises. My core started to melt, sending tingles through my inner thighs.

I wanted to suck in a breath, but instead I bit my lip harder. His eyes flickered, for just part of a second, to my mouth. The same moment they snapped back to mine, our train once again slid to a halt. I glanced up overhead at the map and felt my heart drop.

"Oh no," I gasped. *My stop!*

We'd passed it two stations ago. Before I had time to think, I grabbed my stuff and leapt off of the car…

With the beautiful man hot on my heels.

Grayson

I don't know what the fuck I was doing when I followed her out of the car, but it happened.

I saw her walking away again and something inside of me clicked. The next thing I knew, we stood side-by-side on the platform at the 23rd Street station, just below Chelsea.

The girl started muttering to herself while she dug through her bag, her slender fingers pulling out handfuls of yarn. "…gonna be so late now. Unless I—no, because I don't have—but if I don't then—"

She shook her head the whole time, swinging her ponytail from one side to another. "Did I forget to bring the darn—"

It was hard not to smile at her. Even distressed, she was just… endearing. I pressed my mouth into a hard line, trying not to smirk while she spiraled.

She looked over at me once and huffed, as if somehow exasperated with me. "Here," she said, "Hold this a second."

I'd barely stretched out my hands when she started piling minty green wool in my arms. Next came the wood needles, a hairbrush, a cell phone, a braided-yarn lanyard with keys on the end, and, finally, a multi-colored crocheted coin purse.

"Wait a minute." Unable to help it, I chuckled as I held up the small rainbow pouch. "Is this your wallet?"

The girl nodded dismissively, mumbling random words to herself until she managed to unearth what looked like a *map*. She beamed down at the creased paper while she unfolded it.

"Are you serious?"

She furrowed her brow at the lines on her map, her mouth turning down in a preoccupied frown. "What do you mean?" she muttered back.

"You just handed a stranger your wallet and your phone? On a subway platform?" I pressed, working hard not to scoff at her innocence. "And you're using a *paper* map? Are you insane?"

"Yep," she mumbled sarcastically, almost too quiet to hear while she continued scowling down. "Certifiable."

My lips quirked at her quip. Surprise joined the riot inside of me. I knew she fascinated me… but I never expected to *like* her. "What are you looking for, anyway?"

Her blue eyes ran circuits over the banged-up rag. "I'm trying to figure out where we are."

I shrugged. "Easy. We're in Chelsea, under the intersection of 23rd and 8th. There will be train heading back toward Washington Square in twenty-some minutes."

She blinked at me, then at her map. "How do you know all of that?"

I tried not to stare at her too hard. "Grew up here. Now I go to school here."

Her gaze roamed down over my outfit. A cute little crease formed between her eyebrows. My fingers tingled, yearning to smooth it out.

"You don't look like a student," she remarked, dubious.

I glanced at my Brooks Brothers shirtsleeves and slacks, fighting another smirk. It was considered casual dress at Stryker & Sons. "Occupational hazard."

Part of me wanted to tease her for her weird outfit-of-the-week, but I knew it wouldn't come off as sincere. In frayed denim and a tight, white daisy-patterned blouse with billowy bell sleeves, she looked… bright.

The strip of bare skin between the knot at the bottom of her shirt and the waistband of her shorts made my fingers twitch again. Would she be as soft as she looked? Was her skin as warm as her eyes?

She plucked her taped-up iPhone out of my grasp and sank her teeth into her lip—a habit of hers, evidently. Anxiety stained her sapphire gaze. "You said twenty minutes? And that's the fastest way to get back downtown?"

"The Village isn't downtown," I said automatically, then regretted sounding like a smartass. "But yes."

She did the mumbling thing again. "Even if I could take a cab, I'd still be—what? Fifteen? Twenty-five minutes late? Stupid New York traffic always—" Her mouth trembled while she started taking things out of my hands and ramming them back into her bag.

"Do you need a cab?" I didn't want her to leave, but I couldn't be responsible for that look on her face.

She sighed and shook her head. Her hair swished at me again. "It wouldn't help. I have—had—a class. It's only fifty minutes. At this rate, by the time I get there, I'll miss half of it anyway… I might as well just head to work."

She blinked moisture out of her eyes and gave me a small, shy smile. Under my gaze, her peachy cheeks warmed. Suddenly embarrassed, she dropped her gaze and shuffled back. "Anyway, thanks for not robbing me."

I watched her walk away again. With a perfect view this time, I noted an oblivious sort of grace to the way she moved. The flip of her hair, her hips' subtle sway. Even those horrible shoes couldn't detract from her charm.

By the time I made up my mind, I had to jog to catch her at the top of the stairs, where the station spat us out onto the street. Taxis honked and brakes squealed, navigating the deadlock of a Friday evening.

The dim of nightfall did nothing to cool the sidewalks, even when a humid breeze blew the girl's hair into my chest. A lash of sweetness struck me—the scent of honeysuckle.

Her eyes went wide when I reappeared beside her. Ignoring the unspoken questions plain in her features, I asked her one of my own. "How much time do you have before work?"

She shrank back a half a step. "A little over an hour. It will probably take that long to walk there. It's in Greenwich, so…"

I glanced down at the Tag Heuer strapped to my left wrist—*7:22*—and had an idea. "If I promise to get you there on time, will you eat dinner with me?"

Our gazes clashed again, throwing the same sparks. Her perfect pink mouth lifted into a sideways smile before wilting at the edges. Something sad fell over her eyes like a veil.

"N-no," she whispered, stammering. "I… can't. I'm sorry."

She started down Eighth Avenue, walking too quickly.

"Wait."

The desperate word tore itself from my mouth and she turned her head. For a second, I just stared. Up ahead, with her gold hair glowing under a street light, she seemed like a mirage.

And I was… *afraid*? Scared I'd never see her again. Worried I made her up.

"Just—please," I called, not sure what I even wanted. "I'm Grayson. Will you at least tell me your name?"

Her forlorn half-smile reappeared. Only for a second. "Ella," she told me, already slipping farther away. "It was nice to meet you, Gray."

❋❋❋

Chapter Three

September 2016

Ella

After the initial pang of heartache subsided, I was *pissed.*

"Egotistical, heartless, self-absorbed, yuppie son of a—"

My hip slammed into the turnstile on my way out of the 33rd Street station. Midtown teemed with its usual morning mix. Titans of industry in Brioni suits mingled with GQ'd ad-execs. I easily picked up who was who—anyone important walked with leisurely grace, while the rest of us underlings scurried not to be late.

Ignoring the Empire State Building got easier as the months wore on. It stood just off to my left, but I was too angry to glance at it. I didn't want to see the things I loved about New York. I wanted to stew in my righteous rage.

I turned toward Bryant Park and started the six-block schlep to Idealogue. A decent ad agency with a horrible name. After working there for sixteen months, the play on words still made me roll my eyes every morning. Though, I was just an assistant who worked for a bunch of marketing whizzes, so what did I know?

Just a few blocks off of Madison Avenue, Idealogue had taken over five floors of prime midtown real estate within four years of their launch. I had to admit, our building was one of my favorites. Its forty stories of translucent blue glass gleamed from every angle, reflecting the cloudless morning down at me.

But I could not have been *less* in the mood for gorgeous pre-fall weather.

I managed not to trip in my heels as I hurried through the gray granite lobby, flashing my security badge on my way to the elevator bank. My stomach growled as we ascended, reminding me that I forgot to grab my usual bagel on my way into the building. I tried to ignore the hunger pangs while I smoothed the front of my black sheath dress and picked lint off of the hem.

Idealogue's third level featured a mix of splashy colors and modern lines. It was reserved for "rising stars"—ad execs with a few big accounts under their belt who were still clawing their way up the ranks. In addition to their own office pods, each one had also earned an assistant.

I worked for Marjorie. With attitude for miles and a mind as sharp as her claws, my boss perfectly embodied the word "ambition." She always dressed to kill and had a way with young up-and-coming CEO's. Over the summer, she roped six new accounts, all with presidents under 35.

I took my seat in front of her office pod just in time. Three minutes later, her Louboutins echoed off of the elevator platform. The cobalt heels contrasted her asymmetrical, neon-yellow dress, but matched the dyed ends of her black hair. The spikey gold choker around her neck gave a fashionable air of danger.

I did my best to smile as she approached, but my heart wasn't in it.

"Has Parker been by yet this morning?" she demanded, walking right past me.

I jumped to my feet and scrambled after her. "Um, no," I admitted, hanging her red YSL bag on the hook next to her door.

One glance across the round office space told me Parker was late; his lights were still off. "He's not in yet."

Marjorie rolled her almond-shaped eyes. "Figures. Men. They come in later, go home earlier, and still take 95% of the credit."

Men. They ruin your life, break your heart, ignore your existence, and then buy the building across from yours just to put their name all over it.

I didn't say it out loud, but my face did.

Marjorie paused, tweaking up her tweezed black brows. "You're not your usual perky self today," she observed.

With a single nod, she tossed a credit card at me and turned away to fire up her computer. "I like it. Take my card. Go get us a round of coffee, on me."

By the time I hiked to Starbucks and back, I somehow calmed myself down. I decided not to let Grayson's company business ruin my big day. I worked hard on that book—I wanted to be excited about that.

I *felt* excited. Tingly, even…

Though that may have just been the extra caffeine from my cold brew.

After dropping Marjorie's regular order off on her desk, I slipped back out to mine and dove into my call list. Six messages later, Parker approached out of the corner of my eye.

Yesterday, I might have gotten a thrill from him coming toward me. Most women would. He was undeniably handsome—blond, with warm hazel eyes and a strong, stocky build. He always wore a pair of black brow-line reading glasses while he worked and tended to favor eclectic business attire.

Today, his hunter green vest and tweed slacks made me think of fall. I felt a pang. Autumn was always the hardest season for me… aside from Christmas.

Swallowing hard, I forced a grin. "Good morning, Parker! Looking for Marjorie?"

Parker had a habit of sitting on the edge of my desk. It used to bother me, but I'd gotten used to the intrusion… along with the way my stomach flipped whenever he grinned back at me. "Looking for you, actually."

I tried to sneak in a deep breath. *You knew this was coming,* I coached internally. *He's been flirting with you for months.*

I even consulted my therapist about him on several occasions. Dr. Laura encouraged it—in my self-imposed limbo, I hadn't gone out with anyone in almost three years. She thought a casual date would be a good exercise for me.

Oblivious, Parker went on, still smiling. "I was wondering—are you free for lunch tomorrow?"

Grayson

I warred with myself through four meetings and eight phone calls.

Once I cleared the decks and turned my attention to my creative projects, I thought I'd be able to focus. Normally, the time I spent sketching out new builds each afternoon was the highlight of my day. But I couldn't seem to get that damn Google alert out of my mind.

I should have just deleted it. After all, the woman *clearly* wanted nothing to do with me. Why even bother reading whatever the internet had to say about her?

That was a stupid notion, of course.

How could I have thought I had a prayer of ignoring her name?

I'd never been able to ignore her. Not from the minute I saw her.

At five minutes to five, I gave in and clicked the email. The Google alert sprang open. My mouth dried while I read the one item listed.

For Always, a novel by Ella J. Callahan.

It was an Amazon link to a Kindle book. *Her* book. Brand new, available to purchase for just $5.99. The low price unearthed a long-forgotten feeling of fond exasperation—she had never known just how much she was worth and it always bothered and endeared me in equal measures.

No reviews yet.

That didn't matter though. I knew it was inspired, because I knew her. Still, I hesitated, my mouse hovering over the word "purchase."

I have to buy it, right? I mean, how could I *not*? But, also... *how could I*?

The title alone almost killed me. My chest throbbed so hard, for a second I thought there might actually be a knife twisted into it.

After ten minutes of deliberation, I decided that reality couldn't possibly be worse than what I imagined. I clicked the button and watched the e-book materialize in my online library.

The cover looked simple enough. Yellow. *Of course.*

I clicked past it, forcing confidence. *This is fine. Not bad at all. It's been three years, for God's sake. I can be happy for her.*

Then, two pages in, I saw it.

The dedication.

For Gray, for always.

Chapter Four

September 2013

Ella

"This is completely ridiculous."

As ever, Maggie had a point. She fluffed her afro up off the back of her neck and scowled at me through round rose-gold glasses. "I thought you said what happened with Hot Subway Guy last week was no big deal."

I chewed on my bottom lip and bounced in place. Sweat slicked my lower back until my black tank top clung to me like Saran wrap. "It was."

Maggie's eyes narrowed while she cocked her head. "Then why, exactly, am I standing in Satan's asshole?"

I almost laughed, but the sound caught halfway up my throat. Maggie hated our usual subway stop and I didn't blame her. The Ralph Avenue station was a pit. It wasn't even a "station" per se—just an underground strip of scraped-up concrete.

Usually, the smell was barely tolerable...but heat turned the unpleasant odor into a suffocating stench. Even as twilight cooled the sidewalks above us, the air in the tunnel remained muggy and putrid.

"It's not *that* bad," I lied.

Her dubious, dark eyes scanned the area behind us. She lowered her voice to a growl. "You're not afraid of being mugged in this hellhole, but you're afraid of a handsome man who likes you?" She shook her head. "Ella Callahan, you need therapy."

The truth embedded in her jest stung my chest. She had no way of knowing I tried desperately to get in with student services' mental health counseling for over a year. After what happened to me, every campus officer, guidance counselor, and dean told me the same thing: that it "seemed like" I would "benefit" from "someone to talk to."

Because, apparently, the whole incident was *my* problem, not theirs… or the guy's.

But every therapist wanted special insurance or close to $200 an hour, and I had neither.

So I took up knitting. And yoga. And baking. And filled every available second of my time with work, school, or studying. The less time I had to think, the better. Plus, falling into bed exhausted every night actually gave me a fighting chance at sleep.

"—think it's intimacy issues, but what do I know?"

I tuned back in as Maggie finished her monologue. "Anyway, regardless of *what* your issue is, the problem isn't going away any time soon. I mean…" Her gaze started at my ankles—deliberately omitting my clogs—and ran up to my face, as if proving a point. "*Look* at you."

I glanced down at the toothpaste-stained tank top that would be soon be soaked through with sweat. "You're right," I deadpanned. "I'm *basically* a model."

Maggie's face pinched, annoyed. "Dubious fashion choices aside—you're hot. And the guys will just keep on comin'."

Our subway appeared as I rolled my eyes. "Let's just get this over with."

My anxiety ramped into a roar as soon as the train left Brooklyn. Maggie chatted away. And I counted down the stops until we hit the Financial District.

The usual mix of Wall Streeters filed in. Thankfully, this week, none of them seemed drunk.

"Oh. My God." Maggie's voice dropped to a low murmur. "Is that him? That has to be him. Six-three? Bright green eyes? Hair you want to yank? Bronzed like Adonis?"

I didn't need to look up to know she was right. I suddenly *felt* Grayson's eyes on me, tracing my left cheekbone, then my neck, and the place where my sticky black tank exposed my collarbone.

Instead of turning toward him, I bent my head to Mags. "You're *supposed* to be my buffer," I whispered. "Now, act like we're having a serious conversation so he doesn't come over here."

Maggie glared at me. "We *are* having a serious conversation if you think I'm going to help you cheat yourself out of that fine-ass man over there. Seriously, Elle. *Are you insane?*"

She started to lift her gaze back to him. I elbowed her ribs. "Mags, *stop*."

Her dark eyes widened and leapt back to mine. "Okay, Ella, *seriously*? I don't know if I can help you, here..."

My throat tightened. *Damn it, why didn't I bring my knitting?*

"What do you mean? You *are* helping me!"

Maggie looked unsure. "I mean, I'm here, sure, but… the way he's looking at you… I don't think *anything* is going to stop him from coming over here."

I prayed she was wrong. And right. I couldn't decide what would be worse—having to face Grayson after the way I freaked out… or never speaking to him again.

I knew, deep down, if I didn't ever talk to him, I would always regret it.

Not just because Maggie had a point—he *was* beautiful and I'd probably never meet anyone who compared. But because it was a pitiful choice. The decision to let the fear win.

Sure, for months I vowed that I would never be alone with a guy ever again. But avoiding Grayson meant denying myself something I really wanted, out of fear.

Was I *that* far gone? That damaged?

I didn't want to be.

So, on a brief flash of bravery, I looked up.

Grayson

They were whispering about me. I probably would've been flattered if I wasn't so edgy.

She wasn't in one of her usual technicolor ensembles. I wondered if maybe she was trying her best not be noticed.

An impossible feat. Her face alone would stop most men in their tracks.

That day, her hair hung loose over her bare shoulders in pale blonde waves. Her sexy legs were on display again, capped off with the same hideous shoes she wore every week. And she looked perfect.

While I watched, Ella bent her head closer to her friend. Their opposite appearances were striking. Ella's golden waves against the other girls' black spiral curls; Ella's black tank top next to her friend's rainbow-striped sundress.

For a second, I wondered how they met. Maybe they were classmates, riding to school together. Maybe the other girl's sudden appearance on the C line had nothing to do with me or our weird encounter last week. *Could be a complete coincidence.*

Then the girl cast her dark brown eyes back at me, clearly assessing.

Not a coincidence, then. She's definitely here because of me.

She liked whatever she saw. Turning back to Ella, she shot her an obvious *hot-damn* look and fanned herself. I glanced down at my gray slacks and white dress shirt, smirking.

When I turned back toward them, Ella's sapphire gaze instantly snagged my attention. Her face looked just like it had under the street light on the corner of twenty-third. Sad and indecisive and… longing? *Or maybe that's just what I want to see.*

Ella's phone tore her attention away. She frowned while she read the screen, then showed it to her friend, who rolled her eyes. "Great," the girl grumbled, deflating, "All of this for nothing."

I saw an opening. Three paces later, I arrived at the pole right between their seats. "Whatever it is," I said, nodding at her phone, "it can't be as bad as two drunk pikers trying to fight you."

Ella stared up at me, her mouth trembling between a small smile and a straight line. "Just a cancelled class," she murmured shyly, dropping her eyes back to the cracked screen. "No biggie."

I scrambled for another topic and plucked up the first thing I could think of. "You don't have your knitting stuff today. What will you use for protection if there's another brawl?" When I caught her fighting a grin, I pressed my luck. "Or if some other guy tries to ask you out?"

The girl with her snorted, tossing a look at Ella. "Did you stab him and just conveniently leave that part out of the story?"

Huh. I'm a story.

Ella's cheeks glowed blush, clearly embarrassed to be caught talking about me. I smiled at her. "It's okay. I told my friends about you, too. I've had beautiful girls give me their phone numbers on random subway platforms; but never their actual *phones*."

It was a lie. I hadn't told anyone about her, because she made me feel like a crazy person. What self-respecting New Yorker even *talked* to strangers on the subway, let alone chased them down?

…or walked up and inserted themselves into their conversations?

The friend grinned at me, approval clear in her eyes. "You know what, Elle?" she said, gathering her purse while the train's next stop came into view. "Since your class is cancelled, I think I'll get out here and grab dinner in SoHo. Some of my friends from the theater alliance are meeting at a Korean-Mexican fusion place that's supposed to make amazing kimchi queso."

Ella's mouth dropped open, her expression frozen between pleading and disbelief.

"You know me," the other girl went on, gliding toward the doors. "I'm such a whore for a bowl of cheese."

She stood almost as tall as me. Her brown eyes bored into mine for a long moment, shooting me a warning look. "Nice to meet you, Hot Subway Guy. I trust you'll see that my friend here doesn't miss her stop this week?"

Before I could speak, she wiggled her fingers at us and sauntered off of the car. When I faced Ella, her disbelief had taken a turn toward the accusatory. Her face soured as she watched her friend float away.

I tried for another joke. "I'd probably be offended that you thought you needed a buffer… if I wasn't flattered by my new moniker: 'Hot Subway Guy.' Think I should trademark it? Have some business cards made up?"

Ella's lush pink mouth flattened into a line. Her eyelashes fluttered when she lied. "I have no idea what you're talking about."

I chuckled. "Say I'm a gentleman and I pretend to believe you—will you give me a chance and come have dinner with me?"

Her fearful look tightened my lungs. It also exasperated me. Why was she afraid? She handed me her wallet, so she must have thought I was sane, at least. She talked to me and even smiled at my jokes… so why did she look *terrified* every time I asked to keep spending time with her?

And, if she really didn't want anything to do with me, why didn't she say *no*? She had no problem confronting those two assholes last week…

I figured I'd never know unless I asked.

"Ella."

I liked her name. Delicate and different. It reminded me of fairy dust and princesses and once-upon-a-times. I spent the whole week repeating it in my head—finally *saying* the name out loud felt good.

It rolled out on a deep breath while I rubbed my hand over the back of my neck. "I get it; you don't know me. So, if I'm being creepy or making an ass of myself, just tell me so. I promise I'll leave you alone."

Her eyes softened into warm puddles of blue, rendering them even more beautiful than usual. Her voice hummed, soft but insistent. "You're not," she promised. "I—listen, I'm just… I don't…"

She couldn't get her words out. Instead, she bit her lip and stared up at me, considering. When she opened her mouth, she spoke so fast I barely understood her.

"There's this waffle bar, across the street from my stop. I sometimes go there for dinner if I can. And, tonight, I can. And I guess…if someone else wanted to go there, too, I couldn't stop that person from exercising their right to do so. Since this is, you know, America."

I bit another smile back. Seemed I couldn't control them, around Ella. I'd never met anyone like her. Every time she showed me glimpses of her personality, a strange feeling burst through my chest. Some sort of warmth.

I lived for it. And hated it. And couldn't figure out *what* the hell it was.

I only knew I would suddenly do anything to get to that damn waffle shop, even if I had to pretend we were strangers. Even if I had to actually eat a waffle for dinner.

Our subway chimed, illuminating Washington Square on its map of stops. Playing along with her game, I didn't announce my intentions. I just followed her off, into the station, and up the steps to the street.

Walking behind her afforded me the best view in the whole damn city. Her tight top and shorts put her figure on display. Gentle curves that seemed so natural on her small-but-leggy frame. I wanted to slide my hands down the perfect bows of her hips and pull her body into mine.

Dusk had settled over the city by the time we rejoined it. The humidity seemed more damp than sweltering. Miraculously, when a breeze came through, the weather almost felt cool.

It had been a while since I walked around the West Village. I recognized a few old stand-bys like Papaya Dog and the gothic-style Methodist church down the street. Beyond that, I could just make out the corner of Washington Square Park through the pre-street-light dim.

I felt out of place in my work clothes, with leather loafers and a matching bag. Everyone around us dressed more like Ella—casual street clothes and mismatched fashion statements. With her crocheted Big Bird-yellow purse and funny green clogs, the girl fit right in.

She led me across the street, to a tiny storefront wedged between a bank and a head shop. The neon sign said, "West Side Waffles." Everything—from the awning outside to the checkerboard floor inside—was as yellow as her bag.

West Side Waffles took your desired batter, pressed it in an iron, and let you pick the toppings for it. They had every option imaginable, from whipped cream to curry sauce.

Once we fell in line, I leaned closer and asked Ella, "Is it safe to talk to you yet? Because I have no idea if I should do sweet or savory here."

Relief surged through me when she giggled instead of ignoring me. "If you go savory, you're on your own," she quipped. "I'm getting mine covered in chocolate."

Dessert for dinner. Something a kid would love. A normal kid, anyway. When I was younger, a French chef with a penchant sous vide prepared most of my dinners.

Bewildered by all the options, I just ordered whatever Ella asked for. When she pulled out her little knit coin purse, I already had a twenty folded between my fingers. I reached around her to hand it to the cashier.

"You shouldn't do that," Ella mumbled. "Since this isn't a… whatever."

"Date?" I grabbed our food off of the counter and layered as much charm into my smile as possible. "No, usually I take my dates to restaurants that don't make us carry our own trays."

She gave a cute little snort. "Forgive me. I had no idea I was in the presence of such a gentleman."

A gentleman. Was I? A flurry of flashbacks from my summer of random hook-ups floated through my mind. I almost winced. There were a lot of women…too many, some would argue.

I tried to play it off as flirtatious banter. "Clearly, you don't know me very well."

I hoped for more of her soft little laughs, but my reply troubled her for some reason. A crease folded the creamy skin between her blonde brows.

"What?" I asked, setting down the waffles on the table near the front window. "You were hoping 'Hot Subway Guy' would be a White Knight?"

That earned me a tiny smile. "No," she sighed, sitting down. "I was just thinking… if this *were* a date… that you probably go on *a lot* more dates than I do."

I held back another grimace. What could I say to that? I *did* go on a lot of dates.

Most weren't romantic. I had to attend every museum benefit and university booster gala in the city. Bringing my own companion usually held more appeal than wading through the cesspool of single social-climbers and sorority girls vying for their Mrs. degrees.

A lot of times, I didn't even have a say. My parents often filled the seat next to mine without my input. Once, I had to spend the whole evening with some debutante named Buffy VanHorn. She gave terrible head, too.

For the most part, my usual dating scene didn't bother me. Finding girls was easy enough. Charming my parents' fix-ups never proved much of a problem, either. I figured, hell, most guys could do worse than an open bar, a nice meal, and an easy lay on any given Friday night.

But I didn't think Ella would appreciate that perspective.

"I go to a lot of functions," I hedged. "Though, now that I think of it, I haven't been out with anyone in about… a month?"

Jesus. Was that true?

The last time I took someone to an event was somewhere back in the middle of August. I quickly re-counted the weeks. *One, two, three, four…*

Ella finished doing the math at the same time I did. Our eyes met. And I knew she saw it all over my face: I hadn't touched another woman since the day I saw her.

Ella

Grayson's green eyes searched mine for a long moment.

I didn't know what he was looking for, but he seemed to find it. After a breathless beat, his face broke into the rueful grin I liked best. "Guess I've been distracted."

He shrugged and started cutting up his waffle as though he hadn't just admitted to having a crush on me for a month.

Of all the discoveries I'd made about him so far, his calm confidence was slowly becoming one of my favorites. He was generally quiet, but spoke his mind easily, even when his thoughts betrayed his feelings. It made me feel like I knew him.

But as I sat there, trying to come up with conversation, I realized I knew *nothing*.

At a loss, I decided to start with the last true dialogue we had. "You said you were a student?"

He nodded while he chewed his first bite. "I'm a senior at Columbia. Finance." His gaze dropped down to his lap for brief second. "And, um, Architecture. But that's more of a personal interest than a career path. What about you?"

Two majors? Great. He's too beautiful and *too brilliant.*

"I go to NYU," I replied. "I'm a junior this year."

Genuine interest glimmered in his green eyes. "…studying?"

"Oh. Um. English. I'm going to try to get a job for an ad agency or a marketing firm after school. But I love books, so…"

His reassuring smile made my stomach flip. "Maybe you'll write one someday," he told me. "Or work in publishing."

I felt a blush creep over my face as I thought of the four unfinished novels sitting on my laptop. "Me and every other barista in Greenwich," I mumbled, digging into my food. "Thank you for dinner, by the way."

He nodded once, inhaling another bite of his waffle. "This is good," he told me, pointing with his fork. "I've never eaten chocolate for dinner before."

That didn't surprise me. Everything about him—from the way he dressed to the way he held his knife—exuded *wealth.*

Not just money. Lots of people had money. They wore flashy clothes and threw black AmEx's around. That wasn't Grayson. His dignified air hinted at more than just a bottom line in someone's bank account. He had *breeding*. Refinement. Class.

A wealthy, charming, Ivy League guy who looked like a Greek god.

I could *not* have been more out of my league.

But just in case it wasn't totally obvious, my stupid mouth blurted, "We ate chocolate for dinner every year on Halloween. My sister was the worst. She almost always ate too much too fast and wound up ruining her costume by getting sick."

I wanted to sink down into a puddle on floor. *Oh Lord, I did not just say that.*

But Grayson grinned. "Is your sister older or younger?"

"Younger. Darcy. She's fourteen now."

His intent gaze gave the impression that he was actually *interested* in my pathetic life. Which—let's face it—could *not* be true. But suddenly I couldn't seem to shut up.

"She lives in Maryland, with my mom. That's where I grew up. You probably knew I wasn't from here after what happened on the subway last week."

His smile turned teasing, but his eyes softened. "The map *was* sort of a give-away. And you still seem… optimistic. Most people who grow up here are kind of jaded by the time they're on their own."

I felt my cheeks heat. Talking about myself seemed like a recipe for mortification. Besides, he was the interesting, mysterious one.

"So you're just another jaded New Yorker, then?" I asked, only half-kidding.

He frowned, considering. Then he looked at his watch and instantly cast his eyes away, glancing too quickly to actually check the time.

"Well, I don't think I'm *cynical*, yet… but I'm bored most of the time. Does that count?"

I found it hard to picture his life as lackluster. Someone who looked like him, with his brain, should surely lead a thrilling existence.

"How can you be bored here?" I laughed, gesturing out at the frenetic New York night descending upon us. Then I remembered that he said he'd grown up there. "Which neighborhood are you from, anyway?"

A bit of his ease dissipated as he sighed. "Upper East Side. My father's grandfather started a real estate development firm in the twenties. It does well." He looked from his work shirt, back at his watch, over to me. "I'm interning there, now, actually."

That explained all of his very professional (very sexy) outfits. And why he always got on the subway in the Financial District. And why he paid for dinner with a twenty he peeled off of a wad of money half the size of my fist.

"What does real estate development entail?" I wondered out loud. "Probably a lot of negotiating."

Gray's eyes sparked while he looked at me. "Yes. A lot. And contracts. Zoning. Construction costs, profit margins." His favored self-deprecating smile slid back across his lips. "But I mostly just sit in meetings and act like I know what the hell is happening."

I laughed before I could help it. "C'mon," I needled. "You can't be *that* clueless. They haven't fired you yet."

Gray smirked again. "Yet." Then he shook his head. "Nepotism, right?"

The thought clearly depressed him. And I wasn't about to try to argue the point. Instead, I tried a different line of questioning. "Are your siblings involved, too?"

He flashed another grin, as wry as it was gorgeous. "Only child."

My lungs squeezed while I forgot how to breathe. My brain once again blurted nonsense. "Oh, I see. You're Spoiled Trust Fund Guy."

Mortified, my lips clamped shut. But Gray instantly gave a deep, rich laugh. The sound echoed through me in a warm wave, pressing my thighs together.

He regarded me with bright, shifting eyes. "And you're Quirky Brooklyn Girl."

I scowled, considering. "Yikes. I work in a coffee shop and everything."

Gray's grin widened, overwhelming me with its sheer perfection. "And I spend Christmas in Aspen. Guess we're both predictable."

I couldn't keep a straight face when he smiled at me like that. "Hopelessly," I agreed.

The more we talked about his parent's ski chalet, their charity galas, their summers abroad, the more I relaxed. Because, I realized; I really *had* let my ego get the best of me.

This guy can't possibly want to sleep with me.

There was no chance he'd ever look at me twice after hearing about my rat-infested student housing in Bushwick and bargain-bin shopping habit. I'd probably never see him again after dinner.

When we both finished our meals, he glanced out at the dark street. "You said you work near here?"

I nodded up Fourth Street. "Six blocks or so to the west. Four Foxes."

He stood in one graceful push. For a moment, I was distracted by the way his slacks hung around his—

"I'll walk you," he insisted, grabbing both of our trays and turning to dump our trash in the can behind him. "I like this neighborhood."

He's just being gallant, I told myself, trying to steady my breathing. *It's nothing romantic. Just a nice, well-bred guy, making sure I don't get robbed on my way to work.*

It was easy enough to tell myself that, but harder to actually believe it, especially when I caught him staring as we stepped out onto the street.

Rush hour had cleared, but the Village was just gearing up. Bodies bustled past each other, sirens wailed. I could almost make out the echo of steel drums drifting out of Washington Square Park.

We crossed through the throng of taxis. On the other side of Fourth, I saw the sign for the Golden Swan Garden on the corner. Gray caught my wistful look and shot me an inquisitive glance.

"I've always wanted to go in there," I admitted with a regretful shake of my head. "I walk by it all the time."

Grayson looked over at it, then at me. "You know, it's funny. I've lived here my whole life and I've been to the Village dozens of times, but I've literally never noticed that before." His glowing green eyes traced the side of my face. "If you want to go in, why don't you?"

"The sign says it closes at dusk," I pointed out, gesturing at the darkness around us. "I work nights."

Grayson fought another smile. He seemed to do that a lot. Almost like he was trying not to laugh at me.

It occurred to me that that ought to be insulting instead of adorable. "Something funny?" I asked tartly, narrowing my gaze at him.

He held up both hands in mock-innocence. "Not at all. I just... You're a rule-follower. And you're cute. Sometimes you say things that make me smile."

My chest squeezed. *Don't panic. You knew he thought you were cute because he asked you to go to dinner. This doesn't mean he actually has any interest in you as a woman. Breathe.*

"And then," he went on, turning his eyes toward the sidewalk ahead of us. "Other times, like when you bite your lip or sway those hips of yours... it makes me want to press you against a wall in one of these alleys."

Oh. My. God.

He shot me another one of his sheepish smirks. "I'd never push my luck, though. It was hard enough getting you to let me buy you that waffle."

Somehow, I continued to put one foot in front of the other. After a few moments, he glanced over at me again, frowning. "You're pale."

Even scowling, his mouth made my heart pound. I wondered what those chiseled lips would feel like if I let him take me the way he wanted to. If I let him press his hard body up against mine.

But then I would be between him and a wall. With no way to escape. My stomach seethed at the thought.

I lifted one hand to my head. "Headache," I lied. "I get them sometimes."

He looked around us, scanning the shops nearby. "Would water help? Or maybe some aspirin?"

I pressed my lips together, hoping my rising panic wouldn't make my voice shake. "No. It's fine. I have to get to work anyway."

Four Foxes was still two blocks up. And I needed Grayson to leave me alone so I'd have time to calm down before I walked into the café.

I stopped on the next corner. "The Christopher Street station is just below us. The 2 will take you back up to the Upper West Side, right?"

"The 1," he corrected, and then started to protest. "But, Ella, I—"

"No seriously," I interrupted, "It's okay. I'm good from here. But…"

But… what?

I wanted to see him again. I also knew I could never actually *be* with him.

God. Maggie's right. I need therapy.

His face would torment me later. He looked… confused. Wounded. And, more than that, he seemed genuinely worried about me.

I couldn't leave him with nothing, so I reached into my bag and pulled out the blue felt-tipped pen I ordinarily used to take notes in class. Before I could overthink it, I reached for him.

"Here."

I slid my fingers under his heavy, warm hand, and scribbled my phone number right in the middle of his palm. The feel of his skin sent a charge tingling up my arm.

I watched his chest expand on deep breath. "Ella…"

Ella, what are you doing? Ella, I don't need your number. Ella, this was fun but…

Our eyes locked when I looked up at him, waiting for him to finish his rejection. But half a breath later he hooked his arm around my waist.

The heat from his body washed over the front of mine, bathing my breasts and chasing a chill down my back. The smell of him—that warm, expensive musk—strengthened the pull deep in my belly.

I thought the feel of his body would send me spiraling. Instead, it steadied me. My tremors started to fade. When I relaxed against him, the arm wrapped around my waist tensed. His hand spread across my hip, flexing restlessly.

Bending closer, Grayson lightly skimmed his lips from my temple to my cheek. I swore I felt the caress echo between my legs.

His face loomed inches from mine. Our gazes collided again, bewildered blue to smoldering green.

"I'm *going* to call you," he murmured. "So just… give me a chance. But I don't…" Frustration flared in his eyes. "I won't chase you if you don't want to be caught."

He really *was* beautiful and brilliant.

And, suddenly, I *really* couldn't breathe.

So I slid out of his grasp and backed up. Flashing my most believable smile, I did my best to convince him—and myself—that I could do this.

"Okay," I said. "Catch me."

***

Chapter Five

September 2016

Ella

I'd been seeing Dr. Laura for two years.

Definitely long enough to know when she didn't approve.

While I told her about Parker's proposed lunch date and my mixed feelings, her delicate brown brows folded in consternation.

"Ella," she replied, staring steadily. "I hear your disbelief—which we've determined is needless self-doubt—and I hear your anxiety about re-entering the dating world—which makes sense, since it's been years. But what worries me is the way you describe Parker."

In my head, I rewound my monologue, searching for something objectionable. "I said he was handsome… successful for his age… and nice?"

"Yes." Dr. Laura dropped her pen into her omnipresent notebook. "And when I asked how he made you feel, you said…" Her eyes scanned her notes before she quoted, "'Fine.'"

When she repeated the word back to me, I winced. "Oh."

She shrugged her rounded shoulders, hidden beneath a billowing kimono as per usual. "Don't get me wrong. It's perfectly alright to accept a date with a man you don't have feelings for. Initial attraction doesn't necessarily determine long-term success. Many of the married couples I've worked with started out as apathetic strangers. I only raise the issue because I'd expect you to have feelings a bit more complex for someone you've worked with for over a year. With your anxiety, I'd at least expect a bit of apprehension about how dating him could affect your job…"

I frowned, following her logic. "But isn't it good that I'm not anxious?"

"Maybe," she allowed. "Or maybe you're not worried because you've already closed yourself off to the possibility of a real relationship."

"With Parker?"

Kindness suffused her chocolate gaze. "With anyone who isn't Grayson Stryker."

When everything fell apart, I only survived by telling myself the hurt would dwindle over time. I thought the pain would be faded and familiar by now. But bone-deep dread still sucked the air from my lungs every time I heard his name.

Reading my expression, Dr. Laura softened further. "You asked me to stop asking you this, but I feel I need to do it one last time. Ella—are you certain that there's nothing to be done to repair what you lost?"

Right on cue, guilt joined the despair, swirling into an eddy of misery.

Because I didn't "lose" him… I left him.

"No," I murmured. "Not after what I did."

She opened her mouth to argue. I waved my hands, begging her to stop before she began. Then I pressed my palms into my middle, doing my best to hold the chasm closed.

I'd heard all of her gentle assertions before. None of them would ever undo what I'd done. For the first time, she seemed to accept that claim. "Alright Ella. Moving on, then?"

My head bobbled. "Moving on."

Grayson

For the first time ever, I kicked the shit out of Amir.

My chauffeur-turned-security-liaison, Marco Amir, ordinarily won every round when we sparred. Easily, given his Hulk-like 6'5"-frame. It didn't help that he was also ex-military. And a former cop. And a self-professed gym addict.

As he adjusted the set of his bruising jaw, his dark eyes widened. "Did you take a shot of amphetamines? Because you're on another level."

For Gray, for always.

My teeth ripped at the boxing glove strapped to my right wrist, unfastening it. "I don't know what you're talking about," I muttered, throwing the gloves into the middle of the ring. "You're just pathetic today."

Amir's black brows arched. "Damn. So it's like that, huh?"

My non-existent patience completely unraveled. "It's however I want it to be," I snapped. "You *work for me*, remember?"

In fine form, I tore out of the ring, snatching my duffle bag en route to the elevators. I didn't so much as glance back before stepping into the cart. "I'll see you in the morning. Six. Don't be late."

A military man through and through, Amir kept his reply entirely even. "Yes, sir."

Two floors up, my anger burned off, leaving a puddle of shame behind. I scrubbed the back of my neck, squeezing my eyes closed.

First Beth, now Marco.

I added his name to the list of out-standing apologies I owed others.

Mom, too, I realized. On my ride uptown after work, I bit her head off for pressing me too hard about a date she fixed me up with a few weeks before. Really, I was just appalled that I couldn't even recall the poor girl's last time by the time my mother called to ask me about her.

And Daniel. Known by most as "The Other Stryker," my older cousin basically saved my ass when he stepped up to help me run half of the operations at Stryker & Sons. And, sure, we didn't always agree on various business methods. But he got shit done. And all I ever did was argue with him. Just that evening, I sent a terse email demanding the poor bastard re-do a project that was already totally acceptable, just because I could.

Speaking of bastards…

Graham. My asshole best friend, who put up with more of my moodiness than anyone. I owed him a round of drinks. Or two. Or ten. In fact, I blew him off for the third time in a row the previous week.

And Dad.

Of course. He always sat at the very top of the list. I basically spent my entire existence apologizing to my father, albeit indirectly.

The elevators swung open, revealing my lonely hallway. Another barb of regret pricked at me.

I designed the whole building from scratch… and, ironically, the damn hallway outside of my own penthouse wound up being the only piece I hated. Because the penthouse took up the entire top floor, the elevators *should* have just opened right into it. Instead, I opted to put a narrow strip of blank space between the elevator doors and the stainless-steel gateway to the apartment.

Needless.

My electronic lock disengaged with a swipe from my keycard. I shuffled through the pointless door and leaned back against the cold metal. Emptiness echoed back at me.

For Gray, for always.

In another fit of impotent rage, I threw my shit to the side. In a normal home, a duffle bag that big would have hit something. But I designed my place with surgical minimalism.

White oak, steel, and glass.

I could see the entire wood floor from my place on the threshold. It sprawled in a cavernous circle, only interrupted by the metal island off to the right, an occasional piece of furniture, and the fogged glass that partitioned off the master bedroom, the terrace, and the guest bath.

Ella would hate it.

It was not the first time I'd had that thought. In fact, when I designed the place, I went out of my way to alienate any memory of her. I banished colors, texture, and warmth; opting instead for hard surfaces, clean lines, cool fixtures.

Usually, my spite comforted me. But not tonight.

For Gray, for always.

Ignoring it all, I turned to the left and made a beeline for the bar along the far edge of the great room. My shaking hand poured out four fingers of gin. I gulped it, not even bothering to mix it with tonic.

I panted through the liquor's burn, bracing myself over the ashen bar top with both hands. "Jesus."

After refilling, I wandered over to the glass wall at the back of the penthouse, staring without seeing. I wished—for the thousandth time—that I never rode the godforsaken subway in the first place. That I never noticed the sweet girl huddled in a pile of red yarn. That I never chased her down, asked her out, determined that I had to have her.

But I did.

I *had* to have her. And, when she left, I had to let her go.

While I debated the wisdom of reading past her book's dedication, I took my gin with me into the shower. By the bottom of my glass and the end of my grooming, I reached a decision.

Not knowing what the book was about felt like having a shard of glass lodged in my consciousness. Every time I tried to focus on something else, a dart of pain niggled at me, reminding me that I still didn't have answers.

Holding my breath, I slid under my covers and stared up at the dark ceiling. Finally, I summoned the courage to open the reading app on my phone.

For Gray, for always.

The words stared back at me, proving that I hadn't lost my mind. They were really there.

I tapped past the cover pages, to the first chapter. Three pages in, suspicion kicked up. The characters, the settings. Bits and pieces of dialogue I'd worked hard to forget. It was all too familiar.

A scene in a small park... I scrolled ahead, scanning for the location of an upcoming chapter. *An art gallery...*

My heart fucking stopped.

Dear God.

Chapter Six

September 2013

Grayson

My loft felt emptier than usual that night.

It was one of those trendy places on the West Side, designed to feel big and bare. Usually, I liked it. So, what the fuck was my problem?

I thought about going out, working out, jacking off. None of it appealed to me.

Well, mostly. I considered using the thought of Ella to get myself off. The way her body felt when I held her on the street made my cock twitch.

But every time I thought of her, the way she acted after dinner stopped me cold.

I stared up at the ceiling over my bed, unable to shake the image of her face when she told me she could walk the last two blocks to work alone. And I felt...worried.

She seemed afraid. Of me.

My mind reeled, trying to figure out *why*. Before, I thought maybe she just wasn't into me... But she asked me to come to dinner with her. And she gave me her number, then told me to "catch" her.

Was it all a game? That would be fun, under normal circumstances.

But, for some reason, I didn't want to play.

The way I felt when she suddenly left me in the middle of the Village sealed it—I wasn't messing around here. I wanted her, badly enough to go out on a limb as many times as it would take to have her.

Something told me Ella wouldn't put me through some sort of obstacle course for no reason. The fear I saw on her face didn't seem put-on. It felt genuine. When I pulled her body close to mine, she actually trembled. That couldn't have been part of some act.

I trusted her. In a weird, overwhelming sort of way. I couldn't imagine her ever doing anything to purposefully confuse or upset anyone.

So that meant she was truly afraid. There was only one way to find out why.

Her phone rang five times before she picked up. "Gray?"

For the first time since our walk, I smiled, loving that there were no other guys out there with 212 area codes calling her. "How'd you know?"

I heard her shifting around and tried to imagine what her room looked like. I knew she lived in some bombed-out hole-in-the-wall in Bushwick, built for students, sharing space with her friend from the train.

But I guessed her room would be colorful and warm and covered in knitting. Just like her.

"Guess I'm not cool enough to give my number out to multiple strangers in one day," she sighed. "And I don't think I know anyone else who would call me this late."

Something about the softness of her voice set off the alarm bells in my head. "Are you okay?"

She paused for a second too long. "I'm alright. Work was long tonight and—" She exhaled static into the line. "I'm fine, though."

I only heard all the things she *didn't* say. "And…?"

I would have taken any other girl at her word to avoid a whole dramatic diatribe; and I'd just determined that I trusted Ella. So

I don't know why I doubted her. Maybe because she seemed like the type to downplay her problems to make other people feel comfortable. That only motivated me to dive deeper, though.

A small snort of derisive laughter came through the receiver. "You'll laugh at me," she warned.

I wanted to hear *her* laugh. "If I do, I'll do it quietly," I joked lamely. "According to you, I'm a gentleman."

Except when I'm thinking about your lips. Or your skin.

"Uh-huh." Her voice dripped sarcasm. She clearly knew better. After a long pause, she gave in. "It's um… it's the sky, actually."

"The… sky?"

"Yeah," she rushed on, trying to get her words out quickly. "Back home, I always liked to look out at the sky before bed, to see the moon and the stars. It was—My dad was an astronomy researcher. So, I think I did it to, uh… to see him? Sort of. Anyway. There's a harvest moon tonight and I missed its rise because I was at work, so I knew it wouldn't be at its fullest, but I just looked out my window and—"

Her voice choked off, like she was too embarrassed or too upset to go on. I understood her anyway. "You can't see it, can you?"

The city lights. Their glare made stargazing impossible. For a New Yorker like me, it was no big deal. I never got used to starry nights.

But Ella was, and she missed them. And I actually, miraculously, knew what she was trying to say. "You're homesick."

Her voice lowered to a whisper. "Yeah."

I thought of her in that cramped, warm room, looking out at a blank sky, missing her father. I could tell from the lilt of sadness in her voice that it wasn't an ordinary sort of missing—that it was a bigger, more permanent kind. He must have passed away. "I'm sorry."

I'd never meant those two words as much as I did in that moment. Ella could tell. "You know, Gray," she said, and giggled lightly. "Most people say that because they have to, but… I believe you."

The sinking, soaring feeling swelled up inside of me again, bursting until my throat felt blocked. It dazed and terrified me how the smallest change in her demeanor—a determined slant to her jaw, a pensive sigh, her little laugh—could send me careening toward this unknown cliff.

In the back of my mind, my fantasies of Ella evolved along with my feelings. Before, I wanted to make her wild for me. I wanted her to scream my name louder than she'd ever said any other man's. I wanted her pleading for me to shove into her.

Now, I wanted her even *more*… but differently. I didn't care as much about the ego boost of having her beg or my territorial need to make so her desperate for me that I would have her entirely to myself. All of that seemed selfish and hollow compared to the thought of using my body to give her comfort.

I wished I could hold her, relax her, help her forget about whatever sadness or fear filled her eyes before she left me stranded on the street. Maybe, if I kept at it, we would both be able to forget.

I let my mind run away with me for a minute before forcing myself to stop. Having a hard-on—even if it was more romantically-inclined than my normal erections—wouldn't help me cheer her up.

"You called me Gray," I pointed out, hunting for a subject to distract us. "No one else ever has."

For a second, I swore I could *hear* Ella bite her lip. "You're right. I'm sorry. I'll stop. It's just what I've been calling you in my head for some reason."

I meant to tease her, but my voice was rough. "Don't stop."

Her next words sounded breathy. "I won't." Then her tone dropped lower. "Gray."

Despite all my efforts, my dick hardened instantly. Even so, I found myself with the same dumb grin she always inspired. "Say it again."

She gave another small giggle. "Gray."

My face hurt from smiling. "God. I like that way too much."

"I like it, too," she admitted, back to sighing. "Gray..."

I waited. If she was ever going to trust me enough to tell me why the idea of us together upset her, I knew I had to give her space. That was part of trusting her.

"I don't—" She shifted and I heard a mattress squeal. "I want you to be happy."

It happened again—I read the anxiety shadowing her words, and heard all of the ones she didn't say. "You think you're making me *un*happy?

She spoke through her teeth, probably chewing her lower lip some more. "No. Not yet. But I think... I could, accidentally. Or I would, eventually. I don't know how to explain it."

I tried to imagine how. Ella, with her perfect peachy skin and her silky blonde hair and the sapphire eyes. Ella—funny when she meant to be sharp, intelligent in her shy, quiet way. Genuine. Gorgeous. Would I ever be near her and feel unhappy?

"Not possible," I decided.

"No, seriously," she argued. "I'm not—I just don't think I can be what you're looking for."

The urge to argue sprang up. It took me a minute to calm myself enough to speak evenly. "Ella. *You are* what I'm looking for. And you said you'd give me a chance. Can I see you tomorrow?"

I held my breath while she hesitated. "I work until two tomorrow."

Without a single clue as to what I would do with a girl, in the middle of the afternoon, in the Village, I found myself saying, "Okay. I'll meet you there at two."

She seemed unsure. "Okay..."

"Okay." I nodded, hoping my own determination would somehow seep into her through the phone. "I'm going to hang up now, before you can talk either of us out of it. I'll see you tomorrow."

"You're bossy," she complained, but then gave a resigned exhale. "I like it. You better quit while you're ahead, though. You may be bossy, but I'm persuasive."

Once again grinning like an idiot, I killed the call.

Ella

Sometime between Gray hanging up and my six A.M. alarm, the seasons clicked.

Saturday morning dawned with a chill that swirled through the air and stuck to the sidewalks. The perfect morning for a hot cup of coffee...which meant work would surely be insane.

Across our single room, Maggie's rumpled bed remained was still empty. She was either still at a rave or passed out at a friend's, which left me to my own devices.

It was hard enough knowing how to dress for a busy shift on a cold day without the whole going-on-a-date-afterward situation. I wound up in a pair of gray leggings and a huge, slouchy sweater I'd knitted out of a spool of soft navy wool.

Eying my clogs longingly, I tugged on a pair of Mag's grey suede booties. I didn't know much about dating—and even less about dating someone like Gray—but I knew one thing from Maggie's relentless crusade against the comfy green shoes: they weren't sexy.

And I was almost mostly sure I wanted Gray to find me sexy.

The cold subway was quiet and mostly empty. I spent the whole ride thinking about how Grayson acted on the phone. He clearly understood me, even when I didn't. And he was so sexy and composed—equal parts heat and cool. The enigmatic combination devastated my self-control.

I wanted him, but I had no idea *how* to want him without completely freaking out. For the first time in a long time, putting my hands to use looping yarn through my needles did nothing. Even walking eight blocks in the autumnal chill didn't shake the nerves.

Luckily, work was as crazy as I anticipated. My shift flew by in a rush of pumpkin-spice-everything. The espresso machine whirled constantly, steam billowing every time I made a macchiato or a latte.

"Elle."

After six hours, my manager's voice started to sound a lot like one of the teachers in the Peanuts cartoons. I waved my hand, letting her know I heard her, but continued with the four cappuccinos I had on deck.

"Ella!"

Nikki and her dreadlocks appeared at my shoulder, scowling at me. "Your shift is up. And there's a guy at the counter who's asking for you and staring at your ass. Stalker or date?"

I whirled to find Gray, focusing on my backside with put-on concentration. It was so unexpected, I blurted a laugh. "A little of one and a lot of another," I joked, pulling my apron off and turning to conceal my butt from scrutiny.

Gray flashed the Prince Charming version of his smile, sending a flurry through my insides. His face was so handsome; I almost didn't notice his uncharacteristically casual clothes. While I rounded the concrete counter, I nodded at his charcoal thermal shirt and jeans. "Where are your slacks?"

He came close enough for me to smell the warm cologne on his neck. His green eyes shone down at me. "I gave them the day off. What I have planned for us is a little too… messy."

The suggestive timbre of his voice suggested sex, which should have sent me back into panic mode. But between his scent, his eyes, and the way his Henley stretched over his muscled shoulders, pheromones bathed my brain, turning it to mush. In that moment, the thought of messy sex made my stomach clench.

Then he pulled it out.

Huge, squat, and bright orange.

Another laugh sprang up my throat, breaking our sexual tension. "*What* is *that*?"

He shrugged, employing his rueful smirk. "A pumpkin." Reaching behind himself again, he presented me with a bundle of newspaper. "I told you this would be messy."

The gourd looked bigger around than I was. I tilted my head while I considered its purpose. "Are we going to eat it?" I asked, incredulous.

His low chuckle warmed the inside of my chest and his laugh lines made him impossibly more handsome. "We're going to carve it."

"It isn't even October," I giggled. "Where are we going to go to carve a pumpkin?"

Gray balanced the orange giant under the crook of one arm and wound the other around my waist, pulling me toward the exit. "I told you," he said, casting a glowing green glance over at me. "I have a plan."

For a while, our walk seemed too quiet. The further we went, the more tension stretched between us.

It was my fault. After all, the last time we walked through the same neighborhood, I fled like a coward.

Sneaking a glance at his profile, I hoped I wouldn't find him frowning. But his expression was pensive, trained on the walkway ahead. Still as handsome as ever, but definitely brooding.

Walking along with a man who ought to be a stranger to me suddenly felt surreal. He was a guy from the *subway*. Someone from a different world.

None of it made sense. How did I find him? Why did he like me? For that matter, why hadn't I been afraid of him, that first day on the train platform?

I was always afraid of strange men. A guy who followed me off of the subway and hovered around should have terrified me. Instead, I handed him the contents of my purse.

Gray caught me looking at him and quirked a dark-winged brow. "What?"

I turned my face forward, biting my lip as I shook my head. "Nothing," I insisted, then instantly made a liar of myself by going on. "I just… does this feel crazy to you? We don't really *know* each other."

He hesitated before turning his attention back on the sidewalk in front of us and shrugging one of his broad shoulders. "Isn't this what people do? Meet, talk, hang out. How else am I supposed to *get* to know you?"

I wasn't being clear, but it was hard to put it into words. All I knew was that one day, I was alone; and the next he appeared. Now, he loomed larger in my mind than any other person.

"I'm not explaining it well," I mumbled, more to myself than to him. "I mean, I was on the subway and then you were just… there. Here."

Gray's eyes brushed over my cheek, his gaze warm. "It's like the boats in the park," he said.

Immediately, his features furrowed. Clearing his throat, he cast his focus away from me again, almost seeming self-conscious.

Lost, I shot him a sideways glance. "The canoes?"

He rubbed his hand over the back of his neck. His expression remained stony, but I swore I saw some color creep up his throat, over the somehow-sexy arc of his Adam's apple. "Not the big boats," he said simply, as if that would suffice.

I tried to reason my way through his stoicism, to no avail. Finally, he caught me staring and relented, shaking his head with a sigh. "When I was little my parents used to travel in the summers without me. It wasn't a big deal. I had nannies and it was just a couple weeks… but, to a kid, it felt like *forever*."

Gray kept his eyes trained ahead, as if picturing a scene I couldn't see. "I was...sad? Lonely, I guess. I don't have siblings, you know? So, one day, one of the nannies took me to Central Park; which was fine, but also kind of boring because I'd been there a hundred times with a dozen different nannies. But this particular day, we went down a different route and turned a corner and… it was just *there*. The pond, all full of model sail boats."

"I've seen that in, um, movies," I admitted, feeling like a silly tourist.

He shrugged again, still a bit chagrinned. "It's no big deal, really. But, for a kid… I don't know. I was having a crappy summer, I walked around a corner, and boom. There it was—a whole new reason to love the city, just when I was ready to give up on it. Like magic."

Shame forgotten, he leveled gazes with me, sending a charge down my back. "You remind me of that feeling."

I'm not sure who stopped walking first, but we paused in the center of the sidewalk, watching each other. He studied my face, no doubt reading the awe that filled my features.

Didn't I think the same thing the first day I saw him—that I hated this city? That I didn't know what I was doing there or why I put up with it?

And, then… there was Grayson Stryker.

And I stopped wondering why I was there. Because it felt like I knew, suddenly.

An unspoken understanding passed between us. Another of our odd moments of connection.

I wanted to speak, but I didn't know what to say. Sensing my struggle, Grayson simply offered his hand. I took it and held my breath the rest of the way.

Ten minutes—and a lot of what-the-heck looks from passersby—later, Grayson steered me and our pumpkin into Golden Swan Garden.

My eyes flew to his.

"You said you've always wanted to go in," he reminded me, shoving the black iron gate open with his back. His expression flipped from soft to taunting. "So come in."

I had passed the little corner garden hundreds of times. It was only a few dozen feet of walkable space—but I was always too busy, too late, too tired, or too distracted to walk through.

With cracked sidewalks and black iron benches, the little corner seemed torn from another time; maybe an era when people strolled arm-in-arm and stopped to sit with the seasons.

It was the perfect day to be there. All of the plants were still in summer bloom, even as autumn settled over them. I knew the flowers would die and the trees would start to change color within the week, but, for the moment, the garden was perfectly lush.

"Alright," Gray said, choosing a spot off the center of the walkway. He took the newspaper from me and started to spread it over a patch of grass. "Here's good, I think."

Still in disbelief, I sank down to my knees across from him and took another moment to soak in our surroundings. As I looked around, I felt Gray watching. When I turned, I found him studying me with an intoxicating combination of heat and tenderness.

"Ella," he murmured, forcing my gaze to his. Our connection clicked back into place while we stared. Warmth flooded through my belly. "You're gorgeous."

I wanted to laugh him off. I felt frizzy and overly-dewy from hours in front of the espresso machine. And I surely smelled like a pumpkin pie candle someone sprinkled with coffee grounds.

But it was impossible to deny the depth in his eyes, the lust tempered by scorching sincerity.

I ducked my head while my face flamed. "Thanks," I replied lamely. Then babbled on, "I didn't know what to wear. I usually don't dress for work, cold weather, and a date all at once. I *did* know better than to wear the clogs, though; now my feet are killing me."

His sculpted lips quirked. He ran his eyes down my throat—over to where the wide neck of my sweater exposed my collarbone and shoulder—before they flickered back to mine, still blazing.

"You are horrible at taking compliments," he pointed out, unbothered. "You'll have to get better. Because I don't think I'm going to stop."

I fought the urge to gulp. "What about you?" I retorted. "I bet *you* get embarrassed when someone fawns over you, too."

After a second, his thick brows drew together. "I don't know, actually. Girls don't really give guys compliments like that."

"Huh." I kneeled up and leaned toward him, pretending to inspect his face. "Well, your eyes are obviously…" Words failed me for a second. "Incredible. Which really isn't fair, considering all of…" I waved my hand around his head. "This."

He cocked an eyebrow, bemused. "All of what?"

Rolling my eyes, I reached out and ran my fingers over his sharp jaw. A light shadow of stubble chafed my fingertips, sending quivers through my core.

"This," I said again, my voice softening as I touched the hollow under his cheekbone. "You have the most handsome face in Manhattan."

My hand drifted up to his glossy dark hair, lightly touching one sideburn. "Not to mention, I've only seen hair like this in cologne ads. Or on the covers of cheesy romance novels."

Gray didn't move a muscle, but his eyes followed mine while I traced my gaze over his features. The buzz humming between us drew me closer, until I felt the heat of his throat on my face.

When I realized how close we were, I forgot I was supposed to be making a point. He seemed just as distracted, watching my mouth until I pulled my lower lip between my teeth.

His quiet groan gave me goosebumps. "Ella..."

The next thing I knew, he'd tugged me into his lap and sealed his mouth over mine.

I went into sensory overload. My muscles locked in place while my brain completely whirred to a halt. And, for a moment, I was just sensation.

The feel of his lips surrounding mine, the tingle of stubble against my chin. The way he cradled my back in one arm and reached his free hand up to touch my hair.

Gray groaned again, then slid his tongue against mine in a long, slow glide. Instantly, my nipples puckered. Like he somehow knew, his fingers followed a lock of my hair down to my chest, grazing the outline of my breast through my sweater. My core tightened while warmth spread out from my center, pooling in my panties.

The sound that rose from my throat startled me. Gray's grip tightened while a growl built in his chest. His answering kisses were deeper, less controlled. His tongue wrapped around mine and slipped down it again. He stroked his fingertips along the curve of my bra until I moaned some more.

"Jesus," he muttered, breaking away breathlessly. "You have to stop making that noise or I'm going to get arrested for taking you in this park."

His crude assertion should have turned me off, but, instead, it had me pressing my legs together, trying to relieve the ache at their apex.

A cold breeze blew through the garden. I shivered in his arms, huddling closer to his hard heat. Each time I shifted in his lap, he winced. It took me a minute to figure out why. When I did, my face burned.

"Oh," I gasped, moving to get off of him. "Sorry."

"Uhn-uhn," he replied, holding me tighter. "Come here."

The world shifted as he lowered me onto our pumpkin-carving newspaper and settled alongside me. Lying near him felt so natural;

even more so when he gathered me against his chest and tilted my chin up, considering my face for a long moment.

Sunlight filtered through the trees behind him, bathing his dark head and perfect features. I stared, unable to help myself. He was impossible to believe—a dream.

How did I find him?

I touched his hair, slipping my fingers through the sun-warmed strands. He closed his eyes for a second. When they snapped back open, a new kind of fire rimmed the green irises.

"I don't know what you're doing to me," he muttered.

Before I could think about what he meant, he resumed kissing me, as desperate for the feel of my lips as I was for his.

He kept his hands outside my clothes, stroking my back, the side of my neck, the space between my breasts. I clearly didn't have as much self-control; when the side of his henley slipped up, my fingers followed the fabric, feeling the hard, golden flesh above his hip.

Gray's throat rumbled when I gave in to my impulses and glided my hand higher, following the line of his spine. He softly bit down on my lower lip and I flexed my fingers, scratching his bare skin.

His hips bucked against mine. "God. Ella."

The blood thrumming in my ears echoed the pounding in my sex. I wriggled, uncomfortable with the wetness gathering between my thighs. He bit my lip again, brushing his fingertips over one of my breasts at the same moment, and I whimpered into his mouth.

He murmured my name again, running his hand up and down my leg. My thighs trembled every time his touch came close to the place that ached for him.

"Gray," I whispered urgently, edging on desperation.

He smiled against my lips. "I know. We have to stop... or at least go somewhere private. Before one of us combusts."

Go somewhere private...

For sex.

I was so consumed by my body's carnal reaction to him, I hadn't even paused to consider what we were building up to. Part of it wasn't even my fault—it was him. He got me so turned on, I couldn't remember to be terrified.

Now, though… I remembered.

"We could… carve the pumpkin?"

He blew out a breath, rolling onto his back. "Okay," he exhaled, closing his eyes. "Just give me a minute."

I needed one, too. My entire body felt like a bundle of live wires, thrumming with electric need. I sat up and looked around for something to distract myself from the puddle in my panties.

No one could see us—not that it mattered, at that point. The thought of someone watching mortified me, but I knew it wouldn't stop me from doing it again if I didn't clear my head.

After a few seconds, I looked back down at Grayson. With his shirt pulled up around the hard ridges of his abs, a noticeable erection pressing against his jeans, and his muscled arms up over his head, he looked more beautiful than ever.

Cracking one eye open, he caught me staring and shot me an unapologetic half-grin. "You're killing me," he joked, then glanced down at the bulge in his pants. "I could drive nails right now. And that look in your eye isn't helping."

There was a riot inside of me unlike anything I'd ever experienced before. I probably looked crazy from lust, but I couldn't figure out how to turn it *off*. Embarrassed, I hung my head to hide my face from his view.

"Hey." Gray hoisted himself up. His warm palm pressed against my jaw, bringing my chin back up. "You're perfect. I only meant—I've never been this turned on from kissing anyone. And every time I look at you, it just hits me all over again."

Our gazes locked. I sunk into the green. "What hits you?"

"How beautiful you are," he told me, entirely earnest. A glimmer sparked in his eyes. "How much I want you."

He leaned in and I held my breath, waiting to feel his mouth again. Instead, he reached around me hauled the giant pumpkin into his lap.

"Here." He situated the gourd between us. "This can be our buffer."

I eyed the pumpkin skeptically. "Did you bring any tools?" I asked and nodded at the outline in his pants. "Or are we using that thing?"

Gray's laugh was quickly becoming my favorite sound. And I loved the way it made his eyes crinkle. "I have a pocket knife, smartass."

He patted down his pockets before extracting a steel handle with his initials embossed along the edge—GFS. I wondered what the "F" stood for.

"Okay," he said, considering the task at hand. "What do we do?"

I giggled. "You mean you bought this thing and you don't even know how to carve it?"

Gray rubbed the back of his neck. "I figured you would know. You're from the suburbs. And you told me that story about Halloween with Darcy."

He had listened, even when I was rambling like an idiot over waffles. "Alright," I huffed, pretending to be annoyed. "Give me the knife."

While I worked, he leaned back on his hands and observed me. "Do you still like Halloween?"

The question threw me at first. After being so close, it felt odd to return to small-talk territory. "Umm, not really," I replied, purposefully not looking up. "My dad was really the Halloween ring leader."

From the corner of my eye, I caught Gray shifting in place. “When did you—I mean when did he…?”

I smoothed my face into a reassuring expression. “It’s okay. It was four years ago. I told you he was a scientist; well, he always stayed late at the lab when he was working on something new. It drove my mom crazy,” I recalled out loud, shaking my head when I pictured her nagging him.

“It didn’t snow a lot that winter. Just a little here, a little there. It kept melting and coming back. I guess that’s what makes the roads the most dangerous, though—black ice. He worked late one night and couldn’t see the ice patch on the highway…”

Even after a handful of years, I could still picture him so clearly. His perpetual cowlick, his argyle dress socks. The quiet, dreamy way he smiled at my mom while she flurried around house, always in a tizzy about one thing or another.

Sometimes, I hated that clarity. It probably wouldn’t hurt so much, I figured, if I could forget even a little bit.

“He was brilliant,” I recalled out loud. “Pensive. But he had a great sense of humor. Anyone could make him laugh.”

I stopped when I realized my eyes were filling. “Geez, I’m sorry,” I sniffed, wiping my face and forcing a laugh. “That snuck up on me.”

Gray kneeled up to pull me close. “Hey,” he murmured, “Don’t apologize.”

“I haven’t cried about it in a forever,” I said against his chest. “I have no idea why I’m crying now.”

But, as I said the words, I realized—it was him. Gray. I knew he was listening. I knew he would care. Most people weren’t capable of either, let alone both.

There was something else, too. A feeling I couldn’t quite grasp. One that left me more open and vulnerable than I felt with anyone else.

"I get it," he whispered, nuzzling his face against my hair.

Gray settled us back down on the ground, this time with my body tucked under his arm. I wiped my sweater sleeve under my eyes.

"Tell me more about your family," I mumbled, not wanting to be the center of attention any more. "I mean, I know their names and what they do for work, but… do you get along with them?"

He tipped his head back to look up at the trees. "They're… Yeah, we get along. *I* get along with *them*, anyway." He smirked at himself. "My mom is actually one of my best friends. I have brunch with her every weekend. My dad is… He's a good father. We just…"

Gray sighed. "I don't know how to say this without it sounding like a First World problem. I suppose because it is… He just has a lot of expectations for me. He chose all my schools, my major, my apartment. He's groomed me, you know? To take over Stryker & Sons. It used to be me and my cousin, Daniel, but we had a falling out with my dad's brother. A big one. So now it's all down to me."

I had to agree—it was a high-class problem. But I understood what he meant. He wasn't complaining about his birthright. He just felt smothered. "That sounds like a lot of pressure."

He gazed down at me with shifting green eyes. "Yes."

"And maybe it hurts to think about who you could've been if he wasn't always pushing you in a certain direction," I guessed. "Is that why you have two majors?"

"Yes," he said again. He didn't so much as blink, but I saw his gears spinning. Considering.

I was about to ask him about architecture when he swooped in, silencing me with the warmth of his lips over mine.

That time, our kiss built slowly. After a moment, he laid me back down on our blanket of newspaper and settled over my body. His heat melded into me while he stroked his tongue over mine until I moaned for him again. Cursing roughly, he shifted to put himself between my legs.

Feeling his full weight sent me spiraling into my most terrible memory. Everything inside of me lurched. I tore my mouth from his and made a small, panicked sound.

Gray immediately sat up, frowning while I folded my knees up against my chest.

"…Ella?"

My pulse hammered in my neck, pounding so viciously that I couldn't swallow. Bile rushed up my throat unimpeded. Acting on instinct, I sprang to my feet and turned to run for the nearest trash can.

"Ella!"

I heard Gray rushing to catch up to me. Desperate to be alone, I slapped a hand over my mouth and spoke through my fingers. "I feel sick," I choked out. "I need to go."

He yelled my name again, but I was already running.

Grayson

I spent the rest of the afternoon calling Ella before finally giving up.

It was dark out before I even realized I left the pumpkin, the newspaper, and my knife on the ground in Golden Swan Garden.

Sitting on my sofa, staring at the TV without watching it, I caught myself *hoping* I would start throwing up. That way, at least I'd know she was actually sick and not just… running away again.

After making out for the better part of an hour, I figured I caught any bug she had. But the protein shake and salad wrap I forced on myself for dinner stayed down.

And there I was, for the second night in a row, trying to figure out what the fuck happened. Running through details that made my blood sing in my veins, knowing she was just as hot for it as I was… and having no clue what suddenly freaked her out.

This time the memories… *hurt*? I put so much of myself on the line for her.

I trusted her. Again. Still. And now part of me felt like an idiot while the other piece was almost too worried to function.

What did I do? Did I hurt her or scare her? The thought of harming Ella made me feel like maybe I *had* gotten her fictitious stomach flu after all.

I fell into a troubled, short sleep sometime around one. Six hours later, a dark grey morning woke me. For a long moment, I let myself pretend Ella had come home with me instead of running away. Then I noticed the text waiting on my screen.

The last thing I wrote loomed above her response: *I just need to know you're ok.*

Her reply was as bleak as the weather. *I'm going to be, eventually. I really am sorry about everything, Gray. Obviously there are things I need to work through. Can I text you when I figure it out?*

Helpless anger choked me. I rolled over, turning away from the text, willing myself to forget her altogether.

What a stupid fucking thought.

The following afternoon, I found myself at the gym, pounding my fists into a punching bag, relishing the jolts shooting up my arms.

I deserved the pain. I was an idiot.

Even after I swore I wouldn't text her back… I did. Of course.

I knew I would the second I got the invitation. One of my architecture acquaintances liked to dabble in photography on the side, and he'd landed a gallery space for Saturday night.

The exhibit seemed like a perfect date for me and Ella. I told her so when I sent her a picture of the postcard invite. *It's a public place where I won't be able to tackle you again*, I wrote, only half-kidding. *What do you say?*

But, of course, she didn't reply.

I hit the bag harder. More pain battered through me. *Good.* I was determined to keep going until I couldn't feel anything anymore.

Ella

"So."

I'm sure the decor was intended to help people feel calm. The sandy walls, the warm wood floor, the deep blue couch. A little fountain bubbled on the table next to the door while I fidgeted on the sofa, bouncing both of my legs in turn.

The woman sitting across from me was more relaxed than I ever had been in my life. She settled back in her worn leather armchair and nonchalantly reached for the mug of tea on the table beside her. I eyed the dove grey notebook in her lap, wondering exactly how many pages it would take for her to document my particular brand of lunacy.

At least Dr. Laura Dawn didn't seem cold or severe. When I scrounged together half of my savings and half of my paycheck to pay for one therapy session, I could only hope I'd chosen someone decent to spend the money on.

Tall and long, her soft green kimono-maxi billowed whenever she moved, emphasizing just how thin she really was. Even though her body was slight, she had a naturally soft face, without any lines or angles. Her hair matched—loose, easy curls of short, dark hair that bounced when she tilted her head to the side, assessing me.

When I didn't speak, she smiled kindly. "Your name is Ella?"

I nodded one jerky bobble. "Yes, ma'am."

Her smile grew, changing shades from amused to encouraging. "You can call me Laura," she said. "Or Dr. Laura, if you prefer that."

She slid a slip of paper out from the pages of her notebook. "I see here that you're a student and you paid out-of-pocket to see me for a one-time session. I can also see that you're anxious and, normally, I would give us each some time to get to know one another; but I'm sure you can't afford for me to waste a second."

My head bobbed again.

Her brown eyes softened. "You must be very upset about something," she went on, "to pay to come here. Do you want to tell me about it?"

And, oddly, I *did*. I'd been holding so much in for so long, her offer was irresistible.

"I met a guy on the subway," I muttered while I bit my lip. "Last month. And he's… he's *perfect*. I mean I'm sure he's not *really* perfect but he *feels* perfect to me. For me. Maybe I'm not for *him*, since I'm basically a hobo compared to the girls he usually dates, but—I don't know. He doesn't seem to care about that. Or even notice it, really.

"He just… likes me. Wants *me*. And I know—I *know*—I sound surprised and that's self-deprecating because I should think I'm great and any guy would want to be with me and all that. But, seriously, if you saw this guy you would understand that *him* wanting *me* is like… a miracle. Especially after the way I've acted around him."

Dr. Laura wrote something short in her notebook. "What's his name?"

I blinked, surprised by the simplicity of her question. "Gray."

She gave a small smile. "So you came here to discuss Gray?"

"No." The word jumped out before I could stop it. "Well, yes. Sort of. I need—I need to know if I'll ever be able to be with him."

Dr. Laura's brows drew together. "Surely that's a question you should answer for yourself. Do you feel you could be happy with him?"

I thought about lying in his arms last week. When he held me, everything else melted away. When he kissed me, I believed I'd never think straight again. My body still hummed from the memories alone.

I thought about his laugh lines, his little rueful looks. The way he rolled his eyes but smiled when he talked about his parents. The way he listened, even when I started talking nonsense.

"Yes," I whispered.

She nodded like she trusted me. "He clearly means a lot to you, if you came here today to talk about him."

I knew she was right. I'd been living with what happened to me for a year and a half. I found my own ways to cope with it. I only wanted to confront the issue now because it affected Gray. "I'm worried that I'll hurt him and I don't want to."

Sympathy saturated her features. "Do you feel you're a hurtful person?"

"Normally, no," I sighed. "I'm not doing it on purpose. He wants to be close to me, but every time he tries, I have a panic attack."

Her eyes widened while she jotted down another note. "Have you always had a panic disorder?"

My stomach clenched into a fist. "No."

"So did they develop over time or was there an event that prompted the attacks?"

There it was. The reason I was there. I had to say the thing I managed to avoid for so long. The words I could never scrape out, even when I tried to report what happened to the campus police.

My breath shuddered out of my lungs. "I went to a—I was—"

I almost burst off of the couch and ran. But as my legs twitched, wanting to bolt, I remembered Gray's face each time I turned away from him. And, for just a second, I felt… *angry*. No one got to make him feel that way, not even me. Not because of something that someone else did to me.

The blast of fury gave me one brief, brilliant moment of bravery. I pushed the truth out on an exhale. "I was raped."

I'm not sure how I expected her to react. I figured a psychologist who specialized in young women's mental health probably dealt with assault victims day in and day out. I anticipated questions about exactly what happened—the usual probing, dissecting sort that determine if a girl is exaggerating or delusional.

The campus police had a million of those and my answers, apparently, did not pass muster. Particularly when I couldn't supply them with the name of the vicious stranger who attacked me.

Instead, though, Dr. Laura dropped her pen into her journal and met my eyes. "Ella, I'm so very sorry," she said, utterly sincere.

Adrenaline drained from my body and left me shaking. "It's fine," I rambled tightly, "Really, I—"

"No." Dr. Laura interrupted. "Ella, it's not fine. Now, I may not know the details—and, if you'd like to tell them to me, we can do that. But I do know that what happened to you is creating problems in your current relationship. You must have survived a horrible ordeal, to feel echoes of it when you're with a man you clearly *want* to be with. And that is not okay. Or fair."

I tried to swallow around the lump in my throat, but that only made my eyes water. My voice rasped. "I need to know if I'll ever be able to... *be with* him."

"Sexually?" she inquired, ignoring the blush on my cheeks. "There are a lot of factors that go into that equation, but, generally, I would say yes. Most sexual assault survivors are able to be intimate again eventually. There may be triggers they avoid indefinitely, but, Ella, what happened to you does not have to disqualify you from a fulfilling sex life with a man you desire."

While I chewed my lip, she asked, "Have you had panic attacks when you attempted intimacy with other men? Or just Gray?"

A tremor straightened my spine. "There haven't been any other men," I whispered. "Since... what happened. That was eighteen months ago."

"I see." She made another small note. "And how long have you been with Gray?"

Chagrin made my face flame more. "We aren't really together, yet. He keeps asking me out and last Saturday we had our first—"

Dr. Laura smiled softly. "Sexual encounter? It's okay, Ella. You won't offend me."

My blush deepened again. "Right. Of course not. Yes, we were kissing and… touching. And I wanted him…but then something happened and all of the bad memories rushed up at me. I had to physically run from him to get to a trash can and throw up."

Dr. Laura made a pondering sound. "So you *can* tolerate—and even enjoy—being with him, until a certain point. That would suggest a trigger of some sort. Do you remember what changed in the moments before you panicked?"

I wondered if my face would permanently resemble a beet. "Not really… he was doing all of the same things I liked, before…"

"Did he maybe change positions?" she inquired. "Some survivors have trouble with any position that may resemble their attack."

Closing my eyes, I tried to picture what happened in Golden Swan Garden. "He kissed me…and got on top of me." Queasiness settled over my stomach, twisting my expression.

Her voice was soft. "Was your assailant on top of you when he raped you?"

I juddered, squeezing my eyes shut even harder. "I was drinking… and drugged. I try not to remember." But suddenly I could feel the weight of him again, pressing me into the damp frat house mattress, suffocating me while his palm crushed my mouth and nose.

"Ella?"

I couldn't open my eyes. I bent forward and put my face in my hands. "I think he was on top of me," I gasped. "I couldn't move. Couldn't get any leverage. He had his hand over my mouth."

Silence engulfed the room for a long moment. "We can take a break," Dr. Laura finally offered. "You don't have to push yourself."

It took me several minutes to catch my breath. When I sat back up, wiping tears from my face, Dr. Laura's compassionate expression nearly sent me back over the edge.

"I think you're very brave to do this," she told me. "Gray is very lucky, to have someone care about him so much. But is this what *you* want, too? It's important to be sure you aren't forcing yourself into a sexual relationship you don't really want."

I didn't even have to think about it. "I want him. I don't think I've ever wanted anyone else this way."

Her face broke into another grin. "That's wonderful. In that case, we should use our remaining time to work on your triggers. If we can identify them, you two may be able to avoid them altogether."

The thought made me cringe; laying out a list of no-go sex stuff for Gray sounded mortifying. "And we would have to avoid them forever?"

She gave a noncommittal shrug. "Some couples do, others prefer to push the boundaries. It's a personal choice. I would recommend sticking to your limits until you're very comfortable within them. When and how to approach expanding them? Those are decisions you can make with Gray."

I only had one more bomb to drop. "He doesn't know. And I don't want him to know."

For the first time in our session, Dr. Laura's face betrayed a hint of disapproval. "That's your choice, of course," she acquiesced, diplomatic. "It will make it much harder to honestly discuss boundaries. And, without that information, he'll be at an inherent disadvantage when it comes to understanding you."

I recalled the way he watched me—the way his green eyes shifted between lust and tenderness. I loved that look too much to see any pity in it.

"Do I have to decide right now?"

Dr. Laura smiled again. “Of course not. It’s a very personal decision. In the meantime, let’s ID your triggers and make a plan to work around them.”

“Hold on.” I pulled my phone out and swiped open the message from Gray that I’d been dying to answer for days. I quickly typed out my response: *I’d love to go.*

For the first time in a week, I felt hopeful.

$320 poorer, but hopeful nonetheless.

❊❊❊

Chapter Seven

September 2016

Ella

There was a harvest moon that night.

It was just bad luck. I knew that.

Still, I sat in front of my window and looked up at the blank sky, wishing.

Wishing I'd known what I had when it was still mine. Wishing I'd savored each small piece of it. Wishing it didn't hurt so bad to remember.

Wishing the very best for Gray, no matter where he was.

At noon the next day, Parker took me to Bryant Park Grill.

I wondered how he knew it was my favorite lunchtime splurge in the city. Nestled in the center of the park two blocks from our office, the building always enchanted me. Verdant vines covered the exterior, giving patrons the feeling of dining inside an ultra-modern greenhouse.

Our table happened to be next to one of the tall windows. While I draped my napkin across my lap, I gazed out at the ivy twined just beyond the glass and shook my head. "It's funny… We spend so much time at the firm trying to reinvent beauty; sometimes I forget that simple things can be the most charming of all."

A dimple pooled in Parker's left cheek when he grinned. "You really are a writer," he teased. "You have a mind for poetry."

I decided not to point out that I liked to write novels, not poetry. It was a nice compliment either way. "Thank you," I replied, blushing down at the ivory table linens.

Silence stretched between us, just long enough for me to feel self-conscious. I'd done my best to dress up a bit without seeming too eager; but now my charcoal sweater dress somehow felt too stuffy and too informal at the same time. It didn't help that Parker was his usual charming self, all-too-handsome in a navy suit without a tie.

When the server arrived, he ordered each of us a kale salad and insisted, "You have to try the mushroom ravioli. And the sesame tuna." He requested both before I could interrupt to tell him I only had forty minutes to eat.

"Don't worry," he said, winking while he handed off my untouched menu. "I bribed Marjorie to give you an extra-long lunch."

That was thoughtful of him… Maybe a bit presumptuous to assume I'd be okay with Marjorie knowing about our date… I didn't know how I felt about the issue yet, but it seemed my mind had been made up for me.

And it was probably polite to just eat what he ordered, and not mention that Bryant Park Grill's fish and chips were my favorite lunch in New York. I could always come back by myself after my next payday.

The food he selected turned out to be excellent, anyway. While we ate, he regaled me with stories of his college days at Brown, his desire to eventually start his own ad agency, and his childhood home in Colorado.

It was sort of nice not having to think about what to say. He was funny and interesting, with a creative sense of humor. I laughed between bites and asked questions whenever I could.

By the time the check arrived, I estimated that my half would be well over $50, which meant I would have to cancel my night out with

Maggie over the weekend. Thankfully, Parker snapped the booklet off the table before I even reached into my purse.

He frowned while he fished out a credit card. "Wow," he said, "I'm horrible."

I blinked at him, confused. "What?"

He sighed, leveling his hazel eyes at me. "I brought you to lunch to get to know you and spent an hour talking about myself." He took off his glasses and drug a hand over his face. "Sorry about that. I think you make me nervous."

I had to bite my lip to keep from smirking. The notion that I could make a man like Parker nervous was the funniest, oddest thing he said all day. "Why?" I blurted. "I'm no one."

Oh Lord. Dr. Laura would be so upset if she'd heard that.

"I mean," I went on, "I'm not, like... You shouldn't be nervous, Parker. You're great."

"Ella, you are 'like'," he quoted back at me, waving his hand in my general direction. "I noticed you the day you started working at Idealogue and I still notice you every single day. Multiple times a day. Let me take you out again. Maybe to dinner, next time. And I promise I'll shut up."

I turned my face to hide the blush on my cheeks. "You're interesting to listen to," I told him. "You don't need to shut up."

Parker grabbed my hand and held it up between us. He waited until my gaze met his. "So you'll go to dinner with me, then?"

I couldn't think of a reason *not* to... aside from the obvious. But Dr. Laura would surely have something to say about *that*, too.

"Yes," I agreed, making sure to smile. I added my one weird caveat. "But no dessert."

Parker grinned, even as his blond eyebrows furrowed. "No dessert, huh? I knew no girl could have a body like yours unless she was into fitness."

A perfect cover for my eccentricity. "Yes," I lied. "I, um—I'll have to work off this ravioli on the treadmill later."

I figured he'd never find out that I had never been on a treadmill for longer than six minutes in my entire life. What he didn't know couldn't hurt him…or me.

"So maybe Friday night?" he asked, still gripping my fingers.

I bit my lip again. "I have plans with my roommate on Friday, but I could do Saturday."

For a second, he looked nervous. I quickly added, "If you don't have… something else to do."

I'm not sure how I sensed it, but I just *knew*. He clearly had another date Saturday night. It wasn't all that surprising. That's how most men in the city operated. And some silly office crush followed by one maybe-date-lunch certainly didn't guarantee me any sort of exclusivity.

"No," he decided out loud. "I mean, I did. But I'll cancel it. I'd rather go out with you."

I probably should have been flattered, but I only felt guilty. Now some other girl was going to get cancelled on. *Ugh, this is why I don't date.*

Parker checked his Apple watch and whistled. "Damn. Marjorie's going to have my balls. My hour-and-a-half was up ten minutes ago."

He dropped my hand to put his card back into his wallet and stood up. "Come on," he said. "We can decide where to go Saturday night on our way back to the office."

Grayson

Wednesday, our luncheon with the NYC contractors' union took twice as long as planned. That put my entire day off by two hours. I was irritated.

My dad was *pissed.*

“Fucking money-grubbing pains-in-the-ass,” he muttered, settling into the back of our Mercedes sedan. If his life-long chauffeur, Barnes, had anything to say about my father’s language, I couldn’t tell. The old Brit met my gaze in the rearview, waiting. When I nodded, he peeled away from the curb immediately, speeding uptown as fast the lunch-hour crush allowed. I turned my attention back to Dad.

People always told me we looked nothing alike. I used to think it was a weird comment to make; but as the years passed and our appearances diverged more dramatically, I started to notice it, too.

The one thing I did inherit was his size. We were both tall and broad-shouldered, with long arms and legs to match our statures. My hair seemed to get darker every year and my eyes lighter. He was he opposite—his once-blond hair turned white before it started to fall out, and his eyes went from gold to murky brown.

Mom liked to tease him about his round face. Once upon a time, he hid it under a well-groomed white beard. But, now, when he glowered at me, his round chin seemed to seep into the folds of his neck.

Half-bald and pale yellow, Mason Stryker was still a force. His age and health didn’t seem to matter—Dad remained an imposing man. Even more so when he got angry.

Internally, I sighed. If he blew into the office in a shit mood, it would mean a bad Wednesday evening for everyone.

“They gave us concessions on the health insurance bullshit,” I pointed out, squashing a twinge of guilt. “They only asked for $0.67 more per hour.”

“That’s nearly a dollar more for time-and-a-half,” he groused, hoarse. “Which they always get because it takes their lazy asses twice as long as it should to get anything done.”

I’d learned it was better to act apathetic. If I dug my heels in, so did he. Shrugging, I tried for blasé. “Building in the city is harder.”

I looked out the tinted window at the traffic boxing us in. "Less accessible streets, more transportation delays."

Dad harrumphed.

His poor health had really started to show. He had no patience, very little poise. His suits fit looser, particularly in areas where he used to be broader and stronger than me. Recently, a restless air of discontentment often filled the shadows on his face. It took me a long time to put a name to it:

Helplessness. He didn't tolerate it well.

His Blackberry buzzed in his hand and he turned his glare on it. "Damn it. Your mother."

He always acted annoyed when she contacted him during work, but I knew better. Mason Stryker may have been a man with few weaknesses, but Jacqueline Stryker would always be his Achilles' heel. He adored her and indulged her endlessly.

His muddy, tired gaze softened while he read her message. It accomplished what I couldn't. His mood shifted from hostile to speculative.

"She's asking about our table at the brand relaunch next weekend," he said gruffly, looking out his own window. "She's worried about you. Thinks you need a companion."

For Gray, for always.

In the cold light of day, my revelation about Ella's book felt like a bad dream. The thought of reading all of our memories, twisted around made-up characters… possibly coming to a false happy ending…

It gutted me.

As such, I studiously avoided the app for two days, choosing to pretend I never saw the damn thing. But that didn't keep me from reliving the whole fucking ordeal every time I thought of her.

And I thought of her every other minute, now.

Most of the time, I managed to summon the energy to get pissed off. But, in the rare moments when I was too exhausted to raise my hackles, I just felt dejected.

I thought I'd feel better as the hours wore on and I continued my campaign of avoidance. Instead, the ache in my chest only swelled and throbbed. Sometimes, its immensity made it hard to catch my breath.

"Dad." My voice sounded tight. I sighed, struggling against the weight of my grief. "I don't want a companion, okay? You know I done with all that shit."

Sensing my upset and not wanting to witness it, my father kept his gaze trained on the traffic. "It's been three *years*, Grayson."

I couldn't resent his dismissal. After all, hadn't I firmly convinced myself that I was over her? That time healed all wounds? Hell, a week ago, I would've *agreed* with him.

But that was before.

Before the reminder that she was still out there. Before the confirmation that I had—against all evidence to the contrary—meant something to her, after all. Before this invisible knife lodged itself in the tender space on the left side of my chest. The same place Ella Callahan once conquered.

For Gray, for always.

I suddenly felt my father staring at the side of my face. "Son," he said quietly. "You have to get past this."

My insides squeezed. I forced my feelings down and turned back to the window. "I don't know what you're talking about."

Chapter Eight

September 2013

Ella

I rethought my entire outfit eight times in the space of the twenty-minute subway ride uptown.

The small black dress seemed artful enough back in my room. And Maggie lauded the way it skimmed my body from mid-thigh to bust. Though, with off-the-shoulder straps hugging my upper arms, and slit up the back, I wondered if maybe I put too much of myself on display.

Second-guessing, I pulled the bobby pins out of my hair and let it fall to cover my bare shoulders and chest. Between that and my ruby-red lips, I hoped no one would notice the cleavage situation.

I got off in Chelsea, at the same stop where Gray first asked me to dinner. The memory made me square my shoulders as I marched up the steps.

No more running, I vowed to myself.

Thanks to Dr. Laura, I had a plan. If I ever had a prayer of salvaging my chances with Gray, I had to convince him I could get through a whole date without panicking or trying to bolt. I had a list of triggers to avoid; but it seemed safest, for the time being, to sidestep anything sexual altogether.

After all, he invited me out in public, to a party his friends were attending. I had to make a good impression and prove I was capable of holding my own at upscale events.

Surely we could go one night without jumping each other.

That way, I would make it through the whole evening without an episode. Gray would see that I wasn't psycho. And then, next time we were alone, I could try the trigger-avoidance stuff.

Simple.

Or not.

Because dear *Lord.*

Always beautiful beyond compare in slacks and button-down, Gray was *otherworldly* in a suit.

He stood at the mouth of the subway station, checking the gold watch on his left wrist while the street light above shone off of his slicked black hair and polished leather shoes. His light grey suit complimented both. And the crisp white dress shirt underneath highlighted the golden warmth of his skin.

He'd shaved, revealing the perfect lines of his jaw and cheeks. My gaze instantly flew to his lips, sculpted to perfection, even when he quirked them into a concerned frown.

"Gray?"

When he turned and saw me, the shadows instantly fled his face. He started to smile, then froze. His eyes widened into big green vats.

"Ella. Hi."

He looked down at the sidewalk between us while dread chilled my stomach. *Oh no,* I thought, *it's the dress. It's too much.*

"I'm so sorry if this outfit is wrong. I don't think I've ever been to a gallery opening before. I can go home and change, but it will probably take me a while…"

I expected one of his wry grins or maybe an eye-roll. Instead he looked off to the street and adjusted his gold cufflink. "Your outfit's great," he said unconvincingly.

He checked his watch again, staring for a second too long. "We should go," he concluded.

I'd Googled the gallery, so I knew it was two big blocks away, on the other side of the High Line. I turned to the west and started walking, pulling my red-and-black velvet shawl tighter around my body.

It was cold, considering it was only the first weekend in October. Looking at Gray didn't help. In fact, every time I glanced at him, a chill ran down my back.

He was as distant as I'd ever seen him, his gorgeous face set in remote lines. With both hands in the pockets of his pants, he stared straight ahead and strode on in silence.

"So, um," I started, trying to make conversation. "This is a friend of yours?"

He shrugged a shoulder and kept his eyes forward. "I guess so. Architecture is a small program at Columbia so we all know each other. This guy is also an art major. I guess these pictures are supposed to be 'revolutionary'." He made air-quotes and shook his head. "I'm not sure what that *means*, but…"

"It sounds nice," I commented, feeling lame. "Who else will be there?"

With another evasive lift of his shoulders, he grunted, "Not sure. Probably a bunch of art school chicks and the guys who follow them around. My old roommate is usually one of those. Shithead."

Gray normally had a dry sense of humor, but now he just sounded… cynical. My annoyance accidentally bled into my tone. "Well, if you don't want to go, why are we here?"

For the first time since I arrived, he actually looked at me. A flash of amusement moved through his eyes. "I have to go to lots of stuff like this. I never *want* to. And, like I said, I figured we should try a date where we can't make out. The other kind hasn't gone my way lately."

I couldn't tell if he was angry or just making a point. "Well it hasn't been easy for me either," I retorted, tossing my hair over my shoulder.

He smiled sardonically and rubbed his hand over the back of his neck, casting me a sideways glance. "So you agree we shouldn't hook up, but you thought you'd torture me with that dress?"

I gave an indignant huff. "As if you don't know that suit makes you the sexiest man alive."

His grin instantly melted all of my pique. "It's Armani," he said, giving his sleeves an amused once-over before cocking an eyebrow at me. "Who knew you had such expensive taste?"

That made me giggle. *Maybe I do*. After all, Grayson Stryker wasn't just any guy. If men were chocolates, he would've been the most decadent, expensive truffle in the case. Ironic, considering I would've been a pudding cup.

"It's less about the suit and more about what's in it," I teased, pointedly eyeing his broad shoulders and tapered hips.

Gray's gaze warmed at my compliment. He extended his hand. A peace offering. "Think we can manage this?"

His voice sounded teasing, but his face didn't match. Concern filled the space between his brows until I reached over and slid our palms together with a reassuring smile. "Yes."

Tension leeched out of his body and my heart swelled. He was clearly nervous that I would hurt him by running again. It only strengthened my resolve.

No more running.

Hoping to relax him further, I squeezed his hand while we walked. "So what should I expect at this thing? I've never been to an exhibit opening."

He flashed me the Prince Charming smile that made knees wobble. "Well, it will be a bunch of privileged Columbia students, convincing ourselves we're cool by standing around and acting like we know anything about art."

"Insufferable," I laughed. "It will be easy to keep my hands to myself while you're being a pretentious poser."

He chuckled. "See? My plan is working already."

Grayson

I knew I was screwed the minute I saw her.

She looked so insanely gorgeous, I had to avoid looking at her for the first two blocks. Even after that, the way her dress clung to her body made me lose my mind.

I knew she hadn't chosen it to torment me—it was, all-in-all, a tasteful choice—but anything that tight on a body like hers challenged my self-control.

I'd never seen so much of her peaches-and-cream skin at once. Her bare shoulders, chest, and neck were perfection. The lack of jewelry or straps just tempted me even more.

I wanted to burrow my face against her and kiss her throat. Peal the front of her dress down and find out if her nipples were the same pale pink as her natural lips or if they matched coppery bronze freckles dusting her naked shoulders.

Jesus, Grayson. Get a grip.

Somehow, I calmed down while we walked to the gallery. Mostly, I suspected, because of her temper and her jokes.

We were laughing about the gallery's self-importance when a gust of wind swirled her sweet honeysuckle scent up into my face. When she trembled from the cold, I resisted the urge to pull her body to mine and bury my hands in her blonde waves, repeating the promise I made to myself all week.

I'm not going to touch her. No more pushing.

Never mind the fact that her hand was already twined with mine.

I blew out a frustrated, anxious breath. "You ready?"

"Sure." Guileless, she smiled up at me through pretty, painted lips. "How bad could it possibly be?"

Muted house music greeted us when I held the door open. Ella walked ahead, letting her shawl drop down to her elbows as she stepped into the heated room.

Holy hell.

My mouth dried. The slit up the back of her dress beckoned to me, a perfect arrow to the apex of her thighs. Thin black material clung to her sumptuous hips, accentuating the way her spine sloped into her perfect ass. Without the shawl, I saw that her dress dipped into a V at the center of her back, showing off the flawless curves of her shoulders.

She glanced over at me, sapphire eyes wide. "Wow."

My sentiments exactly.

Oh. The gallery.

To me, it looked just like every other "hip" gallery in town. Basically, a big white room. I could tell Ella was impressed, though. Probably because of the size—this particular space had an echo-y, sprawling quality to it.

I stepped up beside her. "Remember," I muttered, "Whatever you do, don't use the word 'derivative'. That's like yelling 'fire' during a Broadway show."

"This is really fancy," she whispered back.

Her crimson mouth curved, but trepidation filled her eyes. The shy little smile warmed my chest. I bit back the impulse to tuck her close to me and relax her with a kiss.

Instead I tried for an encouraging grin. "So are you."

Her hands smoothed over the front of her dress while she glanced around, clearly doubting my compliment. But, honestly, she looked every bit as elegant as any of the trust fund brats clustered throughout the room.

The dress was fine. It wasn't her fault that she was so ridiculously sexy, no matter what she wore.

I could already feel my body tuning in to hers. When she turned, I turned. When she paused, I paused. The second she swiveled her face up to look at me, I stared right back.

Intensity surged between us, seeping down into me. Her eyes pleaded, beseeching but conflicted. For a second, it seemed like they begged me to touch her. But, half a moment later, a frisson of apprehension replaced the heat.

Anticipation and dread pumped through my veins—the feeling of holding my breath, followed by the realization that I'd be waiting for air indefinitely.

No more pushing.

I blew out a sigh, trying to convince myself I was fine.

It didn't work. I needed a drink.

My gaze broke from hers, scanning over her head until I located the bar in the back corner. "Do you want a drink?" I asked, carefully avoiding another look into her eyes. "The wine at these places is usually terrible but the champagne is probably drinkable."

"You like champagne?" she asked, surprised.

I shrugged. "Not particularly. I usually drink gin. But I'll have champagne with you. Let me go grab some."

Ella clutched my sleeve. "No," she replied. "These are your friends. Go say hi and I'll get our drinks. Gin, you said?"

I blinked at her, dumbstruck. I'd never had a woman get a drink for me. It just wasn't the way people did things in our circle. Usually, the men gallantly offered to retrieve the drinks so they could cluster together at the bar and discuss the Dow or some other bullshit for the rest of the night.

But she wasn't thinking about social order or appearances. She was just being thoughtful.

Before I could argue, she tossed a smile over her naked shoulder and glided over to the bar. I watched her go, my body tingling from the sight of her. I didn't even notice my former roommate and current best friend, Graham, come up behind me.

"Who is *that*?"

God. Here we fucking go. I needed the liquor more and more.

"My date," I snapped, turning to glower at him. "Emphasis on *my*."

"Eh." He shrugged, unbothered by my possessiveness. "I can turn her."

When we lived together our first year at Columbia, girls often got Graham and I confused. Sometimes they mistook us for brothers, but I didn't see it. We had the same coloring, I guess, but his features were darker than mine and he was leaner, rangy.

That night, he had on blush pink blazer that irked me for some reason. In fact, his presence annoyed me in general, though I couldn't explain why. Usually, I liked having one of my actual friends around at events.

My irritation made sense when I caught him eyeing my girl, though. His deep brown eyes glittered while he watched Ella rub the front of one ankle over her opposite calf.

"Where did you find such a snack?" he said. "I don't recognize her from the usual roster."

I probably should have had some lie up my sleeve, but it didn't occur to me to be embarrassed about the truth until I saw the way Graham looked at her. He could tell she wasn't one of us. No matter how gorgeous she was, she didn't have the air of snobbery that set socialites apart.

I watched her smile sincerely at the bartender, looking the server right in the eye. And decided on the spot that I didn't give a fuck what Graham or any of them thought. I didn't want to lie. I didn't want Ella to find out one day and think I was ashamed of how we met.

"The subway."

Graham's mouth dropped halfway open. "What *the fuck* is the billionaire heir to the biggest development company in Manhattan doing on a *fucking* subway?"

I scrubbed a hand over my face, losing patience. "I was downtown and there was traffic."

He followed my gaze back to Ella, who shared a laugh with the bartender as he handed her our glasses. Graham choked halfway through a sip of his scotch. "Holy fuck," he coughed. "Is *she* getting *your* drink?"

I felt my hands fist in my pockets. "Yes."

His eyebrows rose sky-high. "Damn. I need to start riding the subway. Maybe I'll find a hot piece to fetch my cocktails."

He was kidding, but I'd never felt less like laughing. "She's not a fucking servant," I growled. "She's *nice*."

Graham didn't seem overly impressed by that. "Ah. Nice. Novel, I suppose." He squinted at Ella's back, considering. "How is that—you know, in bed? Boring, I would think. Then again, you always *were* sort of vanilla. And sometimes the quiet ones can really bring the—"

Ella turned back in our direction. I cut him off. "So help me God—be polite, or I swear I will tell everyone about the spring break trip when that jellyfish stung your balls and you cried like a bitch."

His face darkened at the memory. "Killjoy," he muttered.

Ella was still smiling her innocent, beautiful smile when she rejoined us. "Is Hendricks decent for gin?" she asked. "They had another kind but I wasn't sure…"

"It's great," I assured her, taking the glass and gulping twice. "Thank you."

Her nervous blue eyes flickered to Graham. "Hi, I'm Ella. Or Elle. Whichever."

While he shook her hand, his stare skimmed over the peachy skin at the tops of her breasts. "I like a woman who isn't too particular. Graham Everett," he told her, flashing a roguish grin. "Let me know when you're ready for an upgrade, gorgeous."

My fingers twitched around my cocktail. *I'm going to kick his ass.*

I expected shock or fear. Instead, Ella giggled. "Ohhhh, you're *that* guy." Amusement lit her gaze when she turned back to me. "He's the shithead?"

A cleansing burst of laughter killed my insecurities on the spot. "Yes," I confirmed, chuckling. "That he is."

Graham had the grace to keep smiling. "I see my reputation has, unfortunately, preceded me. So I'll leave you two to... whatever..."

He winked at Ella, just in case his suggestive tone wasn't clear enough. Then he tossed me a goading, mischievous look. "By the way, Grayson," he said casually, turning to walk away, "I think Olivia is here somewhere."

My stomach dropped. *Fucking. Hell.*

I'd been so pleased about finding a date Ella might enjoy, it didn't occur to me to check the guest list. My eyes followed Graham's mocking smirk to the crowd hovering in the back corner of the gallery. Olivia's curtain of glossy dark hair stood out immediately.

Beside me, Ella traced my gaze across the room. She shifted on her heels and took a hasty sip of her champagne. "This is good," she mumbled, clearly uncomfortable. "But I'm used to the $4 kind you get at Trader Joe's, so."

Another unexpected laugh broke the tension crowding my lungs. Ella shrugged, giving an apologetic grin around the rim of her glass. I tightened the fist in my pocket, once again resisting the urge to reach for her.

It got harder by the minute. She was so endearing. Sincere and silly at the same time.

I loved how much she *didn't* belong there. It was no wonder she immediately caught Graham's eye—she was the only one in the room not walking around with a stick up their ass.

If I wasn't so distracted by her, I probably would have had the foresight to get us out of there. But instead of coming up with an excuse to bail, I fell into her dark blue eyes for a moment too long....

"Grayson!"

I might have cringed. Ella saw me bite back a scowl and turned to watch Olivia float across the wide, white space.

Her blonde brows furrowed, quizzical. There wasn't enough time to explain the whole thing, so I used our remaining seconds to blow out a deep breath and stare hard into her eyes. "I'm sorry about this. Really."

Ella looked even more confused. But when I turned my attention to the brunette approaching, she managed to do the same.

Olivia looked predictably chic in an asymmetrical white dress that hung off of her straight, thin body in an effortless, artful way. Her black hair shone under the cold gallery lights, falling down over her shoulders and curling at her waist. Diamonds the size of marbles winked in her ears, almost the same cool grey as her eyes.

She glided right up to me and kissed the air on either side of my face. "Grayson, love! I didn't know you'd be here!"

Yeah fucking right.

Ever since our parents set us up two years earlier, Olivia Watts had somehow shown up at nearly every event I attended. The only-child heiress of a supply chain mogul, she was as wealthy and well-connected as my family... maybe even more so. My father liked that.

Unfortunately, I found her borderline-insufferable. Even more unfortunately... that fact had not stopped me from hooking up with her. A few times.

Olivia raked her cold gaze over Ella, then pointedly ignored her to grace me with one of her wide, whitened grins. "Stunning pieces, no?" she commented, gesturing around us. "Dunkin is *tres* talented."

I knew damn well she hadn't looked at the photos. No one had and no one would. They were just props in a social farce masquerading as culture.

Yet I found myself agreeing. "Yes," I said evenly. "Groundbreaking."

I expected Ella to shrink back from the conversation. Instead, I caught her smirking into her champagne, clearly hearing the insincerity laced through my fake assessment. It was almost enough to make me smile. She always surprised me in the best ways.

"Olivia, is it?" she chipped in, smiling at her. "I'm Ella, Grayson's date."

Her confidence made her even sexier. My body drew closer to hers, coming to stand with my front left side pressed to the back of her right.

The warm curve of her backside taunted me through my suit pants. I pushed against her automatically and she pushed back, casting a small, knowing smirk over her bare shoulder.

Olivia's eyes hardened while she watched us, her disapproval visceral. I couldn't focus on anything she said, though. I was too busy with the teasing glide of Ella's hips when she shifted on her feet. My free hand smoothed over her side, tingling when I felt her warmth through the thin fabric.

I forced my attention forward just in time to tune in to the end of their exchange. "—nice to meet you," Ella chirped, bright but dismissive. "Enjoy the show!"

Olivia scowled at us, her thin lips pulling down. "You as well," she replied, shooting me a glare while she turned on her heel. "Grayson."

Pride and disbelief blurred together while I watched her retreat. I looked down at Ella's amused expression. "You have to teach me how you got rid of her. I've been trying to get her leave me alone for *years*."

Ella did her best to look confused. "I have no idea what you're taking about," she replied. "I thought she was a *lovely* girl."

While I laughed, I instinctively pulled her closer. The odd, glowing warmth seeped from her body to mine and swelled up inside of me again. Our eyes locked as our laughter faded. We both froze instantly, realizing, too late, that we'd broken our pact not to touch each other.

Ella shuffled back a step and cleared her throat. I found myself bracing for some type of fallout, expecting her to run again. But she just glanced around, looking for a distraction.

"Should we…look at the pictures?" she whispered. "No one else is."

I swallowed a large mouthful of gin. "I told you. No one here knows one single thing about art. Possibly not even the artist."

A spark glimmered in her gaze. "Is his name really Dunkin? As in, Donuts?"

Another laugh sprang up my throat. *Where has this girl been all my life? Maybe I'd actually enjoy going to pretentious functions if I got to spend them with Ella.*

"Yes. Dunkin; as in, Donuts."

Interest lit her eyes. "Well now I really *am* curious. Can we look?"

It was amazing how she made me forget myself. Normally, being the only one in a room of my peers to do something would have made me antsy. But Ella didn't know how we normally did things. Her innocence was so refreshing; it forced me to rethink the usual order of it all.

Of course we should look at the damn pictures in an art gallery. What kind of absurd asshole ever decided otherwise?

She followed me to the corner of the room, where the first piece was labeled with a small acrylic plaque. "*One*," she read, tilting her head while her ocean eyes assessed the print. "Oh I get it. It's called 'One' but they're twins."

Her crimson grin widened, distracting me with thoughts of her lips on various parts of my body. "You were right," she said, "this is ridiculously self-important."

I nodded, hoping to shake out some of the images in my head. "We're just getting warmed up. You might need more champagne."

Truthfully, she was already flushed from the half-glass she'd drunk so far. Her glowing skin looked warm. So warm… especially in the cool, stark gallery light.

She caught me eying the blush on her chest. "I'm a lightweight," she replied, biting her lip and sliding her gaze down my body. "If I have much more... who knows what I'll do?"

The subtle come-on hardened my cock instantly. "You don't need to tease me," I warned mildly, sipping my gin. "I've been fighting an erection since the second I saw you tonight. And I've been replaying that moaning sound you make in my head for two weeks." I gave her a rueful smirk. "You clearly have the advantage here."

The skin along her neckline blazed while her thighs pressed together under her dress. Her sapphire eyes darkened as she licked her lips. "I wouldn't be so sure about that."

Unable to resist anymore, I ran my thumb over her mouth, lightly releasing her lower lip from her teeth before skimming my fingers down her neck and over her collarbone. Her breasts rose and fell while her breathing picked up.

It reminded me of the way she gasped when she wrenched herself away from me in the park. The memory poured over my head like a bucket of ice water. I leaned away from her.

She swayed slightly before standing up straighter. My hand fell to my side. "I'll go get us another round."

Ella

The champagne was either a horrible idea or a stroke of brilliance.

The more I drank, the less I cared about all of the inhibitions that normally made me so nervous.

It got harder and harder to worry about propriety, especially when Grey looked so devastatingly handsome. More than his looks, though… it was *him*. His wry humor and calm charisma. His deep, easy laughter and intense, soul-wrenching stares.

He was lying when he said none of the people in the room knew anything about art. The photos were mediocre, but Gray was genius. He spoke about light and color and lines like they were a form of poetry, making gestures with his hands to help me visualize his thoughts.

I found my body naturally drawing closer to his throughout the evening. By the bottom of my second glass, my breasts brushed his biceps as he explained asymmetry.

He broke off mid-stream and stared down at me, green eyes shining with want and something more…dangerous. They skimmed my chest and my hips in turn.

"Ella," he warned, clenching his jaw and reining himself in.

I fell back a step, nearly dizzy from the desire surging through my center. "You're right," I told him, trying to take a deep breath. "Sorry."

Clearly, he was doing everything in his power not to touch me again. But I *wanted* him to. And we couldn't seem to say apart. Our mutual magnetism was too strong.

He watched my breasts strain against the tight black fabric and adjusted his stance, shifting to conceal the bulge in his pants. "Damn it," he muttered.

The edge to his voice made me just as wet as the thought of his cock getting thicker. Our eyes locked, connecting soul-deep. A wall of heat built between us, condensing the air.

I wanted him, but I didn't know if he could forgive me for bolting on him before. I'd promised myself I wouldn't run, but he had no way to know that. I had to find some way to prove it.

Anxiety pulled at the bottom of my lungs, tugging insistently. But I didn't want to let it win. I'd already done that… and it hurt him. So, this time, I closed the gap between us and reached up to touch his cheek.

"Gray," I murmured, letting my hips press tight to his front, feeling his erection against my belly. His teeth ground harder while his body disobeyed him, stiffening between us. I gave a tiny half-smile. "This was a hopeless plan."

He stared right at me, warring with himself. Without a veil, he let me see all of his raw emotions, all of his doubt, all of his need. There was something so vulnerable about that. The moment of intimacy soothed my apprehension.

Gray watched my face closely. I'm not sure what he saw there, but it settled him. His posture unwound and his hands found my waist, stroking down my sides while a low rumble built in his chest.

He did a sweep of the room, frowning at all the people clustered around us. Casting a glance back down at me, his nostrils flared on a deep breath.

"Fuck it," he decided, eyes blazing. "Follow my lead, okay?"

Before I had a chance to answer, he clasped my hand in his and started off toward the bar. I trailed at his heels, confused and somewhat embarrassed when heads turned to follow our path.

Instead of whisking me out into the cold alley, Gray acted like we were waiting in line for more drinks. Anyone observing us quickly lost interest.

A moment later, he discreetly tugged me into the hallway next to the bar and pushed open a random door. He pressed it shut and turned a lock.

I don't know if he grabbed me or if I jumped him. Either way, I wound up in his arms, burying my face against his white dress shirt. He tightened his grip on me while one hand stroked over the back of my hair.

"I know how this seems, but I need you all to myself," he told me, voice pitched low. "Just for a minute, okay?"

I loved confident Gray, brilliant Gray, and good-listener Gray… but the moments he let himself be vulnerable with me were my favorite. He was normally so self-possessed. But as he clutched me closer and turned his face into my neck, I felt him sink into me like I was a soft place for him to land.

"Okay," I agreed, holding on harder.

Rigidity drained from his broad shoulders while I pressed my palms into his back. In that moment, I realized; he was nervous.

This was hard for him. This event full of fake people he barely tolerated, trying not to spook me… maybe even having feelings for someone at all.

"Thank you for bringing me," I said softly, wanting him to know I appreciated his efforts.

Gray sighed against my skin and leaned back to study my face. "Thank you for coming. And not bailing on me." He gave a wry half-smile that didn't quite touch the swirling depths of his eyes. "Yet."

The look on his face pinched my heart. I couldn't stand that I'd made him doubt me. For a second, I worried that that uncertainty would always loom over us. But then Gray took my face in his hands and sealed his mouth over mine.

It was a soft, slow kiss. Sweet and enticing and far too fleeting. "Please," he murmured. "Stay with me this time."

My fingers threaded into the hair at the back of his neck. "I *want* to," I told him, quiet and sincere.

I'd never meant anything so much, in so many different ways. Gray watched me for a long second, his eyes unfathomable in his handsome, somber face.

"I know you do," he finally replied, stroking over my cheek and tracing the side of my neck. "I believe you."

He cupped my jaw, holding me still while he bent down for another kiss. He hesitated half a breath away from my lips.

And, suddenly, everything seemed absolutely clear. Simple.

I wanted him. And he was there, waiting for me.

So I stretched up and closed the distance between us, wrapping my arms around his neck and falling against his chest.

"God, Ella," he muttered, kissing me back like he couldn't get close enough, fast enough. "It was torture not touching you."

Gray pulled me in tighter, roughly sliding one hand down to my ass while the other grasped the hair at the nape of my neck. He sucked my tongue, sliding the length of his over mine in deep, lush licks. My toes curled while every muscle in my core pulled tight.

Oh my God. This is really happening.

I fought the rush of fear swelling under my diaphragm and ran through my mental list of triggers. The broom closet he chose eliminated most of them. Without a bed or another big surface, it wasn't possible for him to lay on top of me. And the street lights coming in through the windows along the roofline were bright enough that I could see his face—see that it was *him*, the man I wanted so badly, and no one else.

I tried my best not to overthink it. My body knew what to do better than my brain did, anyway. I wanted to feel the heat radiating from his chest, so I tugged the hem of his shirt out of his pants and went for the buttons, moaning at the feel of him under my fingertips.

His body was perfection—tan and smooth from his throat to the defined ridges of his abs. The light layer of hair on his chest tickled my palms while they rubbed over his pecs, making him groan into my mouth.

He broke off suddenly, stilling my hands by placing his on top of them. "Tell me if you want to stop, okay?"

But I didn't. So I grabbed the lapels on his open jacket and tugged him back to me, nipping his lower lip before sliding my tongue against his again.

Gray growled and lifted me onto a low bookcase beside the door, shoving my dress up to the tops of my thighs as he went. I hooked my knees around his hips and yanked his body between my legs, wishing I could get close enough to grind my wetness against him.

He bent to rub his face into my overheated throat, skimming his lips down my sternum at the same time his hands traced the edges of my breasts. I gasped his name, tightening my legs until I felt his erection graze the center of my damp panties.

"Fuck," he mumbled, bucking into me as his mouth found mine, his kisses more intense than before. I felt his hand sweep down my back, releasing my zipper. The pressure confining my breasts disappeared.

"Take your straps off," he ordered, hoarse.

Nerves fluttered in my stomach. Then he leaned back slightly, stripping out of his shirt and jacket so I could see his flawless torso; and every rational thought evaporated.

Fascinated by the sheer perfection of him, I couldn't help but run my hands over his wide shoulders. Unyielding strength flexed under my fingertips while his muscles quivered.

I didn't stop. I wanted him to know how much he turned me on. I wanted him to feel as good as he made me feel when he put his hands on me.

But I was still awash in apprehension, my body at war with itself.

"Hey," he murmured, more gentle than before. "Ellie. Look at me."

The new nickname instantly melted the tense knot in my stomach. Panting, I met his gaze just long enough to see the incredible spectrum of emotion raging inside of him. Fervor lined his face as he leaned into me again, nuzzling our foreheads together before sealing his lips back over mine.

That time, Gray kissed me with a passionate reverence that made my heart ache as intensely as my sex. I whimpered into his mouth and he made a low, soothing sound while his hands drifted over my shoulders to pull the straps down my arms, exposing me.

A rush of cool air hardened my nipples. He broke away, chest heaving, to look down at me.

"You're so beautiful," he groaned. "Every part of you is better than I imagined."

I pressed my heels against his backside, pushing his solid length tighter against me. "I want you," I breathed, desperate, "I'm throbbing from the feel of you."

Hunger darkened his expression. "You think you're throbbing now?" he asked, too softly. His fingers trailed down the sides of my bare breasts until I shuddered. "I've barely touched you, baby," he murmured, kissing the top of my shoulder.

I rubbed against him again, beyond shame. "Then touch me."

He ran one hand up my thigh, coming to the edge of my thong. His thumb skated over my center. "Ellie," he rasped, eyes flashing. "You're *soaking*."

His touch glanced over my panties while I squirmed, afraid I'd go out of my mind if he didn't stop. "Gray," I begged.

His gaze snapped back to mine. "You're so wet already. Has it been a long time?"

I bit my swollen lip, embarrassed. I wasn't sure what to tell him, how much to explain; so I settled for a simple truth.

"No one's ever touched me like this," I whispered.

I was sure I'd put him off when he froze for half of second. Then his mouth crushed down on mine. The strokes of his tongue matched the rhythm of his thumb until I cried out and reared up, needing more.

Gray slid into my panties and touched me skin-on-skin. A garbled moaning sound bubbled out of me while he rumbled against my lips, "You're so *ready*. It's making me so fucking hard."

Desperate to feel him, I reached over and unzipped his pants. He stilled before resuming our kisses, fucking my mouth with his tongue.

Black boxer briefs clung to his massive erection while I sized him with my hands, rubbing his length until a roar vibrated in his chest. The sound tightened my nipples to the point of pain.

Looking for relief, I brushed my breasts against his chest. Gray reached up with his free hand, expertly pulling each peak in turn. I melted as his thumb sank into my pussy. The shallow thrust was just enough to make me clench around him.

"You're going to come," he whispered. "I can feel you."

My grip on his cock tensed while he penetrated me and rubbed two fingers over my clit. Everything inside of me squeezed and then burst with a warm rush of relief. I cried his name, letting go.

"*Gray*."

Grayson kissed me feverishly, absorbing my moans until I broke away to catch my breath. His bare arms enveloped me, burning my naked back. I felt myself shaking, but couldn't focus long enough to think of anything other than the erection now pressed into my belly.

The second my mind rebooted, I slipped down to my knees, pulling his pants and boxers to the middle of his thighs. His cock sprang forward. Magnificent. Thick and hard as stone, with veins pulsing up the sides and a dark layer of well-groomed hair at the base. My mouth watered at the sight of the pre-cum slicking his wide head.

"Ella, you don't have t—"

As desperate for his orgasm as I had been for my own, I sucked him into my mouth.

I couldn't fit him all the way in, but he didn't seem to care. He thrusted in and out while a long, guttural sound escaped him.

"God," he gasped, reaching down to gently cup his hands over my hair. "Don't stop."

I tucked my lips around my teeth and clamped down, giving him more friction, finding a faster pace. His head fell back while he panted, his hips churning. "Damn it, Ella."

Sliding my hands up to his hard glutes, I pushed his cock into the back of my throat. At the feel of his muscles flexing, I moaned over his length.

I added my fist, chasing it up and down his shaft with my lips, swirling my tongue around his head on every other draw. His hands tensed against my scalp while he bucked into my mouth, again and again; then came so hard, I had to swallow around him to get it all. A tremor ran up his frame when I pulled back.

Gray looked down at me like he was seeing me for the first time. At that moment, someone walking past the closet bumped the door handle, rattling us both. He cursed before bending to pull up his pants.

"Let me zip you up," he ordered. "We'll sneak out the back."

Grayson

With loose limbs and a truck-load of post-orgasm endorphins flooding my system, I felt stoned as I led Ella out of the gallery's back exit.

Ellie.

The sobriquet came to me in a moment of near-insanity, but I liked it. It suited her. And I loved the way she alone called me Gray. It seemed only fair that I have a similar claim on her.

In my stupor, the bright street lights at the mouth of the alley looked like hazy halos. I steered us to the main street as purposefully as I could, given my fuzzy head and weak knees. When we cleared the second corner, I reached back for her hand.

But she wasn't there.

Before panic could spiral down through my center, I spotted her. She lingered about twenty yards behind me, eyes squeezed shut, propped up against a building.

Shit.

"Sorry. I'm fine," she lied when I was close enough to hear her. "I just…need a minute."

My body felt so tied to hers, I could sense the anxiety radiating out of her. Instinctually, I braced my arms on either side of her shaking shoulders, shielding her from the autumn wind and any passersby.

"Hey," I murmured. "What's wrong? Is it… what we just did?"

My stomach sank at the thought of her hating what was going to go down as the single sexiest memory I possessed. I tried not to look wounded while she blinked up at me.

"*No*," she promised, fervent. "That was… insanely amazing. And I want to do it again. But I sort of freaked out when we had to rush out like that and I'm just trying to calm down so I can figure out why it upset me."

It still didn't make sense to me, but at least she tried to explain. And she hadn't fled. Yet.

Part of me wanted to comfort her, but another part worried she'd disappear if I didn't keep her close. I slid my arms down to hug her.

"Can I hold you while you figure it out?" I asked. "You're a runner—you have priors."

She giggled weakly, nestling her face against the base of my throat. A second later she relaxed and pulled back to look up at me. "Huh."

Her perplexed expression was adorable. I bit back a smile. "What?"

Color rose to her cheeks. "I think that was it," she mumbled, dropping her gaze to her feet. "I just needed you to hold me."

That thought echoed through me until it sunk in. My entire world shifted on its axis.

This beautiful, funny, bright girl wanted me to hold her. And she felt bad about it.

Looking into her eyes, I could see she was embarrassed to need anything from me. Regret and tenderness vied for space inside my chest, crowding around my lungs.

I tugged her back into me and buried my face against her hair. "I *want* to hold you," I confessed. Just as they had in the broom closet, more words rushed out before I could stop them. "If it were up to me, we'd go home together and I would hold you for the rest of the weekend."

She softened in my arms, sighing. "I'm sorry if I'm being needy."

Maybe she was. I couldn't tell anymore. Because, with her, the word lost all negative connotations. The thought of Ella needing me sounded like heaven.

A second later, I felt her stomach rumble and realized I never fed her dinner. "How about I hold you in a cab and we go eat something?"

She grinned up at me. "Can 'something' be ice cream? I like eating dessert for dinner with you."

The mysterious feeling I had no name for flooded through me. Bliss and awe and fear woven into one undeniable fact: I would've done anything for her.

***

Chapter Nine

September 2016

Ella

I knew it was wrong.

I knew that.

But after four mornings of his stupid billboard slapping me in the face, I couldn't stand it anymore. I convinced myself that I needed to see Stryker & Sons' headquarters—if anything, I argued internally, it would give me a sense of what to expect from their new addition to my neighborhood…

My phone didn't help. The Maps app informed me that the walk was much shorter than I imagined, meaning I had time to make my ill-advised journey and still catch a taxi to be on time for eight P.M. yoga with Mags.

Eight blocks passed in a blur of commuters and cabs. My mind raced along with my heart. *I shouldn't do this*, it chanted. *I shouldn't do this. I shouldn't do this.*

But it was too late.

It was done.

I was there.

Stryker & Sons stretched up into the skyline, all steel beams and smokey curved glass.

It was surreal to find that Grayson was less than ten blocks away. How many days had I pondered, as I sat at my desk or on the subway… how many times did I wonder where he was?

Now, I was there, too.

I imagined he was probably still be inside. His father always worked well into dinnertime. I couldn't imagine Gray operating any differently. I also knew that it would be a catastrophe if either of them saw me. Not to mention the Other Strykers…

Did that stop me, though?

I ghosted in from the crowd teeming on the sidewalk, craning my neck back to admire the edifice looming over me. It was impressive—a twisted cylinder, stacked up into the skyline… and just familiar enough to make my pulse leap.

Because I'd seen the building before.

In a notebook, back when it was no more than an errant idea. One of Gray's doodles, sketched into the margins of some financial accounting assignment he didn't care about.

I remembered the exact moment I first saw it, almost three years before. One of our lazy Sunday mornings in his fashionable loft. He stood at his kitchen island, glaring down at his homework, pouting gorgeously. I wasn't able to resist drifting over to him, running my hand between his broad, bare shoulder blades, rubbing the tension from the back of his neck while I peered around his bicep.

The page presented a jumble of notes and equations, scattered among pencil-grey skyline sketches. My gaze followed the lines of his imagined vista, snagging on a crude version of the very building that now stood before me.

"That one," I'd murmured, hugging his waist with one arm while my free hand traced the cylindrical spire. "That's my favorite."

Gray had given me a bemused, guarded look. "That one, huh?" He considered the doodle, frowning some more before he dismissed his work as he always did, "No. It's too… standard. Doesn't stand out enough."

I used to hate hearing him critique himself. With all his breeding and refinement, I once assumed he was simply a critical person; but I'd learned the only person he ever truly disapproved of was himself.

Brushing my fingers over his jaw, I offered him a soft kiss. "Looks perfect to me," I'd told him easily. "Besides, you'll think of a way to make it stand out. Maybe a garden or something."

He finally cracked a smile, then. One of his wry, rueful grins. "A garden in midtown," he muttered to himself, shaking his head while his eyes ran back over the doodle, his gears spinning. "Huh."

And here it was.

Just yards from the building's automated doors, a concrete park adorned the grounds. Singular and unexpected, the oval patch mirrored the cylindrical shape of Stryker & Son's tower. All statues, with life-size bonsai trees and modern topiary shapes, it was essentially a Japanese landscape, dipped in smooth grey stone.

I recognized Grayson's unique genius immediately. It was his take on my idea. Something to set their skyscraper apart from the masses. Something beautiful and creative, but still understated. Like him.

I sank onto one of the floating slate benches tucked into the rock-trees, feeling a strange burst of pride.

He did it. He took the job at his father's company and made it his. He found a way to use his talent without letting his family down. I always knew he could.

My hand traced the edge of the nearest bonsai statue. The cool stone sent a shiver up my arm while tears built inside my chest.

Somehow, I felt like it was… ours. His brilliance, my reassurance.

We did it.

The pressure inside me broke on a sob as I covered my face in my hands. I tried to breathe through the memories, hoping anyone who walked by would assume I was some random secretary who just got fired and keep walking.

"No, I can't do drinks tonight, but I can do a breakfast next week."

I could have picked the voice out of a lineup of hundreds. It had murmured the sweetest words into my ear, given me wicked commands, woken me, along with kisses, in the mornings. It sailed through the other side of the paved garden, heading for the street. I cracked my fingers over my streaming eyes, peeking out just in time to catch Grayson clip toward a white Mercedes idling at the curb.

The air in my lungs evaporated.

Holy Lord.

If Grayson Stryker was a god three years before, I didn't even have a word for him now. Women turned their heads, mouths hanging open, as he strode past them. His fitted blue suit and white tie made my jaw drop, too.

For a long moment, I stared, rememorizing the sharp lines of his face, the straight slope of his nose, the way his dark hair caught the twilight. White-hot longing pierced my middle. For one insane second, I caught myself wishing he would look at me, just so I could see those green eyes one more time.

In a flash, I realized the real reason I'd come—I needed to see *him*, not the building. I needed to know, once and for all, if I would always want him more than I wanted anything else on the planet, if I would truly have to carry that yearning in my heart forever.

At least now I had my answer.

Grayson

I slipped into my car and fell back against the black leather seat, exhausted.

"Where to, sir?"

To the empty condo at the top of the building I owned. To the bed that was too big for one. To the kitchen I never touched, the wet bar I touched way too often, and the TV that was almost large enough to make me forget I was alone.

I turned my head to look out from the dark glass, exhaling roughly. "Home, I guess."

Lately, it felt like I spent half my time staring out tinted windows.

"Mom, I said I was sorry."

"Well, you better be!" she rebuked. "You may be the CEO now, *mi amor*, but you will *always* be my son. And, like it or not, I'm concerned about your well-being."

I stretched out on my sofa, allowing her to berate me to her heart's content. She deserved it and so did I. I grunted along, repeating my apology a few more times before she wound down.

Finally, she sighed. Her voice took on a solicitous quality that made me uneasy. "Before I tell you what I did today, I want you to remember that I'm your mother and I love you."

Oh God. "Mom…"

"I called Olivia Watts," she admitted, then rushed on before I could react. "And she was thrilled, Grayson—*thrilled*—to be your date next week. Now, I know you told your father that want to go alone, but it's simply unbecoming for one of the wealthiest, most powerful young men in the city to turn up stag at his own gala. And you certainly can't bring one of the random women from your phone apps..."

I would have rather asked every Tinder hook-up from the past calendar year than go anywhere with Olivia Watts. Or "Olivia Twat," as Graham so cleverly deemed her.

My stomach sank. "Jesus, Mom, *why her*?"

"Well, I did try a few other young ladies first," she conceded. "But none seemed too keen on accepting an invitation from *me* when, really, darling, it's *you* who should be making your own social calls."

"I *do* make my own social calls," I gritted, "when I *want* to go out with someone."

"Alright, alright," she relented. "I know I over-stepped. I'm just so worried about you, Grayson. You've seemed so down the last few times we were together. I worry that you're getting lonely. And—before you tell me just how often you're *not* lonely—we both know that one-night-stands are *hardly* a cure for the lack-of a lifelong companion."

For Gray, for always.

"I had my shot," I thought out loud. "I had it all right in my hands and I blew it. You were there, remember?"

Neither of us liked to talk about it. I suspected my mother's despair over watching me lose Ella may have actually rivaled my own. She wanted so badly for me to be happy. When I lost the one girl I ever wanted a life with, she grieved with me.

"Yes," she replied, soft. "Well. Nothing to be done for that now, I suspect. So you'll go with Olivia? Please?"

Ugh. Kill me. "I'll consider it," I allowed. "If I can't come up with a suitable alternative by next week, then, fine. Of course, she can still attend as a guest either way."

I'm not a complete dickhead...

Most of the time.

My mind spun forward to logistics. "It's our brand re-launch, Mom, so I'll be working the entire time. I won't be able to pick her up or take her out beforehand and I'm not sure I'll be much of a date while we're there. But if you'd like her come and sit at our table, I'll be a gentleman, of course."

Mom thanked me and told me she loved me one more time before hanging up. I rested my phone against my sternum and stared up at the white plaster ceiling overhead.

Graham texted me a minute later, asking if we were still on for drinks the next night. I agreed and shot an invite to my cousin, Daniel, knowing he'd want to come talk shop with us.

Eventually, I made my way into my closet, finding the next day's outfit pressed and laid out for me by the housekeeper. I forgot they came on Thursdays… and found it darkly amusing that I didn't notice the difference between my apartment being "clean" versus "dirty." Primarily because I didn't have any personal possessions aside from my own clothes.

And the box.

No one ever would have guessed, when they looked at my rows of polished dress shoes and the athletic-shoe boxes stacked beside them, that one box didn't hold any shoes in it at all. On a whim, I crouched down and pulled out the Nike container, chucking the lid aside and lowering myself onto the floor.

The pieces in the box were all I had left of Ellie—scraps, literally. She was very thorough when she left me, but I scrounged together a few small things over the weeks of misery that followed her defection.

A hair tie. Her handwriting—specifically, the recipe for a soup she once made, scribbled onto a notecard that fell down the crack between my old cabinets and the trash can. A dark green bundle of yarn. A copy of her favorite book of poems.

And one unopened gift.

I wrapped my hand around it, feeling the crinkle of the wrapping paper. A bolt of regret stabbed my gullet, blocking my throat.

I should get rid of it, I thought for the millionth time. *Return it. Sell it. Burn it.*

But who was I kidding? I couldn't even read past the third page of her book.

Besides, would getting rid of any of her trinkets help me forget the way she stroked my hair when I put my head in her lap? Or her small, shy smiles whenever I praised her? Or her adorable embarrassment when she gave me one of her handmade gifts?

No. Nothing ever could.

I'd been trying to forget her long enough to know that some memories would never fade.

Chapter Ten

October 2013

Grayson

Sleep was less of a priority than ever.

After our gallery date, I spent every night lying in my bed, listening to Ella's sweet voice drift through the phone. It didn't matter what she talked about—her classes, her friends, her childhood—I found myself fascinated by every little detail.

"I talk too much when we're on the phone," she complained Thursday night. "I'm not this annoying in person, am I?"

Thoughts of her small, impish smiles and beautiful half-naked body swirled through my mind. "You're not annoying ever," I replied.

Ella's giggle warmed my bones. "Yeah, right," she chuckled. Her voice turned dreamy. "It's late again," she sighed. "Should we go to sleep?"

I sank down under my comforter, trying not to overthink the pull deep in my chest. "In a minute," I replied, not ready to let her go yet. "Maybe two."

For the first time ever, I got to brunch before my mother.

Tavern on the Green was just starting to fill up. Patrons and servers filtered in and out of the greenery-draped façade, a couple dozen feet away from my table in the courtyard corner.

When I requested the far-off spot, I intended to fly under the radar. But even with my dark sunglasses and discrete table, a group of girls I recognized from Zeta took turns glancing over at me. I leaned back in the old-fashioned white iron lawn chair and looked up at the tree canopy swaying overhead, wishing Ella would wake up and text me back.

I knew my mother had arrived when all the heads in my general vicinity suddenly turned to watch the hostess escort her to our table. In expensive jeans and some violet-colored blouse, she looked as casual as someone like her could. Oddly so, actually.

Her thin, pointed face didn't bear its usual makeup. Her lips were weirdly pale while she pursed them and nodded the hostess away.

Looking at me didn't help. Mom slid into the seat across from mine, suspicion pinching the spot between her eyes. "You're here early, *mi amor*. Are you well?"

I expected the barb, but she delivered it less like a mockery and more like an actual question. "Ha-ha," I grunted, leaning over the table to kiss her cheek.

The truth was, I woke up early and couldn't fall back asleep. The anticipation pumping through my body made it hard to even sit still. I kept checking the time, trying to convince myself not to count the hours until Ella came over.

My mother scrutinized my face for a long second. "You *seem* well," she told me. "Much better than you did a few weeks ago. Has work improved?"

The mention of my internship threw me. I'd forgotten all about using it, weeks before, as a cover for my obsession with the "random girl" on the subway. The thought made me smile, now.

"Work is good," I hedged, shaking out my napkin and draping it over my sweatpants.

I should have known she wouldn't take that bullshit. "…and?" she prompted, boring her eyes into mine, smoothing her linen over her lap.

The way she looked at me sent tingles over my scalp. I managed to shrug, feigning innocence. "And....?"

From its place beside my salad fork, my phone buzzed. I grabbed it immediately, knowing it would be a text from Ella, hopefully answering my earlier question about what she wanted me to order in for us that night.

Let's have dessert again, her message read. *I can bake something for us. Or we can each make something... unless you're scared you won't be able to match my mad kitchen skills.*

Hell.

I *knew* I wouldn't be able to, considering I barely knew how to boil water. Still, I found myself grinning while I rubbed my chin, trying to decide if I should talk her out of her adorable suggestion or humor her.

I liked the notion of her wearing an apron... and nothing else. But I wasn't even sure I owned an apron. My kitchen was strictly for take-out storage and reheating.

If I agree, I wrote back. *Do you promise not to make fun of me?*

Her instant reply wrung a laugh from me. *No.*

I set my phone back down, trying and failing to come up with any dessert ideas that wouldn't lead to me burning down my apartment building. When I glanced back up, I found my mom gazing at me. Her eyes swirled, but her mouth tightened with ill-concealed amusement.

She canted her head, still staring, and molded her lips into a reproachful pucker. "Who was that?"

I realized my mistake too late. It had to be obvious I was texting a girl, but some stupid adolescent instinct kicked in and I automatically denied it. "No one."

True to form, she didn't buy my lie for one second. "They made you laugh, so they must be *some*one."

I expected dread. After all, sharing details of my dating life with my mother was never something I relished. But as I sat there, facing her genuine interest, I only felt an inexplicable thrill. And I realized—I *wanted* to tell her.

I just had no clue why. Or even *what.*

I met a girl? Because she was knitting on the train and I couldn't stop thinking about her? So I wore her down with waffles and an ill-fated pumpkin? Then, last week, we almost had sex in a closet in Chelsea?

God. Not that.

"Her name is Ella."

Mom's small smile turned knowing, even though her eyes still seemed oddly far-away. "So this one has a name, hmm? I assume that makes her your girlfriend?"

I deserved that. She was used to me hustling girls in and out of my life so quickly, I never expected anyone to bother with formalities like names. Sometimes, I forgot to get their names at all.

But not this time.

Pressure built in the pit of my stomach, a mix of excitement and reluctance. "I'm not sure I'd call her that." *Yet.* "We've been out a few times." *And she blew the top of my head off last weekend.*

A waiter arrived and filled our glasses with still water. Mom waved him off in her blasé way. The tide of emotion buried in her eyes took on a glum note. "You *like* this girl," she realized aloud. "She must be special."

Is she?

All my memories of her swelled and swirled. Ella's slight little frame nestled into a fuzzy pile of yarn on the subway. The sweet way she combed the hair at the nape of my neck whenever she let me hold her. Her quiet, bubbly laugh. Her favorite hideous shoes. The soft fullness of her curves, melding into my bare chest while I touched her. The fear that sometimes fell over her eyes, and the courage with which she tried her damnedest to push it back.

She *was* special. Extraordinary. Exceptional in the truest sense of the word. I didn't stay up late on the phone with anyone—except Ella. I didn't chase down girls on the train—except Ella. I didn't pursue women who walked away from me—except Ella. For fuck's sake, I didn't pursue women *at all.*

Except Ella.

Ellie.

She was the exception to all of my rules, boundaries, expectations. All the roadblocks that usually kept other women at arm's length… I didn't even notice her jumping those hurtles. Because, with her, they all melted into puddles. And she splashed right through them, in her ugly green clogs, adorably oblivious.

The forlorn look on my mom's face distracted me from my revelation. It occurred to me how odd it was for her to talk to me about my love life without scolding or gushing. I frowned at her. "Are you okay, Mom? You're… subdued."

She watched me for a long moment, clearly turning things over in her mind. Finally, she sighed and gave a shrug. "I suppose I am getting old, *mi amor*," she demurred, dropped her eyes and taking a hasty sip of her water. "Old and sentimental."

Old? I almost laughed. She was the opposite of the dowdy, decrepit society matrons we suffered at every upper-echelon event. I usually had to threaten my own friends to stop salivating over her after a few drinks.

"Mom, seriously," I chuckled. "What's going on?"

Her expression softened as she surveyed mine. "I would like to meet this girl-not-girlfriend," she replied, ignoring my question. "I think I would like her. She has you smiling more. Perhaps brunch, next week?"

A *week*? The thought dampened my palms. "Maybe next *month*," I asserted, sitting back again. "I have to finish sweeping her off her feet."

And, you know, actually make her my girlfriend, first, I reminded myself.

The crazy thought had me shaking my head. It was insane—we hadn't even slept together yet. A situation I hoped to rectify within the next twelve hours.

Mom watched me with increasing warmth. "You should have no issue winning her over," she said. "Just remember, the best gestures don't cost anything."

She picked up her menu, giving her wisdom a chance in sink in. I stared at the list of entrees, unseeing, thinking about my plans for Ella that night. She was supposed to come over, and I assumed we would… do it.

That's how it usually went when I invited girls over. They came, we turned on the TV and bullshitted for a while, then we wound up in bed. Or on the couch. Whatever.

I couldn't put my finger on why, but I wanted it to be different for Ella.

Because *she* was different, for me.

Mom had mentioned a gesture of some sort. It took me the length of the salad course, but I finally came up with an idea. As the server cleared our places, I met her eyes.

"Hey, Mom? Do you have any good dessert recipes?"

Ella

"Are you nervous?"

I counted the pairs of underwear in my leather backpack, then counted them again. *Four.* Surely four pairs of panties would be enough for one night… right? I figured I would change them every time we had sex… assuming we finally *had* sex…

But could men even do it four times in one night? Didn't that only happen in romance novels and on the CW?

"So that's a yes," Maggie said, answering her own question. "Is that what you're wearing?"

I looked down at my tight, striped sweater and overly-ripped boyfriend jeans. "Yeah?" Maggie's dubious brown gaze skimmed over my clothes. I tried again. "No?"

She shrugged. "It's a cute outfit and you look hot. It's just not very... casual-night-in-slash-sexy-lounging, you know? Not very Netflix-and-Chill. It looks like an ensemble for a picnic in the park."

I hated when Maggie was right.

"Well then help me!" I huffed, too nervous to ask nicely. "I'm supposed to be there in an hour and he's all the way up on Central Park West!"

Maggie pursed her lips at my pile of mismatched Goodwill clothing and then held up one of her slender fingers. "Hold please."

With a whirl of her colorful kimono robe, she twirled over to her side of our bedroom. A minute later, she plucked an armful of fabric out of the organizer under her bed. "Here."

It was a long-sleeved white tee shirt, tight but thin. Beside it, she placed a scrunched-up ball of burgundy lace and a heathered pair of dark red leggings. I unrolled the lacy knot to discover that it was a wireless bralette.

"Won't you be able to see the bra under that shirt?" I asked, layering the gauzy white cotton over the maroon undergarment. "And my boobs through the bra?"

Mags rolled her eyes. "That's the whole *point*, Elle. You have to look *accidentally* sexy. It's your first night staying over at his place. It's your first night in with him at all!"

In the week since the gallery incident, Gray and I texted all day, every day, talked on the phone for hours each night, and met downtown for a mid-week lunch of coffee, chocolate croissants, and cinnamon buns….

But we still hadn't ever really been *alone* together.

"I don't want you to think I'm expecting anything," he told me the night before. *"I just…I can't explain it but I want you here. I want us to wake up together."*

I couldn't resist his sincerity…and I knew I'd never be able to resist *him*, either. Besides, I may not have known anything about dating, but even *I* knew that "staying in" to "watch a movie" meant sex.

"Accidentally sexy," I repeated, considering Mag's outfit again. "I guess you're right."

She nodded emphatically. "Of course I am. So wear that, your grey NYU sweatshirt and the flat black boots with the fuzzy socks. The plain, grey fuzzy socks, *not* the Hello Kitty ones. Take your boots and hoodie off as soon as you get there and leave your hair down." Her eyes narrowed, still scheming. "What are you ordering for dinner?"

I smiled despite the butterflies flooding my throat. "We're making desserts for dinner. I'm bringing the ingredients for my double fudge brownies."

Something about that softened Maggie's eyes. "You'll call me if you need me?"

I nodded, buckling my backpack. "Yes."

"And you're bringing your own protection? Because I don't care how gorgeous he is, he's still a man."

Rolling my eyes, I pulled on my grey fuzzy socks and boots. "Yes."

Mags tossed me my hoodie. "And *breathe*, Ella. You're even whiter than usual."

Breathe, I repeated, grabbing my knitting supplies for the long, nerve-wracking subway ride ahead. *Yeah, right.*

I counted on the hundreds of blocks between our apartments to calm down, but the subway ride flew by. The 103rd street station was by far the farthest uptown I'd ever been. It spat me out right across the street from Central Park, two blocks over from Grayson's place.

When the wind started howling, I was grateful for Maggie's hoodie suggestion. In the gathering twilight, the wide, empty sidewalks on the Upper West Side felt colder than most places in Manhattan. There were fewer shops, restaurants, and bars than I expected, leaving most of the tall brownstones residential and quiet. Grayson's place seemed newer than the ones around it. Instead of scuffed old stone, it was a charming mix of antique bricks, plaster ceilings, and exposed steel beams.

There wasn't a doorman, but I had to put in a code to get the elevator to open and then give another set of digits to rise to his level. My foot tapped all the way up to the sixth floor.

Before I could bring myself to knock on his door, I had to do a few minutes of deep breathing. I reminded myself of everything Dr. Laura taught me about triggers and skills to disarm panic attacks. When I finally had a grip, I tapped my fist against the black slab.

I heard a crash, a curse, and the sound of bare feet padding over the concrete floor. Grayson appeared a second later, winded and shirtless, looking a bit harried.

"Hey," he said, "You're here."

That made me smile. "Yep." I held up my groceries. "And I brought chocolate."

Gray reached for me without hesitation, pulling me against his naked torso and grinning down at me. "What I meant was: I'm glad you're here."

His voice melted me. The tension gripping my body started to thaw while his hands stroked down my back. "Come in," he murmured, drawing me over the threshold. "It's cold out there."

His loft was anything but. I didn't know where to look first.

The space was narrow, but long, with a living room near the door, a kitchen in the center, and a bed at the back beneath three tall, thin windows. On the wall beside the door, an old-fashioned furnace burned low.

Clusters of thin, gauzy papers adorned the cracked plaster walls. After a moment, I saw that they weren't just blank pages—they were sketches. Groups of pencil etchings filled the empty white surfaces that gave way to more exposed brick and black metal beams overhead.

"Wow," I exhaled, backing away from him to turn in a circle.

It was obvious a professional had decorated. The furniture was modern and masculine, all black steel and caramel-colored leather. Homey touches like lamps and soft gray rugs offset the cold concrete floor and stark black kitchen cabinets. "It's beautiful."

He shrugged one tanned, muscled shoulder. "It's nice. And it's close to school."

With my nerves muted, I finally noticed how gorgeous he looked. Golden skin hugged every hard ridge of his body, glowing in the warm recessed lighting. I saw that he'd showered recently, leaving his hair wavier than usual on top. The lingering scent of his after-shave gave me a buzz. His sweatpants hung low on his hips, teasing me with of the waistband of his boxer briefs.

Gray stood there, in the middle of his apartment, waiting for me. And it was all I could do to keep myself from sprinting into his arms and tackling him to the floor. But even as everything south of my waist warmed and melted, fear still hammered at my heart.

His smirk turned rueful. "I was trying to find my pots and pans. I don't think I've ever cooked anything here before."

I managed a smile while I followed him into the kitchen. "We'll figure it out," I said, not sure if I was reassuring him or myself.

Grayson

When she reached the butcher-block island, Ella stepped out of her boots and pulled her sweatshirt over her head.

God Almighty.

My mouth dried. She looked so hot. Tight red leggings highlighted her long legs and gave me a great view of her ass. Through her sheer white shirt, I glimpsed dark lace covering her breasts.

When she caught me staring, she bit her lip, nervous. "I wasn't sure what to wear to a co-ed sleepover," she told me, looking at herself. "I've never had one before."

Just like the night at the gallery, when she told me I was the first man to ever get her off, a ridiculous rush of delight swept through me. I loved that she gave me pieces of herself she had never trusted to anyone else. I couldn't explain why, but it meant something to me.

I hugged her close again. "You're perfect," I told her, relishing the feel of her silky hair against my bare chest. "Do you want a drink while I finish raiding my kitchen?"

She giggled softly. "Sure. Do you mind if I look around?"

I shook my head, fighting a wave of apprehension. I'd done a perfunctory clean-sweep before she arrived, but I didn't scour the place. As I handed her a glass of merlot, I hoped she wouldn't notice the dirty laundry kicked under my bed. At least she wouldn't find any condom wrappers, since I hadn't bothered with anyone else in months.

But instead of inspecting my shelves for dust or otherwise, Ella wandered over to the bookcase in the corner across from my bed. I watched her examine my meager book collection, pursing her lips. "Hmmm," she hummed softly.

English major, I reminded myself, wincing. The only literature I had to my name was an embarrassing assortment, at best. "Pathetic" would have been a better word. *Hitchhiker's Guide to the Galaxy. The*

Life of Pi. A few *Sherlock Holmes* books. I shuddered. *The Da Vinci Code.*

"I'm, uh, not one for the classics," I mumbled sheepishly, half hoping she wouldn't hear me.

Ella's dark blue eyes twinkled. "What are you talking about?"

I turned my attention back to the ingredients I had no clue how to use. "The books."

"Oh," she said, as if it never occurred to her. Her grin grew. "*Hitchhikers Guide to the Galaxy is* a classic, in my opinion. But I was looking at your picture." She held up the only frame on the case—a flat black one holding a picture of me and my parents.

It wasn't nearly as embarrassing as my book collection, but it still wasn't great. The only family photo in the whole place… and it wasn't exactly flattering. But it was the only shot I had of the three of us being normal people, not at some society function or in a portrait studio.

I snapped the tipsy selfie the last time we were in Spain, on a trip to celebrate my high school graduation. Three pitchers of sangria had my mom beaming blearily, my father red-faced, and me grinning far too big, half-squinting.

"I like it," she told me, smiling. "It's just so different from the ones online."

Surprise stopped all my useless fidgeting. "You looked me up?"

Ella's cheeks glowed in the half-light. "Of course," she replied, just a notch below defensive. "You know I don't have social media. How else was I supposed to make sure you weren't a crazy person? Or a con artist?"

Her guilty expression tempted me. I crossed my arms and regarded her through narrowed eyes, feigning irritation. "And?"

Her perfect pink lips quirked up. "And you're legit. And handsome. And *everywhere.*" She giggled. "I only looked at the first dozen photos or so, but there were *pages* of them."

With another girl—someone socially ambitious or shallow—I may have been put out. But Ellie was, as ever, an exception. I shouldn't have been surprised she'd looked me up, anyway, given her anxiety and the way we met.

Satisfied by her exploration of the bookshelf, she moved on, traipsing over to the group of sketches hanging across from the nightstand. My dread returned in full force as she canted her head, pausing to examine each one before moving on to the next set.

For a moment, I forgot about which pots I needed to find and watched her drift further into my bedroom. Part of me wanted to race over and tackle her onto my bed.

Instead, I gripped the edge of the countertop and waited. She sipped from her wineglass, floating over to my single favorite place in the whole loft—the corner next to the window, where I kept an antique drafting table.

Her fingers ghosted over the half-finished rendering left on top of the scuffed wood surface. She turned around unexpectedly and caught me observing her once again.

"Gray," she said, beaming, "These designs are incredible."

I looked away on instinct, dropping my gaze to the open drawer of random cooking utensils in my island. "It's just a hobby."

She turned back to the drafting table, her expression clouding with disbelieve. "Didn't you say your father develops real estate? Have you shown him any of these?"

As if he'd actually look. The bitter thought clenched my fists. "Not really."

I heard her sifting through the pages. "You *should.* You're so talented."

I wasn't sure why her praise rattled me, but I suddenly felt my neck heat. "Not really," I repeated, half-shrugging.

My head snapped back up to look at her when she laughed. "Well, I guess that settles it," she sighed, coming toward me. "You're just as bad at taking compliments as I am."

An unexpected grin pulled at my lips, threatening to bloom into an actual laugh. She made me smile when I least expected it. I couldn't remember anyone else doing that, ever.

When her thin brows arched in put-on consternation, I chuckled despite myself. She was close enough to grab, so I gathered her up against me, regaining my equilibrium as soon as we touched. While she looked up at me, her expression softened and sent a pang echoing through my chest.

"Thank you." I didn't know what I was thanking her for. I only knew I felt grateful—for her compliments, that she always knew how to lighten my mood, that she was there with me at all.

Amusement gilded the sapphire blue. "Thank me by turning your oven on. I'm starving."

Grimacing, I hooked my free arm around the paper bag of groceries she brought with her, peering in to try to size up how pitiful my dessert would be compared to hers.

Her smile lit her beautiful bare face again. "I'm going to make brownies," she added. "But they're the extra fudgy, death-by-chocolate kind."

Her attention turned to the array of shit sitting on my countertop. "Is that liquor?" she asked, bemused. "You trying to get me tipsy again, Mr. Stryker?"

God, yes.

I replayed the image of her on her knees all week. Her full, painted lips, the sounds she made when I came in her mouth. But, mostly, how her eyes shone up at me.

The way she worshipped me like a god should have inflated my ego, but, instead, it humbled me. What had I ever done to deserve to have someone like her look at me that way?

"I have no idea what you're talking about," I replied. "You know I'm a respectable man who values my propriety. Didn't Google teach you anything?"

She snorted adorably and rolled her deep blue eyes. "Right. You proved as much in that closet last weekend."

Her fingers grazed the bottom of the special liqueur I'd borrowed from my mother for the occasion. "The label's so pretty," she whispered. "Is that Spanish?"

"Italian, actually." I grabbed the bottle and frowned at it. "It's my mom's. Her parents are from Italy, by way of Spain. I'm using her recipe."

Curiosity filled Ella's face. "What recipe?"

I flashed a tight smile, determined to surprise her. "You'll see." I added another grimace. "And there's less of a chance you'll notice how badly I screw it up if you don't know what I'm making in the first place."

We worked around each other for about twenty minutes. Cooking was entirely novel for me… not to mention having a gorgeous girl in my kitchen. There was something sexy about it—the close quarters, the heat from the stove, the way we had to brush past each other occasionally.

Ella giggled at me more than a few times, but I couldn't blame her. I looked ridiculous trying to chop up Belgian chocolate and whisk cream. At one point, I somehow managed to leave a towel next to the gas range and almost set the kitchen on fire.

She, on the other hand, moved like a pro. Even though she'd never been in my kitchen before, she seemed to have an intuitive sense of where things were and how they worked. Though, when I pointed that out, she called it "common sense" and gave me a patronizing pat on the shoulder.

Within the hour, we had a fresh pan of perfect brownies… and a pot of the most questionable hot chocolate ever conceived.

We set them side by side on the island…and started laughing.

"You win," I admitted, pulling her hip against mine and dropping my forehead to her shoulder in defeat. "I surrender."

"Let's taste them both first and then decide who won. Yours looks like hot fudge. And I know there's booze in there. Maybe you beat me."

God. It kept hitting me over and over again: she was *sweet.* Genuine and kind. It was rare that a girl could look as beautiful outside as she was inside.

I nuzzled against her neck for a second, savoring the scent of honeysuckle mingling with the aroma of chocolate hanging in the air. "Alright. Let's get this over with."

We took plates of brownies and mugs of chocolate sludge over to the rug in front of my couch and sat cross-legged. She settled in, moving slowly, with her oblivious grace and general cautiousness. The low light caught in her loose hair, burnishing the gold waves and slanting over the soft lines of her face. I stared for a second too long and the exposed V of skin at the base of her throat turned pink.

Before she got too flustered, I forced my attention to the fudgy square of chocolate on my plate, going in for the kill.

"My God." I held up the brownie I'd just bitten into and stared at her. "How did you *do* this?"

Her eyes shimmered while she smiled, pleased. "I went through a baking phase last spring. This is probably my two-hundredth batch of these brownies."

I shook my head while I devoured the rest of the square in one bite. "It's amazing. I'm going to need more of these."

When she lifted the mug of hot chocolate to her lips, I flinched. But she took three sips before making a contented sound and giving me a wide grin. "It's *good.*"

"No way." I swallowed a mouthful and looked down at it, surprised. "Huh. A miracle."

She drank more. "It reminds me of a French bakery I love in the Bowery. They make true European hot chocolate that's thick, but not too sweet, like this. Only yours has *liqueur* in it, so I think you win."

I looked over at her. Between the spark in her eyes and the blush on her cheeks, she truly glowed. It suddenly got harder to breathe. The deep well of indescribable feeling echoed inside of me once more.

"You know what?" I murmured, leaning over to kiss her. "I think I did."

"Okay, okay," she shrieked, waving her hands in front of her face to fend me off. "I'll tell you!"

I'd never seen anything more beautiful than Ella, laid out in front of me on the carpet, laughing wildly. Still, I relented and stopped pressing my fingers into her sides.

We were trading stories, swapping embarrassing moments and firsts. I'd just told her about losing my virginity to Marissa Reeves in her Hamptons pool house. The anecdote served as both a humiliating memory and a "first" rolled into one; since I'd slipped on the wet floor during doggy style and wound up falling face-first on the tile next to the bed.

Ella got the whole sordid tale out of me by promising to give me hers after. When she threatened to renege, I had to tickle her into holding up her end of the bargain.

Any qualms I had about our night in being like all the others I'd endured were totally obliterated. Just like every other aspect of our relationship so far—the night had already surpassed all of my expectations in the most unexpected ways.

We never even glanced at the television. We argued about music and food (she thought my musical taste was too basic and I had the same critique of her palette). She tried to teach me how to do a yoga headstand. I couldn't do it, but I appreciated that I got to watch her beautiful body bounce and stretch while she demonstrated the proper technique.

Ultimately, we wound up back where we started, spread out side-by-side on my only rug. Wanting to be closer, I lowered myself to lie beside her. "Alright," I prompted, giving no quarter. "Go."

Ella screwed her face up, pinching her lips at the ceiling. "Ugh. Fine. Okay, so it was my high school boyfriend, Mark."

That didn't surprise me—I could tell she was a relationship person. What *did* surprise me was the sudden, violent urge to hunt Mark down and gut-punch him. The urge only grew when she proceeded to tell me that he took her virginity before junior prom and then dumped her before the dance.

I rolled onto my side and stared at her, noting her pink cheeks and unbothered air. She didn't like the story, but she seemed to have made her peace with it. I ran the backs of my knuckles over her flushed skin, meeting her bottomless blue gaze. "I think I fucking hate Mark."

Her warm little laugh still got me every time. Something in my chest snagged while I watched her chuckle. "It's okay. He got herpes from his next girlfriend so I sort of feel like the universe settled that score."

I couldn't remember ever laughing so much. I fell back down onto my side while we both snorted. Without thought, I found myself reaching for her, tucking her into me. Ellie set her head against my chest, wiggling until she found a spot that seemed perfectly tailored to the curve of her cheek.

I felt sixteen again, in a good way. Knowing what was going to happen, but not knowing *when*. The giddy, uncertain feeling of sitting in a movie with a girl I really liked, hoping I wouldn't embarrass myself whenever things got going.

I couldn't figure out why I felt nervous, though. We were basically together the week before and it was incredible. Wouldn't actual sex just be *more* incredible?

When we hooked up at the gallery, she told me it was the first time anyone had ever touched her like that. Now I knew for sure that she wasn't a virgin, though I never really thought she was. Virgins didn't normally accompany their dates to broom closets. Or give goddess-level blow jobs.

So…what? Those assholes had sex with her and didn't even bother trying to get her off? How was that even possible?

The second I had her to myself, all I could think about was making her come. I wanted to do it again and again, every way I could possibly think of. I couldn't wait to taste her, to feel her body tighten around mine while I was inside of her.

Oblivious to my wild libido, Ella sighed and nuzzled her face against my bare shoulder. I stroked a hand over her hair, loving the way it sifted through my fingers like silky smoke. She gave a quiet, contended hum and my chest tightened again.

I want to take care of her.

That splinter of truth lodged itself in my throat. Suddenly, everything else made sense. It explained why I couldn't stop thinking about making her come. Why I waited by my phone when she had to ride the late train home from work. Why I always listened so intently when she told me about her thoughts and her hopes.

I wanted to take care of her.

As if she sensed the turn in my thoughts, Ella tilted her head back to gaze up at me. Her smile faded when she saw the look on my face.

Our gazes collided, and I knew she felt the struggle raging inside of me. Before I could speak, she closed the distance between us and tentatively brushed her mouth over mine, nervous I would pull away. Even after everything between us, she was still shy. It tightened my throat.

I angled her face and kissed the hesitance out of her within seconds, stroking my tongue against hers until the tension drained from her body. Ella moaned when I circled her tongue with my own, tasting the lingering sweetness of the liqueur and chocolate. She nipped my lip and I hardened instantly.

My hands glided over every dip and curve they could find, touching her body at a slow, unhurried pace. This was the first time we were really, truly alone—and we had all night. I wanted time to memorize each perfect piece of her. Time to feel how flawless she really was.

Her kisses always got bolder the longer I kept at her. My fingers traced the swell of her breast and she whimpered into my mouth, quivering while I stroked my thumb over the lace covering one of her taut nipples. She ran her hand over my stomach and I shuddered, too.

She made a soft sound and glided her touch up my naked back, lightly scoring me with her fingernails. When she reached the nape, she scratched harder. My body went rigid, overwhelmed by the sudden rush of pleasure trickling from my shoulders down to my groin. When she grabbed the hair at the back of my neck and tugged, a growl built in my chest.

Damn. I didn't even know I liked that until she did it.

My cock swelled as I fought the urge to grind it against the spot between her thighs. I wanted us to go slow, but it was hard to pace myself with her. We had chemistry in the truest sense—dynamic, potent, inescapable. It moved between us. Building, burning.

And the bursting, bleeding feeling in my chest only spurred me on. I wanted to sink myself into her deeper than I'd ever been inside anyone else.

Ella ran her hand back down my spine, then surprised me by sliding her fingers into the back of my boxer-briefs. My shy, sweet girl couldn't stop herself—she wanted to put her hands all over me.

I fucking loved it.

When she touched my bare skin and moaned against my lips again, pre-cum slicked the head of my cock. I groaned.

Ella enjoyed my body as much as I enjoyed hers. She left no doubt about that, especially when she gripped my ass and yanked my lower half closer. The feel of her grinding the seam of her leggings against my raging erection made taking things slow less likely by the second.

With nothing under us but concrete and a rug, I knew I had to move her to a softer surface soon. But first I needed to make sure she was ready. When she broke away from my mouth to kiss my neck, I murmured, "I want to take you to bed, Ellie."

She pulled back slightly and looked up at me. Fear streaked through the haze of lust clouding her gaze, but she swallowed and nodded.

I couldn't ignore the way her body tensed in my arms, though. "If you don't want to, it's okay," I promised, trying to calm her with a half-smile. "We can stay here and you can keep torturing me all night."

Her expression softened as she studied mine—looking, I think, for some sort of insincerity.

I ran my hand over her hair, then touched her pale cheek, trying to reassure her. Why was she so nervous? Would she want to tell me the reason? Could I move forward if she didn't?

Fuck it, I have to ask.

"I was wondering earlier… when you said last week that no one had ever touched you the way I did… is this not something you do? Because I'm fine if we don't have sex tonight, Ellie, I swear."

It surprised me how much I meant it. As much as I wanted her, I never wanted to push her or scare her. Still, I was relieved when she frowned and shook her head.

"No," she whispered. "It's been a long time, but I… There have been a few other guys. I just meant that none of them had ever…"

I nuzzled my nose against the side of her face. "Made you come?"

"Right." She sounded so small and embarrassed.

I kissed her again, softly. "That's their fault, not yours. Your body is perfect. And making you come is all I've thought about all week."

She snuggled closer, needing me to hold her tighter. The strange, all-consuming feeling swelled inside of me again. I banded my arms around her in a vice-grip.

"It's more than that," she confessed to spot between my pecs. "I just… there are certain things about sex that I—that I *don't like.* And I feel weird about it because I want you to be able to do whatever turns you on, but there's some stuff I just can't handle."

Shit.

Curiosity and concern roiled through me. "If there's something you need or something you don't like, I want to know. It's important to me, okay?"

She bit her lower lip while her eyes watered slightly. "What if I disappoint you?"

God. A flaming arrow to the heart would have hurt less than the look on her face. I crushed her into me again, holding on as hard as I could.

"You won't," I swore, and meant it. I was already happier with her, on my floor, clothed, than I ever had been inside of a bare-ass naked woman. "But I need to know."

Ella tilted her head to press her face into my neck. "Okay," she mumbled into the crook of my shoulder, sighing. "Can we keep the lights on?"

Watching Ella come in a fully lit room? My impatient dick twitched at the thought. "Yes, please."

She gave a shaky giggle. "Can I take off my own pants?"

That was an odd one, but obviously not a problem. I tried to make her smile again. "Thank God. Those yoga-pants-legging-things are impossible. Saves me some work."

"Gray," she scolded, slapping me lightly and leaning back to flash a half-smirk. "I'm serious."

"Me too," I replied. "Of course you can take them off. I promise it's not a big deal. What else?"

Her face sobered. "Can I be on top?"

I felt my eyebrows rise. "Every time?"

She considered that, forming worry lines on her forehead. "No, I guess not. It's less that I want to be on top and more than I don't want to be trapped on the bottom."

For the first time in an hour, I wasn't hard as stone. Because it was impossible not to click the pieces together in my mind. *She doesn't want to do it in the dark… or have me rip her clothes off… or be "trapped" underneath me.*

Trapped.

That choice of words seemed key.

I watched her face until she finally met my gaze. Our connection cracked into place—instantly filling with all the things she didn't say.

Did someone… *hurt* her?

She blinked and looked down at the spot where our chests met. A dozen questions spun through my head, but none rose to the surface. They all ran together, melding into a murky tumult of outrage and dismay.

Could I ask her? Would she tell me? Did I even have a right to know if she didn't feel like volunteering the information?

I suddenly remembered her face, panicked and pale, that day in Golden Swan Garden. And the evening at the subway station in Chelsea. And the night I tried to walk her to work. She wore the same expression now.

If I push her, she'll run.

Her voice matched her face—an apology and a plea wrapped in one. "You could do any other position though."

Drowning in dread, I'd lost the thread of the conversation. *Position*? Her face made my stomach clutch. I couldn't focus on anything apart from her eyes, two swirling pools of pained mortification.

"Gray?"

Her nickname for me snapped me back to reality. *Positions. Sex. Sex with Ella. Focus on* Ella, *you idiot. She's offering herself up on a silver platter and you're just staring at her.*

"I'm sorry," I said, clearing the hoarseness from my throat. "I didn't mean to hesitate like that. Of course any position you want is fine."

Fine? I sounded like a prick. What was I even saying? Any sex with her at all would be *amazing*. Everything I wanted. I didn't give even a sliver of a fuck which position it was in. And she obviously felt embarrassed. Had I really just told her it was "fine"?

"It's alright," she murmured, quiet but earnest. "I ruined the mood. I understand if you don't want to be with me, now."

Of course she would think that, with the way I was acting. Tears filled her eyes, turning the sapphires to oceans. My lungs nearly collapsed at the sight. *Fuck. How many ways can I screw this up?*

I cupped my palm around her beautiful, ashen face. "Ellie, no."

As if to argue with me, she glanced down to where my erection previously tented my sweats. The bulge was gone, quelled by the sickening thought of anyone violating her.

"It's alright," she said again, rushing to comfort me. "My little list isn't exactly alluring."

Frustration rumbled inside of me. Not *alluring*?

"None of this shit bothers me at all, Ellie. I— I care about you. I just… is there… a *reason*? Or something you want to tell me?"

One lone tear streaked down her cheek, melting into my hand. She stayed silent for a long second. Long enough for me to watch determination steal away the sadness.

"No," she sniffled, glancing away. "There's not."

A war waged inside of me. The part that felt so sure that my instincts were correct, versus the part that trusted her more than I'd ever trusted another person. I wasn't sure which side to give in to.

Ella rushed on before I could decide. "I want tonight to be about us and this crazy connection we have," she said, beseeching me with her bright, wet eyes. "I want that so badly, because I love the way you *want me*… the way you look at me like you could eat me alive. It turns me on and makes me feel beautiful and desired and so, so happy."

Fuck. Her happiness was too big a temptation. Irresistible. *She would tell you if there was something you needed to know.*

I pressed my lips into hers softly, tasting the salt from her sorrow while I hummed my reassurance, giving in to the urge to trust her. "Tonight is still about us. I'm glad you gave me your list. It will help me make sure I don't scare you off."

She blinked up at me. "You're not mad?"

Before I could answer, she surprised me by slipping away and standing up. For one horrible second, I thought she would run again. But she just stared down at me for a long moment.

"Do you still want me?" she asked, barely whispering.

I propped my head up in my hand and let my eyes trail down over her body. The answer was clear and immediate, just like the first time I ever saw her. "Yes."

Ella gave single, certain nod. Then she pushed down her leggings. My jaw fell open while my gaze snagged on the black lace panties covering her from my view.

"Then show me," she breathed, pulling her shirt over her head, tossing it away.

Everything rioting inside of me lurched to a halt.

Holy. God.

"Show me you still want me, Gray."

Ella

Grayson was on me in a second, lunging to his feet to crush his mouth into mine.

He hauled me up against his hot, naked torso and bent my legs around his waist. Surprised, I bit his lip harder than usual and he growled. The low sound vibrated through me, pooling between my thighs.

With almost no effort, he carried me through his apartment until we reached the bed. He set me on the edge and, for a moment, I wondered if I'd have better luck on the couch. I hadn't gotten around to my bed-related issues…

But then he dropped his pants.

And every synapse in my mind sizzled to a crisp.

Oh my…

There could be no man more beautiful than Gray. In the light, I saw everything the dim broom closet had hidden. His long, thick legs; the outlines of his powerful quad muscles; the V carved between his hips, pointing right to his perfect penis.

And he was so *hard*. Visible veins throbbed up his shaft. When he stepped toward me, the thick length bobbed along with his balls. My mouth watered and I swallowed loudly, following the lines of his torso up to his heaving chest; and then, finally, his gorgeous face, set in severe lines.

His voice rasped when he spoke. "Take off your underwear and lie back on the bed so I can look at you."

Gray got bossy when he was aroused. His calm authority sent another swell of desire through me. My nipples hardened while I pulled the bra over my head. His eyes drank me in, slowly roaming over each of my breasts before he pointedly glanced at my panties.

"All of it."

I felt weirdly nervous for him to see me up close, in the light. No one else ever had, myself included. Suddenly, I wished I'd taken Maggie up on her offer to introduce me to her waxer...

I expected Gray to come for me the second my panties hit the floor. Instead, he loomed over the foot of the bed, watching with hot, hungry eyes. When his hand gripped his cock and started stroking it, I gasped.

"Sorry," he said with a wolfish, distinctly-unapologetic smile. "I've been thinking about this exact view every time I touched myself for weeks."

My mouth went slack. He was the hottest thing I'd ever seen. And he thought about… *me*?

Blood thrummed through my ears, pounding in rhythm with my throbbing clit. I pressed my legs together, trying to find some relief. Gray tilted his head, regarding me with his heated stare.

"Tell me what you think about," he rasped, rubbing the broad head of his dick. "What gets you off when you touch yourself?"

I hadn't done anything of the sort since my horrible night at that fraternity. Instead of admitting so, I just shook my head. "I don't think about anything."

That stopped him in his tracks. He froze for a second, staring at me. Then his hands fell away from his body and reached for my ankles.

He gently pulled me to the edge of his mattress and kneeled. His eyes glowed up at me, snapping with verdant fire. "I'm going to give you something to think about, okay?"

Before I could speak, Gray stretched up and kissed me with slow tenderness, as if we had all the time in the world. As if I wasn't pulsing for him. He ran both hands through my hair, trailing them all the way down to my waist, then over my sides, my hips, my thighs, until my entire body tingled.

When he finally pressed my legs open, I understood what he wanted. Hot color flooded my face and I bit my lip, torn between raging desire and a slicing sense of shame.

"I want this," he told me, more solemn than ever as he lightly trailed his fingers over my sex. His gaze snapped back to mine. "Okay?" he asked again, demanding an answer.

I managed a slight nod as my throat dried. "Yes."

Gray stroked my cheek sweetly, soothing some of my anxiety. His gaze softened. "You can lay back and relax… or watch, if you want."

Then he bent forward and kissed me in the spot that ached for him. A startled sound leapt from my throat and he rubbed his strong hands over both of my bare thighs, gentling me.

"You blush here, too," he murmured, letting the words vibrate against my overheated skin. "You're so damn beautiful, Ellie."

So was he. The sight of his broad, golden shoulders and dark head between my legs sent a woozy rush through my head. I nearly swooned when he skimmed his lips lower and touched his tongue to the trembling opening of my sex.

"Gray," I cried, shaking as he plunged his tongue into me.

My body tried to writhe, but he gripped my hips to position me while his wicked mouth licked and sucked me with a passion that left me weak. He started a pattern, slowly unraveling me—shallow thrusts into my pussy, then one long lick up to my clit, which he sucked until I was on the edge of coming before sliding back down again. After his seventh circuit, I thought I'd die if he didn't let me finish.

"Gray," I keened, grinding myself against his tongue. I couldn't take it. I felt emptier every time his tongue teased my slit. "I need you. I want you now."

Another one of his growls reverberated through me. A second later, he tilted his head and sealed his lips around my clit. I shattered.

He continued anyway, giving me the perfect mix of suction and pressure, swirling his tongue to tirelessly draw out my orgasm until I collapsed onto the bed with pinpricks of light dancing behind my eyelids.

When I came to, I felt soft, wet kisses on my belly. Gray nuzzled his face into my naked stomach, groaning softly. "You have the most beautiful pussy I've ever seen. And you taste like heaven. I've never been so hard."

I was still panting. "Then take me."

With no further prompting, he stood and walked around the side of the bed to his nightstand. The sight of his penis curving upward made me ache all over again. The throbbing in my clit had subsided, but I felt emptier than ever.

After placing a condom on the table, he sat with his back to the black iron headboard and met my gaze. "How's this?" he asked, referring to his position.

White-hot longing burned in my chest. He looked like a dream—his muscled body, naked and laid out for me, his massive dick slick from wanting me so badly.

I crawled over to him and reached for the Trojan, desperate to feel him inside me. Kneeling between his thighs, I unwrapped the rubber and slid it down his impressive length.

He surprised me by snatching my hips and pulling me into place. I hovered there for a moment, watching him.

His jaw was tight, his eyes glinting hungrily. Gray was clearly on the brink of losing control. But, even so, when our eyes met, his gaze warmed. He leaned forward to press his forehead into mine, putting us face-to-face and running his fingers down my arms before lifting them to his shoulders.

Any residual hesitation lurking in the back of my head vanished. In one movement, I sank down.

A loud, broken groan sloughed out of him while I cried out, breathless. Gray flexed his hands on my hips, screwing deeper.

Pleasure and pain swirled inside of me. The feel of his cock instantly quashed my empty ache, but he was so *thick*. I was gasping before I'd even taken all of him.

For a second, I worried that the bite of discomfort would trigger me. But all I had to do was look at Gray's face and the past fell away. His wild eyes burned while he watched me move over him. Every time I dropped down, an agonized sound of ecstasy tore from his throat.

I moved my hips tentatively at first, not sure how best to accommodate his length. The more I moved, though, the more the pleasure overrode the soreness.

Gray shook when he hit the end of me, grunting. "*Fuck*. You feel so good."

The gruff tone of his voice made me clench around him. His eyes flashed as he spoke again, urging me on. "Yes, baby. Look at the perfect way you ride my cock. You're such a good girl."

I moved faster, crying out from his dirty praise and the feel of his wide length sliding in and out of me.

He tilted his hips to rub a spot inside of me I'd never felt before. Tension built low in my belly, stretched taut, desperate for release. It made me lose my rhythm, but he didn't care. His hands guided my hips up and down while he rubbed the crown of his cock against the same ridge with every thrust. I tangled my fingers into the thick, dark hair at back of his neck and pulled.

"Jesus. Ella." He bucked his hips harder and reached his hand between us to stroke my clit with his thumb.

Dizzying heat blossomed over my body. The pounding pressure inside of me was so much stronger than I'd ever felt before. I couldn't stop myself from grinding down harder.

"Gray," I murmured, frantic. "You're going to make me come again."

He made a rough noise and caught my lips with his, ravaging me with a deep, sloppy kiss, spilling panted praises into my mouth. Our tongues slid together while our bodies strained to get closer. He held onto me with one hand, using the other to press his thumb onto my clit at the same moment his thick head rubbed the secret spot he kept stroking.

The tension inside of me finally burst, pushing a hot flood of bliss through my veins. I screamed, coming hard. While his guttural growl filled the room, my sex spasmed around his solid length.

"*Ah*, God. *Ellie*."

His cock swelled and throbbed inside of me, his body going rigid. I bent forward and ran my lips over his sweat-slicked shoulder while he jerked, emptying himself into the condom.

One breathless moment later, Gray gently pulled my hair to tilt my head. Hiding his face against my neck, he whispered my name with tender reverence that would have melted me if I wasn't already a puddle. I held him closer, wondering if he'd pull back. Instead he nestled into my shoulder, relishing the contact while we both drug air into our lungs.

After a few moments, he straightened, putting us eye-to-eye. I cupped his jaw in my hands, unable to stop myself from tracing the sculpted planes of his face, the dark slashes of his brows.

His gaze burned, full of fervor and concern. "That was okay?"

Gratitude formed a lump in my throat. My vision swam while I stared back for a long moment, half-sure I'd imagined him.

"It was amazing," I whispered.

He leaned his face into my palm, closing his eyes while he let out a deep breath. "*You're* amazing," he said quietly, winding his arms around me.

A poignant silence swelled to fill the room. Emotion swamped me, filling my throat until I was sure I would cry. Gray held me tighter at the exact moment I tightened my grasp on him.

I pulled back just far enough to look at him, only to find that his expression mirrored mine—dazzled and dazed, struggling to understand what had passed between us. Neither of us seemed to have any answers.

Eventually, he guided my head to his shoulder, tucking me close again. We stayed like that for a while, with his hands roaming my back and my head resting against him.

After a few minutes, it hit me: I did it. I had sex with Gray, because I wanted to and he wanted me. And it was incredible. Which meant there was no reason we couldn't be together, now.

Overjoyed, I leaned back to grin at him. "Can we do that again?"

Gray's deep, gruff laughter filled the space between us, chasing away the disquiet. He raised one winged brow at me. "Liked that, huh?"

When I gave an enthusiastic nod, his cocky grin melted away. He traced his smoldering gaze over my lips, my cheek, my eyes. "I did, too," he whispered.

Gray took hold of my jaw and sealed his lips over mine. The long, slow kiss warmed my bones.

I felt a tremor run through him, down to his cock. When he broke away, the smug smile returned. "We're going to need a new condom if we want to go again. Maybe some water to rehydrate. And possibly another brownie."

I moved to get off of him, but his hands stilled me before I got too far. "In a minute," he whispered, sinking down to put us both on our sides. He pressed me into him and burrowed his face into my hair. "I'm going to hold you first."

Grayson

I woke to a cold chill creeping overhead and a wealth of warmth sprawled across my chest.

Outside, New York had its first crappy weather of the season. An overcast sky swirled in between my building and the next one over while icy rain pelted my window. I watched the beads roll down the smoked glass for a long time, trying to sort through the tangled mess of emotions inside before glancing down at the girl snuggled up against me.

I didn't get very far. Ellie was too tempting.

I couldn't figure out how she got more beautiful every time I looked at her. Lying across my chest—with her lips swollen from all the ways I kept her up all night and her blonde hair in a silky jumble—she was perfect.

My cock agreed. Gazing at Ella only encouraged it. She fell asleep without her clothes. Sometime in the night, my comforter gathered around her hips, offering me a chance to memorize the curves of her naked back in the cool light.

I followed her spine all the way down to the two tiny dimples over her ass. I felt her bare breasts press into the side of my chest. My cock strained more.

Even with so much of her flawless skin on display, I found myself staring at her face for a long time. The soft arc of her jaw, the shadows under her cheekbones, the way her eyelashes fanned over the lavender crescents beneath her eyes.

Something made her scrunch her nose. It reminded me of the first time I ever saw her—how she'd screwed up her face while she stared out the subway window, not bothering to stop knitting for even half a second. As her expression smoothed back out, the familiar tide of unfamiliar feelings swelled up in my chest.

I spent most of our night fighting it back so I could focus on her and her body. But every time we fit ourselves together, every time she cried my name, every time she fell into my arms.... I couldn't deny the rush.

More than happiness, softer than elation. The warmth of contentment and the thrill of joy blended into a type of certainty I'd never experienced before.

No. Too soon.

To distract myself, I ran through images from our first night together, pausing to sear certain moments into the depths of my memory.

The guys she slept with before me were clearly assholes. After one night with her, I could tell no one had ever properly tended to her body before. She seemed awed by all of the things I could do to her—and grateful in a way that left an ache throbbing in my chest.

Just thinking about how she looked when pleasure swept through her made me shift restlessly. She snuggled in closer, then blinked awake. Her shy smile sent another burst of bliss swooping through me.

"Oh, hi."

My grin cracked so wide, it hurt my face. "Hi."

She rubbed her hand over my pectoral and pressed a kiss to my bare shoulder. "Mmm. You're ridiculously hot. *Too* hot before coffee. Scrambles my wits."

Chuckling, I rolled to put us chest-to-chest. "Can't do anything about that, unfortunately. But I can get you coffee," I whispered, sweeping her hair off of her face. "There's something I want to try first, though."

Her wispy eyebrows arched while her peach lips quirked into a smirk. "I find it hard to believe there's any base we didn't cover last night."

I could only think of one. "It's something I've never done before," I admitted, hiding my face against the warm crook of her neck.

Ella wrapped her arms around me and gave a reassuring squeeze. Her affection felt so genuine. Guileless. She never held herself back from reaching for me or pulling me closer. When she hugged me, I knew she wanted nothing other than to give me comfort.

"Tell me," she murmured, running her fingers through my hair and pulling at the nape of my neck. I groaned and she giggled. "I assume it has something to do with the boner pressed up against my hip."

I couldn't bring myself to say it out loud. Instead, I looked into her glowing blue eyes and rubbed my nose down the length of hers. "Are you sore? I don't want to hurt you."

Ella wiggled her hips, testing herself out. "Maybe a little," she conceded, blushing, "But it's, um, deep."

My dick twitched at the memory of working myself all the way into her. A wolfish smile spread across my face before I could help it. "Sorry about that."

Grinning, she rolled her eyes. "Oh yeah, you seem really broken-up about it."

I shrugged. "Okay, I'm not *that* sorry. Honestly, your pussy is so perfect, it's a miracle I lasted longer than five minutes."

And it was *tough*. I'd never worked so hard to keep myself from coming in my life. I hoped it would get easier the more we did it, but she was so tight and responsive…everything I did to her got her soaking.

Even now, I felt wetness against my thigh. Her sapphire eyes sparkled while they sketched my face. "What do you want to try?"

I gathered her body against mine and sealed my mouth over hers. She melted into me while my tongue stroked over hers in soft, leisurely glides.

Ella ran her hands down my back, scratching me lightly until I shivered. She cupped my ass and pulled herself closer, rubbing against my erection. I wanted her so badly it made me breathless.

Fighting the instinct to roll on top of her, I hooked her thigh over my hip and reached behind myself to grab the last condom in my drawer. I hated that there had to be something between us, but I wasn't about to break the moment by starting *that* conversation.

Reaching down, I sheathed myself with the rubber and turned my gaze back on hers. "Tell me if you're too sore, okay? It won't be deep like this, but I think you'll like it."

She nodded, breathing hard, and watched me position my dick to slide into her. With both of us on our sides, I had to pull her to me at the same moment I thrusted forward.

She whimpered while I grunted, relishing the feel of her tightness clinging to the top half of my shaft. Using her leg for leverage, she held herself close enough for me to slip in and out, making us both moan.

Jesus. She felt like heaven. Especially when I found her G-spot and her pussy started clenching around me on every plunge.

I kept up a slow, steady rhythm and turned my attention back to kissing her, spilling all of my groans into her mouth while we moved together. She trembled in my arms, holding onto me while I held onto her.

"Gray," she cried softly, "I—"

I love you.

She didn't have to say it. I could feel it. And it was everything.

"I know," I panted quietly, resting my forehead against hers. "I know, baby."

It was the first time I'd ever made love in my life. Now I knew—it was just as good as fucking. Better, maybe, because it somehow made every feeling inside of me tangible.

I bit her lip softly and wrapped her hair around my wrist, wanting to feel her everywhere all at once. Her body tightened a little more with every thrust. She ground her hips tight to mine, searching for the right amount of friction to set her off.

The feeling was indescribable and irresistible. I shifted just so, knowing the new angle would put pressure on her clit at the same time the head of my cock rubbed inside of her. Her moan echoed off the walls of my apartment, sent tingles racing down my back. I felt my balls draw up, ready to come as soon as she did.

"That's right, baby," I praised as she clenched on me. "Such a good girl. Fuck—you're making me come."

Kissing her roughly, losing control, I growled when I felt her body clutch around mine. We both came within seconds, holding on to each other as we rode out the high together.

Ella

It took an hour for Gray to let me out of bed to make out coffee.

He was so gentle and sexy, knowing just when and how to touch me. Our bodies stayed twined for half an hour and then he held me for another twenty minutes, silently caressing my back and untangling my hair.

When we finally spoke, he offered to run down the street and grab whatever I wanted from a coffee shop. "I can make us coffee," I told him, stretching. My limbs felt soft and wobbly, like Jell-O. "But first maybe I should find my clothes."

Gray grinned. "Yes to the coffee, no to the clothes."

It turned out the lacy scrap I'd worn for underwear was missing anyway. Instead of using any of the pairs I packed, I put on Gray's black boxer-briefs and made my way to the living room to pull Maggie's white tee shirt back over my head.

He sat up in bed and ran both of his hands through his unruly hair, watching me intently. He seemed completely at ease while I rummaged through his cabinets to source a French press and a bag of coffee grounds.

"Do you take sugar or milk?" I asked, embarrassed by the mundane question. How could I know what his penis felt like but not know how he took his coffee?

"Neither," he called back, slipping his grey sweats over his naked ass.

When I returned with two mugs of black coffee, we sat shoulder-to-shoulder against the headboard, listening to the rain. Glancing over at him, I found a gold condom wrapper stuck to his side. We both laughed as I peeled it off.

"I'm going to need to buy more of those," he told me, balling up the paper and tossing it into the wastebasket beside his bed. "We went through the box I had in my drawer."

I tried to count how many we used. A blush crept up my neck. "Oops."

He shrugged and took an unbothered sip from his mug. "Not complaining. Although, we should probably get tested and stuff now that we're... you know."

I giggled. "Having actual intercourse? Yeah, probably."

He rubbed the back of his neck—his telltale nervous gesture, I'd found. "I meant now that we're *together*. I mean, assuming there aren't any other guys..."

If I blinked, I would have missed the flash of vulnerability streaking across his face. I reached over and lured his gaze back to mine by stroking his cheek. "That makes sense," I replied, smiling easily. "I'm already on the pill so at least we won't have to deal with that."

I couldn't tell him that part of the university's post-rape protocol included STD testing... and there hadn't been any other men between that and Gray. I was fine getting checked again, anyway, just for his peace of mind.

He nodded once, decisive. "We'll both go to student health tomorrow."

I couldn't help but grin when he issued orders like that. "Okay, boss. Whatever you say."

Gray's eyes heated. "And then, tomorrow night, we'll do all of this again, without the condoms."

I pursed my lips, considering. Mondays, I usually studied and then went to sleep early so I could catch the 7AM train in for my 8AM shift. If I spent all night in bed with Gray, I wouldn't make it. Then Thursday I had a paper due. Work and class on Friday... more work next Saturday...

"I can do next Saturday night," I countered.

His palm cupped my jaw, turning my head to face his horrified expression. "You expect me to wait a *whole week* to have you again? That's cruel."

I loved how much he wanted me. I ran back through my mental calendar, looking for wiggle room. "Okay, I can do Thursday night."

He narrowed his gaze and shook his head. "No deal. Tuesday night."

I laughed. "Don't you have classes? And your internship? I'm sure you can't do either if you're up all night with me."

Gray gave me his broad, playful smile. "You know, for someone who only slept about three hours, I feel strangely energized for some reason. Weird."

I shoved him lightly. "I'm serious!"

His eyes lingered on my cheekbone while he tucked a strand of hair behind my ear, thinking out loud. "I have an exam Tuesday at four, and I have to be at Stryker & Sons Wednesday, but not until after lunch. So Tuesday night would actually be good."

"Okay, okay," I surrendered. "I'll trade my Wednesday morning shift for a double on Tuesday and come over after. It'll be late, though. And my feet will be sore."

He chuckled while he nuzzled my temple with his warm lips. "I'll agree to late Tuesday night," he murmured, skimming his mouth down to tease my earlobe, "*if* you spend the whoooole weekend here."

I kissed him softly, then gave him a big smile. "Agreed. Thank you for negotiating."

Gray made a face somewhere between bewildered and amused. "You were right," he said, drinking more coffee.

"About what?"

"I *am* bossy," he admitting, smirking. "But you *are* persuasive."

❋❋❋

Chapter Eleven

September 2016

Grayson

I'd tried everything else to forget Ella's damn book dedication.

So I decided to try one last thing.

I scrolled to the T's in my phone book. Specifically, every girl saved under "Tinder."

For a while, I sat parsing the potentials. I wanted someone who would come right away, which meant choosing a girl who had been to my place before. And, of course, she had to be hot enough to distract me.

I also needed to make sure she was one of the dozens who already signed an NDA. They were a standard security practice for me, now, at the behest of our company attorneys. Anytime a girl came over, Amir escorted her up and had her sign on the dotted line before letting her in.

Three candidates fit my needs. I shot off identical texts to all of them, got two bites back, and chose the name least similar to Ella's.

Zoe, as it turned out. I thought I remembered red hair.

Through months of trial and error, Amir and I had the whole thing down to science. As soon as I sent him the pick-up information, I knew Zoe would be at my door within thirty minutes.

"Like a pizza?" Graham had snorted when I described our arrangement over drinks one night. At the time, I figured he was just busting my balls. Now, I saw his point. The whole thing *did* sort of feel like ordering mediocre takeout when I didn't even know if I was hungry.

Or, maybe, like ordering a green juice when I really wanted a steak.

God. *"Ordering?" I'm comparing women to take out now?* I scrubbed my hand over my face and fell back into my sofa, disgusted with myself.

To stave off the guilt, I decided to be as attentive a host as possible. I was standing in my kitchen, staring into my long-untouched wine fridge when I heard the elevator ding out in the pointless hallway I hated.

Apparently, my memory sucked. Because a moment later, a lithe woman with short black hair sauntered into my great room. *Probably better*, my mind determined, noting all of the ways her features diverged from the honey-blonde haunting my memories.

"Hey!" When she spoke, the husky tenor of her voice reassured me, too. After two glasses of some sour red wine she chose, I recalled why I ever selected this girl for a hookup in the first place.

I picked her because I didn't like her at all.

She worked in pharmaceutical sales—a bold, smoldering vixen type who exuded self-importance and erupted into gales of laughter at all of her own jokes. Whenever I glanced away and looked back, I caught Zoe eyeing our surroundings with a greedy gleam in her dark eyes.

Nothing like Ella's sweet little laugh… or her gentle curves… or her peachy blush… or her heart.

When we hit the bottom of the bottle, Zoe bent over the edge of my island, giving me a clear look down her sports bra. She tossed her hair to the side with a beatific smile. "So, where do you want me?"

My eyes jumped from her tits to my living room, considering. I didn't like to take anyone into my bedroom. It felt too personal for a stranger and I hated to change my sheets after. The couch was my go-to—but I thought maybe I'd go with fucking against a wall instead. Or maybe out on the balcony. Zoe struck me as an exhibitionist.

The truth was, I couldn't be bothered to choose.

"Whatever suits you," I told her, straightening to reach back and tug off my shirt. "Anywhere but the bedroom."

She took that as a challenge. Some blend of curiosity and indignation sparked in her dark eyes. "*Any*where?"

Her question made me realize—the bed wasn't the only place I kept off limits. "I'd prefer not to use the shower or entryway either."

She smirked. "Um… why?"

For Gray, for always.

"Just my personal preferences," I lied smoothly, coming around the counter to snatch her up. *Before I change my mind.*

I had to concentrate. It took concerted effort to focus on kissing her. My mind listed off the usual foreplay steps by rote, prompting me every few moments.

Move your hands down her sides. Now inside her thighs. That's probably good enough. Have we been making out long enough for me to stop? What time is it, anyway? Goddamn it. I'm not wearing my watch.

Just before we settled on the sofa, Zoe jerked back, eyes flashing with irritation. "Is something wrong?"

For a moment, I stared down at her, thrown. My mind felt as empty as the hole bored into my chest. Wind whistled through both, along one crystal clear thought.

"I can't do this anymore," I realized out loud, hearing the words for the first time as my mouth ran ahead of my mind.

Zoe's eyes narrowed. "What?"

I didn't know if she meant to express general disbelief or if she actually didn't understand me. And I didn't care. "I'm sorry, but you need to go."

She scoffed, backing away. "Yeah, whatever, Grayson. Honestly? You might have more money than God and a body to rival one, too, but, in bed, you're a six. I can do better."

Her taunt bounced right off of me. "I'm sure you're right."

I knew all of my "dates" would describe me as a lazy lay. The truth was shameful, but undeniable; I no longer cared enough about any of my hookups to put in the sort of effort I used to.

And, now, it seemed, I didn't even care enough to actually fuck them.

Just to be sure, I stared over at Zoe for another beat, trying to feel something. But my body didn't want her. And the rest of me was consumed with wanting Ella.

It's her goddamn book. I growled internally, watching Zoe huff out my door. *I was fine before I saw it. I didn't turn out hot girls who wanted me or lose sleep at night. A week ago I would have taken Zoe right against the island and slept like the dead after.*

I heard her snap at Marco and the ding of the elevator. As soon as it buzzed again, I collapsed on my couch and groaned. "What the *fuck* is wrong with me?"

Not knowing.

Too succinct not to be true, the thought sank down into my center.

If I knew why *she wrote that... If I knew what it* meant... *I could move on.*

But how could I figure any of it out? She made damn sure I couldn't find her or get a hold of her after she left me. And I'd searched her name often enough to know that she still didn't have any social media accounts.

Full of restless anxiety, I stomped to the bar area to pour myself a glass of gin before wandering back to my seat. *Even if I did, by some miracle, locate her… she wouldn't be in New York.*

After our breakup, I tracked down her roommate, Maggie, out of desperation. She told me Ella had left the city, for good. After insulting me fifteen other ways.

If she's really gone, I have to respect that.

As much as I hated Ella for everything she put me through—up to and including her goddamned book—I didn't have it in me to swoop into whatever life she made elsewhere and shit all over it. If she loathed me so much that she literally left the state to get away from me… I couldn't bring myself to confront her, now.

I could only think of one way to find out where she ended up.

"Amir!"

The door clicked open quietly. Marco slipped in and stood at attention, his eyes sharp. "Sir?"

I cast my gaze down into my tumbler. "I need you to find someone."

He didn't speak for a second too long. "If you can't locate this person's information on your own, I'm assuming it isn't someone who wants to be found."

A gasp of pain sliced through me as I remembered the way Ella left… without a single trace. A hoarse wedge blocked my throat.

"Correct."

Jesus. Some part of me already regretted my request and I hadn't even made it yet.

What am I thinking? That I'll find her information and if by some chance she's still in the city then I'll… what? Call her? She blocked me.

And, even if Marco managed to track her down and we *did* speak, somehow… I'd just end up right where she left me before.

Because she's fucked up and always has been, I thought callously.

Damaged. Anxious. Terrified of things that made no sense. *And she never even told me why.*

Perhaps sensing my own hesitation, Amir regarded me with a steely expression. "I trust you know what you're asking for isn't exactly… legal?"

I knew, but I no longer cared. If I didn't get that damn dedication out of my mind, I'd go insane.

"Can you do it or not?" I demanded.

His features tightened. I suspected years of police and military training engrained a deep respect for rules. Even so, he finally gave a slight nod. "Give me twenty-four hours."

Ella

"Elle?"

Snapping to, I straightened in my desk chair and tried to blink the blur out of my eyes. After sobbing into my pillow over my Grayson sighting, I spent a sleepless night snared in a horrible recurring nightmare. And barely made it into work Friday morning.

When I swiveled my chair, I found Parker standing on the other side of my desk. The remnants of a smile warmed his lips, but his blonde brows folded over his glasses as he took in my expression. "Are you alright?"

I swallowed past a scratchy throat and forced an answering smile. "Yeah! I just spaced out for a second there. Did you need my help with anything?"

Parker's grin rebounded. He produced a cold brew coffee with a flourish, setting it in front of me. "I just wanted to see you and bring you this."

A pang of guilt struck my heart. *I cried over another man half the night and this sweet guy brought me a coffee.*

Not that I wasn't grateful… frankly, I'd never needed caffeine quite so desperately.

"Do I look *that* bad?" I quipped, taking a gulp. It was pumpkin spice, which I normally didn't like—but I could not afford to be picky. Besides, the gesture really meant a lot to me. In theory.

"No," he replied instantly, still smiling. "You look gorgeous."

I didn't think my navy sheath dress and scuffed nude heels could really be described as "gorgeous" … and Lord knew my face needed some blush and mascara. Since I barely scraped my hair into a bun, I hadn't even attempted makeup.

Parker helped himself to the corner of my desk, settling there with his own cup of coffee. My sluggish mind whirred, envisioning the picture we presented.

"Do you think it's a good idea?" I fretted out loud. "For us to be… chatting? At the office?"

His lips tilted up at the corners as his hazel eyes ran loops over my face. "I wanted to talk to you about that, actually. I know Marjorie is aware that we've decided to see each other outside of work. She seemed fine with it. Would you be opposed to other people knowing?"

A sharp barb of anxiety poked at my stomach. "I haven't looked up any of the rules in the handbook. I honestly never thought I'd need them."

Fondness filled his features. "You know, I actually believe that. Despite you being beautiful and a total catch."

His amusement faded slightly as he cast his eyes down at his Starbucks cup. "The rules are pretty simple for inter-office relationships. Obviously, we would adhere to professional decorum at all times. And, as the senior employee, I would fill out a form for HR."

Of all the days to have brain fog. "A form…?"

He misunderstood my confusion for reluctance. "Not right now," he rushed to assure me. "I mean, we only went out once."

"And you're seeing other people."

The thought popped out before I could censor it. Luckily, my tone fell somewhere just north of observational.

Even still, Parker cleared his throat. His hands fidgeted with the sleeve on his cup as he rambled, "I was. Well, I mean, I was *going to*. And I was dating someone *else*, too. Before. So I was and I was going to, again, this weekend, but then I went out with you and now I—"

He interrupted himself with a smirk, shooting me a playful, accusatory look. "You make me nervous," he admitted. "First I spent our whole lunch talking about my stupid self and now I can't figure out how to tell you that I've cancelled my plans with any other women so I can focus on this. Because I could tell the idea of me dating other girls made you uncomfortable when it came up earlier."

The look in his eyes heated my cheeks while he added, "But, also, because I really like you, Ella. A lot."

Flashes of my nightmare and my stalking expedition to Stryker & Sons streaked through my thoughts. My face crumpled at the memories.

"You don't know me very well," I whispered. "I would hate for you to miss out on other opportunities and wind up disappointed."

Pure warmth filled the curve of his lips. "That's how I know I won't be—you're one of the kindest people I've ever met. I've never heard you say anything mean or negative or thoughtless. I've seen how intelligent you are. You work hard. Everyone loves you."

He leaned closer, as if imparting a secret. "And, did I mention, you are gorgeous?"

Grayson used to call me gorgeous. He whispered the word to me while we made love, dropped it into the crook of neck with kisses whenever he passed me in the kitchen, murmured it into my palm whenever he nuzzled there.

And the sad truth was: I didn't want another man to say it to me.

Is that it, then? Do I just go through my whole life alone? Turning down sweet, handsome men like Parker until, eventually, they stop noticing me? All because the thought of being close to anyone but Grayson Stryker makes my heart ache?

A knot tangled my throat, leaving my words watery. "Thank you," I told Parker. "It's just… thank you."

Blessedly, he didn't hear the tears in my voice. Another wide smile stretched across his square features. "So, a proper date tomorrow night? Dinner at eight? No dessert?"

I nodded, forcing out one last weak smile. "Just text me the details."

Chapter Twelve

October 2013

Grayson

A boney hand snapped in front of my face, forcing me from my reverie.

I blinked, finding myself in my usual vestibule, tucked into the back left corner of Butler Library. Beside me, Graham glowered.

"What the fuck, dude?" he demanded, whispering. "You've been staring at the wall for twenty minutes. This exam is in, like, five hours. Have you studied at all?"

I looked down at my notes. *Right. Financial accounting.*

I *had* studied… but my brain refused to focus. Every other second, my thoughts wandered back to Ellie.

Less than forty-eight hours had passed since she left my apartment Sunday afternoon, but by Tuesday morning I was like a junkie, jonsing for another hit.

My leg bounced in place while I waited for her to answer my "good morning" text. My fingers twitched every time I remembered the way her skin felt under my palms. Thoughts of waking up to her gorgeous, bare face swirled through my mind. The memory of her laugh echoing through my chest made it ache.

"Grayson?" Graham's scowl morphed into something that almost seemed alarmed. "What's going on?"

I didn't *know*. But ever since I made love to Ella, I couldn't *breathe*. Or think. Or pay attention to anything. I also couldn't stop smiling every time her name popped up on my phone.

I felt… *happy*. All the time.

I shook my head, hoping it might force my thoughts into some semblance of order. "Nothing," I muttered, rubbing the back of my neck. "I'm fine."

My phone made a liar out of me, buzzing. I had it in my hand the same instant.

Good morning, she wrote back. *Although not as good as Sunday morning...*

I grinned, remembering. No morning could ever be *that* good again. Her luscious breasts pressing into my side; her sweet, sleepy sighs while I kissed her awake. The heat between her thighs, the feel of her fingers in my hair.

Briefly, I indulged in the fantasy of waking up with Ella naked in my bed every day. My cocked jerked to life, half-hard from the mere thought.

God. I'd never be on time again. And I'd be grinning like an idiot every single day. Sort of like I was right then.

"Oh, for fuck's sake," Graham hissed, grabbing my phone and flopping back into his chair. I dove for it, but he turned his back on me, huddling over the screen and scrolling up through our text thread.

Panic gripped my chest. If he swiped back far enough and saw the selfie she sent the night before, I would have to beat him to death with my econ textbook.

"Asshole," I snapped, snatching the phone back. "There are *pictures* on here."

My asshole best friend spun back slowly, pinning me with an accusatory stare. "The *girl*?" he said, pitching his voice low in the library silence. "The one from the gallery? You're still *talking* to her?"

Talking, texting, laughing, fucking, making love…

"...yeah." I shrugged and pretended I was suddenly interested in my exam notes. "It isn't a big deal. Whatever."

Like the dramatic prick he was, Graham gave a long-suffering sigh and slammed his book shut. "Okay. Look. It was bound to happen to one of us eventually."

I glared at him. "What are you *talking* about?"

His face was resigned, tinged with a distinct consolatory note. "Grayson. Buddy. You're pussy whipped."

Heat crept up the back of my neck. "Shut the fuck up, Graham."

He shrugged, unmoved. "Like I said, it was inevitable. I'm just glad it's you and not me. Although. She *is* really hot. And—what else did you say? *Nice*?" He made a noncommittal sound. "So that's all cool, I guess. What do your parents think?"

My fists tightened until my knuckles popped. He knew I hadn't introduced Ella to my parents. And he probably guessed that they may not approve. Especially Dad.

The thought of throwing Ellie into his path turned my voice into a snarl. "Why can't you just mind your own business?"

"Because I don't have any," he tossed back. "Because we're friends. And we've *been* friends for years and I've never seen your face do what it was doing a few minutes ago." He waved his hand at my phone. "She's obviously gotten to you."

I hated the way he described it. Like I was a fortress and she was some foreign entity, executing a successful attack. As if she'd done something strategic and insidious.

All Ella had ever done was be herself around me. I was the one who stormed her barricades... because I just couldn't help myself.

And I wanted *more*. I wanted it *all*. As much of her as I could possibly get.

Fuck me. Graham was right.

I sank into my chair as the fight drained out of me. "Alright. Fine," I muttered. "I like her. A lot. And we're... dating."

Graham spread his hands open, palms up, as if to say, *See? That wasn't so hard.* "Dating. Huh. Quaint. Where have you taken her aside from the gallery?"

"Uhh…" *My bed? A broom closet? A waffle shop?* The truth sank down through my lust-addled brain. *I haven't ever taken Ella out on a proper date.*

Graham's glower returned while he watched my realization dawn. "Oh *c'mon.* It's one thing if you're gonna break up the team because you have a good girl. I can accept that. But you're sitting here mooning over this chick and you haven't even *taken her out on a real date*? Or made a plan of attack for the parents? You're Grayson Fucking Stryker. If you're going to do this thing, then *do it*."

Hell. Who knew my shithead best friend could actually be… inspiring?

He rolled his eyes and turned back to his books, waving a dismissive hand. "Go. Call an actual restaurant. Make plans. Tell the girl. Goddamn. How am *I* the one who knows what to do here?"

I gripped my phone in my hand, staring it down, deciding. "You know," I mumbled, standing to go outside and make my calls. "Sometimes I think I hate you."

Ella

"This one?"

Maggie held up a scrap of gold lamé so skimpy, I actually snorted. "Are you insane?"

She rolled her eyes skyward, turning back to the thrift shop's half-off rack. "You can't be so picky, Elle. We're bargain hunting for formalwear. It's a suicide mission."

Sighing, I flipped past a Care Bear tank top and a flannel dickie. "I know, I know."

She *was* correct, after all. When I agreed to go on a grown-up date with Gray, I was so excited I forgot to worry about the fact that he'd already seen my one and only fancy dress the night we went to the gallery.

Mags and I spent Friday afternoon sifting through both of our closets, looking for anything remotely appropriate. Some of her pieces passed muster, but her willowy model's build rendered most of her dresses too long and too tight for someone with my figure.

It certainly didn't help that Gray *refused* to tell me where we were going.

He simply instructed me to tell Maggie I wouldn't be home until Sunday evening… and to wear heels. As if it were *that* simple to plan for an overnight date in parts unknown.

Men. I swear.

Mags held up a velvet halter top, tilting her head at me. "Okay, you're buying this," she announced. "It's three dollars and you're the only person on earth who can carry off this color."

I blinked at her. "It's orange."

"It's topaz," she corrected, holding it under my chin. "And if you won't buy it for yourself, I will. It's perfect for autumn and you obviously need some more sexy date clothes, assuming this boy will be sticking around…?"

I supposed she had a point. Still, I didn't dare say anything out loud. What Gray and I had still felt surreal, like a daydream run wild. If I admitted how hard I'd fallen for him…and how into me he seemed in return… would I suddenly come-to on the subway in stifling August heat and realize I'd just zoned out while salivating over a stranger?

With a begrudging scowl, I snatched the top from her and huffed out an exasperated breath. "That still does nothing to help me tonight."

Maggie looked down at her phone and sighed dramatically. "It's already six and you have to be all the way uptown by eight. There's no help for it, Elle. You're going to have to re-wear the black dress."

She pursed her lips as though the notion of repeating an outfit left a sour taste on her tongue. "I can lend you a different shawl, though…and some other shoes."

Desperation tinged my voice. "Maybe he won't notice?"

My roommate tilted her head one way and then the other, weighing that possibility. "Possibly. Boys are dumb. But didn't you say he has an eye for art and design and stuff?"

Ugh. Right, again. Of course Gray would notice. I'd just have to apologize and promise to find something different for our next date… assuming he wasn't permanently put-off by my bargain-budget formalwear redux.

We paid for my three-dollar future-date top and shoved it into the crocheted bag on my shoulder before making the ten-block hike back up to our neighborhood. By the time our building came into view, the street was dark and my nerves were vibrating. I wouldn't have noticed the glossy white Mercedes idling on the curb if the driver hadn't leapt out as we passed.

"Miss Callahan?"

As with most things, my first reaction was fear. I shrank back into Maggie's side while she, true to form, surged forward, drawing herself up to her full height and eying him shrewdly. "Who's asking?"

The young, good-looking driver offered a polite smile. "My name is Marco, miss. Mr. Stryker sent me to collect Miss Callahan."

He opened the passenger-side door and extracted a large box with *Bergdorf's* emblazoned on the top. "And to deliver this. He asks that we depart sometime around seven-fifteen."

A quick glance at the phone wedged into my frozen fist told me it was already six-thirty. *Oh my God, I still have to pack my overnight bag and curl my hair and shave—*

The driver interrupted my panic spiral by placing the box in Maggie's outstretched arms. He turned back to his vehicle to extract another, much smaller container… and the single most perfect peony I'd ever seen.

Had I told Grayson they were my favorite? I couldn't remember… but he obviously did.

Marco offered both gifts to me. A white card sat on top of the tiny box. I recognized Gray's handwriting from the notated sketches on the walls of his apartment.

> Ellie—We're going to dinner later. But here's your dessert first, of course.
>
> Yours, Grayson

Yours.

Mine.

The word sunk down through the maelstrom of anxiety drowning my lungs. My fear receded, leaving giddiness in its place. "Forty-five minutes?" I asked Marco. "We *have* to leave at seven-fifteen?"

He had the decency to wince. "Afraid so, Miss Callahan."

"Ella," I said automatically, already backing toward our building. "I'll be back as fast as I can."

Grayson

For the hundredth time, I wondered if *any* of it was right.

Turned out that romantic gestures involved a lot more guesswork than I originally anticipated.

Did she like pink peonies or white ones? I went with white. What dress size would fit her better—four or six? I told the personal shopper to select a six.

And milk chocolate strawberries, instead of dark or white chocolate. The St. Regis instead of The Plaza. The Tiffany Suite over the Dior. Champagne, not red wine.

"A drink, Mr. Stryker?"

They knew my name at the King Cole Bar. Would it be obvious I was a regular? Was that a bad thing?

It must have been obvious that I was nervous, because the bartender had offered me a cocktail four times. I kept sipping my water, glancing toward the entrance and then back at my watch every half-minute. *8:08.*

She was late, but Marco texted earlier to tell me they were en route. I couldn't figure out why I felt like I had an electric current buzzing through me. It wasn't like she wouldn't show up…

My watch ticked on. *8:10. Maybe I should tell the maître d' to hold our—*

Every rational thought evaporated as my restless eyes flicked back to the entrance.

And there she was.

Ellie.

I swear to God, my fucking heart skipped. She was somehow—*impossibly*—more gorgeous than ever. The emerald green dress gave her peachy skin a warm glow and looked especially striking against the curled curtain of her gold hair. The strapless bodice molded tightly to her breasts and her ribcage, then flowed into a short skirt that shone slightly as it shifted around the flare of her hips… her smooth, freckled thighs… her long, bare legs….

I'm not going to make it.

It only got harder to breathe as she approached, grinning just for me. Her makeup reminded me of the night at the gallery. She wore just enough to make her sapphire eyes ludicrously large and luminous, but, this time, pink glossed her lips. The sheen on them was the only thing that stopped me from hauling her into my lap and sealing my mouth over hers.

Instead, I managed to swallow down my awe and smile back at her as I stood, lifting her hand to brush my lips over her palm.

"Perfection," I complimented, glancing into her eyes.

She smirked, flicking her gaze down over my slate tie, my navy suit. "You're one to talk." Her sweet little smile turned coy. "Sorry I'm late. Some crazy man only gave me forty-five minutes to get ready."

I laughed before I could help it. "Oh, come on. You're beautiful. It can't possibly take you that long to get ready."

Ellie sighed dramatically. "Spoken like a man." Her eyes sparkled. "Are we having a drink here before we go back to your place?"

I offered her my hand and helped her up into the high leather seat beside mine. "Not exactly." Waving the eager bartender over, I turned to Ella. "Champagne?"

She pursed her lips, obviously uneasy. "Only if isn't too expensive," she murmured. "I can look at a menu and pick something else."

No way I'd allow *that* to happen. The price was of no consequence to me… but if she saw the $250 price tag for the bottle of Dom I selected, she wouldn't be able to drink it.

I flashed a reassuring smile. "I already had them put a bottle on ice for us."

She frowned slightly. "But you like gin."

The memory of her bringing me a gin and tonic and calling Graham a shithead widened my grin. "But you like champagne," I countered. "And tonight is about you."

Guilt darkened the edges of her expression, so I decided to distract her. Nodding at her small gold purse, I asked, "Any yarn in there?"

Ella giggled softly, sending a bolt of warmth through the center of my chest as the bartender set our chilled bottle and two glasses between us. "Not in the purse. In my overnight bag, though."

I nodded as if that was a totally normal thing to pack for a night with a lover. "What color, this week?"

For some reason, her cheeks heated and she dropped her eyes to lap. "Dark green," she mumbled.

"Hmmm." It was the subtlest color she'd worked with since I met her and it embarrassed her for some reason. "What are you making this time?"

She straightened her posture, visibly donning a false air of bravado while she reached for her flute of champagne. "Nothing major," she said simply, then swallowed.

Her eyes flew open. She looked down into the glass and over at my face while I tried not to chuckle at her adorable surprise.

"Is it good?" I asked, as casual as could be. "The sommelier recommended it."

Her eyelashes fluttered. "The soma-what?"

A smile crept past my defenses. "The wine guy."

"There's a wine *guy*?" she asked, wide-eyed. "As in, a man who makes a salary for telling people which wine to drink?"

Good Lord. She was too damn cute.

Unable to resist a second longer, I bent toward her and slid my hand over her crossed thighs. My lips ran up her cheekbone to rest against the whorl of her ear. "I missed you, Ellie."

It was true. I missed her with an intensity that left me reeling whenever I pondered it. Every morning, I woke up and turned to the other pillow, expecting her there. Every night, I fought the urge to charge down to Brooklyn and knock on her door. Every day, her precious texts and phone calls filled my free moments.

And, as stressful as it had been, I actually enjoyed putting together our date. The idea came to me on the heels of the shower I took with Ellie on Sunday morning that left me wishing I had a bathtub. A hotel room would have one, I figured. And then I could strip her down after our date and wash her in the tub... Or strip her down, have my way with her, and *then* wash her in the tub. Or....

Ellie's hand closed over mine while she leaned against me. "Thank you so much," she hummed, her breath catching. "This dress...the strawberries... this champagne...it's all perfect, Gray. No one has ever been so generous or thoughtful to me."

Her gratitude did strange things to me. I didn't want her to think she owed me any elaborate thanks. Because I *wanted* to do things for her; and I would *keep* doing things for her for as long as I could.

But, at the same time, her appreciation made me feel twelve feet tall.

For the second time in three minutes, I only narrowly avoided tugging her into my lap. The heady combination only she inspired decimated my self-control. Joy warmed my chest. Lust, thick and hot, pulsed through my veins. Elation clouded my thoughts, thicker than any buzz.

God, I thought. *I could get through anything during the week if all my weekends were like this.*

I tucked a loose strand of gold behind her ear and pressed a quick kiss to her lips, not giving a damn about the makeup. "I would spend every Saturday this way," I confessed, then sat back and rose my glass to clink hers. "And we're just getting started."

Ella

Gray steadily tortured me through an entire bottle of champagne, half a bottle of red wine, and three of the most delicious courses I'd ever consumed in the single most beautiful restaurant I'd ever seen.

He abandoned the seat across from mine in favor of the one on my left, then proceeded to spend the evening tantalizing me with the briefest of touches. The glide of his fingertips over my forearm; his warm palm squeezing its way over my thigh; a hand massaging the nape of my neck just long enough to send a thrill skittering down my spine.

It didn't help that he was just as charming as ever, at once a flawless gentleman and brimming with seductive charm.

Even though it made him impossibly out of my league, I had to admire his confidence and gallantry. He ordered astronomically expensive plates of food and tested their wine pairings with easy grace; a practiced gesture to subtly flag down a server here, a slight nod of approval there.

Mixed with his wickedly sensual gaze, the combination was devastating. His endless emerald eyes alternated between searing attentiveness and suggestive glances, roaming over my lips, my breasts, my lap....

By the time he fished his wallet out of the pocket inside his suit jacket, I was practically panting for him. As soon as the waiter disappeared with his black card, I slid my hand over the one he had wrapped around my knee.

"Can we go home now?" I whispered, imploring him with my eyes.

Masculine triumph curved Gray's sculpted lips. "We could," he allowed, noncommittal. "Or..."

He reached into his other jacket pocket and extracted another plastic card, setting it on the fine ivory table linens spread between us. "We could go upstairs."

I had to concentrate on not sounding squeaky. "Upstairs?"

The heat in his eyes smoldered. "To a room. It's closer than my apartment."

With the way he was looking at me, closer suddenly seemed like the only detail that mattered. My mouth tingled while he glanced over my lips, then stared back into me again. "Unless you'd like to wait..."

I did not want to wait. Not one more minute. I wasn't even sure I'd make it to the room he so thoughtfully procured in advance. I wasn't even sure I cared that he'd been decently presumptuous in doing so.

Later, I would worry that I should have played coy, been harder to get. Later, I would tease him for assuming we'd spend the night together. Later… when he wasn't looking at me with so much naked desire that I felt all the muscles below my navel clench in anticipation.

Then I decided: if I couldn't be demure, I would be bold.

Gray signed the check and slid his wallet back into its rightful place. I held the key-card out to him, burning my gaze back into his. "Take me now."

He didn't need to be told twice. Half a breath later, he was on his feet, reaching over to help me to mine. Wordlessly, he laced our fingers together and led me out of the sumptuous dining room of the Astor Court restaurant, into the gilded splendor of the St. Regis's marble lobby. Without pausing, he swept me across the floor, over to the bank of antique mahogany elevators.

One glided open. I prepared for him to twirl me inside and tackle me into the back wall… but I didn't anticipate the uniformed elevator operator standing at the button panel, waiting to oh-so-politely ask, "Which floor, sir?"

I could see from Gray's expression that he'd forgotten all about the existence of elevator operators as well. The flash of irritation bolting over his features almost made me giggle.

He cleared his throat, tightening his desperate grip on my fingers as he replied, "Tiffany Suite, please."

Tiffany *Suite*?

My shock barely had time to ripple out from my center, up to my face. The attendant immediately gave a slight bow—an actual *bow*, I swear—and then jumped to his task. "Of course, Mr. Stryker.

So good to make your acquaintance. Is there anything you and your guest require? I will ring for your butler immediately."

A *butler*?

Which century *am I in?*

Gray's free hand cupped his chin, his fingers forming an L-shape as he rubbed his stubble and gave a dark, sardonic smile. "Please don't."

His eyes slid over to me, lighting with humor when he saw the furious blush burning my cheeks, throat, and chest. He gave my hand a reassuring squeeze. "We'll call down if we want anything other than privacy."

If the elevator attendant thought it odd that Gray had basically just announced we were intent on spending the rest of the night naked, he didn't let on. "Of course, sir. I'll inform the concierge accordingly."

Gray gave another of his confident, commanding nods. I stared, fascinated and bewildered, unsure what to make of this new side of him. As bone-melting as I found his cool aura of self-assurance, it also intimidated me.

Suites? Butlers? Hotel employees who knew his name on sight and scrambled to accommodate his every whim?

How was this the same guy who rode my subway line and ate brownies for dinner on his floor? The one who read *The Da Vinci Code* and listened to horribly embarrassing pop music and bought a pumpkin for us to carve together?

The guy who *couldn't wait* to talk to and touch… *me*?

Me.

Me?

For the love of God—why?

As I struggled to come up with any sort of explanation, the elevator deposited us in a long hallway. I followed numbly as Gray led me to a creamy set of double doors and slid his key-card into the lock.

It was worse than I ever could have dreamed.

More beautiful and opulent then my imagination could conjure. So much so, in fact, that as I stood in the foyer—yes, the room had a *foyer*—and took in the shimmering blue-and-silver wallpaper, I actually *groaned.*

"Gray, *no*," I cried, overwhelmed by his generosity and my general deficiency.

His rueful smile softened his face as he shrugged. "It has a bathtub," he said, as if that explained everything.

"A *bathtub*?" I sputtered, peeking into the great room beyond the entrance and finding it infinitely grander than the entryway. "It has a full view of the park. And a chandelier made out of *pearls*. Tell me those aren't real, please. And—and—geez, is that actual *silver-leaf* on the *ceiling*?"

Beside me, his wry smirk became a shade sheepish. "Too much, huh?"

I wished I could make a joke or feign nonchalance. Or simply express gratitude. But I only felt misery.

Because it was suddenly, *vividly* clear just how much I did not belong with him. And that thought, while undeniably true, felt… *wrong.*

"Gray," I murmured, stricken, standing on the threshold of the living space so lovely, I wanted to cry. "Why did you do this for me?"

Silently, Gray turned and stepped closer to block my view. So close, he was all I could see. His hands skimmed up my arms and gripped my shoulders gently.

His gaze burned into mine, solemn and sincere. "Because I could. Because I wanted to—so much so that planning this night was the most exciting thing I did all week, aside from having you in my bed."

He grinned at the memory like he couldn't help himself. "And, really… because there is no one I can think of who deserves more than you."

Grayson

Ella came apart in my arms, moaning my name. I held her against my side, pressing my forehead to hers as she ground against my hand. Even though I'd just been inside of her an hour before, she was so wet and hot, I thought I might lose my mind if I didn't get to push into her again.

We'd already fucked on the dining table in the Tiffany Suite's main living space.

It was quicker than I wanted, but I had no hope of longevity. When she threw herself into my arms, it was all I could do to strip off her dress before I set her on the lacquered white surface, under the chandelier dripping with dozens of strands of pearls, and sink myself into her.

I couldn't resist her. Not when she looked at me like I hung the moon in the sky. Not while I couldn't breathe because I wanted her more than I wanted air.

I didn't even manage to remove her panties or my pants. An oversight I remedied after carrying her to the suite's huge tub and turning on the tap.

I held her in the bath, skimming my hands over her flawless skin while we relaxed. Neither of us had much to say, but the silence didn't bother me. With Ellie's naked back against my bare chest, her soft hair in a sloppy bun that brushed my cheek every time she tipped her head back to smile at me… I'd never been so content.

We wound up in the Tiffany Suite's wide, white bed. Soft bedside lamps haloed Ella's profile, turning her into an erotic silhouette I had no prayer of resisting. It wasn't long before I gathered her into my side and started skimming my hands over her again.

I watched her features shudder and then soften in release. God. She truly was so beautiful, it *hurt.* A painful knot welled in my throat, leaving my voice hoarse while I murmured her name.

"Ella."

Her sapphire eyes blinked open, full of smoky sensuality. They flickered down to my erection, taking on a determined gleam. She settled between my legs and ran her slender fingers over my hips until my body jerked forward, desperate to slip between her perfect peach lips.

If she intended to torment me, she did an admirable job. Instead of giving in immediately, she situated herself on her knees, flashing a brief-but-incredible view of her full breasts, her nipples standing at attention.

I was about to lunge up and haul her on top of me when she bent forward, lifting her ass as she sucked my raging cock into her mouth.

Jesus. Fuck.

The hands I lifted to grab her shoulders landed on her head instead, sifting through her messy blonde bun while she took me into the back of her throat. A growl ripped from my chest. My hips circled, impatient for another orgasm.

But that would mean forgoing the glory of filling her perfect pussy.

"Baby," I muttered, gently pulling at her roots. "I want to be inside you."

Ellie hummed, then doubled down, fitting her fist and her mouth around my entire dick. She sucked hard, clamping her lips around my length and pulling all the way up to the throbbing head.

My body bucked from the bed. A ragged sound sloughed up my throat. I wasn't going to make it through another draw like that.

"Ellie," I tried again, my fingers straining against her scalp. "Be a good girl and come up here."

Tender amusement lit her blue eyes while she looked up the length of my torso. An irresistible blend of seductress and supplicant, she taunted every dominant, masculine instinct I had while somehow sending a rush of warmth through me.

Reeling from the overwhelming rush of emotion, I snapped. One need supplanted all else.

"Enough."

Ellie gasped as I snatched her up and pinned her to my heaving chest, cupping a hand around her face. "You're too good at that," I scolded softly. "And I want us to be—"

One.

I didn't say it. Couldn't say it. But it settled somewhere in my center, crushing me while it shoved the breath from my lungs.

Ella watched my face for a long moment, then reached over to hold my cheeks the same way I held hers. "Gray…" she whispered, infusing my name with feeling.

Her blue eyes burned into mine, returning every emotion I couldn't express. Then, suddenly, they sharpened. "I want to try something."

Instead of shimmying down to hover over me, she rolled and fell onto her back halfway across the bed. My body tensed at the loss of hers, willing me to grab her again. I quelled the impulse, waiting.

She watched me in the half-light, her gaze intense. The rest of her face became a study in indecision. Her front teeth worried the full curves of her lips. A small pucker marred the sweet spot between her eyebrows. Slowly, she reached one hand out to me. "Come here?"

I moved closer to her side, unsure what she meant until she blew out a shaky breath and gave her head a small shake. "No," she mumbled, so quiet the word was barely an exhale. "On top of me."

I froze, unable to believe my luck… unsure if I should take what she offered.

My impatient cock raged at me, throbbing viciously. I might have been able to ignore it, except that somehow, for this woman, my dick and my heart had formed an unholy alliance. In addition to the ache in my balls, a well of want tore through my center—yearning so fierce it paralyzed me.

Because, *damn it*, I *wanted* to get on top of her.

Wanted to feel her soft perfection pressed along the length of my body. Wanted to be able to kiss her while we moved together. To frame her face with my forearms and stroke her hair while she came around me.

I still had no idea why, but I could tell her offer cost her a lot. Fear darkened the indigo in her eyes, blending with her blown-out pupils.

But she trusted me. She wanted to give me a chance to take her somewhere new.

Her actions said more about her faith in me than ten thousand words ever could. Through a thick throat, I could only manage one word. "Ellie?"

My use of her nickname brought a tiny, tight smile to her lips. She wiggled her fingers, beckoning me. "It's okay," she vowed. "I want to."

My Ellie. Sweet and brave and beautiful and offering me the one thing I couldn't refuse.

Her.

So, I slowly rose, planting my knees between her legs and my hands on either side of her shoulders, keeping plenty of space between our chests.

From my new vantage point, I took in the solemn set of her lips, the indecision flashing in her eyes, the way her pulse pounded visibly in her neck. I curved my spine to maintain the distance between us as I bent to brush my mouth over hers, then along the pale, cool skin of her cheek.

"Are you sure you want to do this, baby?" Half out of my mind, ravaged by lust and confusion, I kissed her earlobe and bit it gently. "I'd be happy for you to ride me every day until I die."

I meant it as a light-hearted attempt to break her tension. But the truth of the words struck me as they tumbled out. A stab of panic sliced at my gut. Ella unknowingly chased the feeling with her fingertips, brushing them over my abs and up to my throbbing chest.

Frustration lurked in the background of my tumult. I wished I knew what had happened to make her so afraid of something that felt so natural. Part of me was angry that she still hadn't explained herself.

Staring down at her, I tried to dismiss the selfish stirrings as best I could. Did it even matter, now, anyway? Whatever created her fear was over. And, obviously, she trusted me not to hurt her.

Our gazes connected. Her hands drifted to my shoulders, pulling lightly to bring me closer. And then, with equal parts simplicity and sincerity, she said the single sweetest thing she could have told me.

"I want it to be you."

I could've lived a thousand lifetimes and never been worthy of such a gift.

But I sure as hell wasn't going to deny it.

Drawn by the force of my feelings and her delicate touches, I settled myself over her completely, placing my hands above her shoulders and putting us face-to-face. My straining erection found her center, pushing against her heat.

I felt her exhale in a trembling stream and watched her mouth fold into itself.

"I have an idea," I murmured, slipping one hand between our bodies. "Let's stay here for a minute."

Latching my lips onto her throat, I kissed and nipped at the tender chords there as my fingers found her wet, throbbing clit. I rubbed it in slow, soft circles, working her until she started to rock into my hand again.

"So beautiful," I praised, tracing her features before glancing down to where I was pleasuring her. "I can feel you getting wetter against my cock."

Ella's eyes were dark beams of indigo, never leaving my face. I stretched back up to nuzzle my forehead into hers, groaning quietly when I felt her body clench around the very tip of my member.

She must have liked that sound, because her hands skimmed down my back to my ass and pressed me further into her.

"Keep touching me," she begged, her voice small.

Molding my mouth against hers, I held myself on my left arm, continuing to stroke my fingers over her. Finally, so gradually it made my balls ache, I sank inside her in one long glide. She clung to my pulsing cock, gripping me.

My vision blurred. A deep, endless moan rolled out of me.

Ella's hands flitted to my face, drawing my attention back to her pleading expression. "Go slow," she gasped. "Please."

I took her at her word, easing myself in and out with measured, tender thrusts, never moving my fingers from the swollen bud at the top of her folds. Ella clung to me, her soft breaths gusting across my cheek while she ran her gaze over my face in continuous loops—almost as though she was worried I'd turn into someone else if she dared to look away.

When I found her sweet spot, her eyelids finally fluttered closed for a brief second.

"Gray," she sighed, combing her fingers into the hair at the back of my head. I increased my pace slightly and pressed gently on her clit until I got a full-blown moan. "*Graaaay.*"

Her body was wound tight. I felt her tick beneath me, jerking on every plunge, reaching for a release she just couldn't grasp.

"Look at me," I rasped, nearly out of breath from staving off my own climax. On instinct, I moved with a little more force and ran my left hand through her hair, capturing her eyes with mine.

"It's me," I said, the words rushing out before my mind censored them. "It's me, Ellie. All you have to do is look at me and you'll see everything. You always do. Look at me and see how much I want to take care of you. How much I *need* you, Ellie."

I shuddered when she clenched around me. "I need you so much it's tearing me apart," I panted, thrusting harder, desperate now. "I need you to come so I can fill you up."

A wet sheen brightened her sapphire eyes as she looked right into me. A second later, her hips lifted. She held my gaze, grinding herself against me while she whispered my name and tugged my hair.

Another groan tore out of my chest. I sealed my lips over hers, kissing her with every real, raw feeling bursting inside of me. Ella quickened, whimpering into my mouth and pumping against me faster and faster until—thank *God*—she shattered into a delicious shower of spasms that clutched at my cock.

I barely lasted half a breath before following her over, pouring myself inside of her while I murmured her name into the warm crook of her neck.

Ella

It was a dream I'd had countless other times.

I tried not to think about it… but, whenever I did, I came back to the conclusion that my subconscious clearly remembered more about that horrible night at the frat house than I did.

Because it produced a shockingly vivid nightmare every single time.

Maggie must have known about it; we shared a bedroom and I had woken—bolting upright, panting—at least a dozen times in her presence. After I brushed off her concern with some mumbling about sleep apnea, she never brought it up again.

Honestly, I probably should have warned Gray ahead of time. But as he held me in our afterglow and buried his face into my hair, I could have sworn he'd vanquished the painful memories once and for all.

In the Tiffany Suite, with Gray's naked perfection warming my bones, the past slipped further and further away. So far, in fact, that I forgot to worry about the possibility that pushing my boundaries might have consequences.

When the dreams first started, I assumed they would get better over time. Or maybe I would just get stronger. Yet, as my mind took me back to that dark corner bedroom for the hundredth time, the same fear pulsed through me, as thick and sickening as ever.

Why am I here? *The familiar thought echoes through my head.* Wasn't I looking for a bathroom? Why am I so nauseous all of a sudden? I had two drinks, right? Or three?

The clueless string of questions muddles together into a muck of general confusion. I have no answers and it's hard to summon a sense of urgency about any of it, because I'm promptly hit with a heavy wave of numbness.

I blink at my surroundings, but it gets harder to re-open my eyes each time the lids flutter closed. Why am I so tired?

The exhaustion is visceral, overwhelming all my other concerns. There's a bed in the middle of the room. My feet feel like cinder blocks while I trip forward, managing to crash onto the damp mattress before I fall.

The room swirls as I tumble down, giving me the oddest sensation—like I suddenly cannot locate any of my limbs.

There is a sound across the room. A click? Shuffling?

None of it makes sense. I was just going to the bathroom. Why am I on a bed? Why am I alone? Where are my friends?

My brain is soup. I open my mouth and make some sort of noise, but it isn't a word. When someone actually replies, I am shocked.

"Hmm. Don't try to talk, princess. Just relax."

I do not know that voice, but the pitch suggests a man. Am I in a man's bed? *The notion sends a prick of queasiness through my guts.*

Someone pulls on my skirt. Not me, right? *I try to find my arm, to lift it, but only manage to get it to move a few inches before I lose it again.*

"None of that, little princess," the voice says. A smooth, detached chastisement. "You won't win."

Alarm bells clang in my muddy mind as the danger finally registers. On a burst of sheer terror, I manage to recoil, kicking my weighty legs until my knee connects with something.

There's a quiet grunt; then, all too easily, the man's weight subdues my flails, catching each knee in an iron grip.

"A fighter," he chuckles darkly. "Didn't expect that. You seemed so quiet."

When I can't wriggle loose, I do the one thing I can think of and start to scream. All that gets me is a sharp blow to the cheek, followed by a sweaty palm crushing my face into the mattress.

"Ella?"

Wait. That voice is wrong. It doesn't belong here. It's…

"Ellie?"

Gray.

Reality smashed the nightmare's strangling grasp. I lurched forward, eyes flying open. Panting, I searched the dark room in front of me, frantically scouring for any trace that the dream had been real.

But the hotel suite was as peaceful as ever, serene in its quiet opulence.

"Ellie, baby?"

A warm hand fell on my shoulder and I jumped, squeaking, my body automatically cringing from the contact. Gray dropped his arm instantly. A second later the lamp atop the mirrored silver nightstand ticked on, bathing us in soft light.

It didn't matter, though. My eyes squeezed shut as I hugged my knees into my chest and dropped my forehead to sit on top of them.

The timbre of Gray's voice, rough from sleep, took on a stern note of concern. "Elle. Talk to me."

"Sorry," I whispered. "Bad dream."

There was a long pause. I felt his eyes on the side of my face. "Is there something I can do?"

I didn't know. No one had ever asked. I turned my head, searching his unbearably handsome features.

Sleep-tousled and bare-chested, he looked even more tempting than usual. But my recently-reawakened libido was nowhere to be found.

Gray's face softened sorrowfully. "Ellie," he murmured, reaching a hand out to me. "Let me hold you?"

An invitation, not a command. I slid my palm against his and he pulled me into his arms, holding me gingerly. His hot, naked skin burned under my cheek.

"Just a dream," he mumbled, running his fingers through my hair. "Just a dream, sweetheart."

He gently slid me closer, like he wished he could pull me inside of himself for safe-keeping. "Nothing will hurt you here," he went on, low and soothing. "I would never let anyone hurt you."

His utter sincerity was my undoing. Fat tears spilled from my stinging eyes. I turned my face into his chest, ashamed. But Gray didn't so much as flinch. He continued stroking my back and holding me close, letting me cry. After a moment, he started to hum a slow song. It vibrated under my ear, giving me something to focus on until my tears subsided.

I couldn't place the tune, but it had the lilt of a lullaby, and soon I found myself drifting into a much less troubled sleep.

Grayson

Ella fell back asleep sometime around 4am, but I couldn't seem to follow her lead.

Instead, I laid awake and stared up at the intricate plasterwork on the ceiling, softly illuminated by the lamp I left on to keep Ellie's nightmares at bay.

I'd had my fair share of bad dreams—mostly of the showing-up-for-work/school-without-pants, forgetting-I-had-an-exam, falling-fifty-thousand-feet variety—but none that ever made me wake up in a blind panic.

I hoped I did the right thing. She was wild-eyed, gulping at air like she couldn't remember how to breathe.

Something about her face reminded me of a child's fear. All bewildered innocence. And I thought back to when I was small and my mother would come re-tuck me in after a nightmare.

She used to sing to me, even though she had no real musical talent. That never mattered, though—it was always comforting to listen to her voice, tripping over the forlorn melodies of her Spanish and Italian lullabies. I hummed the first one I could recall.

With her face tucked into my shoulder, Ellie's tears slowed and then stopped. Now, curled sweetly against my chest, it was hard to believe she'd been so terrified just half an hour earlier.

"What happened to you, Ellie?" I mumbled, so quietly she didn't even stir. "I want to fix it."

Impossible, of course. I might have had the excessive influence of the Stryker name, but even that couldn't un-do the past. Money solved a lot of problems…just not this one.

I laid awake for a long time, turning it all over in my mind, staring down at her sleeping face. By the time the first stirrings of dawn hit the Tiffany Suite, three things had become abundantly clear to me.

One: something horrible had happened to Ellie before we ever met.

Two: I had to consider the possibility she might never tell me exactly what.

And three: I would just have to learn to live with that… because I wanted to keep her forever.

Or, at least, for as long as she let me.

❋❋❋

Chapter Thirteen

September 2016

Grayson

"Okay."

On the barstool next to mine, Graham Everett hiked up both legs of his purple pinstriped pants and leaned over his single malt scotch, staring at me sideways. "What the *fuck* is wrong with you?"

For Gray, for always.

I downed half of my gin and tonic in one gulp. "It was a long week."

He scowled at me. "Made even longer by you moping at happy hour. It's Friday. Time to move on."

Graham was the worst under normal circumstances, but he became particularly insufferable when he was right.

A group of young college girls eyed us on their way past the bar, underlining his point. Women were always drawn to the pair of us. Back in college, when our fraternity held mixers, we quickly realized we scored more girls as a set.

He still used it to his advantage. Especially now that he was a third-generation broker—the long hours and stress left him looking haggard and lean under his lavish suits.

"Where's Daniel?" he asked, his eyes following the girls to their table. "He'll be my wingman if you won't."

I snorted. *True.*

Because I invited him myself, I couldn't complain about Daniel coming along. But after a long day in the office, shooting emails back and forth, I really didn't want to talk to him anymore.

"Probably busy swindling some forty-year mom-and-pop shop out of their mortgage because they can't make the payments he inflated," I muttered.

Graham shook his head in mock-sorrow. "Success has made you bitter." He finished his drink and signaled for another. "What's the big issue? Your dad hired him to be in charge of acquisitions and put him on commission. He gets to be the Other Stryker, you guys get good real estate on the cheap, and you have extra time for your architecture projects. I don't see the problem."

Once again, I didn't have an answer for him. Truth was, Daniel and I were never *close*. Back when we both went to Columbia, he had a habit of piggy-backing off of our name. It wouldn't have bothered me, if Daniel's father hadn't embezzled money from Stryker & Sons years before.

Anytime I complained about Danny, Dad reminded me that I wouldn't want to be weighed down by his failures any more than Daniel deserved to carry around his old man's shit reputation. Still, every time my cousin inserted himself into our family dynamic or tried to charm his way up our corporate ladder, part of me wished we never brought him back into the fold.

We really didn't have another choice, though. When Dad got sick, his illness put Stryker & Sons in danger. Or, rather, *I* put Stryker & Sons in danger… of becoming rudderless under my clueless command.

Cue Uncle Ted and Daniel.

I often wished my dad would just let the whole "& Sons" complex go. I knew he and his brother always dreamed of running the business with their boys, but it seemed stupid to cling to that notion after everything Ted did to screw him over.

Three years later, people still struggled to understand why Mason Stryker let his wayward brother back in on the business. For a while, whispers rose behind my father every time he left the room. Finance columns mocked the decision. Stock values dipped.

I was the only one who understood.

He did it for me. Because my sorry ass wasn't ready to run the business alone. And he didn't want to leave me by myself, mired in his shit, when his illness took him out of the game.

To their credit, the Other Strykers hadn't made total asses of themselves. In fact, they sort of took the opportunity and ran with it. Ted acted as a figurehead, with no real voting power or pull; while Daniel crushed every obstacle in his path.

For almost three years they'd actually been… helpful. As good as me, surely. Maybe even better, in Daniel's case.

I liked to tell myself it all came down to his utter ruthlessness. That he wasn't actually way better at business than me… he just didn't give a fuck about appeasing unions, employee morale, or artistic integrity. And that gave him a level of freedom I doubted I'd ever achieve.

It wasn't fair to him. He followed all the laws, upheld our company policies, and deferred to me without question. Which, Graham frequently reminded me, was very big of Danny, considering he was the elder Stryker son; and, originally, first in line for the job I currently possessed.

My mother once suggested any residual resentment I felt for him might have actually been embarrassment. When all my shit hit the fan three years ago, he was there. He witnessed my one true breakdown. And, now that I had to be his boss, I couldn't take any of it back.

In a lot of ways, I owed him. He didn't abandon ship after learning my sorry ass would be the captain. And he stuck by me through the whole breakup process, offering countless bottles of liquor and the phone numbers for some of the sluttiest chicks in Manhattan…

A second later, Daniel appeared, dropping into the barstool at my other side. "Oh God," he snickered, giving me a once-over while beckoning the bartender by waving a $100 bill. "Grayson's on his period again."

Graham snorted. "Not yet. He's still PMS."

After placing his order and flinging his money at the server, Daniel rolled his eyes at me. "What's your beef with this place, anyway? You're a sad sack every time we come here."

The King Cole Bar was a famous watering hole inside the even-more-famous St. Regis hotel. Right off the eastern side of Central Park, it served as a well-established stop for midtown executives and uptown socialites. The three of us had been drinking there since well before we turned twenty-one… and well before I brought Ella there for one of our first dates.

Images of Ellie grinning at me over the same polished bar top swam through my head. Ice knocked my front teeth while I polished off my gin.

For Gray, for always.

"If you're both so worried about my fucking mood, why don't one of you suggest a girl for this thing we have to go to next week? If I don't find a proper date, I have to sit next to Olivia Twat. And I haven't gotten laid since July."

Not that I'd even be able to, if the previous night was any indication.

Graham balked. "Are you *kidding me*? No wonder you've been such a dick all summer." He spun his phone in his hand, already fast at work. "Easily remedied."

Daniel didn't seem surprised. We worked together, attended all company functions together, and both lived in my new Stryker &

Sons apartment complex along the East River. If I had any women around, he would have seen them. Besides, he was too busy eying the group of girls that arrived right before he did.

"Here." Graham set his iPhone on the polished wood in front of me. "Sara Martin."

From his screen, a blonde socialite with obviously fake breasts grinned up at me. I squinted at the photo. "Sorority Sara? You set me up with her last January for New Year's."

He made a face. "No I didn't. I just met Sara like three months ago."

We both looked back down at the Instagram photo. "I swear, Sara is the girl—blonde hair, fake tits, kept calling me 'Papi' while we hooked up?"

Recognition lit Graham's dark eyes. "Oh *Sarah*! With an H. Yeah, no, this is a different chick."

I blinked at the identical woman. "You've got to be shitting me."

Daniel shrugged, signaling for the bartender again. "All stacked blondes look the same. Hell they all *are* the same."

But I knew that wasn't true.

For Gray, for always.

Lured by another flash of cash, the bartender slid over to us. "Yeah, another round here." Daniel pointed to our cocktails. "And I'd also like a round of whatever those ladies are drinking over there; I'll deliver them in person."

Witnessing my cousin work always provided a good distraction. He seemed to have a way with women. Truly a master negotiator. Even when we were sure he'd struck out, he usually managed to turn it around in the end.

Graham shook his head while we watched him carry drinks over to the girls. "I don't get it," he said. "What does he have that we don't?"

I wasn't sure I understood women well enough to judge who they generally found more attractive. But Danny and I didn't look related at all. I inherited my mom's Mediterranean coloring and green eyes while he got his dad's blonde hair and brown eyes. Also like his father, Daniel fell on the shorter side, his build more rounded than square.

Of the two of us, he must have been better-looking, though. His results spoke for themselves.

"Girls love him," I mused. "He's a confident guy."

Graham glowered, gesturing to his purple ensemble, presenting it as evidence. "Look at me. And you're literally a billionaire. Any other theories?"

"Big dick?"

He considered that for a moment. "We all have those."

I didn't want to know how he knew that. "Maybe it's the money. God knows he waves more cash around than I do."

Graham shrugged, still not convinced but losing interest. He turned back to his phone. "So, Sara—yes or no?"

I hadn't even met her, and I was already bored with her. The thought of spending a night with Sara-No-H sounded less enticing than a night with Stryker & Sons personnel spreadsheets. Or even—God help me—Olivia Twat.

My phone buzzed in my pocket, sending a charge down my spine. A sick thrill swelled in my stomach when I saw Amir's text on my screen… along with an attached document.

Like a tap in the winter, my blood ran ice cold, then suddenly heated to boiling. It thickened, pounding loudly through my ears.

His message was concise. *Found her*, it said. *Ella Callahan: 99 Gold Street, Brooklyn, NY. (410) 555-2394.*

Ella

Maggie decided not to torture me with a rave or a burlesque. Instead, she arranged a celebratory dinner at my favorite restaurant downtown, followed by many, many drinks at an East Village hotspot known for its speakeasy ambiance.

Friends from NYU and work filtered in and out, buying rounds and toasting my book even though none of them had read it yet. By one AM, I was ready to call it a night.

It was long past my bedtime and I was way over my drink limit. Champagne, cosmos, and amaretto sours blurred into a haze, ensuring I'd have to drag myself to yoga class by my fingernails the next morning.

Maggie pouted when I told her I wanted to go. She had her eye on the hot bartender at Angel's Share and didn't want to leave before he got off-shift. I waved off her offer to pay for my Uber and called my own.

For once, the roads back to Brooklyn were quiet. Halfway over the bridge, I turned to watch the city lights fade behind me. As they shrank away, a chasm of loneliness rippled through my center. I reached for my phone and unlocked it, only to realize I had no one to call.

Grayson's face floated, unbidden and unwelcome, through my mind. I immediately banished the thought, swiping to open Instagram and give myself a distraction.

Parker's story hovered at the top of my home page. It was a video of a shot girl pouring a row of drinks, posted only ten minutes earlier. With my usual inhibitions strangled by booze, I swiped over to my texts and shot him a message. I figured it wasn't *that* weird… After all, we were supposed to go on a date in eighteen hours.

Before he replied, the Uber stopped on my corner. Out my window, the cursed Stryker & Sons sign loomed large on the dark street, its logo illuminated by an obnoxiously-bright up-light.

I pushed open the car door and slid out onto the street, staring up at the sign while I listened to the car rumble up the road.

"It's not fair," I muttered to myself. "He had to pop back up *now*?"

Just when I was about to have something exciting and new in my life. Just when a viable guy finally got up the nerve to ask me out. Just when my therapy and finances and friendships were finally back on track after everything that happened to me.

Sighing, I turned my back on the sign.

Only to find Grayson Stryker, standing there in the flesh.

Grayson

The car rolled away, leaving a girl in the center of the street.

City lights haloed her silhouette and hid her features. But I knew her.

Her lush blonde hair. Legs a tad too long for her body. The threadbare flower coat.

Ella.

If I got closer, I'd see the specks of warm cinnamon dusted over her nose. The silver rings around her irises that turned her eyes from oceans to sapphires. Probably a peachy blush on the round apples of her cheeks.

Even if I didn't immediately recognize any of those gutting familiarities, some piece of me *knew* her. Always had, from the moment I laid eyes on her. Years after that godforsaken subway ride… my soul still snapped-to the second I saw her.

For a long moment, Ella stood with her back to me, peering up at the Stryker & Sons billboard across the street. Her shoulders slumped under some invisible weight.

When my cab deposited me on her street, our banner caught me off guard. Dumb. I should have recognized the address sooner—after all, I was the one who chose that block over another option four streets over.

Guilt and conceit muddled in my gin-addled mind. I felt perversely pleased that she was forced to deal with the memory of me while I spent the week wrestling her ghost. But some long-forgotten protective instinct still recoiled from the notion of anything hurting her.

And that pissed me off.

Why the fuck should I care? She left me. Decimated me. And now *I* felt bad?

What if she saw me and burst into tears? Or ran off screaming? My half-baked, fully-drunk plan seemed stupider by the second. I was at her *apartment*? Unannounced? *Three years* after *she* left *me*?

I couldn't remember much of my decision-making process, aside from my lungs crunching at the notion of calling her and never hearing back. Again.

In the months after her defection, I must have called her a thousand times. I sent texts daily, left voicemails. Until April, when I realized none of them ever displayed as "delivered," because she had blocked my number. I followed that discovery with a week-long "graduation trip"/bender with Graham in Amsterdam, where—in the midst of a black-out—I deleted her information altogether.

...only to make Marco dig it all back up, now.

Why didn't I just text her? My blurred brain didn't recall. I must have figured it would be better for her to reject me to my face... which now seemed morbidly masochistic, at best.

Or maybe you just couldn't resist seeing her again.

Hadn't it always been that way, with us? I buzzed around her like a moth to flame, no matter how many times she singed my wings off.

I wasn't prepared for Ella to turn around at that second. But she did.

A dart struck me right in the throat, blocking my breath. *Dear God.*

Her coat gaped open, revealing soft curves and a silky blue slip-dress. None of which matched the white velvet boots stretching up over her knees. She drifted closer, moving with the same sensuality that used to make me wild for her.

My eyes snagged on the worn poppy-patterned overcoat—her only one, back then. My fingers twitched, recalling the feel of her bare shoulders whenever I slid the garment off of them.

Her face hit me like a gut-punch, ripping the air from my lungs, cramping my center. Done up for a night out, she was breathtakingly bare aside from crimson lips and dark wings of eyeliner. With her hair in a messy knot at the back of her head, I could trace the lines of her collarbones, her neck, her jaw.

And, Jesus. It all hurt.

Her voice sent a thrill through my body, but her words scraped at the hole in my middle.

"Gray," she murmured, her voice breaking on the name she gave me—the one no one else ever used. "What are you *doing* here?"

Ella

In my very best dreams, I saw Gray.

I saw him the way I tried to remember him—happy. Usually wearing nothing more than his boxers, in the bed that used to be ours. With his thick dark hair flopping over his forehead, some soft electricity glowing in his green eyes. Sometimes, he laughed. Others, he took my face in his powerful hands and brushed his sculpted mouth over mine.

The man standing on my street at two-AM may have been Grayson Stryker.

But he wasn't Gray.

The furious man glaring at me as well have been a stranger. This person was cold and hard, from the set of his shoulders to the fists clenched at his sides.

My amaretto-soaked brain wasn't quick enough for shock or fear. It could only scramble to keep my lungs functioning in the face of his *absolute loathing.*

Oddly, my body still wanted to be closer to his. I edged nearer, hoping I might be able to help whatever horrible tumult had him frozen on the spot. I started to reach for him.

It's me. I'm the reason he's like this.

My hand fell to my side at the same moment his name fell from my lips. "Gray?"

For a moment, he maintained his gorgeous mask of fury. Even murderous, Grayson was every bit as handsome up close as he was when I saw him at Stryker & Sons. His wide jaw worked, grinding. The stubble over his cheeks and chin caught the sheen of the nearby streetlight, along with his eyes. I saw they weren't flat and hard at all. Up close, the seas of green shifted; turbulent, with swells of desolation.

Gray smiled, but it was a bleak facsimile of the grin I once adored. A mockery.

"For Gray, for always," he quoted, his voice oddly even.

I smelled the gin on him, along with rich, musky cologne. Combined with his words, the familiar scent left me lightheaded. *He came because he saw my book… and the dedication… which means… did he* read *it?*

A pulse of nausea swelled under my diaphragm, along with a sickening surge of hope. "You read it?" I breathed.

"Didn't need to," he bit back. "Lived through it once already. That was enough."

Of course he was right. Why should he have to relive his pain for my benefit? He already went through all of it… because of me. He didn't owe me anything. And, besides, the characters in my book found a much happier ending than the one I created in real life.

Even so, my gaze looped over his face again and again, greedy. For years, I only saw paltry copies of his beauty—pictures in tabloids, the odd news story or magazine feature. Pale imitations of the real Grayson Stryker.

I'd imagined this reunion a thousand times… What would be like if I ran into him at the dry cleaners Marjorie sent me to in Midtown? Our favorite bakery in the Bowery? The boats in the park?

I always assumed Grayson would revert to his poised formality. I pictured him making clipped small talk, flicking his eyes at his watch… anything to get away from me quickly. And I wouldn't have blamed him.

But we weren't trading stilted pleasantries, now. This was something different than a chance encounter. Something darker.

A reckoning.

Fear finally fought its way through my cloudy consciousness. *Oh God. What am I going to tell him?*

My teeth sank into my lower lip. Grayson's eyes followed the motion, sparked, then blazed. The look reminded me of the way he used to leer at me when he had one-too-many drinks.

"You're drunk," I told him, trying for stern.

As I put my hand on my hip, my ankles wobbled, undermining any attempted authority. Gray's grin widened and heated, turning predatory. "So are you."

I knew that grin. And it still made me press my thighs together.

I blew out a shaky huff, tamping down my lust and pouring indignation over the embers. "Don't tell me you came all the way to Brooklyn, after three years, for a *booty call*."

He always was adorable when he drank too much. I'd tried so hard to forget that. "Okay," he shrugged, loosening the tense set of his shoulders. His hand reached over to finger a stray lock of my hair. "I won't tell you that."

Sorrow swirled in his eyes while they ran over my face. A bolt of pain tightened the lines of his. I couldn't decide what felt worse—his outright hatred or watching him war with himself.

Desperate to maintain my distance, I backed away and folded my arms. "How did you find me? *Why* did you find me?"

The indecision bled from his expression, leaving another chilly smirk in its wake. "Oh, that's right. You thought you managed a successful disappearance, didn't you, baby?"

How dare he?

I nearly choked. "Ex*cuse* me? *You* just showed up here after all this time. I think *you're* the one who should be justifying themselves."

Gray loomed closer. "*Me*? After *you left me*? For *no reason*? And then waited *years* to dedicate a whole goddamned book to me? I'm not the one who needs to explain."

The surrealism of it all disoriented me. Was I seriously shouting at Grayson Stryker in the middle of my street? At two A.M.?

All the alcohol definitely didn't help. I felt too warm in my vintage coat. My fingers itched to reach for him. Tingles raced over my skin when he got near enough for me to feel the restless energy surging off of his body.

His beautiful eyes became unfathomable, full of too much to separate the light from the dark. With a low rumble, he snapped, "Damn it, Ella," and lifted his hand to brush his thumb over my lip, releasing it from between my teeth.

The air between us changed when he touched me. Our gazes locked—and it was like falling through a hole ripped right through the universe. A vortex to the past. Back to a time where, no matter what, Gray and I connected on a soul-deep level.

The longer he looked at me, the more serious he seemed. His perfect features pulled into a tight mask of agony. His fingertips curled under my chin.

"Please," he rasped, solemn and hoarse. "It's making me crazy not knowing. You have to tell me why you wrote that."

I wanted to tell him that I didn't understand it, either. How could I still love him after all this time? How could I still *want* him when

I didn't even know him anymore? After everything that happened to me… how could I even *think* of him without wanting to die?

But if I didn't have the answers after all this time, I knew it wouldn't be fair for me to ask Gray. Especially in light of how things ended between us.

"I didn't mean for you to see it," I told him, full of every sort of regret. "It's just a stupid book I uploaded online. I never guessed you would see it."

He cupped my jaw in his hand and squinted down into my face, trying to read me. "Well I did see it," he murmured, intense. "So now we have to deal with it."

We.

It would be so easy to fall right into him. Beg forgiveness. Tell him every horrible, selfish detail. Maybe, at the very least, I could release him from the torment of not knowing what drove me away.

But then he'd have a whole host of new demons. And they would ruin him.

He swayed and I saw an opportunity to rip myself away before I could do any more damage. "You should go home and lie down, Gray." I swallowed a scratchy lump of tears. My eyes implored him. "Try to forget about me."

He stared right back, letting me see his devastation and his desire. "You think I haven't tried that?" he demanded, harsh. "You think I haven't fucked every woman I could? Spent more money than anyone should on traveling and shopping and bullshit? Took the job I never wanted just to have *something* to keep me busy for the *rest of my life*?"

He threw his arms out to the sides and stepped away. "I've done it all, Ella," he shouted, tilting his head back to bellow at all of Brooklyn. "I've tried everything! And I still couldn't fucking forget."

His hands fell to his sides. The fury leeched out of his posture, leaving him hunched and panting in the cold. "So now I'm here."

I didn't know how to explain that he *couldn't* be there. That we couldn't be together without ruining his entire life.

The pain echoing through my torso made it hard to even breathe. "Gray..." I said softly. "I can't, okay?"

"Jesus, Ella." Molten misery melted his anger away as he implored, "Stop calling me that."

Tears pricked my eyelids. "Right. Sorry."

He rocked again, nearly losing his balance. I'd seen him drunk, but never so messed up he couldn't maintain his usual air of confident self-control. Concern crowded my lungs.

"Where's your car?" I asked gently. "Or your phone? I can call the car for you."

He patted down his pockets and frowned, blowing out an exasperated breath. "Jesus Christ. This fucking week."

Gray waved off the look on my face and turned to peer down the street. "Fuck the phone. And the car. How far's the subway?" A humorless laugh scraped out of him. "An uptown train out of Brooklyn. I'm coming full fucking circle."

I was just lucid enough to know that was a horrible idea. A guy wearing his watch should not take a subway in the wee hours of the morning.

"That's not safe," I muttered. "Besides, the only trains running at this hour take you to midtown. You'd have to hail a cab to the west side."

Gray's gaze froze over. "East side. I moved."

Right. Of course he did. That made sense. He probably wanted to be near his parents.

Still, I felt surprised. He used to talk about how much he dreaded his inevitable future on the Upper East Side. He wanted something different for himself, back then. But the man standing in the street with me had clearly given up on a lot of things.

Because of me.

I couldn't just leave him out there alone. Not like this.

"Come in," I sighed. "I have a couch and it's cold out here."

Grayson

I woke up with a crick in my neck and an icepick lodged somewhere between my eyes.

"AH-*hem*."

Wincing against the sunlight streaming in behind me, I opened my eyes to find a familiar, unwelcome presence. Maggie Danvers towered over me, glaring.

"Grayson Stryker," she snarled, "*what* the *actual fuck* are you doing here?"

I didn't know. I couldn't remember what happened. I knew I showed up at Ella's doorstep and waited for her. I recalled the way she looked when she appeared on the street, how she tried to convince me to call for a ride but I didn't have my phone. And I remembered almost passing out in the gutter.

After that, my mind became a big blank hole.

With crusted eyes, I squinted up at Maggie's formidable stance. She had her arms locked tightly across her chest, and a glare to rival Medusa's.

I remembered the look all too well. Only, last time I saw it, I was so depressed I couldn't really appreciate all its varying shades of hatred.

At the time, tracking down Maggie was my last hope of finding the girl I loved. But Maggie called me a creep and an asshole for presuming to seek her out; and then firmly crushed any hopes of seeing Ella again by informing me that she'd moved out of the city… for good.

Was it a lie? Or did Ella really leave and then come back? Why would she *do* that?

My skull pounded while unanswered questions swirled through it. Ignoring my headache and my nausea, I hoisted myself up and looked around.

The room was small, but lovely. Fresh yellow paint reflected sunshine spilling through macramé curtains. Plants hung from knit planters in all the corners. There were clothes piled on a big indigo armchair with rips up the sides, books shoved into a bent bookcase.

I recognized my surroundings, even without the memory of how I wound up there.

Ella's room.

Her honeysuckle scent clung to the floral sheets pooled around my waist. I looked down and realized I'd managed to take my shirt and belt off, but not my watch or my slacks. I couldn't find any evidence as to whether I slept alone or...

"Where is she?" I croaked.

Maggie glowered. "On the couch, cretin."

Shame joined the roil in my guts. "Why did she give me her bed?"

"Because she's *Ella*!" Maggie snapped, her dark eyes murderous. "*Of course* she offered her bed to the asshole ex who showed up drunk on our stoop the night she was supposed to be out celebrating her success. And *of course* you let her, because you're a self-involved dickhead who thinks it's acceptable to just pop back up three years later, right when she's finally about to move on."

My hangover made it hard for me to process half of what she said. Still, dread sank down through me when she mentioned Elle "moving on."

It wasn't fair. Didn't I move on? A long time ago, with any girl I could? I grew up, took the big boy job, got the grown-up apartment, dated the women I was supposed to want. Why wasn't Ella allowed to make the same progress?

Because she left you and never even told you why.

And then… gave up her bed for me?

For most, that wouldn't make any sense. But Maggie had a point. Ella always gave to a fault. Seemed some things hadn't changed completely.

"I need to talk to her," I mumbled, dropping my face into my hands. My eyes stung. "Jesus, it's bright in here."

Maggie scowled at the buttery walls. "I tried to tell her," she muttered, not bothering to clarify. "Anyway, no. You can't talk to her about anything. You need to find a shirt and get out of here before you do any more damage. Honestly, boy, why can't you just leave her alone? It isn't enough that your name is right outside our damn door? She's already in therapy twice a week over your dusty ass. She doesn't need anything else to—."

"Maggie!"

We both turned to find Ella in her doorway, wide-eyed and mussed in yoga pants and a baggy tee shirt. Her lower lip looked swollen and her sexy bun had unraveled slightly, giving her a just-fucked looked that swamped my mind with memories.

Oh God.

Maggie re-crossed her arms, not letting up. "No, Elle. This is not okay. He can't just show up and you can't just let him. I mean, for fuck's sake, how did he even *find* us?"

"I know," Ella sighed, floating forward to hover just inside the door. "I know. It's okay, Mags. I'll handle it."

"It" being me. A sour snort stuck in my throat.

Throwing her hands up, Maggie stomped out of the room while Ella edged into it. She hung near the exit, even after cracking the door to give us some small measure of privacy.

For second, I wondered why she didn't just close it… but then she bit her lower lip and my cock stirred.

Right.

I glanced around the room, at a loss. Did I need to say sorry for hunting her down? My pride railed against apologizing to her after what she did to me; but, sober, in the glaring sunlight, I could see I'd way over-stepped. Getting her information against her will was bad enough… *using* it was a complete violation of her privacy.

But, now, the die was cast. I was there. If I didn't ask her the questions that haunted me, would I ever get another chance?

Or, maybe, it was best if I just left. Deleted her information again—in front of her, this time, to restore her peace of mind. I'd even promise to tell Marco to tackle me if I ever asked him to drive me to Brooklyn again.

Hell, I'll sell the damn parcel across the street. Or give the project to Daniel.

My eyes scanned over her belongs, searching for an innocuous item to focus on… until I noticed something missing.

"There's no yarn."

Ella hugged her arms around her torso and frowned softly. "I have some on my desk," she mumbled. "But I don't really have a lot of time to knit these days."

I tried to picture Ella without a pile of wool perpetually spilling out of her bag. The thought sent a pang aching through my chest. The pain made me want to fight.

"Too busy writing, I'd guess."

Her eyes narrowed at the derision in my voice. "While you're busy knocking down every historic property you can get your hands on in order to make a dollar into a dollar-ten," she shot back. "Right?"

She *was* right. And I fucking hated it. Hated it more coming from her, the one person I ever shared my true career dreams with. She was the only one who knew *just* how much I'd sold out.

I tried to scoff, but it sounded more like a growl. "*Historic*? The building across the street was a crack house during the epidemic in the eighties, and, two decades ago, the bottom level was a Duane Reade."

Ella harrumphed. "And *now* it's an artists' co-op. Someone in there could be the next Andy Warhol—but you and your band of yuppie gentrifiers don't care about the future potential of a place. You just tear it down! How do you think we *get* historic buildings, Gray? We have to *let them age*."

Gray.

Hearing my special nickname didn't get easier. It was still enough to wind me. I couldn't force contempt into my tone; I could barely breathe.

"Well you know all about ending things without regard to future potential," I murmured.

A long moment passed. I felt her eyes wandering the side of my face while I stared into her open closet, hoping in vain for any small pieces of the girl I loved. Instead of colorful knitting creations and thrifted vintage oddities, I found a depressing array of business attire. There were even heels in there. But no green clogs.

When she spoke again, her voice was a gentle whisper. "You came over here to tell me off?" she asked, trembling. "I guess that's fair, after the way I left. You never got a chance to tell me how you felt. That must have been so hard. You should tell me now, while you have the chance."

Her kindness cut deeper than disdain. It was too horribly, wonderfully familiar. Just when I'd almost convinced myself that my Ella was long gone… there she was. Her empathy. Her humility. No one had a heart like hers. I could never bring myself to rip into it.

My tone turned wooden. "Maggie was right. I should leave. I shouldn't have come in the first place. I'm sorry for doing that to you."

Ella's breath shook when she exhaled. "I'm sorry, too," she said softly. "For everything."

That's it. I realized. *What else is there?*

I chanced one last look into her sapphire eyes. They shimmered with tears, but her cheeks were dry and pale as bone. I let myself stare for a long moment, memorizing the curve of her nose, the bow of her lips.

Ellie.

I stayed as still as I could, knowing that, once I made my move, we wouldn't see each other again. Desperation sucked at my insides, begging me not to let that happen.

"Can you tell me why?" I rasped. "You never explained, you just…"

Left me.

One fat droplet rolled down her face. "No," she said simply, her gaze steady as could be. "I can't tell you why."

Outrage lurched up inside of me, but her expression stopped me cold.

She looked… devastated. And yet completely certain.

And, for an insane moment, I didn't hate her. Hating her suddenly seemed *impossible*. Like some sick joke of a bad dream so absurdly false, you wake up immediately.

How could I *ever* have *hated* her? Did I, really? Or was it just coping mechanism?

In that moment, I just wanted to go to her. Sweep her small body up into mine, murmur reassurance, and hold her close until I warmed her.

My entire torso ached while I resisted the pull tethered there. "Ellie—"

Her lips wobbled. "I will never be able to tell you how sorry I am," she whimpered. "But I hope you'll take my word for it."

If she really wouldn't give me an explanation, then I had one other question I had to ask, before it drove me insane.

"Was any of it real?"

Pain broke over her sad, lovely, sun-soaked face. "Gray, please—"

My anger resurfaced, climbing up my throat. "If you aren't going to give me a good reason why you left, the least you could do is answer me now. It's a simple question. Was anything you said to me—or anything we *did*—real? Tell me and then I'll leave."

Ella stood still for a long moment. Finally, she dropped her sapphire eyes to her feet and sniffed. "You don't have to leave, Grayson. Because I am. I just came in to say that I'm sorry for what I did to you, back then. And I hope that my sincere apology means you won't feel the need to seek me out again."

Finally, she peeked up at me again. Our eyes locked, as they had so many times before. While my heart hammered, my gaze catalogued every facet of her face.

I didn't know she was leaving, the last time. Now, I knew.

It was the last time I'd see her. And I had to hold on to it.

After years of trying to forget… now I just wanted to remember.

She dropped her gaze first. "I'll be gone most of the day, so you don't have to race out of here. I left a coffee on the counter for you. Maggie will lock up when you go."

I wish I could say that I took my shit and what little dignity I had left and followed her out. But, instead, I sat, paralyzed by pain, and watched her walk out on me again.

It took much too long for my brain to reboot; for my lungs to drag in fresh air, for my jaw and fists and shoulders to un-bunch. When I finally pushed onto my feet, I felt hollow. Like all of my insides had been scooped out, thrown on the cold wood floor, and stomped under her heel.

I found my shirt lying neatly on her vanity, beside a perfectly coiled belt and both of my shoes. Yet more proof that thoughtful Ellie still lurked inside the stranger she'd become. With stiff, jerky movements, I pulled my clothes back on.

My eyes roamed over her makeup table and the photos taped around the edges of its mirror. Each unfamiliar face sent a stab of grief into my gut.

I really don't know her anymore.

I kept forcing the words through my thoughts, but they didn't feel true. Because regardless of the business clothes, the strangers in her photos… I saw her everywhere.

The yellow paint, bright enough to blind me. The hand-stitched plant holders. The mismatched floral sheets on her bed… most likely thrifted from Goodwill or the Salvation Army.

I could picture my Ellie hanging that crystal dream-catcher in her window. I could see her grumbling to herself about her drab professional wardrobe. On an impulse, I kicked up the yellowed lace bed skirt and found exactly what I expected—stacks and stacks of books, propping up the sagging mattress.

Turning back to the vanity, I heaved out a sigh and faced myself in the mirror. *Hell.* I looked about as bad as I felt. Red eyes, greasy hair, cracked lips, a grey pallor mixed with too much stubble.

I cast my eyes down to the array of cosmetics and jewelry piled there. *I wonder if she kept the…* My fingers twitched for the nearest gold chain before I stopped myself. *No. If she sold it, you're better off not knowing.*

The thought sent a burning bolt of hurt up through my diaphragm. *Jesus. I have to get out of here.*

Feeling beat to shit, I slunk out of Ella's room and into their narrow, three-foot stretch of hallway. To the left, it emptied into cozy living room and a little kitchen.

I recognized Ellie there, too. The coffee she made and left out for an unwelcome guest. The bright blue cabinets. Her desk-full of yarn. And one truly heinous orange chair.

Before I caught myself, I hovered over to it. I pictured her curled up there with whatever book or crocheting or coffee. She probably loved the ugly thing, stains and all.

Just like she loved you.

If any of it was real.

Though the apartment was quiet, construction noises echoed from across the street, interrupting my depressing reverie. A jackhammer started up.

We work this early on weekends? I checked my watch and cringed. *God, we're assholes.*

"Pretty fucking inconsiderate, huh?"

Whirling, I found Maggie watching me from the threshold of her bedroom. In a colorful kimono and her own set of yoga attire, she still cut a formidable figure. Especially given the disdainful look on her face.

With my hangover in full effect, our earlier conversation had already started to haze. Although, the part about Ella attending therapy over my "dusty ass" hung clearly at the forefront of my memory.

Why would she *need therapy? She's not the one who lost everything.*

And, God, what I lost. Standing there, surrounded by all things warm and bright and Ellie… it had never been clearer.

Still, one missing piece bothered me. "The clogs," I said, my voice rough. "Where are they?"

Her brows pushed down over her glasses. "The green ones? The most hideous shoes ever known to mankind?"

That description brought a bleak smile to my face. "I loved those things," I admitted. "They were just so… Ellie."

A knock sounded at their front door. Maggie pushed by me, muttering under her breath as she passed, then threw the slab open.

Amir crowded the frame, dwarfing it with his wide shoulders. "Good morning, miss, I'm looking for—"

"The asshole? Yeah he's here." Maggie turned to glare at me. "This a friend of yours, asshole?"

Amir met my eyes from across the small room, then held up my missing phone. "Figured you'd be here when I couldn't get a hold of you, sir. I picked up your phone on the way. It was at a bar in Midtown."

My eyes flickered to the coffee sitting on the kitchen counter. Maggie followed my gaze and sighed. "She'll be sad if you don't drink it. Just… here."

A second later, she handed me a to-go mug and pinned me with a severely pointed look. "I *trust* you'll find *some way* to get this back to me; right, asshole?"

It seemed like she was trying to say something else, but I didn't understand because it made no sense. *She couldn't possibly be suggesting I come back… right?*

Just in case, even though the thought of drinking it put a lump in my throat, I accepted the coffee. "Thanks. I will."

Chapter Fourteen

November 2013

Ella

"Finally."

Grayson's muttered voice came through his front door as he slipped into the loft. My heart gave a pang when I took in his gorgeous, brooding pout, his thick, wind-swept hair, the way his handsome peacoat stretched around his body. "Traffic was a nightmare."

Despite his grousing, I couldn't help but grin at him. He was just so *hot*. It still shocked me every time I realized that we were together—that I had been in his apartment, alone, because he gave me a *key* to let myself in if I finished work before he did.

In the weeks since his trusting gesture, I settled into a special Thursday routine. After my shift at Four Foxes, I stopped by the farmer's market in Washington Square and bought whatever I could find for dinner.

Tonight, because of the vicious chill outside, I had chili simmering on his stove and a batch of biscuits waiting on the island. I was glad for the heat from the kitchen and the warmth from the smoldering furnace next to my perch on the couch.

Gray shook off his coat, revealing the charcoal suit underneath. When our gazes collided, his frown evaporated. His eyes traced my features in his hungry, affectionate way, then dropped down to the yarn in my lap and the knitting needles in my hands. A wide smile bloomed across his face.

"Still using the dark green, huh?"

I felt a blush steal over my cheeks while he emptied his pockets onto the table beside the door. I'd been using the same yarn for weeks, partly because spending time with him slowed my progress and partly because I wanted the current creation to be absolutely perfect. "I'm just finishing up with it, actually."

"Ah, yes. The Mystery Project." Gray grinned as he approached, shrugging off his suit jacket and yanking his ice-blue tie loose while his long strides ate up the distance between us.

He bent and pressed three tender kisses to my forehead. "Hi, baby."

I tilted my head back to catch his lips with mine. "Hi," I hummed, then gave him another smile. "Are you hungry?"

A wicked glimmer lit his green eyes. "Starving."

I giggled. "For *dinner*, Gray."

Surprise lifted his dark, slashing brows. He glanced over his shoulder. "You cooked again?"

I tamped down the instinct to feel self-conscious. "Just chili. And cheese biscuits."

His mouth softened into a disbelieving curve. "I love chili."

Satisfaction washed through me. One of the many things I learned during our weeks together; Gray loved simple food. Having grown up with private chefs and catered holidays, he relished the basic, home-style meals I whipped together. The week before, he enthused over my fried chicken and macaroni until I was sure I'd have a permanent blush from all the unnecessary admiration.

I shrugged, aiming for a casual air. "It's so cold out. I figured we needed something hot." My fingers roamed over his chilled cheek. "Do you want to take a shower or change your clothes? You must be freezing."

His smile took on a wolfish quality. "I'm starting to warm up. But, yes, we should *absolutely* take a shower."

Heaviness pooled between my thighs. Then I remembered… "Actually, I can't."

Gray had every right to look at me like I'd lost my mind. In all of our time together, I'd never ever turned down an offer to get naked with him.

His frown returned with ferocious force. But he didn't argue or question me. "Okay… I'll just… be back in a few minutes, then."

I bit my lip, uncertain. I had never had a real boyfriend before… and it was embarrassing to tell a sex-god like Gray that I couldn't be intimate with him because my period decided to arrive during my French Literature class that morning.

Reading my face like a book, Gray cupped my cheek in his large, cool hand. "Is everything alright? You're chewing your lip."

Ugh. Mortification heated my neck and throat. But I didn't want him to feel rejected all weekend because he didn't know the cause for my denial.

"Yeah," I replied, forcing a small shrug. "I just, um, started my period today."

Later, I wished I took a picture of his face in that moment. His features quirked into a frozen mask of bewilderment that, upon reflection, was actually pretty hilarious. In that instant, though, I just wanted to melt into the rug under the couch.

Finally, he smoothed the shock from his expression. A wry smirk tugged at his sculpted mouth. "I'm an idiot," he announced. "I've always been in casual relationships before so I've never been with a woman consistently enough to—" He stopped himself and cleared his throat. "Anyway. This makes sense."

I cringed so hard my face hurt. "I'm sorry to have to tell you."

Gray shook his head adamantly. "There is nothing for you to apologize for." He dropped another kiss onto my face, then stayed close as he murmured, "I want to know these things so I can understand you and take care of you."

Comprehension sifted through his eyes. "Did you not want to shower with me because of this?"

I swallowed a lump of embarrassment. "It's not that I don't want to shower with you. I just didn't want to lead you on when I can't…"

The heat flared in his gaze again. "How long do we have to wait?"

I blew out a breath and answered honestly before I could think better of it. "Three days, if you're not squeamish. Five if you are."

Gray chuckled. "Alright, then." A teasing light joined the molten desire in his eyes. "Three days of foreplay? I think this will be fun."

He kissed me again. A slow, lingering kiss that melted for a whole different reason. "Come shower with me?" he asked against my lips.

That time, I was in his arms before I even finished nodding.

Grayson

Adorably rumpled from our shower, Ella settled herself on the barstool next to mine with her usual thoughtless grace.

I was already a quarter of the way into my bowl of chili, speechless at how delicious it tasted. I did manage an appreciative groan, though.

Ellie cast her smiling eyes in my direction. "You like it?"

Nodding, I swallowed and turned to her. "You'll have to be careful," I grunted, only partially kidding. "Or I'm going to get used to this."

She was so damn cute, engulfed in one of my black tee shirts, frowning at me. "Chili?"

I couldn't resist leaning over and kissing her shoulder. "No. This. You. Here with me at the end of the day." Her eyes glowed while we looked into each other and I finished my confession. "I love it."

The way she beamed at me stole my breath. "So do I."

We ate in comfortable silence for a moment. After a bite of one of her biscuits, I was truly in awe. She was so industrious—cooking, baking, knitting, writing. Always making something out of nothing.

My eyes flickered to the pile of dark green yarn left abandoned on my couch. "Are you ever going to tell me what you're making?"

Her smile turned secretive. "Nope." Then she shot me a pointed glance. "Are *you* going to tell me how work was?"

Touché.

It only took a few weeks for her catch on to how much I hated my internship at Stryker & Sons. And while I fastidiously avoided the topic, she made sure to ask about it as often and as innocently as she could.

I glowered at her for a moment. "It was *fine*."

She pretended to consider my reply for a moment before casting me another searching look. "'Fine' like 'I had a turkey sandwich and it was fine,' or 'fine' like 'I got bit by a shark but they sewed my leg back on, so now I'm fine?'"

A laugh escaped me before I could help it. "Well, Stryker does have its fair share of sharks…" I pictured the other interns, all well-heeled and ruthless. "But I'd say it was more of the former than the latter."

Ella's face softened but her eyes stayed sharp. "What did you do?"

I thought through my rounds. They were always more extensive and in-depth than the other interns—and, of course, I "got to" sit in all the executive financial meetings, too.

"Well, I balanced some accounts. Then I went to a meeting with the insurance guys. A lunch with a city commissioner and my father. A budget meeting. A presentation on a new build-out in Jersey. Sat in on a conference call or two. Drank three coffees somewhere in there." I shrugged.

Ella smirked at me. "Internal accounts or external accounts?"

I wasn't at all surprised that she knew to ask such an intelligent question—and that realization almost made me smile. "Internal."

"Insurance salesmen or insurance liability guys?"

I smirked right back at her. "Liability."

"Which city commissioner?" she asked. "Was it Bollero? Pro-labor, pro-union? Man, I bet he hates you guys."

"He does," I admitted, truly grinning, now. "So we took him to Peter Luger's and the third martini seemed to work wonders."

Ellie's musical giggle sent a rush of warmth down my back. She shook her head in mock disapproval. "Shameless, Mr. Stryker." Her glowing gaze traced my face. "Did you show your dad any of your sketches today?"

My gut tightened, hardening into a wad of lead. "No."

The curt response fell out of my mouth and sat between us, sucking all of the air out of the room. Ella worried her lower lip with her teeth and turned back to her dinner, poking at it with her spoon. I watched her warily, noting the way her mouth tightened bit by bit until she finally blew.

"Why not?"

She asked me about the sketches before, but had never probed into *why* I refused to show them to my father. I had a few different answers, each more pathetic than the last.

Because they aren't good enough. Because he'll never understand me. Because if I show him and he mocks me or dismisses me, I won't be able to keep pretending I still have a chance at that dream.

But my dumb ass didn't tell her any of that. Instead, I let it all well up into a seething pit of frustration and self-pity. Then I snapped at her.

"Because I don't *want* to, Elle."

She blinked at me, taken aback, then swallowed hard. Color leeched from her face. "Oh," she murmured, then added in a sarcastic mumble. "Sorry I asked."

I was suddenly angry. So much angrier than I had any right to be. So angry I could think long enough to figure out why I was overreacting.

"No, you're not," I argued. "Because this isn't the first time you've asked and I've already told you no, but you don't want to let it go."

She leaned away from me, her expression frozen. She stared for a long moment—and I got more pissed off by her scrutiny with every second that ticked past.

After several beats, I burst, nearly shouting, "*What?*"

Her mouth wobbled at the lash in my voice, but she drew herself upright, holding her ground. "Look around us," she said, soft and solemn. "Your sketches are everywhere. You draw them in notebooks and on napkins. They're hanging on your walls. There are some rolled up in your bag… you drag them all the way downtown with you every day, Gray. I don't think *I'm* the one who doesn't want to let it go."

Correct. On all counts. Of course. But I was too far gone to concede.

"I told you I don't want to talk about this," I gritted out, glaring at her for the first time ever. "Why can't you respect that? God knows there's shit *you* won't talk to *me* about and I don't harass you over it!"

Her stricken expression sent a burning bolt of shame through my chest. *Fuck me. What am I doing?*

"Alright," Ella relented, her voice subdued.

She turned her face to her lap and slid from her stool, carrying her half-eaten bowl of chili into the kitchen. I watched her rinse the dish out, tension pulling at my shoulders and my neck.

As the irrational anger cooled, half a dozen explanations and apologies bubbled to the surface. I tried to sort through them and put together a coherent thought. Before I managed one, she slipped away, walking into the bedroom area and bending to pick up the clothes I stripped her out of for our shower.

"Ella?"

She stuffed her legs into her jeans before replying. "Hold on."

I watched in rapt dismay while she somehow changed out of my shirt and into hers without revealing any more than a strip of her lower back.

When she floated over to the living room instead of coming back to me, I lurched to my feet. "Ella."

She waved a hand over her shoulder. "It's fine," she lied, gathering her things into her worn leather backpack. "I'm going to go. You had a long day and I'm stressing you out."

My throat swelled as she packed her knitting away. I should have told her that she wasn't making my day worse—that, actually, she was the only part that had given me any sort of joy.

But everything got trapped inside of me except, "You don't have to go."

"I think I want to," she whispered, still not facing me. "Can I call you tomorrow?"

I didn't know what the fuck to say. She wanted to leave. I'd never force her to stay. And it was my own fault she wanted to get away from me.

Defeated, I sighed. "Sure."

She got all the way to the door before I caught sight of her face. Just a quick glimpse of the profile, mostly in shadows. But it was enough to see that she had tears in her eyes.

At a loss, I surged toward her. But I was too late, and the door slammed directly in my face.

***

As if my day didn't suck enough ass already.

I hadn't slept.

Ella's tearstained face loomed in my memory every time I closed my eyes. I tried calling her three times before she finally sent a no-

nonsense text telling me she got home safely and she would call me back the next day.

Friday morning turned out to be fucking freezing, with an ominous veil of dark clouds and cruel gusts of wind that whipped. I got to Stryker & Sons almost forty minutes late, with a coffee stain on my tie and fingers so numb I swore they'd break off on the door handle.

Ella never called.

By 11:54, I was as jittery as junkie, checking my phone twice a minute, debating how pitiful I would seem if I called her again. That's when it appeared—a text from my father. Two lines. No debate.

Family lunch today. 1:00pm—Keens.

Son of a bitch. 1:00 uptown meant that, at noon, downtown, I was already late.

I blew out of my temporary office and hustled up two stories to the executive floor, hoping my dad was late as well. But he wasn't ensconced in his office. In fact, according to his secretary, he hadn't come in at all.

A troubling premonition struck me as I stood in front of his vacant desk, looking down at it and then out the window to the gloomy view beyond.

Something was wrong.

I stuffed the feeling down, battling it back with all the reason and denial I possessed. By the time Marco and I fought our way uptown, it was 1:17 and I realized I had my phone on silent in my pocket for the whole ride, lost in the tumult of my mind.

"This fucking day," I muttered, pulling it out as I stalked from the curb to the restaurant. Ella's name glowed up at me, along with a text I didn't have time to open before I found myself inside.

Just as well, I figured. I wanted to give her my full attention when we spoke, so I wouldn't fuck everything up again.

Ironically, I felt relieved. The eerie sense of dread gripping me relented.

What a stupid asshole I was.

I picked my parents out of the lunch crush, weaving my way to the corner table my father no doubt procured through bribery. He sat with his back to the wood-paneled wall covered in framed memorabilia, dressed very casually, by his standards, in a navy quarter-zip sweater and matching slacks.

My mother sat at his side, impeccably styled in a black cashmere sweater with a fur collar. Her head bent toward his while they continued their intense whispering, oblivious to my presence.

Instead of greeting them, I dropped down into the seat across from my dad, beside my mom. "A beautiful day to be summoned," I quipped, more acerbic than I intended.

My father scowled at me, not bothering to hide his disapproval. "You're late."

"So was my invitation," I shot back, turning to kiss my mother's cheek. "Hi, Mom."

She gave me a tight smile. "Was there traffic, *mi amor*?"

I shrugged, unfolding my napkin and draping it over my lap. "It looks like it might rain sometime in the next 48 hours, so, naturally, everyone on this goddamn island forgot how to drive."

Dad's voice lowered into a menacing rumble. "Don't curse in front of your mother. Or any lady. I taught you better than that."

He did. I couldn't argue the point. "Sorry, Mom," I muttered, annoyed that I felt guilty. "I had a bad morning."

I expected her to fuss over me or maybe give me a dressing-down. Instead, she cast a loaded look at my father before sipping at her glass of still water.

My dad watched her in his Jaqueline-specific way—always carefully observing her emotions, ever-ready to leap to her rescue or offer her comfort. I watched those looks my entire life, and never understood them until that moment.

Because of Ella.

Didn't I constantly look to her, trying to gauge how I could make her happy from moment to moment? I knew I did.

Giving Ella joy made me more content than ever before. Her happiness had become my happiness.

I needed to tell her and apologize and do better. And I would. I couldn't wait to, actually. Just the thought of making things right with us, making it up to her, put a smile on my face.

Until I realized both of my parents were staring at me.

"I told you, *amado*," Mom murmured to my father, smirking slightly. "He's different. This girl he has is special."

Dad's somber eyes felt heavy on my face. "Hmm," he replied, assessing. "I see."

I wasn't sure what he saw or if I wanted him to see anything, really, but our waiter arrived that same moment. I didn't bother to choose a meal; I knew my father would speak for all of us before we had a chance.

"A dozen oysters," he proclaimed, proving me right when he handed off the stack of menus without consulting anyone else. "And three wedge salads. Prime rib for my son. Petit filet for my wife. Rare. And lobster for me. Thank you."

His tone brokered no argument. And damn it if I wouldn't have chosen prime rib for myself, anyway. The bastard never forgot anything.

As soon as the waiter walked away, hastily scribbling his orders onto a pad, my father pinned his focus on me once more. "Well, we need to meet the girl, then, Grayson."

Surprise shimmered through my chest. "You… *want* to meet Ella?"

"Ella," my mother sighed. "Such a pretty name."

Dad's mouth twitched at my mother's approval. "Yes. If you're serious about this woman, we *need* to meet her."

I picked up on the subtle emphasis all too keenly. Meeting my girlfriend wasn't a desire, but a duty he had to the business. Which implied that, if she didn't seem suited to being a Stryker—and all that that entailed—Ella would not merit his approval.

I must have made one hell of a face, because my father hastened to add, "But of course we want to, as well."

Images filtered through my mind. Ellie's ugly green clogs, her tangled piles of pilfered yarn, her makeup-free face and mismatched thrift clothes. None of it would garner their respect and all of it was entirely treasured by me. I sat back in my chair, weighing my words and my loyalties.

"I want her to meet you guys," I admitted, keeping my face straight. "But she isn't anything like the other girls I've dated and she isn't from our social circle. I won't bring her around if you're going to disapprove of her on that basis. She's one the best people I've ever met and I want her exactly as she is. If she feels she has to change to be accepted by my family, I'll never forgive myself. Or you."

An endless silence stretched over our table. Mom seemed genuinely astonished, with her painted lips pursed into a frozen O. But my dad simply stared at me. I met his gaze unflinchingly, awaiting a reprimand but refusing to call back anything I said.

So slowly that I couldn't be sure if I was imagining things, the disapproval in his eyes faded into something I never expected.

Pride.

"Alright," he finally acquiesced. "We will keep that in mind when we meet her and do our best to keep an open mind."

The oysters arrived, along with our salads. I started to eat, thinking that my day had taken a startling turn for the better. All I needed to do was make amends with my girlfriend and spend the night holding her and all would be right in my world.

Or so I thought.

"Listen, son."

Son.

My father only called me that on special occasions. Graduations, milestone birthdays. When I crashed a rented Aston Martin into the gate of our Aspen house. The time I had a pregnancy scare with a girl from prep school and he saw the health clinic charge on my credit card bill. Any time we argued about my future at Stryker & Sons.

Realizing no one else had touched their food, I set my fork on the edge of my salad plate and looked back and forth, from my mother's ashen face to my father's hard expression.

"Yes?"

"We asked you to come meet us today because there's something we need to tell you." His voice was steady and cool, but I caught the moment he reached for my mother's hand under the tablecloth. My heart lurched.

"I went for a physical a month ago," he said. "And I have cancer."

Ella

"Elle, I swear to the Goddess, I will throw your phone into the East River."

Maggie's eyes bugged out as she shot daggers across our tiny room. Slowly, I lifted my hand off of my phone.

"It's not like him to not respond to a text," I grumbled, settling back into my pillows. "It was just a stupid fight. I didn't think he'd still be mad today."

My roommate shrugged. "Boys are idiots. Give him another day to get back to you and then move on."

Everything inside of me balked. "*Move on?*"

I didn't like a patronizing pity in Mag's eyes. "Yes, sweetie. Guys ghost girls all the time. If you haven't heard from him by tomorrow—or Sunday at the *very* latest—then you may as well call him Casper."

I couldn't even comprehend the notion of never speaking to Gray again. We'd only been dating for six weeks, but we had already experienced so much together. And everything he'd done for me—our ultra-romantic night at the St. Regis, ensuring we had dessert before every date, countless small gestures and presents, giving me a key to his apartment, always eagerly making plans for us—suggested he truly cared about me. Maybe even as much as I cared about him.

I looked at the dark green scarf curled into a careful pile on my desk. I'd finished it throughout the afternoon, needing my knitting to keep from spiraling into a panic attack.

With each hour, I found myself looping yarn faster and faster. Until, ironically, my gift for Gray was finished. I tied the final knot on the subway ride uptown, just before we rolled through Wall St. and he didn't appear.

By the time I got all the way back home after class and my work shift, I was more worried for Gray than I was about our relationship. But it was after midnight and I was in Bushwick, with no way of getting to him except a series of very long, extremely sketchy subway rides.

What if something happened to him? a voice in my mind hissed. *You have to make sure he's okay.*

I snatched my phone up and dialed his number before Maggie could even notice. By the time she glared at me, it was already ringing. To my amazement, Gray actually picked up.

"Ella."

His voice sounded wrong. Gruff and thick. "Shit. *Ella*. Jesus, I'm sorry. I was going to call you as soon as you texted me and then—" His sentence choked off, leaving me without an explanation.

I didn't care anymore. Fear for his well-being consumed all of my vanity. "Is everything alright?"

There was a long, tense beat. "No. I—it's—" He blew out a breath. "Something happened. It's… don't worry about it. I'm fine."

I didn't buy it for a second. "What kind of 'fine'?"

For the very first time since we met, Gray's voice cracked. "Shark bite."

Thoughtless, I started packing. *Underwear, socks, phone charger.* Maggie caught on to my mood and appeared at my side, handing me a folded outfit and my toiletry bag. I took both, then reached for the newly-finished scarf.

"I'm coming over," I told him. "It'll take me a while, though."

Gray huffed out a disgusted snort. "God, I'm such an idiot. If I had just *called you*, then you'd already be here. And now it's the middle of the night and—*fuck*. I'm sorry, Ellie."

It occurred to me that I shouldn't assume he wanted my company. "Do you want me to come?" I asked.

"Yes." The lone word was barely a murmur. "Please. Let me call a taxi for you?"

Ten minutes later, my cab surged across the Brooklyn Bridge. Without a knitting project, I had nothing to do but bounce my foot on my knee.

My driver was an older woman. She caught my eye in the rearview mirror and gave her head a shake. "Mmm," she clucked. "Honey, you've got it bad."

I used my key and slid into Gray's apartment. For some reason, though it was after one A.M., finding the place in darkness threw me.

"Ellie?"

His rough voice called from the other end of the loft. I crossed the space as quickly as I could, dropping my bag at the end of the bed and kicking off my boots. The second my coat hit the floor, his hands found my waist and tugged me down onto the mattress. Before I could breathe, his arms enveloped me in a vice-tight hug.

"Ellie," he said again, hoarse. "I'm so sorry. For last night and not calling this afternoon."

I buried my face against the crook of his neck, inhaling the faded scent of his aftershave. There was another smell, too—one I recognized from the rare occasions when he drank liquor. The juniper scent of gin.

Fear tightened the knots of apprehension in my stomach. "It's okay," I soothed, reaching up to brush my hand over his hair. "I overreacted when I left. I'm sorry, too."

His grip on me tightened. "No," he whispered, pulling back to look down at me. His desolate eyes glittered in the dark. "Don't apologize. It was my fault. Forgive me, Ellie. Please."

I squeezed my arms around his neck. "I forgive you." My nose grazed his stubbled jaw, inhaling a stronger whiff of liquor. "You've been drinking…"

Gray's eyes closed. His forehead leaned heavily against mine. "I was in a bar all afternoon." His mouth quirked into a bleak mockery of a smile. "Hiding."

It was serious, then. I knew he wasn't someone who ordinarily put off unpleasant tasks or avoided his problems. The fact that he purposely spent the day evading the situation instead of facing it spoke volumes.

Instead of questioning him, I rolled onto my back and pulled him along with me, settling his head on my chest. I expected some hesitation, but his arms immediately snaked around my waist while he nestled into the hollow at the base of my throat, squeezing his eyes shut.

"I got your text as I was walking into lunch with my parents," he started, a rough murmur in the dark. "I meant to call you as soon as

I left. But after everything they told me, I walked straight out of the restaurant and into a bar across the street. I thought I'd just have a drink and sit and process. But one drink turned into, like, ten, and then it was dark and I was hailing a cab… You called me right after I fell into bed."

That seemed true, considering he smelled like a bar and still had on his rumpled button-down shirt, but no pants. "Here," I mumbled, adjusting him so I could unfasten the stiff garment and slip it off of one of his arms. "Lift up?"

He did, grunting while he pulled the shirt down over his wrist, then tossed it behind him. His gaze seemed bleary while he stared down at my sweatshirt. Strong, shaky fingers gripped the hem and tugged lightly. "Can I…?"

I nodded and arched my back, letting him remove the bulky top to reveal the camisole underneath. Gray settled his face back against my breasts a second later, moaning quietly while he huddled into me.

"Ellie. You always feel so good."

Gray. My heart gave a pang. He really *was* drunk. Sympathy pierced me and I held him closer. "Whatever is wrong, it will be okay," I promised, despite not knowing if the words would hold true. "I'll help you, if you want me to."

Gray clung to me. His eyes slowly blinked closed. "It's not the sort of thing anyone can fix," he mumbled, growing heavier on top of me. "Least of all me."

Did someone die? Were his parents getting divorced? For a long moment, I grappled with the urge to demand an explanation.

In the end, my anxiety won and I asked, "What happened, Gray?"

When he didn't answer, I worried I pushed too quickly. But then I heard a soft rumble and realized it was a snore. He had fallen asleep, still clutching me as if I was his very last chance at survival.

Grayson

I woke up wrapped around Ella like a particularly parasitic strain of ivy.

The windows behind my bed revealed that it was barely light out. I guessed, based on the throbbing in my head and burning behind my eyelids, that I only slept for four or five hours. Beneath me, Ella laid completely motionless aside from the slow rise and fall of her chest.

I carefully freed myself from our tangle, stifling a grunt of pain as I hauled myself upright and slumped against the headboard.

Cancer.

The word sent a slice of panic right into my gullet. I fought to breathe around it, tried to swallow it down. But nothing softened the cold sting of fear prickling through my body.

Sitting in that bar hadn't helped me process as much as I hoped it would, but it did give me enough down time for the facts to sink in. My dad had cancer. It spread. And he was dying.

The doctors wouldn't tell him when, though, as they had a slate of experimental treatments lined up in an effort to expand his estimated lifespan.

My mother clung to that hope in a cheerfully desperate—almost *manic*—way, endlessly patting my father's arm in a nervous gesture she meant to be comforting and repeating, over and over, "There are so many *options* now."

Dad let her. Even though I could see the truth all over his face. Read it in every line and every shadow. In the way he held my gaze, man-to-man, and shook his head almost imperceptibly.

This cancer would kill him. And he knew it.

More importantly, he wanted *me* to know it.

The rest of the meal passed with the disconnected, surreal horror of a nightmare. While Dad did not plan to offer me his medical treatment plan, he *did* proceed to lay out his entire succession strategy for Stryker & Sons.

And it was fucking *crazy.*

Because it all came down to *me.*

Blowing out a ragged sigh, I turned to stare at Ellie's sweetly sleeping face. Her familiar features were more comforting than whole bottle of gin.

The full bow of her upper lip, the lavender half-moons under her fanned-out lashes. The thin blonde brows she loved to quirk at me and the smooth plane between them that creased when she got worried or confused. The small dusting of freckles on each cheek—cinnamon flecks the same color as her perfect nipples. They matched the constellations on her shoulders, the beauty mark on the inside of her left thigh...

My lips lifted into a weak smirk. I knew that nothing and no one else could have possibly made me smile at that moment.

But that was just… *Ellie.*

I wanted to wake her up and ask her the one question that plagued me more than all the others. *Can I do this?*

If taking over Stryker & Sons was the only way for my dad to be at peace… did I really have a choice?

Would she still want to be with me if I had to become an executive at twenty-two? A CEO at twenty-five?

Would I ever be home for dinner or free for vacations? Or would I turn her life into the one I'd always hated—an endless social whirl, carefully contrived for maximum self-promotion and minimum connection?

Though flawless in my estimation, Ellie was no Jacqueline Stryker. My mom thrived in her role as a society wife. She adored shopping, luncheons, party planning; and handled being the center of attention with a blithe air of poise that made her untouchable.

Ella, on the other hand, radiated genuine kindness. She was shy and quiet and without pretense, so guileless and wholesome that it put an ache in my chest. She didn't have a conniving, jaded bone in her body.

How could I take someone so pure and plunge her into my mess?

How could I do it *without* her?

If I was going to surrender to the Stryker mantle and give in to my father's plans… I needed Ellie. From the moment I saw her on that subway, she became the silver lining of my life. I wanted her with me in every possible way. As long as I had her, I would endure anything.

My gaze wandered to the clusters of sketches taped up around my room. Her words from our fight returned to me. *"I don't think I'm the one who needs to let it go."*

The memory brought another bittersweet smile to my lips. *Insightful as ever, my Ellie.*

Half an hour later, the sketches were sorted into a pile on my island, where they would go out with the recycling. I stood over the stack for a long moment before turning away and crossing the room, making my way back to Ella as quickly as I could.

Ella

Sunshine slanted through Gray's trio of windows by the time I woke. I found him asleep next to me, frowning, with one muscled arm raised over his handsome face and the other bent across the naked expanse of his torso.

Grateful for the privacy, I slipped into the bathroom to splash water on my face and attend to my hygiene. Then I tiptoed into Gray's kitchen and started simmering some water for his French Press.

When I spun from the stove to the island his sketches stopped me in my tracks. I took in their placement—haphazardly stacked, at best, on the corner of the granite countertop over the pull-out trash can—and looked up to scan the walls, noting that he had removed every last drawing.

Were they gone when I came in? Did he do it while he was drunk? I vaguely recalled him stirring sometime in the wee hours of the morning… Did he wake up and take them down?

I knew Gray well enough to know that I wasn't witnessing the aftermath of rash action. He got impatient when impassioned, but the sketches were not torn. The edges appeared pristine, the pieces of tape folded decisively around the corners they once secured.

He took them all down slowly and carefully, as if each meant something to him; yet, they were clearly going out with the garbage the next time he changed the bag.

I bit my lip as I sifted through the thin pages, brushing my fingers over some of my favorites. They boggled my mind. How could he not see how talented he was?

The blend of practicality and whimsy, hard and playful, seemed so singularly *Grayson*. I couldn't bear the thought of his creativity moldering in the trash… being crushed by a dump truck… disintegrating…

Besides, I *wanted* them. They were little pieces of his mind. How could I let him throw those away?

I knew I couldn't force him to keep the pages. That would have been akin to him asking me not to delete a chapter in one of my books, just because he liked it. And if getting rid of his sketches would somehow make whatever he was going through easier, how could I deny him that right?

Would he notice if I took one?

A little devil on my shoulder told me he probably wouldn't. The stack contained more than three dozen pages… Surely, if some went missing, no one would be the wiser….

And, that way, I would have a couple, in case he ever regretted throwing the rest out.

After leafing through them as quietly as possible, I secreted nine of my favorites away, rolling them up and carefully slipping the cluster of scrolls into the pocket of my backpack. I narrowly made it back to the kitchen undetected before the kettle started to whistle and Gray rolled over, yawning.

I busied myself, stirring the simmering water and the coffee grounds in the French press while he padded over the cold concrete floor. His hard body, still deliciously warm from the bed, settled against my back. A pair of bare, muscled arms hugged my waist while he wordlessly rested his chin on my shoulder.

Turning my face into his, I brushed a kiss over the prickly slash of his cheekbone. "Good morning."

Gray didn't reply right away. He turned to press his nose into the crook of my neck and exhaled heavily. "Thank you for being here," he finally murmured, gruffly somber.

I twisted in his hold. Gray instantly hauled me into an embrace, squeezing the air from my lungs.

"I need to apologize," he muttered against my shoulder. "For a lot of things."

"Gray, you don't have to—"

He pulled back and looked down at me. His green eyes flashed as his warm hands framed my face, capturing my complete attention.

"No," he insisted. "I do. Because you were right. And I made you cry, Ellie. There is no excuse for that, no matter how mad I was at myself or you or the situation. So I'm not going to make an excuse. I'm just going to say, again, that I'm so sorry and I'm going to do better next time."

His thumb drew a path from the corner of my mouth to my temple. The electricity in his eyes dimmed, then blinked out. His gaze shuttered.

When he continued, he sounded too formal, almost businesslike. "And I'm sorry I didn't call yesterday. I was out of my mind. Please forgive me for the lapse in judgement."

I recognized the cool, professional tone this time—he was hurting. Trying to be strong.

Staring into his brilliant depths, I gently stroked my palm across his face. "Tell me what happened."

His façade cracked right before my eyes. Pain sliced across his features. A wince marred his brow while his chiseled lips parted. I heard the grit in his jaw as he finally bit his words out.

"My dad is dying. He has colon cancer. It's spread quite a bit. His prognosis isn't good."

His pain was my pain. It sank its claws into my chest, tearing at my heart. I think I gasped. "Oh, Gray."

I wrapped my arms into a vice around his neck, pulling myself up his body. One breathless moment passed before he spun me around and lifted me onto the island, stepping between my legs to hide his face against my chest. I held fast, clasping him to me with all my might.

A slight tremor rolled through his body. "I didn't know what to say," he whispered, inside a confessional. "Ella, he sat there telling me he was dying and I just…"

His thick, silken hair rubbed my forearms as he shook his head. "He's *Mason Stryker*. He's always in command. Always the guy everyone else looks to. He's unyielding and influential and… *invincible*. How could he…"

Die.

I understood what he meant, even if he didn't yet. Four years earlier, after losing my own dad, I felt the same baffled disbelief. The feeling had yet to dissipate. I still grappled with a jolt of shock every time I remembered that he was gone and would never come back.

I wondered if it could be different for Grayson, though, since he had the benefit of knowing it would happen. They had the one thing we hadn't—*time*—and that seemed a small mercy, at least.

Not knowing where to begin, I pressed soft kisses onto the crown of his head and waited. Minutes later, he huffed out a tattered sigh.

"I should tell you everything," he exhaled, nuzzling my neck. "This changes a lot of my plans with the company. I'm sure my schedule will have to change, too. I won't have as much free time…"

He was worried about how much time he could devote to me? When he just found out his father was dying? The notion seemed equally sweet and silly. Part of me wanted to reprimand him or maybe tease him, but the moment felt too fragile.

Instead, I vowed, "I will help you. You can do this, Grayson. I know you can."

He leaned back far enough to bring us face-to-face. "No, listen," he insisted, his eyes bright and wild. "I want you to know what you're getting yourself into because you deserve to make an informed decision. I thought I had decades before I'd have to step into his place at Stryker. And now it looks like I may have three years instead of thirty.

"He wants to officially begin his succession plan in May, as soon as I graduate, but he expects me to start acting in the capacity of a chief operating officer immediately. He's talking about having me take over entire *teams*, projects… he said something about an office," Gray rambled, shaking his head as if to clear it.

"Honestly, it was all like a sick blur to me at the time so he'll have to tell me again. But the bottom line is: my life is going to become really busy and the stakes will be much higher than I anticipated. I'll have to get a different place over winter break—something closer to the office, downtown, probably with a home office in it. But, Ella…"

He stopped speaking long enough to spear me with a penetrating stare. "I want you to come with me."

Come with him? To work? To look for an apartment? To help his parents?

"I don't think I understand," I replied, "You need help finding a new place to live?"

"Yes. I need you to help me find a place... for *us*, I hope." His regard intensified. "I want you to live with me. I want to come home to you and take care of you and let you take care of me."

Elation burst through my chest, swift and instinctive. But while my body and heart and soul all clamored for me to accept without hesitation, my mind whirred with worries.

He's not in his right mind, I thought. *Just look at him.*

Gray was... raw.

Reddened eyes, cracked lips, the faint scent of gin clinging to his nude skin. He looked haggard and paler than his olive complexion ordinarily allowed.

"We don't have to make any decisions right now," I hedged, my voice tremulous from suppressing the desire to instantly agree.

His throat worked on an audible swallow. "Please, Ellie," he mumbled, resting his forehead into mine. "I know this isn't even a fraction as romantic as you deserve. And I know we've only been together for a couple of months but I— I can't explain it. I just know that you are the most important thing to me, now. As long as we're solid, I'll be solid."

My heart broke. Whether from aching for him or bursting with joy, I did not know. But it shattered into a pile of glittering shards right on the spot, sending a rush of tears to my eyes.

Gray's mouth molded into mine, skimming softly at first and then settling in. His lips were dry, but warm. And needy.

He needed me so much that I could *feel* it pouring off of him as he fisted the hair at the nape of my neck and held me closer, licking into my mouth. The velvet heat of his tongue started an answering pulse between my thighs, so close to where his boxer briefs outlined his manhood.

The bulge grew more insistent as I kissed him back, angling my face to run my tongue over his and softly graze his lower lip with my teeth. A helpless groan escaped him, vibrating through me as he broke away, turning his attention on the sweet spot just below my left ear.

"Please, Ella," he rasped, biting the lobe. "Move in with me."

Before I could reply, his mouth landed on my neck, his teeth scraping the tender place where it met my shoulder before his tongue swirled smoothly over the sting. He dragged kisses over my collarbone next, feathering it with just the faintest brush of his lips until both of my nipples furled into tight buds.

His knowing hands skirted the sides of my breasts, tormenting me, then skimmed down to the curves of my hips. While one dipped under the edge of my yoga pants, the other slid beneath my cami, roaming up my spine until he found the place where the built-in bra left its indentation. He paused there, sweetly massaging the mark with his fingertips.

His lips gentled against my shoulder, his desperate kisses turning reverent. "Please, baby," he whispered, softly kissing a path back up my throat.

Then his gorgeous face loomed in front of mine again. Our connection snapped into place, offering me a glimpse of his inner turmoil—lust, entreaty, determination. And something else. Some stark, brilliant force that enthralled and intimidated me in equal measures.

"I would love to move in with you," I whispered, because it was true. "But I want to do it the right way."

As I said the words, a thought occurred to me. "It would be your parents' place, right? Or the company's?"

Still holding my gaze captive with his, he nodded, somewhat reluctant. "At first. But I assume I'll have a salary of some sort," he added, giving a humorless smirk. "Eventually."

A found myself smiling back. "We can live off of ramen noodles in the meantime," I offered. "And discount peanut butter from Aldi. There's a guy at the Ridgewood location who gives me $2 off the dented jars."

Gray's grin flashed across his face, there and then gone the next second. A smoldering look replaced his levity. "I want you with me, Ellie. I don't care how much $2 peanut butter I have to eat or who owns the damn apartment."

He wanted me. He meant it. He was offering me a real future, with him.

It changed me.

His sincerity fit all of the broken pieces of my heart back together. Different than before. The smooth, colorless pane was gone. A kaleidoscope of vivid color forged from jagged edges beat in its place.

And I suddenly knew, so certainly, that I loved him.

Which made my answer an easy one.

"Alright," I whispered, blinking back more tears. I added my one condition. "But only if we can ask your parents for their approval. I don't want to disrespect them by moving in with you before we've met or living in their company's property without their blessing."

Gray surprised me by agreeing instantly. "Absolutely. Let's set it up." He flashed a beautiful, cocky smile—the sort that told me he knew he was going to get exactly what he wanted. "How's tomorrow?"

"Gray, *I swear*," I growled.

His swoon-worthy grin twitched before he clamped his lips into a tight line. He held his hands up in a gesture of innocence. "I wasn't laughing."

But obvious amusement danced in his vibrant eyes. After a very somber Saturday, his good mood Sunday morning would have been completely irresistible… if it didn't come at my expense.

Muttering under my breath, I yanked a hairbrush through my loose locks for the fortieth time before pulling half of the hair back. I grimaced at my reflection.

Gray's lips wobbled, threatening to pull into another smile. When I huffed out an unladylike curse and started to undo the hairstyle I just attempted, he lost his internal battle.

"Grayson!" I cried as he sputtered, unable to hold back his chuckle. "This isn't funny! We have to leave and I look like—like—"

Me.

I looked like plain, old Ella Callahan. Not nearly dazzling enough to impress the Strykers, surely…

Gray pushed away from his place against the doorjamb and drifted into his luxurious bathroom, still smiling at our reflections in the wide mirror.

"You look beautiful, Ellie." His grin broadened. "Like I said the first twelve times you asked."

I *had* asked a dozen times, at least. Which was only half as often as I asked him for advice on what to *say* to his parents.

Because he didn't have a chance to talk to them in person beforehand, we decided it would be best for me to act clueless about Mr. Stryker's diagnosis. He also warned me off of several random topics—the stock market (it was not a good week, apparently), Gray's infamous uncle (who embezzled from the company some time ago), and his architecture double-major ("Just…" he sighed, shaking his head, "Don't get him started.").

With his warnings replaying in my mind, I worried my lips with my teeth and glanced down at my clothes. I had on the most sophisticated cold-weather outfit I owned—a tight black sweater and fawn faux-suede skirt, with ribbed black tights and borrowed black-leather ankle boots.

None of it matched the multi-colored floral coat I dug out of a Goodwill bin the previous winter, but there was no help for *that*, since it happened to be the only coat I owned.

"This skirt isn't too short?" I fretted.

"Hey." Grayson's fingers lifted my chin, putting us face-to-face. His eyes glowed with warmth—an intoxicating blend of mirth and tenderness. "Listen. You are perfect. I'm proud to introduce you to my parents exactly like this. You don't have to do anything to your hair or change your clothes. It's just brunch. And I think you look gorgeous, as always."

His fingertips traced the short hem on at the back of my thighs, trailing over the place where they met. A heated languor collected low in my belly.

"Mmm," he rumbled, kissing my forehead. "So gorgeous."

"No, you," I murmured back. It was true, after all. In black slacks and a thick, cream V-neck sweater, he could have stepped out of a men's magazine.

Sighing, I let him lead me away from the mirror. The natural wave in my loose hair would have to suffice, since I didn't have my straightener or hairpins at Gray's apartment. I'd redone my makeup two times, also to no avail. The eyeliner, mascara, and concealer usually seemed sufficient… but now…

I started digging through my backpack for lip gloss, praying I remembered to grab it when I ran home the night before to get my outfit. Out of the corner of my eye, I saw Gray's brawny hand reach past me to pluck up the green scarf.

Oh Lord.

I spun on my heel, lunging to snatch it from him and stuff it back into my bag. But Gray held it carefully in front of his face, inspecting it with a wide, boyish smile.

"A *scarf*," he exulted, glancing over to flash his heart-melting grin at me. "I knew I'd figure it out eventually."

For some reason—either my own embarrassment or his ungallant urge to snicker at my bad hair day—I reverted to a frosty tone. "Yes, it's a scarf. One I spent three weeks knitting. *For you.*"

Gray's expression froze. The teasing twist gradually drained from his lips. His eyes heated. "You made me a scarf?"

Pinned by his intensity, I no longer felt quite as haughty. "Yes," I mumbled, dropping my eyes to pretend to examine my fingernails. "I saw the green yarn and thought it would bring out your eyes."

Before I glanced back up, Gray was on me. He practically tackled me into the nearest wall, cushioning my back with one arm wrapped around my waist while his other hand fisted the scarf between our bodies.

Instinctive fear swelled in my throat, but his lips chased the nervous pulse, trailing hot, open-mouthed kisses up my neck until he reached my chin, my jaw, my cheek. He gentled himself as he brought his lips to mine, brushing slowly, offering me a soft kiss full of gratitude and veneration.

A second later, he broke away, once again staring down at me, grinning crookedly. "I love it," Gray told me.

To my horror, he looped it around the strong column of this throat, then stepped back to let me drink him in. "What do you think?"

"I think..."

My heart sank. The scarf did, in fact, highlight his arresting emerald gaze. It did not, however, stand up to his masculine elegance. Draped against the fine cashmere of his sweater—which probably cost more than I made in a month—my yarn creation looked hopelessly crude.

"...it's nice of you to even try it on."

Gray frowned at me. "Try it on? I'm wearing it out." My mouth dropped open while he flicked his gaze over his watch. "Are you ready? We should leave now."

Gaping, I shook my head at him. "Gray, don't be silly. You can't *actually* wear that."

He slipped his expensive black peacoat over the mismatched sweater and scarf, ignoring me. "Gray," I tried again, whining. "Come on."

All buttoned up, Grayson was more handsome than any man had a right to be while chin-deep in thrifted yarn. He flashed a deliberate, panty-dropping grin.

"Let me get this straight," he said, holding out my own coat and helping me shrug into it before setting his long, capable fingers to work on my buttons. "You made me this scarf?"

I scowled at him. "Yes."

"Because you thought the color would complement me when I wore it?"

My eyes narrowed. "Yes."

A dark, winged brow arched, lending him a supercilious air. "And scarves are for going outside? In cold weather?"

"Yes," I gritted a third time.

He widened his smile, sensing a sure victory. "Then what could possibly be the problem with me wearing this very nice scarf out on this cold autumn morning?"

"Aside from the fact that I may choke you with it?" I asked, shooting him a murderous look.

The triumphant tinge to his smile doubled. His eyes softened with unfettered affection as he reached into the pocket of his coat and pulled out a jewelry box. My heart stuttered to a stop.

"Well," he intoned grimly, playing along, "If you're going to kill me on our way to brunch, I suppose I should give this to you now while I have the chance."

He held out a flat, crimson square with *Cartier* embossed on the top.

"Grayson," I murmured, my throat thick. "I can't take that."

His grin turned teasing. "You're in a fighting mood today," he pointed out, unbothered. Wryness crept into his tone as he shot me a look full of mock-admonishment. "Though I sort of figured giving you a present for no reason wasn't going to go off without a hitch."

Despite my misgivings, it seemed my shaking fingers had a mind all their own. They reached out, tracing the edges of the red leather case before I could help myself. Pressing his free hand underneath mine, Gray held me steady and set the box in my palm, flipping it open as he withdrew.

"There," he said, satisfied. "Not so bad, right?"

Not so bad?

The words echoed through my blank brain. When compared to the necklace nestled into the container's velvet clasps, they were an insult. Blasphemy.

Because it was truly, simply *beautiful.* A thin gold chain adorned with two delicate circles, linked around one another. Tiny gold screws studded one, while a row of flaw diamonds encrusted the other.

I didn't realize I had tears in my eyes until my vision swam, turning the necklace into a watery swirl of gold. "Gray," I whispered, cupping both of my hands around the box. "I *love* it."

Grayson appeared at my side, lifting the gilded chain and bringing it up to my neck. "I went for a walk yesterday while you were at work and somehow wound up in the jewelry store," he murmured, clasping it before trailing his warm fingers around either side of my throat, settling the entwined gold circles into the hollow above my sternum.

"This piece made me think of you." His eyebrows furrowed as he tried to make sense of the memory. "Made me think of us."

He paused to press a slow, chaste kiss to my temple. "I wanted to give it to you before we go to brunch because I want you know: whatever happens today has no bearing on how I feel or what I want."

His hand held my cheek the same way I held the Cartier box. With tenderness that threatened to make my wet eyes spill, he turned my face in his direction, showing me the certainty saturating his features. "You look beautiful," he told me again. "Now let's go."

Lafayette was the trendiest French eatery south of Midtown. Occupying a sprawling corner unit that ate up a third of the block, the restaurant felt much cozier than it ought to have thanks to its romantic, turn-of-the-century décor.

Antique walnut floors, curved leather booths, brass fixtures, milk glass with antique bulbs. Like a piece of Victorian Paris, somehow tucked between NoHo and the Bowery.

Gray ushered me in from the cold, removing my coat with his usual understated gentility. Manners totally at odds with all the dirty things he whispered to me during our cab ride downtown.

If I ever worried my period would scare him off, I now had twenty-six minutes of proof to the contrary. He was counting the minutes until the end of his "three-day purgatory." I decided not to mention that, if my morning hygiene routine was any indication, he'd probably be good to go as soon as we got home from brunch…

While our hostess escorted us to our table, I pondered all of ways I could surprise him as soon as we walked into the apartment.

"Keep thinking like that and I'll sequester us in the ladies' room before you've even had a mimosa," he muttered against my ear, scorching me with his heated words and hungry eyes.

"It would be your fault," I returned, shrugging. "Torturing me in the cab like that."

His smile took on a rueful note. "You've turned me into a mad man. And it's been *days*. I want to fuck you into next Wednesday."

And that was the last thing Grayson Stryker said to me before I met his parents.

With an unrepentant grin, he waved his arm at their table, tucked into one of the rounded corner booths. I narrowly resisted the urge to smack his chest, where my lowly green scarf still hung in stark contrast to his gorgeous sweater.

The second I saw them, it was painfully clear where Gray's insanely good looks came from.

His father was an imposing man—even seated, he looked as broad and tall as his son, if a bit thicker around the middle. While their facial features didn't seem too similar at first glance, a second look revealed that Mr. Stryker was certainly responsible for the wide set of Gray's square jaw and the thick ledge of his brow.

His mouth held a tight, grim quality that told me he frowned a lot, though I could not see whether lines creased his face beneath the well-trimmed white beard that matched his short hair.

Something about him instantly intimidated me, and I doubted I was the only one. The hostess escorting us quailed under his tawny, dismissive gaze.

Gray's mother, on the other hand, was an exotically beautiful woman. Her flawless olive complexion put even her son's to shame. Her raven hair gleamed as it fell in artful waves to her chest, complementing her fine-boned features. Here, I saw where Gray got his slashing cheekbones, the blade of his nose, and his lovely green eyes.

Unlike her counterpart, Mrs. Stryker oozed easy charm. The sympathetic smile she shot the hostess smoothed the sting of her husband's glower. She swung her face back to him the same moment, giving him a small shake of her head while her verdant eyes sparkled with laughter. Clearly, his bad temper amused her.

And he liked it. While I watched, Mr. Stryker's ice melted under his wife's admonishment, giving way to begrudging fondness. So quickly I wondered if it even happened, he winked at her.

And, thus, they were both smiling when Gray finally said, "Mom? Dad?"

Realizing we were there, they both rose. Mrs. Stryker personified poise in her caramel-colored cowl-necked sweater dress and heeled boots. Wearing a charcoal sport coat and dark jeans, Mr. Stryker moved much the way Gray did—economic but graceful—as he extended his hand toward me.

"Ella, is it?" he intoned, piercing me with the same look that sent the hostess scurrying off to hide. "We've heard a lot about you."

Grayson

I felt sure I must've been dreaming as Ella reached for my father's hand with a smile bright enough to light up the whole table.

"Mr. Stryker," she replied, her clear, sweet voice ringing with sincerity so rarely found in pleasantries, "I'm thrilled to meet you."

Her intent sapphire eyes swung to my mom. Her smile, if possible, became even more beatific. "Mrs. Stryker. Thank you both so much for joining us for brunch."

My mother nearly died from delight. "Darling girl," she said, beaming, "I think that you stole my line. But, please, you simply must call us Jacqueline and Mason. Right, *amado*?"

"Yes, of course," my dad put in gruffly.

With my parents on the booth side, Ella and I slid into the individual chairs opposite them. I instantly reached over to rest my hand on her thigh and opened my mouth, prepared to break the awkward silence threatening to descend.

Ella once again surpassed all expectations and jumped in. "This restaurant is decorated so well," she commented, casting an appreciative glace at our surroundings. "And the location is brilliant."

The absolute genius of her simple statement flattened me. She somehow fit both of my parents' true passions into one easy sentence.

Mom and Dad both started speaking at the same time.

"This block is—"

"The fixtures—"

They looked at each other and laughed. Any uneasiness surrounding our table floated away as Ella and I joined in, chuckling.

Mom waved her manicured hand at my father, urging him on. "What about the block, *amado*?" Her sly gaze slid to mine, flashing a conspiratorial look.

Dad launched into the history of this particular block of New York City real estate. True to form, he knew every previous owner, who currently held the deed, and the future investment projections. I half-listened, wondering if I would eventually wind up as pedantic as him if I took his place in the company.

God. What a bleak prospect.

Ella, on the other hand, *actually* listened. And, damn, she asked the most intelligent questions. Better questions than I ever thought to ask him. That probably should have irritated me, but, honestly, I just loved watching the wheels of her mind spin. She followed his endless monologue with rapt attention, her eyes sunny.

Pride felt like a living thing inside of my chest, fighting to burst out. For the thousandth time, I wondered how I ever found her. Gratitude joined the swell of admiration.

While Dad spoke to Ella, my mom caught my eye again. Her thin black brows knit together. "*Mi amor*, why are you wearing a scarf at the table?"

I smoothed my hands over Ella's gift, the pride in my chest somehow doubling. "I didn't want to check it," I told my mother. "Ella made it for me."

At the sound of her name, Ellie and my dad both looked at me. She spied my hand on my scarf and narrowed her eyes. "I hope you're not boring your mom about my hobby."

Ignoring her bid for modesty, I smiled at my parents, explaining, "Ella can knit anything. Clothes, purses." I sent Ellie a searching look, remembering the first day we ever spoke. "Wallets."

"Gray," she chided, flushed. "You're bragging."

"Ellie," I returned, smiling at her. "You're talented."

Her rosy cheeks darkened, but her lips quirked. She arched her brows at me. "So are you."

"Then you are well-matched," my mother interjected, offering us an approving nod. "Do you have any other hobbies, Ella?"

My girl demurred, lowering her lashes to avert her shy eyes. "Just a couple."

Without thought, my hand slipped beneath the curtain of her hair and started to knead the tension from the back of her neck. "Ella also teaches yoga and writes novels. And she bakes the most incredible desserts."

Ellie clearly didn't approve of herself as a topic. She sent me another narrow-eyed look, then turned to smile at my mother. "I loved your hot chocolate recipe," she told her. "Gray made it for me on our first date."

I thought back to that night… the first time I ever experienced the wonder of being inside her. It was impossible to stifle my smile, even as my cock twitched in my slacks and I cleared my throat, shifting in my seat.

"Was that our first date?" I asked Ellie, trying to distract myself and failing miserably when I recalled her painted lips around my erection. "I thought that gallery show counted as the first."

Light shifted in her luminous eyes. "One could argue it was the pumpkin in the park," she pointed out. "Or the waffle restaurant."

A teasing air filled her face. "Although, you did warn me that wasn't a real date, since cafeteria trays were involved."

It took all of my self-control to tamp down the urge to kiss her smile. Instead, I settled for bringing her hand to my lips for a quick peck. "I stand by that statement. You deserve actual dates. That was just me following you like a puppy." Our gazes connected, tunneling into one another, soul-deep. "But, then, who could blame me?"

By that point, I'd all but forgotten my parents were even there. My mom's voice interrupted our reverie.

"My goodness," she said softly, offering a small, wistful smile when we both turned back to her.

My father stared at me like he'd never seen me before. I wondered if I was imagining the maudlin look in his eye—I'd never seen any such sentiment there before. Instead of addressing it, I coughed again, hoping to jolt them from their obvious shock.

It worked. "How did you two meet?" Dad asked, his voice blustery.

Ella turned to me, panic flaring in her eyes. After half a second, I understood. She was nervous to tell them the truth, worried they wouldn't approve of her if they knew.

I didn't give a damn.

"On the subway," I said, smiling broadly at her. "Ella was knitting a million miles-a-minute and I couldn't look away."

Ellie's apprehension broke on a bubbly laugh. "No," she argued. "Grayson was *existing*, and *I* couldn't look away." Her touch feathered over my cheek before she cast my mother a warm, impish smirk. "He's unfairly handsome."

Embarrassment heated my face as she giggled some more, adding, "And he's terrible at taking compliments."

To my surprise, both of my parents laughed. I caught Ellie's eye and gave a small head shake, awed by her once again. She flashed a winning grin and reached for her menu.

"So," she said gamely, "What's good here?"

Ella had me at a disadvantage and she knew it.

Days without her body combined with three hours of watching her charm my parents while I sat there, basking in her perfection, unable to truly touch her, coalesced into a need so acute I thought I'd die if I couldn't have her.

I lunged for her the second our cab pulled away from Lafayette, dragging her body into my lap before she could buckle her seatbelt. "Gray!" she squealed, tittering as my mouth found the pulse in her throat, licking at it. "We're in a cab."

I looked over her head, meeting the cabbie's eyes in the rearview mirror. "Two hundred dollars if you forget everything that happens in this cab for the next thirty minutes," I growled, only half-kidding.

Ella smacked my chest, her scandalized eyes flashing. "*Grayson!*"

But the cabbie nodded and I went back to work on her neck, nipping the sensitive patch of skin just below her ear. She jumped, but didn't pull away. Her voice lowered to a gentle whisper. "Gray."

"Mm hmm?" I was busy nuzzling my face into her hair, inhaling the honeysuckle scent that made my hard cock strain underneath her.

"Did they like me?" she whispered.

Her small voice tempered my lust just enough. I pulled back, pinning my gaze into hers. She looked so nervous; part of me loved how much she cared, while another part raged against the notion of her suffering anyone's disapproval.

Wanting to restore her good humor, I quipped, "If I don't have a text from my mom gushing about you by the time we get home, I will give you two-hundred dollars, too."

Ella's answering smile sent a throb through my raging erection and a wash of warmth through my center. "I like her. She has your sense of humor. And she might be the prettiest woman I've ever met."

I did not want to talk about my parents with my arousal pressed into my girlfriend's ass, but I sighed, relenting for her sake. "And my dad?"

Her eyes went wide again. "He's… scary." She laughed lightly, the sound breathless. "I think he liked telling me about the building, though. And that story about the time you two went sailing. I can tell you get your work ethic from him. And the Stryker Intimidation Factor."

She always surprised me with her jokes. A startled laugh blurted out of my mouth. "The *what*?"

Her expression turned sheepish as she smirked and shrugged one of her delicate shoulders. "You both give off this air of… unapproachability? I think that's a word. Anyway. It's somewhere between superiority and authority. You're bossy like he is."

I wasn't sure I liked that assessment. My brows knit together while I frowned at her. "I am not."

Humor shimmered in her dark blue depths. "Yes you are," she told me, her look taking on a sensual gleam. "When there's something you really *want*…"

Very deliberately, she ground her amazing ass down into my lap. Even though I knew it would prove her point, I couldn't resist positioning her the way I wanted her.

A mocking glint filled her gaze. All sweet innocence and sexual heat, she asked, "Was there something you wanted now?"

Holy hell.

The second she gave me the green light, I was going to devour her. In the meantime, I grabbed the hair at the nape of her neck and crushed my lips into hers, groaning.

She let me kiss her, opening her mouth for the glide of my tongue. Shivering in my arms, Ella pressed herself down onto my raging erection. Her fingers threaded into my hair, tugging until

I bit her lush lower lip. Her nipples hardened into needy points I felt through her bra and sweater.

When a whimper escaped her, she broke away, casting a nervous look at the cabbie. He was completely indifferent, but I knew she wasn't.

With a quiet sigh, I balanced her butt on my thigh instead of letting it press into my groin and pulled her side into the space under my arm. She brushed her lips over my cheek, a lingering kiss so sweet that my heart hurt.

"I can't believe they invited me to Thanksgiving," she mumbled to herself.

It honestly shocked me, too. In as long as I could remember, I never once recalled my father extending such a personal invitation to a family holiday. It was always just the three of us and whatever help my mother required to pull off a traditional meal.

I frowned, pondering their offer. As much as I loved the idea of having Ellie with me for a major family holiday, I knew she probably wanted to go to home to her *own* family.

"*I* can't believe Thanksgiving is in three weeks," I replied wryly. With Ellie in my life, time slipped past faster than ever. "I'm assuming you have to go home to Maryland?"

I didn't mean to pout when I said it, but I did. Ella giggled softly, silently calling me out by tracing her fingertip over my lower lip. While she stared at my mouth, the humor gradually bled out of her expression, leaving it subdued.

"Actually, I planned to volunteer at one of the shelters on Thanksgiving," she murmured, a slight grimace pinching her brow. "I'm sure they need extra help…"

It sounded like exactly the sort of thing she would do. Industrious, kind, generous of spirit. Images of my sweet, lovely Ella passing out food to people in need warmed my heart.

I tightened my hold on her. "Will your sister and mom come with you?"

Ella dropped her gaze while she fiddled with her new necklace. "Oh no. I'll volunteer here, in the city. I, um, couldn't afford a ticket home for Thanksgiving. So, my sister is going to her friend's house and my mom picked up a holiday shift at the hospital. It's double-time, so…"

My hand snapped up to frame her chin, turning her face back to mine. "Wait. You're going to be here? You're going to be alone?"

Ella forced an overly-bright smile. "No! I won't be alone! I'll be at the shelter!"

My answer struck me immediately. "Absolutely not. I'll buy your ticket."

A first-class ticket. She could drink champagne and think of me.

But she shook her head.

"My mom really needs the overtime," she confessed, chagrinned. "I don't want to show up and wreck her plans. Besides, you shouldn't spend your money on me, Gray."

She was *all* I wanted to spend my money on. Buying her the necklace currently strung around her neck gave me more joy than purchasing a hundred bags of shit for myself.

I couldn't argue with the rest of her reasoning, though. I had no idea what it must be like to rely on hourly wages to support two grown daughters; I wouldn't pretend I did by gainsaying her.

Money—as far as I could tell—was the one fundamental imbalance in our relationship. Her one lack where I had a bounty. Because, honestly… I had a *ton* of money. My family's money. Our company's money. My own money in a lavish, as-yet-untouched trust fund.

I hated watching her struggle and stretch when I could literally fix everything with the snap of my fingers… or a call to the right accountant.

School tuition, her rent, her food. All of it would amount to one tiny fraction of a speck on the huge white canvas of my net worth.

I'd broached the topic before, but Ella steadfastly declined. She seemed comfortable accepting my romantic gifts and allowing me to pay for things in my own apartment. Otherwise, she always reached for her wallet when we were out—though I caught worry lurking in her eyes every time she glanced at a total on the register and started to fish around for her crocheted coin purse.

As much as I loved that thing, it had become a goal of mine to never see it again.

"Could I help with your other expenses?" I offered, brainstorming. "All the yarn you can use and all the $2 peanut butter you can eat, on me. Would that help your mom?"

She frowned, pensive. "Your company is already going to pay for our rent after Christmas break, assuming your parents didn't hate me and they're okay with me moving in with you. Anything more would just make me feel like I… Like I couldn't keep up? Or that I'm not enough?"

"Not *enough*?" The phrase outraged me. "Ellie, don't *ever* think that. You're everything."

The words leapt out in anger. I meant to say them to her some other time, very soon, preferably when we were naked and in my bed. Our bed.

Instead of recoiling from my tone, she froze. Her eyes misted. I opened my mouth to start apologizing, but her lips curved into her small, shy smile.

She leaned her face back into mine. "No, you," she replied.

I held her even closer, inhaling her. "Please come to Thanksgiving," I whispered, not above begging. Then inspiration struck me. "I bet my mom would love help in the kitchen. And I'm sure you make an *amazing* pumpkin pie…"

Just as I suspected, at the prospect of being helpful, Ella brightened. "I do have a good recipe with brown-butter caramel… But it won't be weird, Gray? I mean, I'm not family."

On cue, the never-ending tide of adoration swelled inside of me. *One day*, my hopeful heart said. *I want her to be.*

⁂

CHAPTER FIFTEEN

October 2016

Grayson

Family: Matilda and Darcy Callahan. 727 Edmunds Way, Ellicott, MD.

After seeing Ella in person, it felt wrong to read about her and her family in the dossier Amir assembled. My stomach churned, revolting. My fingers drummed restlessly against the cool metal of the island under the folder while my eyes skipped down over the next few lines.

Matilda—nurse technician, Spring Grove Hospital Center. Night shift lead tech.

Darcy—student, Centennial High School. Senior class treasurer. President of the Gamer's Guild. General member: Girls in STEM, honor society, science honor society. Part-time IT assistant, Howard County Library.

Finances—

My conscious gripped me. *No.* I couldn't do it. It wasn't my business how Ella's mom kept her bank accounts or how she kept them.

But Ella's info…

Stapled to the opposite side of the file, a collection of papers contained every minute detail of Ella's life. Her bank balance. Her income. Her weekly schedule, as determined by phone records.

I thumbed through the edge of the stack without really reading any of it. Information blurred past me. Things that made perfect sense—

like her weekend gig as a yoga instructor—and random curiosities I wished I could ask about—like the fact that she graduated a semester later than she should have, despite always being a great student.

Her current address, phone number, and work information stared up at me from the top page. I didn't bother to save it.

After all, she had me blocked. Did I really think she would take me off of her blacklist after I showed up drunk on her stoop? Bellowing at all of Brooklyn about how I fucked my way through the Upper East Side in a pitifully unsuccessful attempt to forget her?

She even said there was no reason for us to seek each other out again.

But there was a lot she didn't say, too. I still had no explanation for why she left. I still had no idea if everything we had between us meant anything to her.

Did I make it all up? Is that why she was able to leave so easily?

But, then, why did she dedicate the book to me? Why did she let me come upstairs instead of leaving my sorry ass on the street? Why did she make me coffee before she fled?

My gaze snapped across my kitchen, to the travel mug Maggie gave me, along with her insistence that I find some way to return it. Why would she suggest that if she knew I didn't have a way to contact Ella? Was she trying to tell me I would get through, if I attempted a text or a call? Was she trying to tell me not to give up, even if I couldn't reach Ella by phone?

I stared down at the digits with my heart hammering in my temples until I couldn't anymore.

Ella

I spent Saturday afternoon lying in my bed, inhaling the cologne clinging to my sheets and crying until I had to flip my pillow over to avoid drowning.

Sometime after twilight fell over Brooklyn, Maggie tapped on my door. "Elle? You left your phone out here and it's been going off. Do you want it?"

My phone? What time is it? Who would be texting me?

I bolted upright.

"Oh my God!" *Parker.*

I cursed repeatedly while leaping out of bed and lunging for the door. When I scurried past Maggie to get to the bathroom, she followed me with wide eyes.

"You okay, babe?"

"No I am not okay!" I wailed, beyond any sort of poise. "*Grayson Stryker* showed up at our apartment in the middle of the night and *ruined my life*! I can't get his *face* out of my head. My sheets smell like *him*. And he *took* my *favorite* coffee mug."

I reached for her wrist, tugging it up so I could snatch my phone back. Hysterical laughter burst up my throat when I saw the time. "And I have a *date*! In SoHo! In *an hour*!"

Maggie's eyes sparked. "With Grayson?" she asked.

"No! With Parker! Remember, Parker? The nice, normal, handsome guy who wants to date me and also happens to be my *boss*?!"

Maggie grimaced. "Well, technically, *Marjorie's* your boss, but—"

"But nothing!" I cried, waving at my blotchy, swollen face. "I am never going to make it, Mags! I have to leave in twenty-five minutes and I can't even think straight to figure out how to start getting ready!"

She grabbed my upper arms and shook me lightly. "Okay. OKAY. I can help you. Just… sit on the tub and do your breathing exercises. I'll be right back."

I dropped down to the lip of our bathtub. My head fell into my hands as I started to count, pulling air through my nostrils and forcing it back out of my mouth.

Maggie returned a moment later, holding a green plastic eye mask. "This is ice-cold," she explained. "I keep it in the freezer to put on my face during allergy season. It de-puffs."

She tied the cold gel-like compress over my face. I gave in, closing my eyes and focusing on the chill stinging my cheeks. A second later, I smelled some sort of hair tool heating up.

Mags climbed into the tub behind me, brandishing a curling wand. "Just keep breathing. I'll have you out of here in twenty."

Gratitude put a fresh lump in my throat. "Thanks."

"You'd do the same for me," she shrugged.

After five minutes, she untied the mask and roughed up my hair, pulling the coiled strands into loose waves that fell down to my chest. When she stepped in front of me and looked down, her expression registered surprise. "Huh. The mask actually worked. Perfect."

She set to work on my makeup next, only speaking to give me directions. "Eyes closed. Okay, open. Suck in your cheeks." After some eye shadow, mascara, blush, and press powder, she clapped. "You're done. What are you wearing?"

I planned to spend the whole afternoon preparing—physically and mentally. I was supposed to shave my legs, moisturize, choose a perfect ensemble. Now, I had to snap into survival mode.

"Jeans," I decided. "I didn't shave."

My roommate pursed her lips, considering. "What about the topaz halter top?"

The memory of what happened the one time I wore the autumn-hued halter for Grayson swirled through my mind. Pain lanced my stomach. "No."

"Wear the cream sweater, then. The one that falls off your shoulder. And a lace bralette under so he'll see the straps."

Without waiting for approval, she dipped across the hall and returned with the whole outfit, tossing it at me. "I'll get your purse. Your train leaves in seven minutes."

I wound up in the corner of a subway car, riding the C line uptown, with knitting in my lap.

I did my best not to look up, not to focus on the fact that I was right back where everything started. In that moment, with the weight of my regret smothering my heart, it felt like it all happened days ago, instead of years.

My weary eyes prickled, out of tears but not out of sorrow. For the hundredth time, I considered everything I could have done differently. All the mistakes I made.

The image of Grayson, standing under my street light, pain cutting across the masculine perfection of his face, flashed through my mind. My eyelids squeezed shut, once more attempting to blot it out. My fingers moved faster and faster.

The yellow wool started off as placemat; but my anxious fingers looped too quickly and accidentally turned it into a table runner before I hit SoHo.

Grayson

"*Mi amor?*"

My surroundings filled me with the surreal, detached horror of a bad dream. Sarabeth's. Weekend brunch. My mother, staring at me, wondering why I couldn't concentrate.

And Ella.

Ella playing in the back of my brain like a song stuck on repeat. Loudly, with the volume knob broken off.

I'm going to text her, I decided. Then, *No. Fucking idiot. I can't. I won't.*

Today, Jacqueline Stryker cut a particularly flashy figure in bright red. Luckily, the waiter didn't bother hitting on her… because my darkly-clad father sat at her side with his arm stretched across the booth, behind her shoulders.

I noticed they did that more, now. My mother seemed to huddle into him at every opportunity. He reached for her just as often. It didn't take a genius to see why. Dad was clearly unwell… and getting worse with every month that passed.

A team of New York's finest physicians managed to slow cancer's progress, but could not reverse it. With each new scan, we saw more and more. His days were still numbered, but no one knew the precise figure. It made sense that my mother longed to be as close to him as she could for as long as possible.

Watching them, a fresh bolt of helpless anger cracked through me. Along with another, wholly-undignified emotion.

Jealousy.

I felt jealous. Of my dying father. Because at least he knew he was about to lose the love of his life forever. At least he had time to hold her and soak up everything they had together.

Ella had shown me no such mercy.

Another flare of outrage seethed in my gut. *Definitely not texting that b—*

But she wasn't a bitch.

Not then, not now. Never.

Even when she stood on the threshold of her small, yellow bedroom, breaking my heart for the hundredth time; she was still just… Ellie.

"Grayson?"

That time, Mom's voice successfully jerked me back to reality. I blinked at the pair of them. "Hmm?"

"Have you slept?" she tutted, pushing my coffee cup at me. "You look exhausted."

I haven't slept since I found out my ex-girlfriend wrote a book and dedicated it to me. Reaching for an excuse, I flashed a grim smile. "Just doing my job. CEOs don't sleep. Right, Dad?"

He had the grace to look slightly chagrinned. "I have said that," he admitted. "But, surely, you knew I was exaggerating. You need rest to do good work."

Rest made me think of Ella's twin-sized bed, with its honeysuckle sheets. *She gave me her bed. She wouldn't do that unless she felt bad… or just wanted me there.*

None of it made any goddamned sense. The further I got from our encounter, the more suspicious I felt. More certain than ever that *something* happened, back then, to make her leave.

But, *what*?

I kept recalling her small, sweet face when I begged her for an explanation—the pale mask of certainty. *"No, I can't tell you why."*

She never said there wasn't a reason. Only that she couldn't tell me what it was. That distinction seemed crucial, suddenly.

And I had to know the truth.

Forgetting where I was, I pulled my phone out of my joggers and shot Amir a text, telling him to go back five years and pull every record he could find. If I was going down the Ella Callahan rabbit hole again, I was damn well bringing a flashlight this time.

"Grayson!" Mom's pinched tone matched her face. "*What* is wrong with you?" Her emerald eyes trailed over me, then flashed to the empty place beside me on the booth bench.

Well.

Not *empty*.

"*Dios mio*," she gasped. "Your scarf."

I scowled. And lied. "I lost my other one."

Her gaze snapped at me. "Grayson Frances Stryker. *Vergognati!* Do not lie to your mother. I have not seen that green scarf since—"

Her exclamation reminded me of being caught with porn in my dresser back in prep school. It meant, "be ashamed." And, damn it, I *was*.

So ashamed of myself for ever even opening the fucking shoe box… let alone pulling out the handmade scarf… and—*God help me*—wearing it.

Motherfucking hell. If a more pathetic sap than me existed, I didn't want to meet him. And now, of course, my mother had noticed.

The gleam in her gaze fell somewhere between desperate eagerness and indignation. I hadn't seen the look in years… not since we banished any mention of my ex-girlfriend from our family discussions.

Still, it made sense. Ella charmed my parents as thoroughly as she enchanted me. When she left so abruptly, she hurt them, too. Especially Mom.

I couldn't afford to give her any hope. Even if I figured out what made Ella run… and why she still refused to tell me… There would be no future for us. I would never trust her again.

"Mother," I clipped, cutting her severe look. "It's a stupid wad of yarn. There's a cold front and I lost my other scarf. That is all."

But Jacqueline Stryker didn't quail so easily. Her gaze narrowed at me. "Grayson—"

"Mom."

"*Mi amor,* you've been so *off* this whole week," she whined. "Your father and I both noticed it. Marco, too."

When I scowled, she rushed on. "Now, don't give me that look. I *asked* Marco if you were okay and he was *very* vague, trying to cover for you. But a mother *knows*, Grayson. All of this strange behavior *and* you've suddenly refused to find female company for a business event... Now, *the scarf…* I can't help but wonder if there's something going on with—"

"That's enough," I snarled, more vehement than I intended. "I won't talk about this anymore. We all agreed, remember?"

Guilt bled into her expression, tightening the lines around her lips. "It's only that, if you did want to talk about it, there's something I—"

Dad reached over to cup my mother's face. "Darling," he muttered, his features stern. "Leave it be. Grayson is right. We all agreed. Besides, we have other things to discuss."

He turned to me. "Have you decided where you want to move the Brooklyn marketing campaign? I got your memo about going in a different direction."

For a moment, my mind reeled. It was jarring to go from such a personal issue to a professional one. But, then again, it wasn't *all that* professional.

The desire for a new marketing campaign came on the heels of Ella's disapproval the previous morning, as well as the realization that we were disturbing her neighborhood without appealing to it in any way. It occurred to me that we needed to try to hook the locals on our new development. Clearly, the firm who came up with the original promotional materials wasn't up to the task.

My father went on, listing some of the other marketing firms we often called in to tweak roll-outs. I half-listened as the gears of my mind started churning. A new idea greased the wheels.

If I want to figure out why Ella left me, I need to get us in the same room and watch her. Between that and whatever Amir digs up, I'll figure it out. And then I can finally put it behind me and move on.

For good.

For Gray, for always.

"I have a new place in mind," I announced coolly, reaching for my coffee. "It's a work in progress."

Ella

Monday morning found me standing in our kitchen, facing the Roommate Post-Date Inquisition I somehow avoided all day Sunday.

As I finished the horrible review of the most humiliating night of my life, Maggie's face froze into a mask of horror.

"You *cried*? On your *date*? *The whole time*?"

I sipped from my inferior coffee mug, missing the one Grayson stole. "Not the *whole time*," I muttered. "I was fine at dinner. He did all of the talking, thank God. But then he took me to a romantic comedy and I *lost* it…"

Gaping, Mags blinked at me. "What did you *say*? Did you explain yourself?"

I winced, gulping down more coffee. "I told him our dog died."

"We don't *have* a dog!" Maggie cried. "Ella!"

I waved my arms, fending off her disapproval and my own chagrin. "I know, I know! But there was a dog in the movie and it was the only excuse I could come up with for why I wound up *sobbing*."

I groaned, folding my forearms over my head and pressing my nose into the kitchen counter, muffling the rest of my confession. "He was so embarrassed. He kept apologizing and offering to ride home with me in a cab… and I just *could not* stop crying. I'll be lucky if he ever speaks to me again."

Maggie cringed. "No text yesterday?"

"Nope." Not that I expected him to. "If I were him, I would run for the hills, too. He probably thinks I need to be medicated. Which, honestly, at this point, I would agree." I scrubbed two hands over my barely-made face. "And, now, to make matters worse, I have to go see him *at work. Forever*."

My roommate flung her arms around me in a hug. "Oh, Elle," she sighed. "I'm sorry this weekend sucked so much. When do you see Dr. Laura again?"

"Thursday," I sniffed. "And I'm counting the minutes, trust me."

Maggie gave me a sympathetic pat on the shoulder and stepped back. For a long moment, we both sipped from our mugs in heavy silence.

Her eyes slid over to me. "Just out of curiosity, what was our dog named?"

"Waffles."

She clinked her cup into mine. "RIP Waffles."

I expected to slink to my desk under a grey drizzle of mortification. Instead, I walked into a tornado-like whirl of panic.

The entire floor flurried. Other secretaries fluttered this way and that. Ad execs hollered to each other from their pods. Off to the side, I spotted two of our company's owners, along with our entire PR team.

Drat. If I'd known every important executive would be on my floor, I would have attempted more than throwing on the same dress I wore the previous week and working my hair into an inelegant braid.

I probably wouldn't have *succeeded*, considering my fingers trembled on every twist and barely managed to smear mascara over my lashes… but still.

And then—because the universe had apparently decided that my life would devolve into a never-ending comedy of errors—Parker darted right into my path. I jerked back, halting him on the spot. "I'm so sor—" he started, but the words died when he recognized me. He drew himself upright, letting the handful of files clutched in his left fist fall to his side.

"Ella. Hi."

Shame stuck in my throat, squeezing my voice up an octave. "Hi. Good morning." Unable to bear the pity in his hazel eyes, I dropped my gaze to the documents he held. "Anything I can help you with there?"

He actually *grimaced.* "No. Thank you. You better get over to Marjorie."

Sufficiently chastened, I hung my head and started off toward my pod. I only made it four steps before he spoke to my back.

"But, Ella? I need to talk to you later. Okay?"

Oh Lord. I wished I could tell him that wasn't necessary. I already heard his rejection loud and clear. And I totally understood. He didn't need to explain himself for my sake.

Instead, I simply waved my hand as nonchalantly as possible. "You got it!"

You got it? Ugh. Hating myself, I shuffled away even faster than before. *I never should have agreed to go out with him in the first place. I knew it was a bad idea. How could I even try to have feelings for another man while Grayson Stryker walks the earth, let alone the streets of midtown Manhattan? So stupid—*

My internal criticisms stuttered to a stop when I reached my desk and found Marjorie pacing her office with concerning vigor.

Wait. My head swiveled, taking in her obvious anxiety and the climate surrounding us. *Something is wrong.*

My boss's outfit was another give-away. She called it her Power Suit. An electric pink pantsuit that she always wore with sky-high black Alexander McQueen heels covered in vicious gold spikes. She reserved the ensemble for closing major deals.

"Marjorie?" I asked, slipping into her office. "What's going on?"

Before replying, she pitched a packet of papers over to me. "Start reading. We have eighteen minutes." Her sharp almond eyes snapped over to me. "And, for God sakes, fix your hair, Callahan."

Thrown, I glanced down at the document. *Proposed Marketing Roll-Out for Gold Street Development—Stryker & Sons.*

"Holy fuck."

The curse hissed out from my numb lips before I could stop it. Marjorie suddenly stopped, whipping her head to stare at me. "What was that?"

Hands vibrating, I blinked blurry eyes at the title again and again, hoping it would magically change. Acid rose up my esophagus.

"I'm sorry," I mumbled, "I only meant…"

No, that's exactly what I meant. Holy fuck.

For the first time ever, Marjorie *laughed.* "Holy fuck," she finished for me. "Yeah, my thoughts exactly. This account is worth two-hundred-million-dollars. That's a two-hundred-thousand-dollar commission, Ella. We got word midday yesterday that Stryker himself is personally coming in to hear our pitches. Every junior exec made one."

"C-coming in?" I stammered. "*Today*?"

Marjorie gave a single nod. "Like I said. Eighteen minutes. We're all meeting in the conference room."

Black spots danced along the edges of my vision. "Y-you said *Stryker* himself is *personally* coming?" Dread welled in my middle. "Which Stryker?"

There were four after all… and only one I needed to avoid at all costs.

Marjorie seemed impressed. She paused, raising her brows. "There's more than one?"

My weak stomach clenched. "Yes. There's Mason Stryker, the former CEO, who was in the process of retiring, last I heard. And t-then, there's his brother and his nephew." I swallowed my stammering with a mouthful of bile. "And, then, of course, the *current* CEO…"

"Grayson Stryker," she finished, reading the name from her own stack of papers. "Yeah. He's all over the tabloids. Supposed to be a real swinging dick."

My brain automatically conjured images of that dick. Amazingly clear images, considering how long it had been since I *saw* it… My cheeks and neck flamed.

"Wait." Marjorie's narrow eyes turned to slits. "You *know* him?"

I didn't have time to explain. I needed to know whether I had to flee the building. "Is he the one coming to the meeting?"

My boss crossed her arms, casting me a severe look. "Yes. And so are you."

Grayson

Eight goddamn blocks.

This whole time, she was only eight fucking blocks away from Stryker & Sons.

The realization infuriated me. "*This* is her building?" I demanded, sitting forward in the back of the Mercedes. "You're sure?"

Amir turned and cast me staying glance. "This is *Idealogue's* building, sir. That *is* why we're here, yes? To meet with *them*?"

I didn't miss his slight emphases. *God, get a hold of yourself, Stryker.*

"Yes," I replied, working to sound even. "Of course." I consulted my watch. *8:56.*

The next time I looked, three minutes had passed. Our elevator announced our arrival on the twentieth floor—Idealogue's executive level. I waded through a throng of owners and higher-ups, shaking hands and maintaining a straight face.

This was one of the few areas of my job where I excelled.

My father called it "Professional Poker Face." Ella used to refer to it as "The Stryker Intimidation Factor." In any event, I found remaining impassive often got me the best results. It was the most basic tenant of negotiation. People scrambled to accommodate you once they realized they needed you more than you seemed to need them.

Amir and I followed the group into an ultra-long conference room *packed* with people. Along with the corners and walls, all thirty seats were full, save for one. I scanned the expanse as quickly as I could, searching for a familiar flash of blonde.

When I didn't see her, something inside of me hardened. The owner pointed me toward the one available chair and the urge to be an ass overrode my control. I shot him a look and gestured at Amir.

"My associate will need a seat as well."

I hated when people assumed I treated my head of security like an accessory. He was a person, after all. Their guest, technically.

Everyone fumbled to produce an extra place. I caught Marco's slight eye roll as he dropped into it. Mocking me, I knew. Because he correctly pinpointed the real reason for my mood.

The other company owner started in on their philosophy and their vision. Honestly—and I would never admit this to anyone—most firms just repackaged the same buzz words.

Synergy. Maximize. Modern. Visionary.

My eyes skipped around the fringes of the room until the president addressed me directly. "So, Mr. Stryker, tell us—what are you looking for in this campaign?"

I almost smiled. It was amazing how often marketing and PR people wanted me to do their jobs for them by bringing fully-formed ideas to the table. But I wasn't there for a fluff-job. If I had time to do my own damn marketing, then I would.

"I'll know it when I see it," I told him, reaching for one of my favorite phrases. "Why don't you have your junior execs show me what they've come up with?"

More scrambling ensued. *Good,* I thought uncharitably. *The more these people shuffle around the more likely I am to catch a glimpse of—*

Ella.

There she was. In the far back corner. Trying to disappear behind a fiddle leaf fig tree. But the aubergine of her outfit stood out against the white wall at her back. And she was entirely too pretty to ever blend in.

Pretty, puffy-eyed, and pale.

A fist tightened around my gullet, crushing it. I grappled with the fierce urge to lurch to my feet and throw myself across the room. She looked so small and scared… and, suddenly, I just wanted to protect her from whatever upset her.

Unless… A cold prickle hardened my lungs. *It's me. I'm the reason she looks like that.*

With her head firmly bent over her shoes, she didn't see me recognize her. Still, my gaze tracked her every move. The way she shifted from one foot to another. Her fingers twisted in the sides of her skirt. The tension pulled tight across her shoulders and the way it emphasized her collarbones, peeking out from under the V-neck of her purple dress.

Look up, Ellie. Look at me.

I used to give the same command while ramming my cock into her. I loved the way lust hazed her sapphire gaze, the way adoration beamed from the indigo irises when our bodies moved together. Just locking gazes with her used to be enough to make me come.

Now, I was simply desperate to see if she was alright.

At my elbow, Amir made a muffled coughing sound. To anyone else, it probably sounded completely normal; but he meant to help me regain my focus, before someone noticed me ogling one of their assistants.

Reluctantly, I turned my attention to the guy presenting his thoughts. He wore square-framed glasses and a tweed blazer with leather elbow patches. Some of his ideas earned nods from me; and two actually compelled me to stop frowning. But the poor guy didn't stand a chance next to his co-worker. The second she stood, all eyes snapped to her fuchsia jumpsuit.

The woman—Marjorie, as it turned out—proceeded to present a concept that was head-and-shoulders above the others. Not only were her ideas better, more fully-formed, and thought-provoking…

she also, somehow, put together a whole visual presentation literally overnight.

After two years as a CEO, I knew greatness when I saw it.

Before she even finished her pitch, I held up my hand. The entire room held its breath until I smiled. "Marjorie, was it? This is excellent. I want it."

My head snapped to the right, where the president sat beside me. "Her plan is good. Don't touch it. My lawyers will contact you about contracts this afternoon. In the meantime, I wonder if we could clear the room to finish flushing out the concept? Let your other employees get back to work."

I wasn't learning anything by making Ella hover in the corner and stare at her feet. Besides, if being in the same room as me made her *that* miserable... I'd let her leave without so much as a private word.

For a moment, the president seemed flummoxed. Then, he began waving people toward the doors. "Thanks everyone! Great work. Marjorie? You and your assistant will stay behind."

Marjorie nodded, her expression giving nothing away. I admired her self-possession. Especially a moment later when she shocked me by turning her head slightly and saying, "Elle?"

My soul seized as Ella slunk out of the corner and traipsed to Marjorie's side.

"See that Mr. Stryker has what he requires," Marjorie said, her tone brokering no argument. "Then go retrieve copies of everything for him and send the electronic parcel."

With a slight bob of her head, Ella turned to walk up the length of the long room until she stood opposite Marco and once again looked down. I just barely caught the peachy pink warming her cheeks before she faced her shoes.

"Mr. Stryker," she murmured softly. "Can I get you something?"

Look at me, Ellie.

"Coffee," I said, unable to help myself. "Do you have a travel mug, perchance?"

My attempt to goad her landed. Her head snapped up, blue eyes flashing with a quick burst of irritation. "No, *sir,*" she shot back, scowling at me. "Our office doesn't supply them. I would offer you my own, but I'm afraid it went missing over the weekend."

And, damn it, I knew I was supposed to hate her. But I couldn't keep a straight face when she got sassy like that. "Hmm," I sighed, rubbing my hand over my jaw. "Maybe someone took it."

Her nose twitched adorably while outrage filled her fine features. "I don't know anyone that horrendously rude."

Until that moment, I forgot how easily she made me laugh. A guffaw snorted out of me before I could help it. "A stranger, then?" I posited, playing along, hoping to hold on to the levity between us, if only for a moment.

But Ellie's face shuttered. "No," she said, so softly. Her eyes traced my expression with a tender blend of regret and wistfulness. "Never."

Her meaning hit me squarely in the chest. And she was right. We would never be strangers.

It was suddenly everything I could do to keep from lunging for her. *I can carry her out of here*, I thought, manic. *I'll put us both on a plane and we can just fly away forever. To an island where nothing else exists and it's just us.*

But what would that do?

She didn't want me.

I cleared my throat, hiding my reaction to my own depressing thoughts by glancing down at my navy suit. "Just the coffee, then, Miss Callahan. Thank you."

Without another word, she scurried past me, around the front of the conference table. Just before she cleared Amir's seat, her heel caught on the carpet, sending her flying forward.

Automatically, I leapt up. But Amir's reflexes were quicker. He spun and caught her easily, with one arm locked around her waist. Ever professional, he had her upright two seconds later without so much as touching his fingertips to her form.

A deeper, rosier blush stained her neck and chest. Her words came out watery as she cast my bodyguard one fleeting glance. "Thanks, Marco."

And then she disappeared, rushing out of the conference room unsteadily.

Marco and I exchanged a loaded look that was interrupted by a harrumph. I swiveled in my chair, finding Marjorie two seats over, staring. Her right leg crossed over her knee to display a spikey heel.

"Listen," she said calmly, her eyes hard. "I know you own more property on this island than anyone else. I'm sure that entitles you to a lot, including my respect. But it does not entitle you to my assistant. If you're only here to get to her, I'm not interested in working with you."

Well, shit.

That *was* the reason for my visit. Initially. But I admired Marjorie's ideas almost as much as I respected her nerve.

I kept my face straight. "You're making bold assumptions. She could be a complete stranger to me."

Marjorie flipped her gaze from me to Marco and back again. "She knows your security guy," she pointed out, utterly confident. "And you called her 'Miss Callahan,' despite me neglecting to mention her last name."

Fuck me. I had to get a goddamn grip.

Backtracking, I shrugged. "Alright, so I know her. That doesn't mean I don't like your ideas. Or want to work with you."

She regarded me shrewdly. "Even if I fire Ella tomorrow?"

It took every ounce of my self-control to remain impassive. The truth was, I'd never forgive myself if my half-baked impulse to come to Idealogue wound up costing Ella her job. I wanted to un-riddle her reasons for leaving me… not take away her livelihood.

"Even then," I lied, entirely even.

Another insane idea occurred to me. Riding on a tide of nerves, it flowed out before I had a chance to truly consider it. "Though," I went on, "as a show of good faith, I'd like to invite you both to a company event this week, at our headquarters. It will be an excellent opportunity for you to meet the team you'll work with."

And an excellent opportunity for me to see Ella again.

Just to observe her, I reminded myself. *To figure out what she's hiding. Nothing more.*

Marjorie's perceptive stare took on a challenging edge. "Sounds like a good plan. I'll have to see if Ella is free. And her boyfriend, of course." She tipped her eyebrows up. "That is, *assuming* we'll be afforded plus-ones…"

Boyfriend. My blood chilled, thickening into slush. My ears pounded while my brittle heart tried to shovel muck through my veins.

She has a boyfriend. My mind reeled. *Of course she does. I mean, Jesus, the girl is so beautiful, I practically stalked her. Followed her out of a damn subway. Found her apartment in Brooklyn. I'm fucking sitting here right now.*

But why wasn't this supposed boyfriend at her place on a Friday night? And why didn't I see anything in her apartment to indicate she had any regular male guests?

Not that that meant anything. Before this whole insane mess, I had girls over all the time… and my penthouse still looked like a museum dedicated to bachelorhood.

In the end, I really only had one option. So I bit out, "Of course, I insist you each bring a plus-one. You'll be my personal guests. My assistant will forward appropriate details and arrange for a car."

Marjorie's sharp smile had a distinctly feline quality. "Excellent."

She waved her hand and I noticed Ella hovering just beyond the glass doors to the room, waiting for a signal to enter. With her grace restored, she floated in and set a cup of hot coffee beside me. Black, just as I always liked it. Just as she made it for me two days before and three years before that.

She also produced a second cup—tea, complete with a saucer. She set it in front of Amir. "Two teaspoons of honey," she murmured, giving him her shy smile. "Right?"

I felt a stab of envy so vicious I thought I might actually snarl. *I* wanted that smile. And she was giving it to my driver? And, apparently, a *boyfriend*?

Amir's dark eyes softened as he took in her kind gesture. "Thank you, Miss Callahan. You shouldn't have gone to the trouble."

She rolled her big blue eyes. "Call me *Ella*, Marco. *Please*. Sheesh."

That was another thing I loved about her and forgot all about—her filler words. She used them in place of curses. *Sheesh. Geez. Drat. Goodness.*

Yearning burned a fresh path of pain through my chest. *Goddamn it.* How many different ways could I miss this girl? The one woman I could never, ever trust again?

I hated myself for it. I hated her for it. But I didn't hate either of us quite enough to control the wild need to be as close to her as I could for as long as I was allowed.

"Miss Callahan," I interjected, my voice a touch harsher than I intended. "I wonder if we might get a tour of the offices after our meeting concludes. I'm sure Marjorie has other business to attend to and I'd like to see where my team will be working when they come here to collaborate."

Marjorie's eyes never left my face, even as she called, "That won't be a problem, will it Elle?"

Ella shot me a look somewhere between appalled and accusatory, then faced her boss with a much more solicitous expression. "Not at all."

Ella

In case Saturday night left any doubts as to the questionable state of my mental health, Parker found me hyperventilating in the stairwell.

After Marjorie informed me—in front of Grayson and Marco—that we'd be attending an event at his office later in the week, it was all I could to nod, walk out of the room, and make a mad dash to the stairs before I hurled all over the conference room. The implications of such an occasion whirred through my mind while I bent over the stairs and did my best not to pass out.

I knew Marjorie—she suspected something was going on and secured an invitation to Grayson's party to test me. If I failed the test, she probably wouldn't have any qualms about replacing me.

Not to mention, the contracts wouldn't be signed before the event.... And her two-hundred-thousand-dollar bonus hung in the balance. If I didn't attend, would Gray revoke his offer? I couldn't do that to my boss. She may not have felt much loyalty to me, but I had tons for her.

She gave me my first real job, straight out of school, with nothing to recommend me save for the fact that she liked the shoes I borrowed from Maggie for my interview. She taught me everything I needed to be successful at Idealogue and worked harder than any of her colleagues by half. I respected her. And, though she may not have realized it, she needed me to play along with whatever Gray was up to until he signed their agreement.

Which meant, of course, I'd have to go to Stryker & Sons.

It took twenty minutes to be sure I wouldn't heave my breakfast all over the stairwell, then another three to start breathing effectively again. Thankfully, I'd mostly finished my panic attack before Parker burst in. And he didn't seem to notice.

"Ella!" he exclaimed, flashing a surprised smile. "Hey. I've been looking for you. Never thought to check in here. Were you… on your way out?"

I forced myself to stand up straight and smile back, ignoring the desperate tightness squeezing my diaphragm. "No. I've just been running between our floor and conference room, fetching things for Marjorie."

His grin deepened, rendering him truly, undeniably handsome. *Lord. Why can't I just like* this *man instead of the one two floors up?*

"I thought I was the only lunatic who took the stairs," he quipped, coming closer. He nodded at the papers in my hands. "Do you need any help?"

I shook my head. "No. She's done with these. I was just…" *Preparing myself to spend time with Grayson Stryker.* "Coming back down."

With a chivalrous flair, he pulled the door to our floor open for me and then reached for the stack of documents. "I told you earlier I wanted to talk to you," he reminded me. "Do you have a second now?"

I had to fight the incorrigible urge to giggle. It was all just so hopelessly, ridiculously *awful.* And, now, I was about to be dumped by a guy I wasn't even really dating… minutes before giving my ex-boyfriend/the current love of my life a tour. Of the offices where I worked with the guy dumping me.

"Sure," I blurted, giving up. "Sure. Let's talk."

Parker's smile wilted at the edges. "About this weekend…"

I changed my mind, reaching out to halt him by placing my hand on his arm. "Parker, you don't have to do this, okay? I know I was an absolute basket-case this weekend. And I'm so sorry, truly. I completely understand why you don't want to go out again."

His blond brows furrowed. "What? Ella, no. I just wanted to apologize for not texting or calling yesterday. I slept late and by the time I woke up, we had the memo about Stryker coming here. Honestly, I worked for eighteen hours straight on that pitch and just totally forgot to text you. I'm really sorry."

Of course. The poor guy just worked for the better part of a day and a night only to get shot down. By my ex-boyfriend.

I tamped down a flare of guilt, trying to focus as I patted his sleeve. "It was such a good pitch." *Not as good as Marjorie's, but…* "Really cutting-edge."

His jaw clenched while his lips parted, the expression caught between a cringe and a smirk. "I thought so. Is Marjorie up there gloating?"

I thought of her satisfied smile while Grayson perused her work. "Marjorie?!" I asked, feigning offence. "Never!"

Parker's laugh filled the space between us. "Thank you," he chuckled, drawing closer. "I needed that one."

I went to shrug, but his hand halted me, floating up to tuck a loose strand of blonde behind my ear. My lungs clamped onto my next breath, refusing to let it go until he retracted his touch. Panic instinctively rose inside of me.

Oh Lord.

My instincts kicked in and I turned my head to avert my face. Inadvertently flinging my gaze over to the elevators, where Grayson watched our exchange, his green eyes blazing.

Grayson

She made him laugh.

She touched him.

She let *him* touch *her*.

Dear God. I didn't know I could hate a perfect stranger. And, despite all the times I claimed otherwise, I realized I never truly hated Ella until that moment.

When she turned and found me gaping at her, a swift bolt of regret sliced through her features. Her sapphire eyes held mine, beaming at me from across the entire floor. Almost… beseeching?

But what the fuck could she possibly want from me? After leaving me for dead and ruining me with her book, and, now, this?

All I had ever done was love her. More than I knew I could. Deeply. Wholly. With every single thing I had in me, I loved Ella Callahan. When she disappeared, I mourned her. Spent every night alone for a year, missing her.

She called me back into her life with that dedication. Those words that drug me back to her doorstep after all the progress I made toward letting her go.

For Gray, for always.

It was a lie. She had another man. She wouldn't even answer my questions. She didn't deserve one goddamn thing from me.

But was I really just going to walk away?

Chapter Sixteen

November 2013

Grayson

November blurred by in a bittersweet slog.

I spent my days arguing with my father when we were together and doing my best to make him proud whenever we weren't.

If we found ourselves in the same room, proximity turned to animosity within minutes.

We couldn't agree on anything. He wanted to start transferring CEO duties to me within *months*, well before I even finished my degree. I asked him if the cancer had spread to his brain and eaten away his common sense.

He started issuing pop quizzes, dropping monumental choices on me without warning and expecting hypothetical answers on the spot. I decline to explain my theoretical solutions out of spite.

He wanted to begin giving me family properties, signing over assets and bank accounts. I recoiled from every contract he pushed at me, claiming I wanted to hire lawyers to read them first.

He often brought up random, morbid requests about Mom, his funeral arrangements, his eventual obituary. I avoided each death discussion with dogged denial.

But whenever he wasn't around, I somehow sprang into action. I comforted my weeping mother over our weekly brunch. I called doctors, specialists, researchers, and hospital directors. I snuck into meetings, listened in on high-level calls, asked his assistant to forward me all of his correspondence so I could start to learn when and how he replied to various issues.

I thought I'd be miserable. The truth was, most days, I didn't really have time to be *anything* apart from busy.

And, at night, I had Ella.

Thank God.

I'd never been one to pray or look to the stars, but I found myself thinking those two words every single evening when I slid into Marco's car and the events of the day tumbled over me, threatening to crush my lungs inside my chest.

Then, I remembered who I had waiting for me at home. And I could breathe again.

We weren't officially moving in together until the week after New Year's, but Ella spent most nights with me, anyway. Like she could sense I needed her there.

She didn't take up much space, though, carrying her life with her in her backpack and never leaving behind more than the occasional yarn fuzz. I couldn't wait to get into our place and have her stuff all around me.

I envisioned a lot more color, in every way.

That seemed to be Ellie's special gift—she took my drab existence and made everything brighter. Her soft little laugh, her unexpected jokes, the light in her eyes whenever I caught her looking at me.

It didn't hurt that we couldn't seem to keep our hands off of each other. After my long days of school, traffic, work, and more traffic, there was nothing better than finally having Ella under me, on top of me, around me.

Every time I pushed inside of her and our gazes connected, she healed me just a little bit. Enough to keep on fighting through the next day.

I loved sharing space with her. Her honeysuckle sweetness clung to our sheets, my suit jackets, the towels… along with threads of her shimmery gold hair. I didn't mind doing schoolwork or conducting Stryker & Sons business at home anymore; not when I could catch glimpses of blonde and soft curves while I worked.

I loved looking up and finding her brooding over her laptop screen, perfecting some part of her book. Or quirking her eyebrows just so while she peered in the mirror. Or—my favorite—bending into one of her yoga stretches. I collected those pieces of her, snapping mental Polaroids to look back at later.

Each day seemed to reveal new facets of her personality, too.

She was clean, but not neat—she would scrub our bathroom grout with a toothbrush, if I let her, but then left every single toiletry she owned in chaotic clusters on the countertop. She liked to sing while she baked, but only the first half of one song before launching into the start of another. She hated to study—always sighing quietly as she turned textbook pages and grumbling under her breath when she had to take notes—but her eyes lit up when I offered to quiz her.

We did a lot of that. Helping each other. She asked me financial accounting questions while I shaved or folded my laundry, often brushing kisses onto my shoulder or my cheek if I got several correct answers in a row.

I proofread her papers for her. She used too many commas, but otherwise wrote brilliantly. Usually, I was so dazzled by her mind that I wound up tossing the paper aside and pulling her into my lap.

On the weekends, we agreed to forget everything except each other. I spent most of that free time looking for new ways to make Ella smile. I'd discovered she loved to go for long walks through Central Park early on Sunday mornings. With a coffee in one hand and a poetry book tucked into her multicolored coat, she forced me to leave the walkway and led me to a big oak tree. I thought she was crazy, until her sweet smirk and sparkling eyes conned me into lying with my head in her lap while she read out loud.

Two poems in, I was hooked. Her calm, lilting voice changed everything. Perhaps because she treated each piece like its own priceless treasure, honoring the authors' every whim by pausing and adding inflection wherever the prose called for it. On her lips, verses I'd run my eyes over a dozen times without finding any value transformed into pearls. It helped that she combed my hair and let me nestle my cheek against her body while she read to me.

Ella also adored chocolate, in general; the Met, but specifically the exhibit for 18th Century France; and making love anytime the weather turned gloomy. That last one actually posed a problem at work—as soon as the sky darkened outside my office window, my cock turned semi-hard. I knew as soon as we both got home, Ella would come to me.

Staring out at the overcast view, I almost felt her warmth spread over my lap. The soft suction of her lips on my neck. The way she would hum and sigh before propositioning me—always modestly shy and nervous, as if I would ever turn down the opportunity to be inside of her.

I glanced around at all the shit on my desk and then out at the rest of the empty executive floor. Being the day before Thanksgiving, my father and I were the only ones in the office.

Fuck it, I decided. I was going to go home to my girl and spending the rest of the holiday weekend focused on her. I packed up my messenger bag and ducked into my father's suite on my way out.

"Leaving so soon?" he asked, not looking up from the ledger in front of him. "Did you at least check your email?"

We hadn't stopped fighting since Halloween; I couldn't blame him for his out-right hostility. But I still snapped back.

"Yes," I clipped, scowling at him. "I also finished all of the insurance contract reviews you told me to read."

He continued scratching his pen at his paper. "And?"

"They suck," I said succinctly. "I'd go with someone else."

His mouth curved into a grim smirk. "*Who* else?" he asked, not looking up. "You're going to be the CEO. If you don't like the deal one firm gives you, then *you* have to find a different one."

Truth was, I already had another agency in mind. I just fucking hated the way he *assumed* I didn't think that far ahead. Torn between my desire to argue and my longing for Ella, I pawed at the back of my neck and checked my watch.

3:16. If I hurried, I could take her to bed before dinner. A perfect plan, because she wanted to watch the Charlie Brown Thanksgiving Special later—a prospect I found equal parts cringe-worthy and endearing.

"Can we talk about it on Monday?"

He paused for the briefest of seconds, then resumed writing. "We can discuss it tomorrow. From what your mother tells me, she and Ella will be in the kitchen most of the afternoon."

Ha. "I'm not working tomorrow," I informed him. "Apparently it's a national holiday of some sort."

That finally got him. His Montblanc clattered onto his desktop as he pinned me with a severe look. "CEOs don't *get* days off, Grayson. When I'm gone and you're running Stryker & Sons, there will *never* be a day when you aren't responsible for this entire company. For the livelihood of tens of thousands of people and their families. Do you understand that?"

I didn't, weeks before. I had a whole list of other reasons to resent my fate. But, as the month went on, I started to see that—in addition to being complicated, stressful, and devoid of any creative substance—my future role also represented the greatest responsibility one could possess in the world of business.

His point hit me squarely in the chest. If I failed, people would lose their jobs. Thousands and thousands of people. Ordinary, hard-working families like Ella's. Their homes, their children… it all depended on *me*.

I swallowed a wad of dread. "Gosling Liabilities."

My father blinked, taken aback that I resisted going for his bait and bellowing at him. "What?"

I pulled the files out of my messenger bag and set them on top of his ledger. "They're the insurance company I would go with, if it were up to me. They're smaller than some of the others we've considered, but their operation spans seven decades and three generations, like ours. I've called a couple of their top clients for references; they were all excellent."

He considered the contract in front of him before turning his attention back to me, his amber eyes assessing.

Always assessing. Weighing my words, my worth, my capabilities, my commitment.

Would any of it ever be enough?

Without waiting for his reply, I backed toward the door. "And, now, since—as you so graciously pointed out—this is my last holiday season as a free man, I'm going home."

To Ellie.

Ella

I finished pulling the third pie out of the oven minutes before I heard Gray's key in the door.

He appeared, windswept and gorgeous in his peacoat, slacks, and my horrible green scarf. The moment our eyes met, he hit me with his Prince Charming grin… but I caught a glimpse of his face before that—all tension and anxious lines.

He wore such expressions far too often. I caught him frowning all the time. While he showered, when he sat at the counter for his morning coffee, pretending to watch the TV. Almost as much as I caught him doodling his design concepts into notebook margins or on paper towels.

His sketches were gone… but I knew he still thought about them. Most of the drawings he did now were evolutions of previous ideas. I recognized some from the pieces I secreted away before he tossed the rest.

Hoping to make him laugh, I gestured to the island full of desserts. "Did someone order pie?"

His grin split into a chuckle as he shucked his outerwear and strode right to me. "I think we ordered *one*, not three," he retorted, raising his slashing brows at the platters of baked goods. "Is that *bread*?"

Oh right. "Rosemary focaccia, Parker House rolls, and a sourdough loaf," I replied, shrugging. "I didn't know which would complement the meal best so I just made them all."

Gray dropped his forehead to mine, eyeing me with censorious amusement. "You know you're not a caterer, right? You're a *guest.* The most important guest, as far as I'm concerned."

"I'm *excited*," I told him. "And I didn't have any work or school today, so I was bored. I *wanted* to make stuff. Besides, whatever we don't eat, your mom can save. And then they'll have it for breakfast or whatever."

I didn't want to mention that I thought storing away baked goods in the freezer might help his mother out down the line, once his father started treatment and their schedules changed. So far, he avoided discussing his dad's cancer treatment as much as possible.

Gray's gaze softened as it traced my face. "That was thoughtful. Thank you."

His touch skimmed down my body, sending tingles to my core. I wanted to slide my hands under his sweater and ask him to take me to bed. But I knew he probably wanted time to decompress first….

And maybe he wouldn't feel up to it all, considering I wasn't exactly my most alluring self at the moment.

He didn't own an apron, so I wound up working in one of his undershirts. And I had flour all over my leggings… possibly some caramel splattered on my cheek.

Sighing, I settled for kissing his neck.

His stubble tickled my nose when he chuckled again. "Ellie? Is there something you wanted?"

Drat. He knew me too well. "Not until you're… settled," I demurred. "Do you want a drink or something? I can wait."

An odd silence stretched taut between us.

"You know what?" he said. "I can't."

Moving all at once, he snatched me straight up. I gasped as he hauled me into his arms and set off for the bed. His lips crushed mine, silencing both of us with the lush slide of his tongue.

Depositing me on the mattress, he toed off his shoes and impatiently tugged at his trousers, his expression full of fervor. I grasped his mood and quickly started to undo his shirt. Gray stripped it off, then pealed his undershirt off of my torso with one fluid pull.

He stood over me, his erection bulging against his boxer briefs, and flicked a pointed look to my leggings, silently asking if he could take them off for me. Even after two months… he still remembered my unexplained boundaries. He still cared. The thought put a lump in my throat as I lifted my hips and nodded at him.

He held my gaze the entire time he pulled the bottoms off, along with my panties. His hand reached up to brush over my face as he dropped to his knees between my bare legs.

"Ellie," he murmured, his face a mask of ardor. "I—"

I love you.

He never said the words. I didn't, either. But, in certain moments, I *felt* them. They were as real as his fingertips on my face.

Gray caressed the length of my throat, down over my collarbone, until he skirted along the outside of my breast, furling my nipples. He watched my breasts respond to him with hot, stormy eyes, gliding his other hand up over my thigh.

Our gazes clashed when he slipped his thumb into my folds. I sucked in another short breath when he grazed over my clit, finding me wet. His eyes dropped to my sex.

"You're so slick and hot." Lust tightened his features and he groaned. "I just want to—"

He couldn't get any of his thoughts out. It wasn't like him. But before I contemplated it too much, he made a frustrated sound and bent to seal his lips over me.

His tongue lashed at my swollen bud while his hands held my breasts, pulling at my nipples. I cried out. He growled, licking lower, teasing my slit.

"Ah," I keened. "Gray, you're so good at that."

Grayson didn't so much as smile. He doubled down, licking back up to my clit, tracing along the edges of it. When I moaned, he hummed his approval and stayed put, focused on the exact right spot, working it until I couldn't take anymore.

My head fell back while I ground up into his mouth, coming loudly. Deliciously impatient, Gray tore away from me the second the last aftershock rebounded through my core. Instead of tossing me back onto the middle of the bed, he shoved his boxers off and sat beside me before reaching over and flipping me on top of him.

"Like this," he rasped, positioning us. His green eyes glowed up at me, full of intensity I didn't understand. "Like the first time."

I remembered the exact position, the very moment he first pushed inside me—the night he gave my body back to me in a way I didn't believe anyone ever would.

Truly, I'd loved him ever since.

Gray remembered, too. He moved my legs to straddle his lap and ran his fingers down my arms before guiding them to rest on his shoulders. I sifted my hands through his hair while I hovered over him, absorbing his bright, shifting gaze, the tense set of his jaw.

He *needed* this. He needed… me.

My soul fit itself around that small, simple truth, obliterating all fear.

"Gray," I whispered, brushing my fingers over his cheek. "You know I love you, right?"

A sting slashed through his features. "God. Ella." He wrapped his hand around the back of my neck, bending my face to his and locking our eyes. "Yes," he murmured, hushed, "I know that."

Our lips brushed at the same moment the tip of his cock found my opening. He stifled a grunt and swallowed hard, still holding our foreheads together.

"You know that I—" he started, "That I—Ella, you—"

His brow creased as he struggled to get the words out. I ran my fingertips over the lines, hoping to erase the evidence of his stress. He huffed a sigh, exasperated with himself. Compassion pierced my heart.

"It's okay," I said softly, "Just… take me now. Please."

With a pained growl, Gray lunged, pulling me down onto his erection while capturing my mouth with his. He was impossibly hard and burning hot, scorching my depths from deep inside. Sharp, sweet pleasure trembled through me.

The solid girth satisfied the ache inside of me, steadily thrusting bliss into my center. One hand went to my hip, setting our pace, as his other caressed my head.

"*Ella*," he moaned, the deep sound reverberating inside my chest. "You feel so perfect. This is all I ever want." His hold on me tightened as his eyes snapped open, snagging mine once more. "This, us. You."

The pulse in my sex matched the beating of my heart, both so urgent that I felt like they would tear me apart. I sobbed, digging my nails into the firm flesh of his shoulders and grinding myself down onto him harder.

"God, baby, *yes*." Gray nestled his face against my breast, drawing my nipple between his lips. He tugged it lightly with his teeth. My head fell back into his hand while I thrust my chest closer to him, crying out for more.

"You're such a good girl," he growled, gripping my hip and yanking me forward. "Ride me like this," he commanded, bossy as ever. "Look at me."

I straightened to stare down into his face. His tumultuous eyes captivated mine as he adjusted the slide of his cock to hit the secret place he knew by heart. The ridge of his crown slipped over it again and again, tightening my core on every plunge.

Still holding my gaze with his, he licked his thumb and reached between our bodies, adding soft circles over the top of my clit. Incoherent pleas burst out of me while I grabbed the hair at his nape and tugged. As he roared in response, his thumb slipped lower, ghosting along the place his tongue traced earlier.

My entire center clenched in climax, releasing with a shower of spasms. Grayson snarled. Pinpricks of light exploded across my vision as I rode him, pumping his cock into the trembling echoes of my orgasm until he shuddered.

His hands lost their finesse, clutching at me restlessly. His cock pulsed, releasing a molten flood.

Gray immediately wrapped me up against him, hugging me hard. His lips grazed the side of my throat and he said my name hoarsely. I heard the tremor in his breath before I felt his hands shake. Instead of pulling back, he nuzzled deeper into my unbound hair, clasping me closer still.

Hiding. From me?

"Gray?" I stroked the back of his head, the broad, sculpted plains of his back. "It's okay… It's fine if you don't say it. Or if you don't…" A painful pang struck my heart. I choked back a chunk of humiliation. "If you don't love me. That's okay. We don't have to feel the same things at the same time."

He somehow found a way to pulled me tighter against him. "Ellie, *no*. That's not it. I—I'm sorry."

His entire frame vibrated. He made a low, disgusted sound, still concealing his face against the curve of my shoulder. "God. I'm a fucking wreck."

My hands slowly smoothed the quivers arrowing down his spine. "Did something happen?" I asked.

Gray stayed silent for a long moment before defeat washed through him. His vice grip slackened. "What if I can't do it, Ellie? What if I can't handle running a whole company and other people lose everything, because of me?"

I couldn't imagine Gray failing so completely. He was too perceptive and much too cautious. Not to mention charming, talented, and brilliant.

"Why would you ever think that?" I demanded, though I could only think of one reason. "Did your dad say something to you?"

A humorless laugh scraped out of him. "Doesn't he always?"

Helpless outrage climbed my insides. "I wish he would stop that," I muttered, brushing his hair back as I scowled over his head. "You're working so hard…"

Grayson sighed, finally straightening to show me his tight expression. "He doesn't accuse me of being lazy. He more just… He's not *wrong*, Ellie. No matter how much I work, there will always be *more*. He wants me to wrap my head around it but it just…"

Infinite work. "That must feel impossible."

"Yes," he agreed, eager to be understood. "It does. But, then, I look across the damn hallway and see my dad and realize; *no*, it's not impossible because he's been doing it for twenty years. So, if he can do it, why can't I even *comprehend* it?"

I smoothed the left edge of his grimace. "You can do it, too, Gray. I know you can. Maybe it won't look the same way your Dad makes it look, but you can find your own way to do the job." I hesitated, wanting to say more but not wanting to set him off. "When you're CEO, maybe you could even find a way to do some of the things you like. On the creative side..."

Instead of furrowing into a frown or slipping into an impassive mask of dismissal, his face took on a far-off, brooding quality. "Maybe... I don't know *how*, but..."

He needed time to think about it. I didn't mind—after a month of meeting steadfast resistance, I was grateful he seemed to consider the suggestion at all.

I realized I was still spread over his lap, buck naked. *Probably not the best way for him to contemplate his future.*

"I'll be right back," I whispered. Slipping away, I made for the bathroom and shut the door.

Grayson

Ella claimed that it was "common sense" to order wildly exotic takeout the night before Thanksgiving. Sort of as an antidote to all of the traditional American fare to follow.

She chose Chinese and I teased her mercilessly about her concept of "exotic" cuisine. We had a picnic on my floor as Charlie Brown's Thanksgiving special played in the background. I found I didn't even mind it. Watching genuine delight sparkle in her eyes was well worth any second-hand embarrassment.

While she flipped her focus between dumplings and television, I spent my meal trying to swallow the distinct sense that I fucked up irrevocably. I knew it took a lot of courage for her to confess her love to me… because I'd yet to summon that sort of bravery.

She trusted me and I left her hanging. Why didn't I just tell her weeks ago? It seemed so stupid, now, as I watched the screen bathe her sweet features in flashes of light.

Of course I loved her. My whole world began and ended with her. Every other fucking thing—my degree, the business, my family's reputation, the money—could go to hell for all I cared. The only one I truly needed was Ella.

I loved her so much, I couldn't imagine living without her. I couldn't recall what my life even looked like before her… and every time I tried, I wanted to recoil from the memories.

I remembered a lot of boredom. Cynicism. Dread.

But Ella changed all of that the day I saw her knitting on that subway. She made me smile and laugh. She brought magic and color and joy to my life. I never wanted to go back.

Now, I was too late to tell her how I felt. I had to wait and make it as special as possible. I couldn't disappoint her again by blowing it off and blurting out a declaration that was less than she deserved.

She deserved everything.

Possibilities whirled through my mind while we got ready for bed and settled under the covers. *I could get another hotel suite. Though, I've already done that. Maybe a vacation somewhere… but then I have to wait until after the holidays, which is another five weeks. That's a long time.*

Clichés like sunset at the top of the Empire State Building or a walk in the gardens felt too trite. And Ella didn't care about flashy restaurants or shopping or expensive baubles.

Although…

She truly loved the necklace I got her. She hadn't removed it once since the day I put it around her neck. I suspected it had nothing to do with the piece's cost, but more to do with how I just had to have it.

I still didn't really understand why it jumped out at me. I only knew that that particular necklace struck me as a representation of us—the one circle studded in metal screws, the other brilliant with its row of shimmering diamonds. I was plain and cool and quiet; Ella was precious and delicate. I tried to hold everything together; and she glittered effortlessly, throwing rainbows wherever the light touched her.

I drifted toward sleep with my girl tucked into the crook of my arm, imagining what other pieces I might buy for her. *Maybe a matching bracelet, engraved. I can etch "I love you" right into it. Then, she'll always have it right up her sleeve.*

Or, maybe, I'll engrave it into a ring.

Under Ella's cheek, my heart broke into a sprint. My eyes snapped open, staring up at the dark ceiling overhead.

God Almighty. A ring? *Where the fuck did that thought come from?*

I looked down at the woman in my arms, her beautiful face relaxed in sleep.

Who are you kidding? some steady voice inside of me replied. *You know this is it.*

And I did. I *knew*. So completely, I found it hard to fathom.

We'd only known each other for three months. She still surprised me. Often. And sometimes I caught her looking at me like she couldn't begin to guess what I'd do next. But, for all we still needed to learn, we understood each other on an intimate level unlike anything I even dreamed possible.

All of the huge changes in my life affected her, too. I saw the way she worried about me, how she scrambled to try to help with business issues beyond her realm of experience, how incredibly patient and flexible she had to be with all the new demands on my time…

I already asked so much of her, without ever truly *asking*. Making her my fiancée would afford her the respect she deserved for being my partner. Moreover, it would signal to the rest of Manhattan how serious I was about our relationship.

Oddly, the concept of never touching another woman again didn't faze me as much I expected it to. I didn't even notice other women anymore, for the most part. Not sexually, anyway. They were just… there. I found I had trouble even recalling their facial features a few seconds after I left them.

I smoothed Ellie's silky blonde hair back from her face, revealing all of her unforgettable qualities. The sweet slope of her button nose, the way her eyebrows tapered off slightly too soon, the cinnamon flecks dusting her skin. It was the only face I ever wanted next to me in bed.

Because she's the One.

Ella

Grayson and I huddled together under his duvet and watched the Macy's Thanksgiving Day Parade on his computer, even though we could hear the cheers from the actual event echoing in the streets right outside his apartment.

I could tell he felt bad about the day before. He kept sighing into my hair and dropping random kisses on my shoulder. Every so often, I caught him examining my profile in a troubled, searching way. Eventually, I just started smiling at him whenever he stared. He realized his mistake quickly, casting me a rueful smirk in each time I silently called him out.

Later in the day, while I traipsed back and forth from my bag at the foot of his bed to the bathroom mirror, he sat at his island and worked on homework until he had to get in the shower. I floated over to his open notebook, hoping to catch a glimpse of his latest doodle.

But there weren't any sketches in the margins.

Glancing over my shoulder to be sure he wouldn't catch me, I flipped back to the earlier sections of his notes. There, I saw dozens of familiar structures I used to discuss with him. I grinned when I noticed that he'd used a whole page to sketch out a formal rendering of one of my favorites.

The cylindrical tower had an ornate glass spire on top. To catch light, I imagined. At fifty stories, it would make an arresting sight.

My grin grew when I saw he had added a feature I came up with; drawn in stark lines, a garden surrounded the base of the building. Under the whole structure, his precise handwriting labeled the rendering.

Stryker & Sons. Headquarters: Manhattan.

A tingle shot through my fingers, aching to tear the image out. It *was* my very favorite, after all…

I wondered what would happen if I just "accidentally" dropped it on Mr. Stryker's desk. Would he finally recognize his son's brilliance?

The shower tap sputtered off. In a moment of panic, I ripped the page from its spiral and flipped his notes back to the current page. My coat laid draped over the adjacent barstool, much closer than my purse, so I shoved the picture into the multicolored wool pocket as quickly as I could.

Grayson toweled off and slung the bath sheet around his waist. A few seconds later, I once again caught him eyeing me strangely through the bathroom mirror. This time, I stuck my tongue out at him and he burst into laughter.

"If you don't want me to stare," he muttered a moment later, brushing past me on his way to the closet, "stop being so painfully gorgeous all the time."

I laughed, hoping I didn't sound rattled. "Covering up your weirdness with compliments won't work. Nice try, though."

His rueful grin momentarily fried my mind. "Weirdness, huh?"

I nodded, grabbing my topaz halter top and making my way back into the bathroom. Mags was right—the autumn hue flattered my coloring. Unfortunately, the piece also highlighted my chest… and made wearing a bra impossible.

Fidgeting with the ties, I grimaced at my boobs, doubting the wisdom of my ensemble. Along with dark-wash skinny jeans and heeled booties, the whole thing felt overly casual. Although Grayson insisted his family Thanksgivings were "jeans-and-a-nice-top" sorts of affairs that didn't necessitate anything fancy.

Biting my lip, I adjusted my favorite necklace and pulled my hair back. It made the cut of the top seem even more revealing… but I had to help Jacqueline in the kitchen—and I figured the Strykers wouldn't appreciate any blonde hairs in their stuffing.

"Do I need a sweater over this?" I called from my spot in front of the mirror. "What do you think?"

Stepping out into the main room, I fussed with the way the top draped over my waistband before looking up. Only to find an awe-struck Grayson, shirtless, standing stock still. Bright green eyes ran over my body in a loop. I noticed his chest expand on a quick breath and bit back a giggle.

"Gray?"

His gaze flashed to mine. "Yes?"

I did a half-twirl, showing the way the halter and my hairstyle bared my back. "Do I need a sweater?"

Hunger darkened his expression. Tossing his own shirt onto his bed, he closed the distance between us with long, graceful strides.

"No sweater."

He was on me in seconds, hugging me into his naked torso and crushing his lips into mine. Strong hands slid up to my exposed shoulders, fingering the line of my spine to the nape of my neck. He cupped his palms around my head and pulled back, leaving me dazed as I blinked up at him.

"Ellie," he murmured, running his nose down the length of mine. "You are so beautiful, sometimes I don't believe you're real."

A rush of delight poured through me. I had no idea what to say to such a glowing sentiment. I bit my lip again. "Thank you?"

Gray smiled briefly before heat melted the amusement off of his face. "You've already done your hair? Your makeup?"

I nodded, still chewing my lip. His eyes flit down to the watch on his wrist. "Damn it," he sighed. "It's almost one."

"Are we late?" I fretted. "I thought you said the car was coming at one."

"It is," he grumbled, pouting in his singularly sexy way. "But right now, I want to take this top off of you with my teeth and throw you back into bed. And there's no time."

A devious idea came to me. "How about I surprise you, later?"

His frown dissipated. "Surprise me?"

With a decisive nod, I slipped out of his grasp. "Yes," I determined out loud. "You'll just have to wait. Right now we have to figure out how on earth we're going to carry an entire island's-worth of desserts down to the car."

Turned out my worry was unnecessary. A few moments later, the doorbell buzzed and two very well-groomed men in dark suits appeared on the threshold. I knew one from many car trips in Stryker & Sons vehicles—Grayson's usual driver, Marco.

The other was an elder gentleman with peppery hair and a downright remarkable scar sliced through his right cheek. Gray introduced him as his father's personal driver and security liaison, Barnes. The man didn't speak when I introduced myself, but he offered a calloused handshake.

After we carried down the trays of baked goods and settled into the white Mercedes, the situation finally sank in.

"Marco!" I gasped, sitting forward to clutch the back of his headrest. "Won't Abuelita be devastated that you're missing Thanksgiving? You need to go home right now!"

The driver offered a warm chuckle at the same second Gray asked, "Abuelita?"

I turned to cast him a scolding look. "Yes, Gray, Marco's grandmother. *Abuelita*. Did I say that right, Marco?"

He turned slightly, just enough to show me his broad grin while still keeping his eyes on the road. "Yes, Miss Callahan."

"*Ella*," I begged, though it didn't matter. I told him to call me Ella every time we met and he never did.

"Of course, Miss Callahan."

With a huff and an eye roll, I fell back into my seat. Gray scooped up my hand and brought it to his lips, kissing my palm while I groused, "Fine, then. I'll call you by your last name, too." I swiveled to look at my boyfriend. "Gray, what's Marco's last name?"

Adoring amusement gilded my boyfriend's features while his eyes tracked mine. "Amir."

"Mr. Amir," I repeated. "How could you defect on Abuelita's Thanksgiving?"

His smile took on a wistful note. "Duty calls, Miss Callahan. I heard there was a lovely lady stranded on the Upper West Side with a truckload of pastries."

Gray feigned jealousy. "Don't make me deck you, Amir."

That would certainly be a fight to behold. Marco was huge—barrel-chested, corded with muscles over every inch of his over-sized frame. But they were almost the same height… and I knew first-hand how strong and quick Grayson could be…

Marco grinned at the windshield. "Apologies, sir."

All joking aside, I felt terrible that anyone would miss their family holiday to squire me around. My lips pulled into a grimace.

"Will you at least take some desserts to her, Marco? Or a pie? I made three..."

"Don't worry about Abuelita," Marco told me. "She's been cooking for days. And I should make it home in plenty of time for dinner. We're Colombian. We won't eat until after dark."

He shared their traditional Thanksgiving meal selections—a mix of Colombian dishes his grandmother cooked, some adopted American fare, and even a couple of Syrian foods to honor his father—while we meandered through Central Park and the Upper East Side.

Without my knitting, I was grateful for the distraction. The closer we got to the Strykers' penthouse, the more I tapped my fingers against my door. When we stopped at the curb, both chauffeurs exited to begin unloading the trunk. Grayson reached for my face, cupping it in his hands before brushing a slow kiss over my mouth.

"My parents think you're wonderful," he assured me. "Try not to be too nervous, okay? It's just dinner."

For one surreal moment, he seemed like a mirage. His navy turtleneck and slacks covered every bit of him aside from the hands wrapped around my head and his starkly gorgeous face. Such handsome features looming inches from my eyes left me dazed and quivery.

"Okay," I whispered, trying to exhale. "I'll try."

But my assumption about a penthouse turned out to be entirely incorrect. In reality, it was much, *much* worse.

The Strykers didn't own the top level of the Park-facing brick facade... they owned the *entire building.*

The entire *mansion*, actually. All five stories of prime, pre-war Manhattan real estate.

I'm not sure why I was surprised. After all, I looked them up. I knew their staggering net worth. It just never occurred to me that a single person or family could even *own* so much space in a city like New York.

Huddled in my heinously inappropriate Goodwill coat, I froze on the sidewalk in front of the impressive structure. Wind whistled between me and the façade—its iron gate, intricate stone-work, and flickering gas lamps. My head tipped as I craned it back to see the top story, shrouded by tall trees and a screen of ivy.

A very unladylike word escaped from between my teeth. I didn't notice Gray standing beside me until he barked out a laugh. "No one's ever had quite that reaction," he chuckled, bending to kiss my cheek. "C'mon. It doesn't feel as big inside."

Liar.

It most certainly *did* feel just as big inside.

After clearing a set of woven iron doors, we confronted the true entrance—two wide slabs of stained mahogany twice my height. Instead of knocking, Gray slipped a key card into a concealed slat along one door's hinge. A heavy metallic click echoed in the stone vestibule before the door fell forward, revealing a two-story foyer with a sweeping arc of stairs. It reminded me of princess movies, where paupers underwent magical make-overs and got presented at the top of grand staircases.

"Did you have to take prom pictures on that thing?" I muttered, eyeing the polished wood warily as Grayson slipped my coat from my shoulders.

"Prep school doesn't have prom." He dropped another kiss to my bare shoulder. His electric green gaze snapped with amusement when our eyes met. "But we could role play, if you want."

A blush stole over my face while he hung our coats in a hidden closet, camouflaged into the textured gold wallpaper and pristine white wainscoting. I blinked at the panel as he closed it.

My dismay got the best of me. "You *grew up* here?"

Gray cast a wolfish grin in my direction, taking my hand and tugging me deeper into the foyer. "Mom?" he called, normal as could be. "I'm home!"

An excited squawk sounded from some room off to the left. Heels clacked over the polished parquet floor.

"*Amorcitos*!" In her bright fuchsia maxi dress, Jacqueline somehow looked elegant as she flew into the entryway, hurling right into Gray's embrace. Kissing both of his cheeks, she leaned back to smile up at him.

"Isn't he the most beautiful boy?" she asked me, shaking her head at her son's features.

"He really is," I agreed dryly. "It's truly unbelievable."

"Okay, okay," Gray mumbled, rubbing a palm over his nape. "That's enough." He spun his mom to face me. "Here, fuss over Ella."

Mrs. Stryker immediately gathered me into her long, thin arms. An expensive blend of perfume swirled around us. "*Que linda*," she sang, patting my cheek. "Of course."

She linked her elbow through mine and started to lead me through the tall archway she appeared from. More wallpaper and wainscoting gave way to a red rug that shimmered like spun silk. Aside from that one pop of color and a matching modern art piece as wide as the wall it graced, the sand-pale furnishings blended into obscurity. A back wall of windows displayed what appeared to be a private courtyard, full of autumn-stripped plants.

"Now, Ella," Jacqueline started, regaining my attention. "We simply must talk about where you got those luscious desserts! They look so fabulous, I almost don't want to serve them! Lord knows my women's league compatriots would appreciate them far more than these heathens."

Until she mentioned "these" heathens, I didn't notice Mr. Stryker, sitting off in the corner of the gigantic living room. A stack of newspapers sat beside him on a well-worn leather loveseat.

When our eyes met, he inclined his head slightly. "Ella. It's nice to see you again."

"You as well, sir," I replied, my voice a touch too high. Then, to Mrs. Stryker, I replied, "Of course, serve whatever you'd like and keep the rest for your ladies! I can always make more, if you need it."

Gray's warm body filled me with relief when he pressed into my back and wrapped his arm around my belly. His voice dripped disapproval. "I keep telling Ella she's *not* our caterer."

Jacqueline's beatific face filled with incredulity. "When Marco brought them around the side entrance I thought for sure you must have ordered from a bakery, but…. You *made* all of those desserts, dearest?"

Another flush heated my neck. "Yes, ma'am."

Gray touched two fingers to my chin, turning my face to his. His eyes sent another burst of calm through me. "Ella loves to cook," he said, then smiled at me. "I think I've gained ten pounds in the last month, just from having her feed me."

Well, *that* wasn't true. Lord knew I saw him naked often enough to be sure… Though I couldn't exactly *say* that in front of his parents…

As if I wasn't already mortified, a heated gleam warmed his gaze. My blush doubled.

"I'm grateful, Ella," his mother said. "Thank the Lord *someone* is feeding him. Though, you certainly didn't have to go through such trouble for us."

"It was no trouble," I insisted. "I wanted to bake and Gray was out most of the day yesterday."

His dad harrumphed, picking up another section of his paper and snapping it open. "Nine to two is hardly most of the day." Then, the elder Mr. Stryker shot me a rueful smile so similar to my boyfriend's version that I almost gasped. "Of course, if I knew there was homemade pie waiting for him at home, I might have been more understanding."

I giggled, but Gray's eyes hardened. He hated the way his father monitored his work time. I suspected Mr. Stryker only did so to help him learn. He wasn't the warmest person alive, but he obviously loved his family and wanted Grayson to succeed.

Slipping my hand into Gray's, I flashed him a small smile. "Homemade bread, too," I put in, playing along. "But I made him order Chinese for dinner, so he isn't *that* spoiled."

Jacqueline and Mason laughed. Gray's face softened while he stared back at me. "I'm *very* spoiled. Ellie made fried chicken last month and—"

I interrupted with a groan, unable to help myself. "Not *again* with the fried chicken! I told you it was no big deal! You have to stop bringing it up *every day*."

Solemnity smoothed his features as he turned to his parents. "This was life-changing chicken."

"Better than the roast chicken at *Le Père Claude* in Paris?" his mother replied, raising her black brows. "Or the butter-basted chicken at *Trattoria Sostanza* in Florence?"

He replied without hesitation. "Yes."

Jacqueline seemed impressed. She grinned at me. "Then I'm very glad I've enlisted your help, *mi querida*."

Just like the morning we had brunch, three hours with Grayson and his parents somehow wound up feeling like three hours of foreplay.

Part of it had to be the way Gray looked at me, not caring a bit who saw. His burning green gaze trailed over my neck, my shoulders, my back, my chest, leaving fire in his wake. His mother and I chatted while we worked in their massive mahogany kitchen, ignoring Grayson as he watched me intently.

Part of it was the way each new story from his childhood made me love him a little more. The memories his mother spun through as we stirred and sautéed painted clear pictures of the boy he once was.

One so similar to the man he grew into—thoughtful and cautious, but confident and charming.

And kind. Always kind, it seemed.

Though, those stories didn't surprise me. Even when he melted my panties off with his sexiness; or got angry with his father, ranting about the company... He treated everyone with consideration, because he respected others.

It still felt like a miracle every time I looked up and found myself in his family's lavish kitchen, with his eyes on me.

By the time we completed all the kitchen prep, I couldn't wait to steal a moment alone with him. I waited for his mom to excuse herself—to go raid the *wine cellar*—before I slipped my arms around his waist and beamed up at him.

"The stuffing just has to bake for another twenty minutes and then everything is done," I told him. "Think we could squeeze in a tour before dinner?"

My boyfriend's brilliant eyes laughed at me. "Are you sure you want to do that? You were freaking out in the foyer. And there are four more floors."

I reached up to touch his solid jaw. "Any pearl chandeliers?"

He cracked a wide grin, remembering what we did in the Tiffany Suite. "No, none of those."

I tugged him toward the entryway and its sprawling staircase. "C'mon! I want to see where the famous Grayson Stryker grew up."

With a self-deprecating roll of his eyes, he came along, grumbling. "Fine, fine. But it's a big place. We may not have time for all of it and you're going to wish you'd worn your clogs."

Three stories and multiple intimidated gulps later, Grayson led me back down to the second level. He intended to show me his childhood game room, but a large framed collage hanging on the wainscoted hallway wall caught my eye.

The huge frame felt different than the rest of the Strykers' art. All the other pieces were clearly priceless works by professional painters. These pages weren't paintings at all—instead, the gold shadowbox held an assortment of…

Sketches.

My heart snagged, skipping a beat. I ran my eyes over the familiar lines and shading. They appeared clumsier, less refined than the drawings I knew so well. But I knew.

I ran my fingertips over the cool metal frame surrounding them. "These are yours."

For a long moment, weighty silence swelled behind me. Then, a heavy sigh. "Yes. They are."

I turned and found him frowning over my shoulder, considering the shadowbox with a brooding air of regret. As I watched, resentment chilled the expression. "Various doodles and other nonsense from art classes over the years. My mom kept it all, without my knowledge. The same week I started interning at Stryker & Sons, this magically appeared."

He always sounded so CEO-like when he got upset.

Shaking his head, he smirked without humor. "I think it's a protest, of sorts. She doesn't approve of my father's insistence on keeping creative work out of my hands. But she doesn't argue with him where business matters are concerned. One of their standing rules. So, instead." He nodded at the frame. "She hung this."

Did she do it to make Mason mad or to cheer Grayson up? It obviously bothered him. I imagined it bothered his dad just as much. "Why?"

The bitter edge melted away, leaving him starkly serious. "I guess to make him walk past it every day. So he would have to look at what he's making me give up. And, maybe, to remind me, too. She claims she only did it because she loves the drawings, though."

A bit of his sexy scowl returned. "I guess that might be true. She shows it to *everyone*."

I giggled at his pout. "Everyone? Like who? The mayor? Oprah? The president?"

Gray's wry smile told me he wasn't entirely kidding when he replied, "Only two of those. Or one, technically. But I tend to think of Mrs. Clinton as a former president."

My jaw dropped. "As in *Hilary* Clinton?"

Gray loved to shock me. His most devastating grin lit his gorgeous face while he wound his arm around my waist. He gave a blasé shrug. "She and my mom go to the same dermatologist."

A laugh blurted out of me. "You're *absurd*."

I loved the way his entire demeanor warmed as soon as mine did. Sometimes, it seemed like I could put him in a good mood simply by being in one myself.

He pulled me into his hard body and dropped his forehead to my shoulder. "This top is absurd—*absurdly* sexy." He skimmed his lips over my collarbone. Teasing me. "Mmm, Ellie. I can't wait to get you home and claim my surprise."

An impulse took hold of me. My eyes flickered over his head, to the open guest bathroom across the hall. I fisted his sweater in my hand and pulled him along.

"Come get it right now."

Gray staggered after me, confused. I closed the bathroom door behind us and flipped on the lights. The soft halogens bathed the marble floors and sink, winking off of all the gold accents that matched the wallpaper.

"Ellie, what—"

Before I lost my nerve, I reached under my ponytail and untied the halter. Gray froze on the spot, his eyes falling to where my hands clutched topaz triangles of fabric over my breasts. Already breathless, I felt my chest rising and falling under my hands. "Do you want it?"

Gray's eyes darkened. "Now?"

I reached for him, dropping my top. "Right now."

For a moment, Grayson didn't hesitate. He crushed his mouth onto mine as his fingers found my naked back. Growling into my mouth, he pressed me between the marble sink and his hard body.

My fingers fumbled with his belt, tugging the strap from the buckle. At that, he paused for a beat before resuming his kisses.

"Ella…" he warned, speaking into my bare skin. "We don't have time, baby."

"This will only take a minute," I promised, looking up into his eyes and pulling at his turtleneck. "Take this off. I want to see you."

Something soft and electric sparked in his depths. He traced his gaze up my body while I lifted the hem of the sweater up around his ribs. Our gazes met, but his thick brows folded together as he studied my face.

"But then I won't be able to hold you," he murmured. "…after."

Tenderness swelled inside my heart. I dropped his shirt and brushed my thumbs across his cheeks, then smoothed the frown off of his lips. His eyes swirled, hungry, with an edge of indecision.

He needed me to distract him, so he could let me give him what we both wanted. I stepped back, out of his reach, standing in the center of the wide powder room with my bare breasts standing at attention. His focus moved from my lips to my nipples, then back again. I watched as he adjusted the fall of his slacks, cupping his burgeoning erection.

"Ellie. You're killing me."

He was on the ropes. He only needed one more push. In my peripheral vision, I noted an ornate antique vanity with a matching stool.

Perfect.

I held out my hands. "Come over here."

Guiding him down onto the stool, I slipped his sweater off as I went. The second I straddled his lap, he grabbed at my hips, pressing my center against his straining erection. Desire deepened his eyes while his cock twitched against my inseam. He cupped the sides of my breasts, staring at them. "This is the best surprise anyone's ever given me."

He thought fondling my breasts was his surprise? I shook my head, then I moved to drop onto my knees, tugging his slacks down with me.

He gave a surprised grunt that I ignored. Kneeling between his legs, I eyed his perfect cock, then gazed up at him, imploring, "Let me. Please."

He groaned as I wrapped my hands around him and squeezed, pulling my fingers up the length of his shaft. His stance widened. "Fuck," he muttered, burning his gaze over my bare tits. When his stare moved to my mouth, he licked his lips. His cock pulsed in my palm. "Ella..."

I swallowed him before he could overthink it, moaning when I tasted the pre-cum slicking the broad head. His hips bucked, encouraging me to suck him in deep. Running my hands up his thighs, I cupped one around his balls while I used my other arm to pin his torso down.

"Jesus," he panted, his fingers finding my hair. "Ellie, you're so fucking hot."

Searing arousal trickled through my core, gathering between my legs. I loved when he praised me for making him feel good. I loved the way he tasted, the way he watched me with hot, heavy eyes. I loved how his thick cock filled my mouth, stretching my lips.

When I took him all the way into the back of my throat, he cursed harshly, tunneling his fingers into my up-do and pulling at the roots of my hair. With another rough groan, his cock swelled against my tongue. I sped up. His entire body tensed.

"Look at me," he growled, beyond all reason. "Now."

When I turned my gaze to his, the expression on his face almost made me burst. My moan vibrated along his length, sending him over the edge. He came in a gushing torrent, filling my mouth as though it had been days, not hours, since he last came.

I barely had a moment to catch my breath before he hauled me back up into his lap, pressing kisses all over my neck and naked chest. "God, baby," he murmured into my throat. "What's gotten into you?"

I didn't know, but his question made me smirk. "I wish *you* had gotten into me," I teased, squirming over him. Wetness pooled in my panties. "Going down on you makes me horny."

Renewed intensity clouded his gaze. Gray wasted no time unbuttoning my jeans and sliding his hand over my center, collecting the moisture from my sex and bringing his fingers to his lips. I swayed in his lap, so turned on I felt dizzy.

"Mm," he whispered, stroking over my opening again. "I'm going to lick this sweet pussy later. But right now, we're almost out of time."

He cinched his muscled arm around my back, pressing our exposed torsos together. Then he ducked his head, capturing the tip of one breast between his lips.

I gasped, grinding my sex against his fingers while he sucked my nipple. He nuzzled between my tits before moving from one to the other. His middle finger sank into me as the heel of his hand pressed over my clit. He held still, letting me work myself into a frenzy against his palm.

"Gray," I gasped a few minutes later, losing my breath when he lightly nipped at my chest. "Gray, I'm going to come."

A low snarl rumbled in his chest. "That's my good girl. Come all over my hand."

I obeyed his command as he took my mouth in a wild, violent kiss. His tongue mimicked his finger, plunging into me until

I couldn't breathe. Pleasure overtook my body. I shook while he held me close and swallowed all of my whimpers.

Gray turned his face into the crook of my neck and rested there. "You're heaven," he murmured, huddling closer. "I don't want to move."

For a long, perfect moment, he clutched my body tightly to his. His hands stroked down my spine in soothing caresses while I slipped my fingers through the damp hair at the nape of his neck, tugging the way he liked.

Banding his arms tighter, he pretended to hold me captive. I giggled breathlessly. "But we have to get back out there."

When he still didn't move, his mood caught up with me. He was worried about not being able to hold me the way he normally did. I pulled back and gave him a reassuring grin.

"Really, it's okay," I promised, framing his perfect face with my hands. "I wanted that."

Now, with his lust satiated, his gaze turned tender. Vulnerability bled into his irises. "Are you sure? You won't run out the front door?"

I hugged him closer, offering reassurance and giving myself a moment to think. Was I really okay if we just went back out to the dinner like nothing had happened? Would I feel used?

I couldn't imagine regretting what we'd just done together. It was something I wanted to give to him, the way he gave so much to me. The fact that he happened to be skilled enough to return the favor in two minutes was just a bonus.

"I'm sure," I told him, smiling as I stepped off of his lap and fixed my jeans. I did my best to affect a teasing, haughty tone. "You'll have to wait for your cuddles, Grayson Stryker."

Just as I started to reach for my top, I caught him staring at my boobs again. He flashed a wolfish, unapologetic grin. "Just storing this image for later," he told me. "I wanted to untie that top the minute I saw it."

Rolling my eyes, I refastened the halter straps with a bow and turned to the mirror. Surprisingly, I didn't look too mussed. My hair needed to be shaken out re-tied; and my lip gloss required reapplication. But, otherwise, our quickie wasn't long enough to do any real damage.

Gray finished pulling down his shirt and fastening his belt in one move. He stepped up behind me, dropping a kiss on the crown of my head while his hand pressed flat against my belly.

"You look perfect, Ella," he said softly, brushing his lips over my bare shoulder. "I've never been so proud." His panty-dropping grin nearly stopped my heart. "Now, let's get you back out there before they realize you served me dessert before dinner."

Grayson stayed close for the next hour. He hovered at my elbow while I removed various dishes from the double-oven. Then he followed me to the bar to help me refill wine glasses.

"You don't have to shadow me," I stage-whispered, giggling at him. "I'm really okay."

Confusion crept over his face. "I know," he said, sincere and puzzled. "But I don't know if *I* am. I'm so used to staying with you, after. Walking away feels… wrong."

No matter how many times I tried to shoo him towards his family, he stuck by me. He even kept up his campaign at dinner, eschewing the seat across from mine for the place at my side. Keeping his hand in my lap, he alternated between teasing swipes of his fingers against the inside of my thigh and soft knee squeezes.

His parents made an embarrassing fuss over the food, complimenting me so often I thought I'd have a permanent blush by the time we cleared the polished oak table.

"That was wonderful, Ella," Mr. Stryker said for the third time. "Grayson told us you were talented. Seems he did not exaggerate."

The three bottles of wine we consumed over the course of the meal didn't help me keep my cheeks from glowing. My face flamed as I ran my fingertips along the table's edge. "It's really nothing."

Gray snatched one of my hands up and pressed a kiss to the palm. His eyes warmed as he smiled at me. “It was delicious, Ellie. Almost as good as the fried chicken.”

His mother’s musical laugh filled the room. “He really does talk about it all the time, doesn’t he?”

“Oh, yeah.” I shook my head. “It’s definitely not the healthiest meal or the most graceful; but I suppose I’ll have to make him more if I ever want him to stop pestering everyone he meets.”

A twinkle lit Jacqueline’s eye. “Perhaps we could persuade you to make some for all of us… next month, in the Hamptons. We’ll be at our East Hampton compound for Christmas this year. We’d be *thrilled* to have you join us.”

On our very first outing to West Side Waffles, Gray told me his family always spent Christmas in Aspen. I wondered why they would suddenly change a solid tradition. *Maybe Mr. Stryker isn’t supposed to travel too far from his doctors.*

My head swiveled automatically, facing Gray. His face—a wilted half-smile and eyes that swirled with resigned sadness—confirmed my suspicions.

I couldn’t help myself; my fingers stretched out to graze his clenched jaw. A beseeching bolt of hope cracked through his features, leaving me defenseless.

He needs me.

I offered Gray a grin, hoping to melt away his consternation. “I’d love to join you all.”

My boyfriend held my hand against his cheek. “Are you sure? What about your mom?”

“We’ll work it out,” I assured him. “I can probably do both. I’ll just look up flights later and change my tickets.” *And hope to God there isn’t an up-charge…*

“Not necessary,” Mr. Stryker put in, his voice gruff. “You’ll have our jet at your disposal, of course.”

Another gulp stuck in my throat. *A jet?*

Grayson's eyes softened as he traced my face. "Maybe I could come with you? I'd love to meet your mom and Darcy."

A shimmer of joy fluttered through me. "Got to make sure I don't trash your plane, huh?"

My silly joke earned surprised spurts of laughter from all three of them. The appreciation I glimpsed in Gray's eyes doubled into adoration. The same smoldering look he gave me the night before, when he couldn't quite get his words out.

Love.

I hoped so, anyway. Because my heart felt close to *bursting*.

And his gorgeous, glowing grin didn't help one bit.

His parents began discussing which day they should plan to make the trip out east to open up the house. Gray turned to me, his expression a fervent mask of gratitude.

"Spending time with you is all I want for Christmas," he murmured, kissing the center of my hand one more time. "Thank you, Ellie."

My chest throbbed. I tried for a weak smirk. "You didn't want a horrible sweater to go with your pitiful green scarf?"

His grin expanded. "If you made me a sweater, then you'd have to see me in it every week." A teasing spark settled in his eyes. "Think I could get away with wearing it to work? Or the gym?"

As I giggled, he took my face between his palms, pulled it to his own, and placed a gentle kiss on my lips, not seeming to care if his parents saw. Holding me still, he closed his eyes and took a deep breath, as if drawing strength from our closeness.

Jacqueline's knowing voice cut into our moment. "Grayson, *mi amor*, I'm afraid it's time to make our customary call to Nonna and Papa."

He only leaned back enough to cast me a rueful smirk. "My grandparents, in Spain. They don't eat dinner until ten PM over there and they're expecting me and Mom to FaceTime them."

Gray caught my inquisitive glance toward Mr. Stryker. "Dad usually doesn't join the calls," he explained, dropping my face and straightening in his chair. "The language barrier makes it hard."

Jacqueline shrugged gracefully. "My husband's Spanish is good and his Italian is passable, but only a rare few can catch on to Spitalian."

I blinked at them. "*Spit*-alian?"

Gray took on a long-suffering air. "Like 'Spanglish' but with Italian. Spanish-Italian. Spitalian." His cheekbones darkened slightly. "Apparently I invented the word when I was six and no one wants to let me forget it."

Gray blushing was almost as sexy as Gray pouting. So when he combined the two, I thought my panties might spontaneously drop. I felt my teeth sink into my lower lip as I looked up at him, somewhere between snickering and melting. Imagining his deep, sexy voice flowing over a melodic romance language sent quivers to my core. "I didn't know you spoke any Italian."

He caught the bent of my thoughts in a second. Flirtatious warmth ignited in his eyes while he stood. "*Solo un po. E non bene.*"

While I struggled to translate, he bent to kiss my cheek, lingering for a just a second too long. "I'll be back in a few minutes," he promised. As he stepped away, a wry, mischievous twist pulled at his sculpted lips. "*Ciao, bella.*"

Jacqueline began teasing him in their made-up language while they vacated the dining room… leaving me alone with Mason Stryker for the very first time.

For a moment, I stared at my plain fingernails, uneasy. Even when I wasn't looking at him, the Stryker Intimidation Factor permeated the air, filling me with a thick wash of apprehension.

When I finally looked up, I found him regarding me with calm concentration. "Ella."

I swallowed hard, hoping my eyes weren't big as saucers. "Yes, sir?"

His dark brown sweater turned his tawny eyes into golden beams. They carved my face with laser focus, searching. "I wonder if I might ask you a question. About our company."

Alarm stuck in my gullet. "Stryker & Sons? I'm happy to try to answer anything you ask me, sir, of course. But I cannot imagine one single thing I would be able to help you with. Usually, when Gray tries to discuss difficult decisions, all I can do is listen…"

The set of his square jaw softened. "In my experience, that's a big help, Ella. Don't ever underestimate the value of a sounding board for a CEO. Each decision we make has many components—sometimes saying them all out loud can give valuable perspective."

A glimmer of pride sparkled in my center. "I hope so. He works so hard… I wish there was more I could do to help him. Sometimes, I wonder if he would be better off with someone who knows more about…" I gestured around the opulent dining area. "All of this. I feel completely out of my depth most of the time."

His version of Gray's self-deprecating smile graced his bearded face. "I'll tell you a secret—most of us are, at your age. I was for a very long time. I've been the CEO of Stryker & Sons for two decades, but, in the beginning, I was just like Grayson. One of the most valuable lessons my father taught me was how to admit when I didn't understand something. And bring in experts who could teach me. Which is why I feel compelled to seek your counsel."

Dear Lord. On *what*? Yarn? Yoga? How much butter to put in caramel? *Two sticks.*

"About my son," Mason clarified. "You seem to be the top expert these days."

Like a moron, I actually pointed to myself. "Me?"

Mr. Stryker sat back, folding his hands on the table. "Yes. I know we've only met a handful of times, but I've truly never seen him as happy as he is in your company. You seem to understand him in a unique way. So, I need to ask you… do you think he can do this?"

My answer came immediately. "Yes."

A slight curve tipped up one corner of his mouth. "Perhaps I should rephrase. I know he's *capable*. He's insightful and cautious. Respectful and calm… to others, anyway. People respond to him as an authority figure. He can negotiate without giving too much away. He does well with numbers. His contract skills are progressing rapidly."

Mr. Stryker's contemplative expression took on an edge of compunction. "My son could do anything he set his mind to. I know he's dedicated himself to this job, despite his misgivings. I only mean to ask you, Ella—if he has to do this job for the rest of his life, will he be happy?"

My mind leapt to the sketches ensconced upstairs. The designs I stashed away. The doodles in his notebooks. The drawing secreted in my coat pocket.

"He's torn," I whispered, admitting it out loud for the first time. "He has a creative passion that he thinks he has to give up in order to be a good CEO. I'm afraid… if he does that… he'll always resent letting it go."

Mason's face furrowed into a frown. "The sketching, you mean? I know my wife likes to believe he was the next Frank Lloyd Wright, but I haven't seen a new design from him in ages. I assumed he gave the hobby up."

"But he's studying architecture," I pointed out. "And the drafting table in his apartment… the sketches on his walls…" As I spoke, I saw he had no clue what I was talking about. A sudden flash of inspiration brought me to my feet. "Hold on. I'll show you."

Before I lost my nerve, I strode out to the foyer and retrieved the folded piece of notebook paper from my coat pocket. When I returned to the table, I took Grayson's seat beside Mr. Stryker and carefully placed the sketch in front of him.

Mason went completely still for a long moment. "What is this?"

I bit my lip, chagrinned. "I sort of stole it from Gray's financial accounting notebook. It's an idea he was working on when we met. It's evolved a lot. I caught him working on it all the time, up until recently."

While he stared at the paper, I rambled on. "I know that Stryker & Sons is a development company, more oriented toward buying up land and turning profits by breaking it up or tearing things down… But I just keep thinking… couldn't there be some value in a talent like Grayson's? He's so creative in this wonderfully sensible way. I know he can't really be an architect if he's going to be the CEO… but I think if you found some way to honor his artistic side, he would feel much more fulfilled."

Mason held up the sketch. Disbelief colored his voice. "You *saw* him draw this?"

"Yes, sir." I nodded. "Many times. The garden was my idea, actually. Of course, he managed to make it more unique and practical than I imagined."

His gold eyes ran over the page again and again. "This is very good. Much more evolved than his work in high school. I suppose I would have anticipated as much, had I known he still drew." He snagged my gaze. "Would you mind if I kept this?"

Eagerness overrode my sense. Without thought to consequences, I blurted, "Of course! I have the others."

He stared right at me for a long, tense second. "You have other versions of this building?"

I sank my teeth into my lip again. "Not exactly, no. Grayson recently got rid of all of the sketches hanging in his apartment and I sort of… I kept some of them without telling him."

An edge of desperation crept into my tone. "I just didn't want him to get rid of everything and then regret it one day. I figured I could keep some of the best ones safe, just in case he changed his mind. I didn't tell him because he's had a hard time letting it go, and I didn't want to undermine his hard work…"

Mr. Stryker frowned at the picture some more. "You said I should find some way to honor his artistic side. You think he would be happier doing the other duties of a CEO if he also had time for creative projects?"

My nod gave away my frantic optimism. "I really think so. I've tried suggesting it to him before, but he says it wouldn't work. And I don't really understand all of the intricacies of your job, so I tend to believe him, but, maybe... Is there any way he could run Stryker & Sons *and* have time to work on the creative side of the business, too?"

Mason Stryker, a world-famous titan of industry, met my gaze head-on. "Not if he intends to stay in a relationship with you."

He said the words so calmly, I didn't know how to process them. Did he mean it as an insult? A hint? A grievance? Or perhaps just… a fact?

A thick wash of shame poured through me. My hands shook as I fell back into my seat. "Oh."

With regret filling the lines of his face, he looked grimmer than ever. "You are a lovely girl, Ella. I see why my son has fallen for you. And I think you are good for him. I don't want him to lose someone he cares for so much. But if he does what you're suggesting I allow, the personal time he's managed to maintain thus far would vanish. And, to be frank, with the way he looks at you and talks about you… I'm just not convinced that that's a compromise he'd be willing to make."

We sat in complete silence, staring each other down, considering. I knew he was right. Grayson would go ballistic if anyone suggested he give up our relationship over work. And, with a tsunami of guilt swamping my stomach, I realized I wasn't willing to make that sacrifice, either.

Mr. Stryker read my expression and made a reassuring sound. "Now, dear, don't feel responsible. This isn't your doing. I hardly think you're the only obstacle here. Even if Grayson were single, he probably still wouldn't be able to do two full-time jobs. Especially since one is so demanding."

But I already felt fully responsible. A pleading grimace pulled at my mouth. "Isn't there anyone else who could help him?" I begged. "Someone to take up some of the slack when—"

I only narrowly caught myself. Mason's face hardened anyway. "When I die? It's alright, Ella. I assumed he told you. It was kind of you not to bring it up sooner."

"I'm so, so sorry," I rushed on, the words tumbling out of me. "Grayson asked me not to discuss it and he gets so depressed when we do that I just—"

A frustrated sigh broke into my words as I scrambled to compose my thoughts. "I want you and Mrs. Stryker to know that I'm deeply, sincerely sorry that you are going through this. You're such wonderful people and you raised an amazing man. It kills me that you may not get to see him become all that he can be, because I know he will do such great things. I apologize if Gray broke your confidence. He was out of his mind when he found out and I think he just... he needed me. But—now that I know, and *you know* that I know—I only hope that I can be helpful to you all, somehow."

Mason dropped his eyes to his lap and gave a gruff cough. "Yes, well. Thank you, Ella. My biggest regret in all of this is what it will do to my family. I remember what it was like to lose my father, though I was much older than Grayson is now."

Without thought, I reached for his hand, hoping to offer some small measure of comfort. Mr. Stryker's head snapped up, pinning me in place with his gold gaze.

"He's a strong person," I assured him, holding fast. "He will find a way through it. I lost my dad when I was seventeen and I did okay. Grayson is much tougher than me. He can do this, sir. I really believe that."

Mr. Stryker stared at me for so long, anxiety started to knot my insides. Finally, he pulled his hand back and abruptly stood. Without glancing at me again, he strode to the exit.

"If you'd excuse me," he muttered and then disappeared.

Grayson

"You wanted to talk before dessert?"

Barnes caught me on my way from the kitchen back to the dining room, informing me that my father had issued a summons. He "required" my "audience"—or so his British director of security claimed.

Minutes later, I hovered on the threshold of his study, pissed. I didn't have the patience for his workaholic bullshit, especially after telling him I'd be taking the day off to enjoy my final Thanksgiving. All I wanted was to have a piece of pie and then whisk Ella home and spend the rest of the night with her. Naked.

He waved me in without looking up from the document in front of him. "Come, sit."

Clenching my jaw, I stalked to the overstuffed armchair across from his white oak desk. I noticed—not for the first time—how much the room reminded me of my mother, not my father. He filled his office at the company with floor-to-ceiling bookshelves, antiques, and oriental art. But this room matched the rest of our house—light wood, a metallic sheen in the wallpaper, sleek furnishings and comfortable chairs. A berry-red rug. A Rothko hanging across from his windows. Though, with nightfall settling over the Upper East Side, the only light in the entire room came from two dim wall sconces behind him.

As soon as I settled in, he faced me, revealing a determined expression. "I've made a decision about the business."

"Dad," I started. "I thought I told you that I wasn't doing this today. Ella and Mom are waiting for us—"

Without a word, my father held up a piece of paper. *My* piece of paper. A page from my notebook. One of my drawings.

"Ella." We said her name at the same moment—him as an explanation, me as an expletive.

Betrayal hit me square in the chest. My fingernails dug into the arms of the leather chair. "That's trash," I told him, trying not to grit my teeth. "She shouldn't have shown it to you."

My father smoothed the sketch out in front of him. "It is trash," he agreed. "All wrinkled and creased. I'll need you to draw up a proper one before I can present it."

Everything inside of me seized. "Pardon?"

"That parcel we assembled in midtown should be a perfect spot, don't you think?" he carried on, still not looking up. "We're slated for demolition in March. That only gives us three months to revise the plans and draw up the specs for this building. I expect the materials will be costlier than anticipated, but we'll spare no expense to make it just right, of course. As our headquarters, it will serve as a showpiece for our clients and the rest of this city."

Finally, his eyes leapt to mine. "That is, if you'll design it."

"But how—what—" I swallowed, shoving down a rising tide of elation, not daring to hope I'd heard him correctly. "I'm supposed to be training to take your job. How can I do that and design a building in midtown Manhattan?"

He crossed his arms and shrugged slightly. "I don't know. But your girlfriend seems entirely convinced that you can do it. She said she believes that all you need is a chance. She showed me this sketch to convince me of your talent."

My heart thudded unevenly. *Ellie*. My God, what had she *done*? My throat dried. "She said all of that?"

He nodded. "Yes. I warned her that the workload might jeopardize your relationship, but she seemed quite determined. She asked me if there was anyone who could help you with some of your executive duties, to give you more time to function in a creative capacity. So, I'm going to call your uncle."

I thought my head might explode. I had only been in the kitchen for twenty minutes. How the hell did Ella manage to turn my entire life around?

"Uncle *Ted*?" I guffawed, incredulous. "Dad, he tried to embezzle company funds. You almost had to have him arrested. What the fuck are you thinking?"

Instead of taking the bait and fighting with me, my father simply frowned. "I'm thinking that I'm dying. And you're my son. And I love you."

The thickness narrowing my throat constricted. My eyes burned. "Dad..."

He interrupted. "I had no idea you were this talented or this invested in architecture. I thought it was a passing phase. If having a hand in the creative side of our company will make all of this better for you the way Ella thinks it will, then I'm going to call Ted in to help you manage the business side of things."

It was an insane idea. "We can't give him any actual power, though, right?"

Dad smirked. "We don't have to. I'm not dead yet. But he's the only one who knows the company the way I do. He'll act as an advisor. And maybe we can even bring your cousin in as another support. You know I never liked that he wasn't part of the business. My grandfather started Stryker & Sons for all of us. Perhaps, eventually, you and Daniel can run things together."

I hadn't seen my cousin Daniel since his Columbia graduation and subsequent defection to Europe. He'd been gone almost two years, backpacking and posting pictures on Instagram. But, despite his questionable Photoshop tendencies, I had to admit… the thought of having someone else in my corner sounded like a huge relief.

"We don't have to decide tonight," my father went on. "I just wanted to tell you what I was thinking and ask for a formal rendering of this piece. Can you have it ready by Monday?"

I was trying—really hard—not to get excited. Not until it was a done deal… Still, I found myself grinning. "Yes. Monday."

He nodded tersely, like he hadn't just handed me my dream on a silver platter. "Good. You better get back downstairs, then. I'm sure dessert is set out. I'll be right behind you."

Dazed, I wandered to the door before he stopped me in my tracks once again. "Son."

My stomach clenched. "Yeah?"

He glanced up at me, dead serious. "If you don't marry that girl, you're an idiot."

❋❋❋

Chapter Seventeen

October 2016

Grayson

"Son."

The moniker, which used to fill me with dread, now only gave me a small prick of sadness. How many more times would I experience my father's gruff disapproval before I never heard it again?

Turning away from my office window, I found him standing just inside the etched glass door, considering the sleeves of his tuxedo instead of looking at me. "I trust you've practiced your remarks?" he huffed.

"Of course." My left hand absentmindedly went to my jacket pocket, where I'd stashed a notecard with my talking points. "Mom's collected Olivia?"

Dad moved from fidgeting with cufflinks to yanking at his black bow tie, still scowling. "Yes," he muttered, "I expect they're well on their way by now. Barnes has them."

The thought of Olivia Twat—who I found wholly objectionable just one week ago—left me curiously blank. A small flicker of annoyance flared in my chest, then dropped down to the pit of numbness stretched taut through my middle. The same blanket of nothingness that smothered every other feeling over the past three days. Ever since leaving Ella at Idealogue Monday morning, I'd dedicated myself to absolute apathy.

That evening, when Amir handed me a stack of files he gathered on her past, I directed him to remove them from my apartment altogether, along with my shoebox of scraps, the green scarf, and the gift I never brought myself to so much as unwrap. He did so without so much as a word. Inspired by his indifference, I also deleted Ella's book from my Kindle library.

Since watching the digital volume disappear from my other titles, I felt oddly empty. As if my mind and my heart had both undergone a factory reset.

Just one final obstacle stood between me and the rest of my life, sans a certain blonde.

The godforsaken gala.

The thick curtain of numbness suffocated my frustration before it even began. I checked my watch.

6:38.

Hell bent on distraction, I ran through a list of the evening's requirements, checking them off. We had catering, entertainment, valet service, a silent auction for a charity aiding urban homelessness. The ballroom on the second floor of our building would serve as the venue—over the week, it had been lavishly appointed with all the trappings of an elegant event. Or so I was assured.

As my second-in-command, Daniel, did most of planning, along with his father, my mother, and, of course, my omniscient assistant, Beth. It was a dream-team as far as parties were concerned. My father and I were honestly lucky. If left to our own devices, my mother liked to claim, we'd surely plan the dullest event in the history of the city.

"Everyone in Bed by Nine, if your father picked the theme," she'd chortled to me. "Or, An Evening of Brooding Silence, if you had your way, *mi amor.*"

She wasn't wrong. Without the distractions I used for years… and without Ella's memory haunting my every move… I mostly spent my time alone, surrounded by quiet.

It probably isn't healthy for me to be by myself every *night… Maybe it would be good for me to take Olivia home. I know she'll be willing…*

But she also wouldn't have blue eyes that beamed. Or sweet touches that gave instead of taking. Or a heart that made my knees weak.

Swallowing hard, I checked my watch again. *6:38*. Still.

Damn it.

Dad harrumphed while he tugged on his tie, pulling the whole thing off kilter. Without a second thought, I crossed over to him. "Here. Let me."

It was fucked. I unraveled the knot to start from scratch. While I adjusted the black silk, I realized… I was looking down at him. My father—who always seemed to tower over every other person in every room—was now smaller than me.

The moment catapulted me back in time to so many occasions during my adolescence when he'd fixed bowties for me. I remembered looking up at my father, wondering if I'd ever figure any of it out. How to tie the damn bowties, how to run our family interests. How to be a man.

But here I was, tying his tie. Running his company, making remarks in his stead.

And I still wasn't a man. Not a good one, anyway. I still needed him to teach me.

Tamping down the hoarseness suddenly blocking my throat, I asked, "Any advice for me tonight? Things I need to do?"

Dad raised his head, pinning me with his muddy eyes. As if he could read my thoughts, he said, "You don't need me. You know what to do. You've taken this company in hand and run with it, exactly as I always knew you could."

Exactly as Ella knew I could. The thought broke through my careful cover of indifference, sending a stinging barb of grief into my chest. *She never doubted me, even when I doubted myself.*

Finished with his tie, I stepped back, dropping my eyes. "You grossly overestimate me," I replied, masking sincerity with ruefulness.

"No." The steady ferocity of his voice made me look back at him. "I *under*estimated you. On purpose. Because I knew I had to in order to make your education as thorough as possible. But, secretly, I always had high hopes for you, Grayson. You've exceeded them all."

His regard softened and intensified at once. "Which is why I'm announcing my retirement tonight, before your remarks."

Dismay washed over me. "No," I denied. "We have a plan. You're retiring next summer. Fall, even."

Mason Stryker rarely acknowledged his weakness. He shifted on his feet before admitting, "I'm sicker than I expected to be, Grayson. You know that. I can't even tie my damn bowtie. I'm not saying I'm dying tomorrow or even next year… but I *am* dying, son. And I want—"

He stopped himself. But I knew what he wanted to say. "You want to be home, with Mom."

He cleared his throat. "Yes. I do. This company has been part of my life; the biggest part, some could argue. But you and your mother… you *are* my life. *She is* my life. And that's what I want to spend the remainder of my time focusing on."

It made sense, of course. And I'd always known, in the back of my mind, that this day was coming. But that didn't stop the surge of gag-inducing terror that scraped up my esophagus.

"Fuck," I hissed, gulping down the riot. "Dad, don't do this to me. Not now. Not tonight. I can't—" *I can't handle with losing you and Ella at the same goddamn event.* "I can't run this place without you."

He didn't waver. "That's not true, son. Besides, this is why we brought Ted and Daniel back in, if you recall. They'll continue to help you. And I'm not dead yet. You can always call me, if need be." His scowl evaporated into a pensive line. "But I really don't think you'll need to."

He turned to the door, gesturing at the title carved under my name. "You *are* the CEO of Stryker & Sons, Grayson. You've done it. Congratulations." With his head bent, he made to exit. "You should be proud."

Ella

In all my horrible imaginings of what the night would bring, I never expected to feel a swooping sense of awe.

Pride, I realized. It erupted through my chest as I stepped into the lobby of Stryker & Sons, my head turning to take in its modern splendor.

As airy as it was immense, the first floor stretched before me in a perfect oval. Beneath my heels, snow-white marble gleamed in every direction, interrupted only by one single black vein that started in the center of the oblong expanse. The dark fissure widened from one small point into a gaping onyx chasm, stretching back to engulf the bank of matte black elevators at the far side of the lobby.

Over the place where the vein started, a chandelier the size of an SUV dangled from the high, curved ceiling. Dozens of octagonal ebony orbs clustered into artfully unbalanced groupings. It gave the whole room an elegant, intimidating edge.

Gray. It was like I'd stepped inside of his mind. Which would have been heartbreaking, if I weren't so amazed.

"Incredible, right?"

Parker's low voice rumbled just behind my shoulder. A thick wash of shame flowed over me. *I'm mooning over Grayson Stryker while on a literal date.*

But at least I wasn't crying over him.

Yet.

There was still plenty of potential for another breakdown. If one of the Strykers spotted me, I was toast. After everything that happened before I left Grayson… not to mention the *way* I left him… I would be lucky if all they did was kick me out.

I'd done everything in my power to make sure that didn't happen. My black evening gown—snagged from the formalwear section of the Goodwill on 61st—had to be the most boring item of clothing I owned. Completely devoid of any frills, beading, flounces, or color, it had a high, straight neckline that covered everything from the base of my throat to the points of my shoulders. The cut narrowed at the waist, then fell in an A-line to my feet.

I'd even sewed up the top of the skirt's slit, stitching it down to the knee. I curled my hair and left it hanging around my face, hoping the voluminous curtain of blonde would be enough to conceal my facial features should anyone bother to look twice.

The velvety red staining my lips was too flashy. It still made me twitch whenever I thought about it, but Maggie *insisted*, pointing out that, while I didn't want to bring any extra attention to myself, I still had Parker to consider. He graciously agreed to come as my date, despite having lost out on the big account. And, in Mag's words, the least I could do was put some color on my mouth so I didn't "look like a widow in mourning."

I was sure I'd never live down the guilt I felt for asking him to coming with me. At the time, I only did it out of desperation. If I had to be at the gala for Marjorie's sake, I figured I better bring a man along to protect me from a certain Mr. Stryker.

And myself, for that matter.

While I took in the glory of the lobby, Parker paused to remove my coat. Around us, the others moving toward the elevators still had their outwear on. But I couldn't exactly blame him for wanting to remove mine as quickly as possible. The threadbare flowers easily marked me as the most gauche person in the room.

With his hand at the small of my back, he guided me forward. "This place is insane," he commented, looking up at the glowing glass prisms overhead. "I wonder who designed it."

"Grayson Stryker."

It hurt to say his name. I'd done everything in my power to avoid even thinking it in the days since I last saw him. Every time I did, I recalled the smoldering hurt in his green eyes as he turned away from me at Idealogue… and inevitably lost myself to the grief that never felt very far away, these days.

But I had to make sure he got credit for his brilliance. I wanted everyone to know that he was so much more than the beneficiary of his family name; he was talented and capable enough to merit all of his success on his own.

Parker slanted a doubtful look at me. His tone fell close to condescending. "I don't think the CEO designs buildings, Ella."

I decided it wasn't worth arguing the point… or revealing just how well I knew our host. An embarrassed blush heated my cheeks. "You're probably right. Of course."

It was shaping up to be a very long evening.

Grayson

This will be the longest night of my life.

The uncharitable thought blurred through my mind as Olivia wrapped her arm through mine. "Grayson, I simply adore what you've done with this space," she cooed, flashing her even, white teeth. "The lighting is inspired. I've never seen a chandelier quite like it. And the decision to go with stone floors instead of carpet! I detest ballrooms with carpet."

In truth, I commissioned the chandelier to be a slightly smaller version of the showpiece hanging in our lobby because I didn't feel like designing a whole new concept for the ballroom. And I picked stone over carpet to cut back on up-keep costs.

Still, the room looked good. I'd own that.

My team had outdone itself, decking out the enormous space in sheer white panels of gossamer that hung from the domed ceiling. The curtains lent the whole space a softness it desperately lacked, and helped whole affair feel warmer and more intimate. Thousands of faux candles, grouped within or behind each panel, finished the effect.

I noticed Amir, standing beside the platform erected for the evening's entertainment, following our every move with his eyes. Even in a black tuxedo, he looked ready to leap into action at any moment.

His arms crossed over his chest, giving away his irritation. Events always made him twitchy. Little did he know, at that point, I almost *wished* someone would shoot me.

My attention flew from the corner beside the event stage to the Rolex partially hidden by my tuxedo's shirtsleeves. *7:42.*

Over my date's head, my mother cast me a disapproving look, scolding me for glancing at the time too often. Or maybe for the expression on my face—which, I realized, probably came off as tense, at best. Not wanting to be rude, I tried to smile as I turned to the woman pressed against me. "Have I complimented your dress?"

Her lips tightened, then smirked. "Yes."

Well, then. I probably kept mentioning it because it was the one true compliment I could muster. She was dressed to kill in a low-cut, open-back evening gown. As we made our first turn around the room, she stole the attention of every other man we passed.

Rightfully so. With her long black hair hanging over her bare shoulders and her lithe frame wrapped in ethereal silver, she looked hot.

I wasn't blind. Just detached.

Yet, not *completely* indifferent to *everything*. Because I kept catching myself scanning the perimeters of the ballroom, searching for one particular face.

My eyes dropped back to the watch on the wrist Olivia clutched. *7:43*.

Mom launched into a spirited discussion of silk versus satin. Covering for me, bless her. I saw my opening and took it without a second thought.

Gently orienting my date toward my parents, I flashed a charming grin. "I'm afraid my hosting duties have only just begun," I interjected, slipping out of her clutches. "In fact, I see the mayor just arrived and I owe him a photo-op. Mother, Father—you'll escort Olivia to our table?" With fingers and lips as numb as my insides, I lifted Olivia's hand for a perfunctory kiss. "If you'd all excuse me."

I caught my father's face as I spun for the entrance—exasperated amusement at having his own social evasion tactics used against him. After all, I learned from the best. Which is also why I knew how to make it seem like I was charging off to slay a dragon while actually discreetly looping around to the bar.

I looked at the person behind the counter without seeing them. "Gin. All of it."

"A man on a mission."

I recognized the voice even before my uncle's hand fell on my shoulder. My hackles instantly rose as I resisted the urge to shrug him off.

"Ted," I returned, taking my three-finger pour of liquor and quaffing it before anyone else noticed me. "Excellent work on the event. I'm fielding compliments left and right."

My uncle—a shorter, rounder version of my father—laughed heartily. With his rounded torso and tuxedo tails, he looked a bit like a penguin.

"Do feel free to send those my way, my boy," he drawled. "Particularly if they come from anyone as delectable as your date. What did Mason say her name was?"

The bartender replaced with first drink with a second. This time, I managed not to knock it back in one slug. Though, God knows I wanted to. Particularly after admitting, "Oliva Watts."

"Watts?" His jowls furrowed along with his blond brows, which promptly rose toward his receding hairline as he placed her name. "Dashwood Watt's only daughter? The supply chain heiress?"

The urge to paw at my tie had me taking another hearty draught. "The very same. We go back to Dalton."

He glanced over at our table, where my mother and Olivia held court over a group of other ladies, each holding flutes of champagne. Impressed, he regarded me with newfound appreciation. "That's a smart match there, my boy. Practically dynastic."

I knew all the society papers would say the same thing the following morning. Two of the country's wealthiest families, drawn together by their young, successful heirs.

It made quite the story. Especially next to photos of us. As Mom like to point out, Olivia may not have been at the top of my list, but she and I took "lovely" photos together. Part of me suspected that was the primary reason my mother called her in the first place.

Ted continued, but my focus faded while I did another sweep of the room. There were so many people—almost fifty-tables-worth. In the sea of formalwear, I found myself searching for a hideous-floral-coat-covered buoy.

Across the teaming expanse, a flash of blonde caught my attention. In a black evening gown, the fair, petite girl stood with her back to me. Chatting with someone tall and dark… dressed in an outlandish burgundy tuxedo.

No one would wear such a thing but my best friend. Graham Everett.

Would Ella seek him out? I didn't know, but it seemed possible. She always like him. She used to claim she saw some indefinable redeeming quality in him that other women had yet to unearth.

I felt my feet move of their own volition. Tossing my uncle a parting clap on the shoulder, I excused myself.

It took twice as long to cross the room the second time. I had to stop multiple times to shake hands, meet dates, inquire after absent parties. All the while, my eye trained on the girl standing with my best friend while my blood ran hot-and-cold through my ears.

Finally, I got close enough to see. It wasn't Ella at all, but another curved blonde. Graham shooed her away when he spotted me and closed the gap between us.

"Grayson Fucking Stryker." His crooked grin and bleary eyes told me the scotch in his left hand was not his first. Or second.

Still, I was relieved to see him. *Nothing like a ballroom full of business contacts to remind a person who their true friends are.*

"Graham." I nodded after his date. "*You* brought someone?"

It was rare for him to bring his own escort. He once told me he considered taking dates to formal events like bringing your own sandwich to buffet. Or shooting fish in a barrel instead of using a pole.

"Eh." He shrugged, unbothered by his hypocrisy. "I figured, what the hell?"

"Feeling lazy?" I taunted.

Graham smirked around his glass. "Grayson, the days are shorter, the weather is colder, and your boy is *tired.* This summer wore me the fuck out. I should be at home, icing my balls. But, you know, this is your party, so. I'm here. I opted for a sure thing. Sue me."

Amused, I sipped my cocktail. "What's her name?"

There was a chance he wouldn't remember. That had happened before, too. Instead, he flashed a shit-eating grin. "You don't recognize her? It's Sarah."

"*Sorority* Sarah?" Damn, he really *was* tired. Circling back to women he'd already conquered. "Or Sara-With-No-H?"

Graham squinted over at his date. "Hmm. Excellent question."

"You're fucking with me," I decided, finishing my gin.

His thick brows rose. "Wish I was. I honestly can't remember… I guess we'll see if she calls me Papi later. Which reminds me—where might one find an empty office without a camera in this place?"

There was only one. My office. And the answer was, "Absolutely not."

Graham's dark eyes regarded me suspiciously. "You're wound tightly this evening. Could that have anything to do with a certain silver bombshell I saw on your arm? You didn't tell me you were bringing Fatal Attraction."

I grimaced. "Strategic decision."

My watch informed me that I had fifty-some minutes until I had to be on stage to make my remarks. The notecard in my jacket pocket started to burn a hole through my shirt.

He noticed. "Seriously," he said, glowering. "You good?"

Damn. I really had to look freaked out for him to take note of my distress. I lowered my voice, ensuring we weren't overheard. "My father is stepping down tonight. He's passing me the reins. In an hour."

Most people would congratulate me. Pump my hand, kiss my ass. Instead, Graham's frown deepened.

"And you're losing it," he guessed. "Typical Stryker. You know, you're always too damn hard on yourself. It's not like you don't know what you're doing. You've been running your family business longer than I've even been working at mine; and if I could get my old man to hand me Everett Alexander, I'd be doing cartwheels, not having a panic attack."

Panic attack. Ella.

A prickle of awareness skittered over my nape. My head snapped up, my gaze picking through the crowd around me until it landed on a group about ten yards away.

And, *dear God.*

There she was.

Tucked into the throng, as unassuming as could be in a plain black dress with her hair hiding half of her face. She had a drink in each hand as she hovered behind a group of executives from Idealogue, clearly not part of their circle.

I realized she had gone to fetch a cocktail for her boyfriend—the blond guy I saw her with at her office—but he'd yet to so much as acknowledge her effort. The champagne she got for herself was more than half-empty, indicating she'd been waiting behind him for some time.

An instinctive swell of anger flooded over my numbness, drowning it. *Jackass. Turn around and take your fucking drink.*

As I stared, Ella chewed on her lower lip and looked down at her feet. She shifted on her heels, scrunching her nose, hating them. Probably missing her green clogs.

You don't know that, my pride sneered. *She's a totally different person now. You don't even know her anymore.*

But some small, sure part of me knew that wasn't right. The truth struck me while I watched her. Each pinch in her features. Every flash in her eyes. Her posture, her poise.

She was still Ellie. And I knew her better than I'd ever known anyone else.

Loved her more than I'd ever loved anyone else.

The truth ripped at the old wound I'd fought so hard to keep closed. Freed from the scab of apathy, my heart opened, bleeding. A week's worth of pain poured out. Hell, three years' worth.

God only knows what I looked like, but—right in the middle of that horrible moment—she happened to glance up. Our gazes locked and held.

Her entire demeanor changed. Softened. Her expression melted into tenderness. It beamed from her blue eyes, warming my face as they traced my features with pure, undeniable adoration.

Just like the very first day, on that subway… Ella saw me. She saw everything.

She swayed toward me. A second later she looked away, searching her vicinity for a place to set the drinks down.

Is she… coming over to me?

That had never happened before. It was always me, chasing her down. Her, running from me and us and all the things we could have been.

But she set the drinks on the nearest cocktail table and cast a quick, guilty look at her coworkers before spinning my way. Our eyes met a second time. Entranced, I wandered away from Graham without so much as word.

Over my shoulder, someone called my name. *Probably just Graham, wondering what the fuck is wrong with me.* My attention shifted for a fraction of a moment before I dismissed the noise altogether.

By the time I looked back at her, though, Ella had stopped cold. Fear filled every line of her lovely face, turning it into a beautiful, horrible mask of absolute dread.

"Ella," I called out, moving faster to get to her. "Wait."

The quicker I moved, the more terrified she appeared. Before I could reach her, she pivoted on her heel and all but ran from the ballroom, weaving through the crowd as she dashed toward the elevators.

Something inside of me snapped.

I would not let her run from me. Not again. Not here. Not after everything she already put me through. I refused to let her go without some sort of explanation, at least.

She flew into an elevator and it closed behind her. By the time I got to the bank, Amir closed in beside me, having witnessed the entire exchange. He whipped out his phone and pulled up the security feeds.

"She got in a lift that was on its way up," he mumbled, checking the footage to see which button she pressed. His thumb stabbed the call button for me, summoning another cart. "Fiftieth floor."

That made sense. The system shut down the rest of the building automatically at eight P.M. Marco set it up that way, ensuring all the other buttons in the elevators would lock after hours. My floor usually required a key-code, but Amir left it unlocked for the gala in case I needed to dip upstairs at some point during the event.

"Go down to the first, in case she turns the elevator right back around when she gets up there," I directed, already pressing the button for the top floor. "If she tries to leave, have her wait for me."

I'd be damned if Ella Callahan got away from me again.

Ella

By the time my logic caught up to my adrenaline, the elevator spat me into the top floor of the building. The second the doors folded open, I leapt out, needing fresh air and room to breathe.

Too late, it occurred to me that I should have gone down instead of up. When I heard a different cart ding behind me, I rushed forward, into whatever dark floor I selected in my blind panic. My knees went out, sending me to the ground. My body doubled over until I felt cold marble against my forehead.

Another ping sounded at my back. Renewed horror surged through me.

"Ella!"

I recognized the voice, but not the fury. In all the time Grayson and I spent together, he'd never said my name with such violent bitterness.

"Ella!" he shouted again. "Goddamn you! I know you're up here."

I tried to breathe. To squeak. Anything. But every muscle in my body clenched tight.

Footsteps surged toward me, coming closer. Suddenly, they stopped, then broke into a run. "Ella? Jesus. Did you fall?"

He dropped to his knees at my side, his hand going to my curved spine. "Talk to me," he ordered, gruff with concern and frustration. "Say something, Ellie."

I tried, but the only sound that escaped came from the sobs wracking my body. Grayson sighed quietly. "Oh, baby." His hand slid up to cup the back of my head. "You're okay."

He didn't know how wrong he was. I'd never been less okay. But he continued anyway.

"You're safe," he murmured, bending close. "We're safe. I'm here with you and I won't let anything bad happen to you."

Little did he know, *he* was the bad thing happening to me.

Even so, his deep even voice and the warmth of his touch started to dissolve my hysteria. Because, danger or no, he was Gray—sure and steady and oh-so-beloved.

Gradually, he unfolded me and pulled me upright. My terror drained away, leaving me chilled and mortified. "I'm so sorry," I mumbled, moving to give him space. "I'm so, *so* sorry, Gray."

In the unlit gloom of the abandoned office floor, shadows filled his features, shading under his sculpted cheekbones, around the stubble kissing his wide jaw and his etched lips. He ground his teeth together as his emerald eyes shifted, full of turmoil.

His pain sliced my soul, carving it to tatters. Tears slid down my cheeks. “I’m so sorry for all of it, Grayson,” I cried. “I never wanted to hurt you. I hate myself for it. And I hate myself for being here, now, putting you through it all over again.”

The ledge of his dark brows lowered over his eyes. They flashed at me, betraying his wrath once more. “Then *don’t*.”

He shoved to his feet, pushing both hands through the thick waves on top of his head before he started to pace. “Christ, Ella, you can stop this bullshit anytime you want! Just *tell me* what the fuck happened to us. Tell me so I can finally fix it or forget it or accept it, instead of keeping me wrapped up in this mystery and all of the misery that comes with it.”

I rose unsteadily, trailing after him as I pled for understanding. “I can’t, Gray!” I wept, tripping over my heels. “I told you that. It isn’t that I don’t *want* to—*I can’t explain*.”

It was too dangerous. For him. For me. For people we loved.

But, as much as I wished he would comprehend… he didn’t. Outrage twisted his gorgeous face, turning his expression into a cruel sneer I’d never seen before.

“I suppose you *can’t* answer my other question, either, right?” he bellowed, his baritone echoing off the semicircle of glass partitions dividing the vacant floor. “All these years. All this fucking torture you put me through. And you still won’t even tell me if what we had was *real!* If what I spent *months* mourning was ever even there to start with!”

He’d asked me as much on Saturday morning. And I declined to answer, hoping to spare him from further heartache. Even though it killed me to deny him.

But he didn’t see it that way. He thought I refused to reply out of some selfish fear. An instinctive rush of indignation rose inside of me, pushing out the truth.

"*Of course* it was real!" I shrieked. "How can you even *ask* me that? I *loved* you, Gray! And I *know* you felt it. What you and I had… it was *always real*."

Deafening silence pressed down around us. I watched my words sink in, knocking him back a step. His entire frame went taut as his chest heaved, dragging in air.

Then, with a desperate growl, Grayson lunged.

His arms hauled me up into his large, powerful chest, pinning me there while his lips crushed mine with bruising force. My nails clawed at his tuxedo jacket, somewhere between shoving him away and holding on for dear life. When I gasped, he invaded my mouth, sliding deep on a possessive plunge.

The dam holding me together collapsed. Years' worth of longing and love and passion spilled forth, soaking into my soul. Alive with the joy of being in his arms again, every nerve sang out, tingling in my toes, my fingertips, the tips of my breasts. He chased the tremors with his large, warm hands, smoothing them over my arms and clutching at my back to bring our chests flush.

A simmer started low in my belly as he stroked his tongue over mine in lush licks. My hands slid up over the broad strength of his shoulders, grasping the hair neatly combed at his nape and tugging it until he emitted a low groan so carnal it sent a rush of wetness down my thighs. When I moaned in response, he yanked me higher against his torso, holding me there as he turned and strode deeper into the office.

I tried to wrap my legs around his body, seeking pressure against the ache at the apex of my thighs, but my dress trapped my knees together. With a grunt, Grayson set me against the cool glass of the nearest partition and dropped to his knees to fist my hem. Tugging hard, he tore the whole thing right up to my hip.

Oh my…

I didn't have time to react. He rose just as swiftly, reaching up to capture my chin in an iron grip. Hungry eyes smoldered down at me, his jaw worked while he gritted, "I am so fucking mad at you."

My breasts grazed his chest as I forced my lungs to expand. "Do you want me to go?"

I would have understood if he sent me away forever, ripped dress and all. In his shoes, most people probably would have. But instead of snapping back or shoving away, Grayson sank his gaze into me for an endless moment, searching. Whatever he found left a sharp, bright gleam in his eye.

One breath later, I was back in his solid grasp. His hands skimmed down my legs, hitching them up and bending them around his abdomen as he carried me through one final portal. A heavy glass door swung shut behind us.

Dizzy from desire, I pulled back just long enough to get a fuzzy image of our surroundings. An office. His, if the size and view were any indication. Not to mention the way he promptly pushed the contents of the desk aside without a second thought.

He settled me on the edge of the smoked glass, parting my thighs to step between them while he panted down at me. His verdant eyes burned into mine once more. "I don't care if it kills me, later. I need you right now."

But he was still. Waiting. Asking me for permission, giving me a chance to stop him.

Love washed over me in a heated rush. I reached up to stroke his cheek, committing the fierce lines of his face to memory. He surprised me by nuzzling roughly into my touch, his stubble scraping a sensitive spot along my wrist where my pulse thrummed.

I sensed the struggle within him. He didn't know if he wanted to pleasure me or punish me. For a brief moment, while our gazes melded into one another, his gentler instincts took over. When he pressed his lips against the center of my palm, the familiar gesture broke me.

"Take me," I whispered, going for his fly. "I need you, too."

On a gruff moan, he sealed our mouths together, slanting his open lips over mine in that delicious way that never failed to make my nipples pucker. His fingers made quick work of the zipper at my back while I shoved his boxers and tuxedo pants out of my way.

His cock sprang out to me, just as large and magnificent as I remembered. Thick, with veins visibly throbbing up to the wide head. I took him in my hand the same second I saw him, tugging on the pulsing shaft until he groaned against my tongue. I worked him harder, closing my fist over the crown every time I slid my touch over him.

While I gloried in his perfect body, Grayson tore into mine. I felt his rage in every move he made. The tender, sensual man who used to take me to my limits was gone, replaced by a thundering tempest.

He yanked my dress down, tore the straps of my bra from my shoulders, and cupped his hands around my breasts with surprising alacrity. When I increased the pace of my hand, he growled and bit my lower lip hard enough to bruise.

His fingers flew from kneading my tits to pushing past my panties. When he found my slick center, he snarled and pulled back to stare down at me. Watching with turbulent eyes, Gray played over my swollen folds until I whimpered.

The sound brought a haughty smirk to his sculpted mouth. Any trace of affection drained from his gaze. "You're soaking wet," he told me. "Like you haven't had any in ages. Doesn't your *boyfriend* ever get you off?"

His callous derision stole my breath just as much as his fingers on my aching center. I swallowed against a hoarse lump of hurt while the muscles in my core gave a vicious twinge.

"Doesn't he rub you here?" The pad of his forefinger glanced over my throbbing clit. I gasped, pushing up into his expert strokes.

"Or… here?" He slid back to dip the tip of his middle finger into my trembling sex. It clutched at him, trying to pull his touch deeper. He made a tormented sound. "Goddamn it, your pussy is so greedy. What's the matter? Your new man doesn't *fuck* you the way I used to?"

Pain slashed into my heart, piercing the most tender place. "Gray," I cried, my eyes filling. "I—"

What could I say? I knew I'd shatter into a million pieces if he kept taunting me; but I'd die if he stopped touching me.

"You *what*?" he demanded, swirling his fingers over me again. "Let me guess. You're *sorry*? Just not sorry enough to do anything about it, though, right, sweetheart?"

Despite the hurt pinching my stomach, my clit sent tingles down my legs. I shook while I replied, "I *am* sorry."

He pressed harder, eliciting a moan I couldn't control. "I don't believe you, Ella," he growled. "But, right now, I don't give a damn. I'm going to fuck you over this desk anyway. Give this needy pussy something to remember me by."

I hated that he made it sound like a threat, but I still wanted what he threatened. The pain in my chest and the pleasure trembling through my core fought for supremacy. Like he was ripping me in half.

Still, I couldn't resist giving him the affection he deserved. Even if he didn't think me worthy of the same reverence.

I started at the hard line of his jaw, brushing my lips up to his ear. I pressed my face against his neck, humming softly while my hands went back to stroking his burgeoning cock. I gripped him exactly the way he liked, relishing the steely velvet feel of him and tightening my grip slightly on every pass.

His body started to sway into my hand, pushing the shaft through my fingers faster and faster while he increased the pressure against my pulsing clit. He teased my slit again, groaning when I spasmed around his fingertips. His balls drew tight.

"Goddamn you, Ella," he murmured, his eyes shifting while his features hardened. "I hate you for doing this to me."

I'd never known such pain. A sob broke from my lips before I could help it. Then another and one more after that. "I'm so sor—"

"Don't." His voice whipped between us. "Stop apologizing and take off your panties. Now."

My heart hammered into my ribs as I hurried to obey him. Still fully dressed aside from his open trousers, Gray stretched over the expanse of his desk and slid a drawer open. The same second my underwear hit the floor, a condom landed in my lap.

"Put it on me."

I hated the cold bite of his voice. But I loved *him*. So desperately, I could barely breathe.

Blinking back tears, I tore the foil wrapper open. His hips shifted restlessly as I sheathed his erection. Before I drew another unsteady breath, he pulled me forward and thrust into me.

Just like the rest of our encounter, pain-filled pleasure marked the moment we collided. After years without him, his thick cock took my body to its absolute limit. He stretched me full, quelling the empty ache inside of me while sending a burn through the tender tissues. The stab pushed a fresh round of wetness to my eyes and they finally spilled over.

I expected Gray's hands to fall to my hips and position me the way he wanted; but, instead, they cupped my cheeks, raising my face to his. Our gazes locked. He saw my tears.

All of his harsh lines faded, revealing anguish that saturated every plane of his perfect face. Shame swirled over me, squeezing my eyes shut as more tears rained down onto my bare chest.

"Ellie."

I thought I imagined him whispering my nickname. But then his arm banded around me, holding me against his torso while his other hand stroked over my cheek.

"Look at me."

Unable to resist the unexpected warmth in his words, I lifted my eyes back to his. Gray stared right into me, offering wounded windows into his battered soul. His fingertips chased the tears from my face.

Without another word, he started to move, giving small, gentle thrusts while holding my gaze. The sting persisted, but I couldn't focus on it. Not when I had the only man I'd ever loved pressing his forehead against mine, watching my every move with tender concern.

One of his hands fell to my lap, slipping between our bodies. He circled his thumb over the aching bud at the top of my folds. I lost my breath, biting my lip while my eyes fell closed.

He nuzzled our temples together. "Good girl. You're pulling me in deeper," he rumbled. "And *pulsing*. Fuck, you feel so perfect."

I turned my face into his cheek, panting. "So do you. I missed you."

I felt myself throb all around him while my body tugged his further into mine, desperate to clench down on him when I came. His thumb slid slightly lower, rubbing a very bottom of my clitoris. Everything inside of me seized, then burst. A rush of liquid heat melted through my core, bathing his cock while he rocked into my release.

"Dear *God*, Ellie," he gasped, pumping his hips harder. His voice tightened along with all the muscles in his back. "You came so hard, but your pussy wants more. It's still gripping me. Begging me to keep fucking you."

"Yes," I admitted, breathless. "Please don't stop."

He adjusted the angle of his drives, stroking over the bundle of nerves hidden deep inside my sex. My head fell back as a fresh round of need surged through my center. I bucked against him, grinding into his touch and the rock-hard slide of his erection.

"Gray," I cried, mindless. "Oh my God. *Gray!*"

My core clutched at him, drawing ravenously at his thickness as I came for a second time in as many minutes. Grayson's answering roar echoed off the walls of his office, reverberating through me as he fucked me through my climax and buried his face against my shoulder before giving into his own.

As he finished, a mournful moan rolled out of him. The serrated sound made my heart stutter. I reached up, stroking my hands over his hair to soothe him while he shook.

For one sweet moment, he stayed in my arms and let me love him. I held him as close as I could, knowing it might be the last time I ever had the chance. He seemed to feel the same way—his muscled arms enveloped my entire frame, pulling me into him and holding fast.

Behind him, a crash ricocheted through the empty floor. Grayson sprang back, disengaging with a brutal curse. "Someone's here. We need to go."

Grayson

With every second that ticked past, the temperature in my office dropped. Plummeting us from our warm afterglow to frigid unease. While I fumbled to right my tuxedo, Ella dropped to her knees to scour for her underwear.

I read it in every shadow on her face: she regretted what we'd done.

I knew I should, too. And the fact that I couldn't seem to summon even a shred of remorse left me… *enraged.*

What the fuck was wrong with me? This woman was the very last person I could ever trust. She'd gutted me more times than I cared to count.

All the times she ran from what we had. Leaving me without so much as a word. Disappearing completely. Dedicating her book to me. Being as light and lovely as ever when I finally managed to hunt her down. Refusing to explain herself. Making me want her. Letting me have her.

With her panties back on, she rose on shaky legs. I noted the way she held her torn dress together over her thigh; how she kept her eyes cast down and her head bent in shame.

And, because I was the stupidest sap in the history of the world, I felt *bad*. And then instantly hated myself for pitying her.

Self-loathing sank through my center, spurring me into action. I tossed the evidence of our hook-up into my trash can and pushed my work back to the center of my desk.

Work, I reminded myself. *My job. My father. My family's entire legacy. The single most important speech I've ever given, which I'm supposed to be preparing for right now.*

Meanwhile I was upstairs fucking my ex on company property and, in the process, very nearly falling right back in love with her despite still having no clear answers as to why she ever left me. Or why she tried to run from me again that night.

The truth of that thought soaked into my soul, numbing it. *She's still just as damaged and flighty as she was back then. Loving me three years ago didn't keep her from running scared and nothing ever will.*

My shame expanded into a mushroom cloud of dread. *I can't afford to do this. I can't fuck up my life like this again.*

I needed to go.

But, still, I stood there and stared. Hoping, against all reason, that she would *say something*. Explain herself. Anything.

In the end, though, she didn't even lift her face. I heard her crying, but refused to go to her. Couldn't, even though part of me desperately wanted to abandon all pride for her once again.

No. Not this time. Before the ache in my chest could override my determination, I stuffed my hands into my pockets and strode past her.

My voice was hollow. "If you'd excuse me, I'm expected on stage shortly. There's a service elevator to the left of the regular lifts. It will take you down to the garage. If you'd please use that to exit, I'd appreciate your discretion."

And then, for the first time, I left her.

Chapter Eighteen

December 2013

Grayson

"What the fuck are we doing here?"

Graham did not stop bitching for one moment during our lunch. He hated the holidays, the cold weather, final exams, Christmas music, his mother. He bought her an expensive brooch at Bendel's anyway, though. Because, in his words, "I'll get my money back when the old bitch kicks."

We had a half-assed tradition of gift shopping together. It started back in our freshman year, as way to be sure we didn't buy sorority sisters the same trinkets and piss them off. Now, he objected to my final stop on our outing.

Cartier.

"I'm meeting my mom. I need her opinion," I grumbled. "You can go text one of those chicks who gave you their numbers at the restaurant."

Graham's face stretched into a shit-eating grin. "Your *mom*? Oh, shit. How do I look? Is my tie straight?"

He had on the most absurd pink suit I'd ever seen, but he also got three phone numbers over lunch. Though, two of them tried to flirt with me before moving on to him. Now he'd try to get his revenge by flirting with my mother.

At my murderous glare, his smile grew. "I can't help that she's the sexiest woman on the Upper East Side."

I cocked my head to side, considering. "I can't decide if I should punch you or drop-kick you."

Unbothered, he brushed at his sleeves. "This suit is silk, you animal. At least wait until we're inside."

"Oh you're not coming inside," I informed him, then checked my watch. 1:57. "In fact I think it's time for you to go."

After a few more MILF jokes, Graham hailed a cab and melted into the crush. Three minutes later, my mother's Maybach arrived.

Barnes' grim figure appeared to open the rear door. Mom slid from the backseat, dressed impeccably in a creamy dress with a matching fur-trimmed coat and tall suede boots.

Her eyes smiled at me as she kissed both of my cheeks and slipped her arm through mine. "So what's with all the secrecy, *mi amor*? Where are we going?"

I didn't have the balls to tell her my plan over the phone. That seemed stupid now that we were standing in front of the jeweler.

Still, I hedged my reply. "I need help choosing something for Ella."

The gleam in her eyes doubled. "Ooh! How exciting! A Christmas gift?"

God, am I really doing this? "Something like that."

I led her out of the Fifth Avenue throng, under Cartier's signature crimson awnings. Holiday greenery and twinkling lights surrounded the doors and windows. A doorman nodded to us as we entered. "Mrs. Stryker. Lovely to see you again, ma'am."

My mother offered him a cool smile as we passed. I caught him lift his wrist to speak into a hidden mic there—likely heralding the arrival of one of their best customers.

Sure enough, not one minute later, a saleswoman dressed in festive green met us in the center of the polished marble foyer.

"Mrs. Stryker," she purred. "So good to see you again. Doing a little holiday shopping today?"

Amused, my mom cast me a questioning look. I cleared my throat. "Actually, we have an appointment. Under Grayson Stryker."

The saleslady quailed slightly, chagrinned. At the same moment, my mother's brows snapped up. "We do?"

"We do," I nodded, forcing confidence. My gaze dropped to my watch. A Rolex—lest anyone question my net worth. "Two PM."

"Of course, Mr. Stryker," the woman replied, recovering her poise. "Right this way."

She directed us up a grand staircase, under several more holiday garlands. The second floor opened into a large room full of creamy curtains and display cases. We walked right past all of them, to a semi-private vestibule. Sheer ivory fabric draped down from the ceiling, obstructing our table from view.

By the time we both took our seats, my mother was staring at me like she'd never seen me before. Even so, she waited for the greeter to excuse herself before she turned to me, gaping. "You called ahead?"

I half-smiled. "I've been here twice in the last two weeks. This is just the final decision."

Concern pinched her pretty features. "*Mi amor*, I'm sure whatever you choose will be very dear to Ella. And she's not a fussy girl... I'm not even certain she would want you to go to such an expense."

Ordinarily, she'd be right. But this was different.

Our concierge joined us before I could reply. The elegant older woman, Bridget, lacked the thinly-veiled avarice her younger counterparts couldn't quite conceal. I found her on my second trip to the store and immediately determined that she would get my commission. The fact that she proceeded to spend nearly an hour weighing the merits of various pieces without once pushing one on me only sealed the deal.

Bridget smiled warmly at me. "Mr. Stryker."

I stood, offering her my hand. "Grayson, please, Bridget. And this is my mother, Jacqueline. She's here to help me make a final decision."

"Lovely." She set a portable leather case on the table top and took the chair across from ours. To my mother, she added, "Your son has excellent taste, madam. And he's been very patient about finding just the right thing. If he were my son, I'd be very proud."

Mom grinned at me. "Oh, I am."

I cleared my throat again, attempting to dispel the whirl of emotion rising in my chest. "Yes, well. This is an important decision."

Again, Mom looked bemused. "It's only a Christmas gift, darling. I know Ella will adore whatever you select..."

Bridget and I shared a conspiratorial glance. A tiny smile played at her lips. "Shall we show her?"

I breathed through an exhilarating rush of nerves, waving my hand at the case. "By all means."

With care, she opened her special briefcase and extracted four ring boxes, opening each before lining all four up to face us.

I watched my mother's mouth fall open. "*Dios mío*," she breathed, swiveling to clutch my arm. Excitement gradually filled her face. "Grayson!?"

I had to chuckle at her obvious delight. "Don't get too excited," I muttered. "She hasn't said yes yet."

The sick stab of fear that sliced into my center had almost become commonplace. In the weeks since Thanksgiving, I spent every free moment plotting my proposal... and worrying that the whole thing might scare Ella off for good.

On the other hand, if she agreed, I'd have everything I could ever want.

For one single question, the stakes were alarmingly high.

Mom bounced in place, abandoning all pretense of sophistication. A stream of Spitalian and English hurled out of her. Something about finally having a daughter... and grandchildren...

I gulped again, swallowing my apprehension and turning back to the jewelry. *One thing at a time.*

"Well," Bridget started, sensing my resolve. "As I said, your son's taste is beyond reproach. He's narrowed it down to four beautiful pieces."

Her French manicure brushed over each case in turn as she described the rings. "The canary yellow diamond. A four-carat stone, set in twenty-four carat gold. As you can see, aside from the bold color choice, it's fairly plain."

Mom pursed her lips at the yellow diamond. "Ella does like color."

I pictured her that morning before school, dressed in hot pink tights, an orange corduroy jumper, and a sky-blue turtleneck. All with her crazy flower coat and infamous clogs, of course.

A wide grin pulled at my lips. "Yes, she does."

"Color can clash, though," Mom added, in her element. "Especially with formalwear."

Bridget nodded at me. "We had the same thought. As you can see, the other rings are more traditional." She gestured to the flashiest in the bunch—a huge cushion-cut stone surrounded by two rows of tinier rocks, all set in a shimmering diamond band.

Mom picked up the case, moving it under the lights. The ring glittered from every angle. "This one is a show-stopper," she murmured, transfixed.

Secretly, it was my least favorite. I couldn't picture my girl wearing something so ostentatious. But I also wanted her to have the very best. And the concept of a ring that would stop other men in their tracks—marking her as mine the second they saw her—held some appeal...

Bridget swapped the case for another. "And this is an ultra-classic brilliant cut. Platinum band. Modern setting. We have the option to add a halo…"

I could see that it didn't thrill my mom. "Too plain for me," she admitted. "Though I believe Ella prefers simple pieces."

I held my breath while both women turned to the final ring. A flat, soft gold band with an intricate antique claw held one wide, flawless oval diamond. Before I realized what I was doing, I plucked up the case and held it between my palms.

"I picked this one," I confessed. "I'm not quite sure *why*…"

Bridget frowned ponderously. "Well, the four carat center stone has the highest ratings possible for color, cut, and clarity. It is an unusual piece, though. Vintage. We recovered that stone from a Victorian heirloom. The setting is from the 1920s."

Old. Not at all my style. And, probably, not what most girls dreamed of when they pictured their engagement ring…

I only knew that it somehow reminded me of the chilly mornings I spent huddled with Ellie in Central Park, listening to her transform pointless prose into poetry. And the nights we sat on the floor in front of my furnace, spoiling our dinner with liqueur-spiked hot chocolates. And the spun gold of her hair when sunlight slanted across our bed.

With a resigned sigh, I set the box back in our line-up. "So, Mom, what do you think?"

A sheen of mischief glossed her gaze. "I have an idea. We will both close our eyes and point to our favorite ring. That way, we can eliminate the other two."

I smirked at her silliness. "Mother. We're in Cartier."

She squeezed my arm. "Oh, no one can see us! And it'll be fun! Come on!"

In the end, I agreed because it had been far too long since I saw her so happy. "Fine. On the count of three?"

"Perfect."

I played along, closing my eyes. As she counted down, I found I didn't have time to overthink. I pointed to the vintage ring and opened my eyes, only to find my mother and Bridget grinning at me… and both of Mom's hands firmly folded in her lap.

"See? You knew which one all along." Humor and pride swirled in her eyes. "Ella loves *you*. Your opinion is the only one that matters, Grayson."

Fresh emotion clogged my throat as Bridget swept the other three away. "We have a winner," she agreed.

I picked up the ring again, staring down at it. Certainty settled inside of me.

"I'll need it insured," I whispered, trying my best to remain practical. "And gift-wrapped."

Ella

Maggie stuck her tongue out at me. "Ew, no. Next."

With a sigh, I flung the red poncho into the box on my left labeled, "Goodwill." I figured most of the clothes were from there, anyway. Might as well send them home.

The last item was a rainbow striped sweater. My roommate wagged her head back and forth. "Eh. Keep it. It makes your boobs look good."

With a laugh, I dropped the shirt into the box on my right and plopped back onto my mattress, glancing around at the empty walls. My half of our tiny room seemed barren already, and I hadn't even moved out yet.

"I can't believe this is really happening," I mumbled.

Maggie alternated between over-protective, cautionary tirades about how fickle men could be and wistful sighing. Today, it seemed, she settled on the former. Her brows arched in a look of pure mistrust. "So how, exactly, is this all going down?"

I rolled my eyes. "We've been over this a thousand times! You know the plan."

"Right, right," she grunted, scooting back on her own bed. "You're putting all your shit in a storage facility in Midtown?"

"Near the new apartment," I confirmed. "Yep."

Mag's eyes narrowed. "The alleged apartment?"

Laughing, I chucked a balled-up poster at her. "Are you implying that my boyfriend is only *pretending* to have an apartment for us to share? You think he's trying to lure me out of Brooklyn and having me move all of my stuff uptown into a storage unit for… what? Kicks?"

She pouted, stubborn as ever. "I'm saying that this all happened so fast that my head is spinning!" she huffed. "Do I at least get to *see* this apartment?"

"Of course you will! As soon as we're moved in."

In truth, I hadn't even seen it yet. I only knew it was located in one of the Strykers' holdings—a building in the Flatiron District, where I could be relatively close to school and work and Grayson could run back and forth from their company's current location downtown and the site of their new building.

Ever since his father decided to give Gray a chance by moving ahead with his concept for their new headquarters, my man exceeded all expectations. He finished strong on his finals, went to work with renewed dedication, and hunched over his drafting table at every available opportunity.

Pride warmed my heart every time I thought of him, concentrating on his latest round of sketches, tracing and re-tracing lines, perfecting each angle. Where he used to come home weary and brooding, now he surged into his apartment each evening with a smile and went right to his drafting table to add new notes.

"I have pictures," I offered to Maggie, not for the first time. "I told you, we can't actually get in until the second of January. The current tenants' lease lasts until the end of the month. But when I gave notice with student housing, they told me I had to have my stuff out of here by December twentieth. So I got a temporary storage unit. It's basically a closet. And cheap. They let me pay cash since I'm using it for two weeks."

Maggie crossed her slender arms. "Mm hmm. And how much did you have to give Grayson for the apartment?"

"Nothing!" I cried, exasperated by her interrogation and Gray's ridiculous generosity. "He pays for *everything*. I looked at my account yesterday and swore the bank made a mistake; then I realized, I haven't grocery shopped or paid for my own coffee in *months*. Last week, I thought I needed to buy tampons and then I found *three boxes* under his sink. The fancy ones, too. And I swear he slips twenties into my jeans whenever he gets a chance—I never take out cash but I keep finding it in my pants!"

Maggie glowered. "I think I hate you."

Before I could backpedal, she flashed a teasing grin. "I'm just *kidding*, Elle. If anyone in this whole city deserves a Prince Charming, it's you."

Most of the time, I really did feel like I lived in a fairy tale. Only better, somehow, because as romantic and wonderful as our story was, it was also *real*.

He bought me *tampons*. We argued over the right way to fold *bath towels*. His generic pop music made me groan; and my everything-on-the-side restaurant orders usually earned me a few muttered grumbles when he called for takeout.

It all seemed imperfectly perfect… aside from the fact that he still hadn't told me he loved me.

While I, to my eternal shame, proceeded to tell him again. Twice. Both times during the throes of passion.

He felt bad about it. I saw guilt in the tight set of his jaw every time I caught him staring at me.

By now, the guilt was old news. And honestly? It was his new, jumpy-yet-solemn stare that made my stomach flip. And not in a good way.

The strange look started a few days before. The day he finished his finals and then went to lunch with Graham. He burst into his apartment an hour earlier than usual, arms full of bags, rushing like a fugitive hoping to conceal himself.

When he found me sitting in my usual spot with my American Literature notes spread out in my lap, he froze. Obviously, he didn't expect me to be home… and, for the first time *ever*, he didn't seem to want me there, for some reason.

Of course, after stashing his bags in his closet and pulling himself together, he then proceeded to order us dinner, quiz me for my final, and reward me for my correct answers by putting his head between my thighs.

So, clearly, nothing was *really* wrong… right?

I placated my misgivings by telling myself that I didn't know one single thing for sure. After all, he never *said* he felt guilty. Or nervous. Or weirdly intense. Those were all inferences I made.

As far as concrete evidence, all signs pointed to a man who loved me every bit as much as I loved him.

When we weren't talking about his budding building or my move uptown, Gray devoted a hefty portion of our conversations to making sure I wouldn't want for anything. He asked me questions about my favorite types of décor, color preferences, snack foods I liked to eat.

It took me a few days to realize he wasn't just playing a question game with me—he wanted to know so he could adjust things to my liking. Already, I'd received a mile-long text from Jacqueline "confirming" my favorite foods… all relayed to her by my boyfriend. She also verified my favorite Christmas movies, holiday desserts, and the type of pillow I preferred.

Before Grayson, I wasn't aware one could *have* a pillow preference; but he was nothing if not thorough.

I knew he'd be mad when he found out I did the whole move uptown by myself, but I didn't want to burden him. Besides, Maggie said she didn't mind. She said it a few times, actually, since I kept apologizing all the way down the block to Goodwill; and maybe a couple more times as we rode the subway with my five boxes, two suitcases, and our purses.

While I tried not to panic about the possibility of someone robbing us blind, she told me about the new apartment she found in DUMBO. It sounded way nicer than student housing. I was grateful for that—I knew I'd feel bad if I got to move into a gorgeous new pad and left Maggie stuck with some stranger in her room.

By the time we stuffed ourselves and my crap into a cab, then unloaded it all at the storage place, we were both out of things to say. We stood on the freezing cold sidewalk in silence, both trying not to cry while we said goodbye.

Finally, Maggie threw her arms around me and hauled me up in vice-tight hug. "You'll call me? If Prince Charming turns out to be a dickhead on a donkey?"

I wanted to laugh, but instead tears flooded my eyes. "I'll call you *no matter what.* And I'll see you in a couple of weeks, I hope? We can go thrifting before classes start?"

Mags nodded as she reached into her purse and pulled out a gift bag. "For you," she said, cracking half a smile. "…and Prince Charming."

That reminded me; Gray was waiting for me. Maggie and I hugged again before she disappeared into the subway. I decided to hail another cab, figuring I could go a bit over-budget on transportation since I'd be eating with the Strykers for a week.

By the time I pushed my suitcases into the Upper West Side apartment, my cheeks were numb. Which may have been a good thing, actually, because Grayson in grey boxer-briefs and nothing else typical set them on fire.

Oblivious to his sexiness, he stood at the kitchen island, frowning at his laptop. "Hey," he called, distracted. "I'm just emailing the movers. When did you say you had to be out of there? I thought you said the twentieth but that can't be right because that would be two days from today and, surely, I'm not *that* incompetent."

I giggled, unwinding my red scarf and kicking my clogs off. My bell-bottoms were soaked around the ankles from sloshing through city slush, so I shucked those, too, leaving me in a periwinkle sweatshirt and embarrassing pink panties.

"The deadline is the twentieth," I confirmed, sidling up to his hard, hot body. "But don't bother with the movers. Maggie and I just finished putting my boxes into my storage unit thirty minutes ago. It's all done."

As I predicted, disapproval pushed Grayson's bushy brows down over his eyes. "Tell me you're kidding."

I shrugged, reaching around him for a sip of his coffee. "I didn't want to add all of that to your plate so I just took care of it," I said again. "Easy peasy."

With a frustrated sigh, Grayson settled his arms around my middle. "You *are* my plate," he said, then shook his head at himself. "Jesus. I really *am* an idiot. But you know what I mean, right?"

"Yes," I chuckled, running my palm across his stubbly cheek. "I know. You're my plate, too."

With a flash of his heart-stopping grin, Grayson ducked his head. His lips moved softly over mine, then settled in for a kiss that chased the chill right out of my body, leaving me breathless and flushed.

He finally pulled back to run his nose down the length of mine. "Thank you for trying to take something off of my list."

"Trying?" I scoffed, teasing him. "Pretty sure I *succeeded*."

While he laughed, his gaze traveled over my shoulder to my suitcase. He spied the gift on top of my bag. "Maggie got you a present?"

I slipped away to retrieve the silver parcel. "It's for you, too."

Grayson snorted a smirk. "*Maggie* got *me* a present?"

I shrugged. "She said it was for both of us. Probably something for the new apartment." I pushed it at him. "Here, you open it."

With an expression of pure suspicion, he reached into the tissue paper and rustled around, extracting…

Grayson's rich laughter filled the room. "What *is* it?"

But—oh *God*—I knew what it was. I knew *exactly* what it was.

My entire body turned red while I covered my face and groaned. Gray laughed some more, speaking through his chortles. "Seriously, you're going to have to fill me in here. Is it a… pipe of some sort? Or a paperweight? A unicorn horn?"

That tipped me over the edge. The pink glass—shaped like thick, swirly icicle—really *did* look like a unicorn's horn.

I shook with laughter, shaking my head. "No! It's a—" I made a completely unladylike snorking sound. "A—" I couldn't breathe deeply enough to speak. Even if I could, I didn't know which word to use.

"A watch holder?" he guessed. "A freezer ornament?"

"*A dildo*."

Gray turned the textured glass tube in his hands. "*Oh*. I see it now." He held the piece out to me, giving a blasé lift of his shoulders. "A pink glass dildo. Naturally. You know, I'm relieved. Because I honestly don't know how we ever could have survived moving in together without such an essential."

I giggled some more, rolling the thing between my palms. My face furrowed while I considered the logistics of it. "Won't it be *cold*?"

His muscled arm snagged my waist while he chuckled quietly. "Not if I put it in your mouth first."

A fresh blush warmed my chest. I bit my lip. "Hmm. I see."

His emerald eyes swirled. "I'll let you warm it up and then I'll put it inside of you while I suck on your clit. Give you something to clamp down on."

Well, then.

Mischief played around his sculpted lips. "You know what? I think you need a demonstration."

I eyed the dildo, imagining all the surprises he might have in store for me. I wanted them, but not as much as I wanted something else.

"But I just want you," I told him, cupping my hands around his face.

All humor melted away, leaving his features stark. Vulnerability softened his gaze. "Just me, huh?"

Why did it feel like we weren't talking about sex anymore? It didn't matter. My answer was the same, no matter what he meant. "Yes. Only you, Gray."

He gathered me into his arms, bringing our bodies together. "Always."

❊❊❊

Chapter Nineteen

October 2016

Ella

Ruined.

I'd felt that way many times, in the years since that one horrible night at that one horrible party. But I don't think I ever truly *believed* it until I found myself shuffling through Stryker & Sons' garage, with my dress ripped up to the hip, my coat lost to the coat check I couldn't access, and my phone God-knew-where.

Not to mention my heart, which I also left upstairs. Laid in front of Grayson's desk like some sacrificial offering. And eviscerated like one, too.

"Miss Callahan?"

Halfway across the expanse between the elevators and the sloping drive up to the sidewalk above, Marco called after me. My shoulders tweaked up at the sound of his deep voice, steeped in surprise.

Oh Lord. My mortification was complete. I was torn, tear-stained, fleeing the scene of a sexual encounter and my subsequent abandonment.

And he caught me.

With no other option, I turned to face him, doing my best to smooth my puffy, reddened features and offer him a small smile. "Hi, Marco."

His face was awful. So full of pity. My stomach twisted as he replied, "I saw you on the security cameras by yourself… do you need help?"

"Do I need *help*?" I wasn't even sure how to respond to that question in that moment. A manic giggle almost burst out of me. "Well…"

His face furrowed. "Let me get you a car, Miss Callahan. Do you have… anything? Your coat or a purse, maybe?"

"I had both," I admitted. "But I… there's a problem with my dress, as you can see… so, I really just need to leave now."

The truth was, even if my dress wasn't in pieces, there were almost half a dozen reasons why I couldn't go back into that ballroom. And all of them made me feel sick.

Unable to stand the seething nausea in my middle, I turned and started scurrying away. He hollered after me again. "Miss Callahan?"

I kept walking, not sure I'd even make it out of the garage before I vomited and Grayson's monitoring system caught the whole humiliating ordeal on camera.

"Miss Callahan!" I heard jogging. A warm hand settled on my shoulder. "Ella."

It was the very first time he had ever used my real name. Surprised, I paused just long enough for him to lightly grip my forearm and pull me toward a row of waiting Mercedes'.

"We have a ton of extra drivers for tonight; I insist you take one of our cars," he murmured, low and concerned. "And I'll do my best to get your personal belongs back to you after we clean up the event."

His kindness sent another rush of tears to my eyes. "Thank you, Marco."

In the comfort of a white sedan, my ride back to Brooklyn passed in a blur of deep-breathing and sob-swallowing. I found our apartment door unlocked and didn't even have the energy to be annoyed. Instead, I shuffled inside and stood on the threshold, looking around our place like I'd never seen it before.

Like a deluge, the enormity of everything that had just happened crashed over me. For the second time that night, I went to my knees, unable to stand up to the fear and sorrow strangling me.

Sometime later, Maggie emerged from her bedroom and found me. Her footsteps dashed across our living room. She dropped down to my side and held fast, waiting for the last of my weeping to subside.

When I finally sat up, she sighed. Sympathy filled her dark eyes. "Did your carriage turn back into a pumpkin?"

I sniffled. "Yes."

"And Price Charming?"

"A dickhead on a donkey," I quoted, not meaning it. But wishing I did.

Grayson

I woke to a vicious hangover and enough self-loathing to fill up my bathtub and drown myself in it.

In the shower, I cringed every time I remembered my actions from the night before. The way I taunted Ella while I was touching her. The glimmer of tears on her pale cheeks. Walking past her and asking her to leave without being seen, basically calling her a shameful secret I wished to keep hidden… moments after coming inside of her.

Banishing all thoughts of Ella didn't help, either. I still had plenty of regrets to haunt me all through my morning routine.

I was distracted during my speech. I didn't even hear Dad's or Daniel's. I all-but ignored Olivia and my mother for the duration of the evening. And I decided to cap off the night by drinking so much gin, I didn't really remember the details of how or when I got home.

I knew I had truly fucked up when I walked into my kitchen and found all of the Ella items I asked Marco to dispose of sitting on my kitchen island. A message, clear as day, from my right-hand man. Only, I didn't understand *why*.

With an aching head and a hollow chest, I lowered myself into the backseat of my car ten minutes later than usual… only to find a stone-faced Amir regarding me through the rearview mirror. *Glaring* at me, actually.

"Sir," he clipped.

Was he… pissed off?

"Amir," I returned. "Is something wrong?"

Marco's stony face didn't so much as flinch. "Your mother called. She asked me to pick her up on our way into the office. Is that alright with you?"

Damn it. She was going to be pissed, too. I fought back the urge to avoid her, knowing it would only make for one more apology I'd eventually owe.

"Fine."

We worked our way up Fifth while I leaned my head back and tried to get it to stop thumping. When we pulled up to my parents' townhome, my mother stood waiting on the sidewalk, looking elegant in a black sheath dress. As anticipated, the climate in the car fell from chilly to glacial as soon as she slid inside.

Without so much as looking over at me, Mom crossed her legs and smoothed her skirt over her knees. "Marco? Close the partition, if you would."

Before I could speak, she held up a staying hand. The glass partition between the front- and backseats slid up while she rummaged in her purse and produced three pills. She held them out, still not meeting my gaze.

"Mom?"

"Ibuprofen." She waved her fist at me until I took the meds from her. "They're for your headache," she informed me. "I'm assuming you must have one after draining all of the Tanqueray on the island of Manhattan."

Her cool rebuke chastened me. I swallowed the pills without argument and leaned back into my headrest once more, shutting my eyes. "Mom, I—"

"Save it," her voice clipped. "Honestly, Grayson. Don't even think about lying to me again."

I didn't plan to lie her… did I? I supposed I would have fib, to tell her I was fine and my behavior didn't stem from some deeper issue… but she had no way of knowing any of that.

Confused, I sat forward and turned to her. "What do you mean?"

Mom cast an uncharacteristically nervous glance at the front seat and the tinted glass separating us from my head of security. She swallowed hard before looking back down at her hands, twisted together in her lap.

"I saw you. Last night."

My stomach dropped to my feet. "You saw…"

"You," she whispered, finally raising her sharp emerald eyes to mine. "And Ella."

Oh dear God. My mind reeled, spinning back through the series of events I'd tried desperately not to remember.

But I did. I remembered all of it. Including the way Ella held me at the end, offering all the same comfort and adoration she used to give me unconditionally. And how we heard a noise that made us jump apart.

"You *saw* us?"

Venom seeped into her gaze and her voice. "Yes," she hissed. "Your office is made of *glass*, Grayson. I went upstairs to fetch some aspirin for your father and…"

She shifted, obviously uncomfortable. "In any case," she went on, "You are a grown man and the CEO of the company. I'm not going to scold you over your sex life."

I felt a flush crawl up my throat. "*Mother*."

At my note of outrage, fury snapped in her eyes. "As your *mother*, I would hope I raised you better than to do something so private in a public place," she continued, scolding even though she said she wouldn't. "Your place of business, no less. Honestly, son. It's disgraceful to display a woman and your intimacies that way. A gentleman protects his partners' privacy."

Hell. She was right. I was reckless with Ella. And I certainly didn't protect her, during or after.

If I was honest with myself, I knew that was the real reason I wound up drinking so much. When I couldn't quite convince myself that she deserved the callousness I displayed, I tried to numb the shame of way I treated her with liquor.

It didn't even work. No amount of gin could banish the fear that I harmed her. I'd barely taken any of her past triggers into account. And I rammed into her without a modicum of control. Recalling the tears that studded her lashes the moment our bodies connected still made me want to wince.

Satisfied by whatever guilt she saw on my face, my mom started to cool. She pinned me with another searching look. "I think you should tell me how this happened."

The last week blurred through my throbbing brain. "We got—I was—Last night was an anomaly, I promise." I rubbed at the back of overheated neck. "I ran into her there, last night and… you know Ella and I have a history. We were just overcome by it for a minute. That's all."

Her fury returned, flashing in her eyes. "I said: *no lies*," Mom bit out. "Try again."

I didn't know what to tell her. Because, really, I didn't even know what to tell myself. How to explain what happened between me and Ella—in the past or over the last few days—and why it occurred. For fuck's sake, I'd been asking myself the same question all morning. Night. Week. For *years*, actually.

But, as I sat there, steeped in guilt, staring at my mother's irate face, hating myself… the answer finally seemed clear.

"I love her," I admitted, to her and myself. "I never managed to stop."

"Finally! The truth." Mom ran her gaze over my face, her lips falling into a pensive frown. "*Mi amor*, if you love her then why are you letting her get away again? You could not find her, before. But now you know where she is and you know she still obviously has feelings for you… why can't you rebuild things?"

Outside my window, the Upper East Side blurred into Midtown. Unable to help myself, I wondered if Ella would be going to work soon. My jaw hardened as I reminded myself, "What she did was unforgivable. I could never trust her."

"Well, I certainly understand the trust issue," Mom relented softly. "By why is what she did so unforgivable? If she truly got scared and ran away… can't you have some compassion for that?"

Truth was, I did. At that very second, vicarious pain pierced my heart. The image of Ella slumped on the floor of my office, struggling to breathe, hit like gut-punch.

She always squeezed her eyes shut and furrowed her brow during panic attacks, as if fighting through every second by sheer force of will. If what happened three years ago was simply the result of her temporarily losing her grip, I knew I would forgive her almost instantly.

But there had to be more to it than that. And she still refused to explain herself.

Instead of delving into the riot inside of me, I blew out an unsteady breath and reached for a tidier, yet equally true, response. "Well, for one, she hurt you guys, too. How could I be with someone who would run off the way she did… knowing what the circumstances were with Dad's illness… our family vacation… She never even apologized. I can't move past that."

It was Mom's turn to look ashamed. Her skin paled as she mashed her lips together. "Grayson… there's something I need to tell you. I almost told you last week, at brunch, when I noticed your scarf, but your father felt it was best for me to leave the past in the past… Now, after what I saw last night, I no longer believe it *is* in the past."

Before I could react, she reached into her purse and extracted a yellow envelope. My scalp prickled at the sight of the curved handwriting on the front. Recognition hit me.

"It's from Ella," Mom whispered, blinking down at it. "She mailed it to me about three months after... the incident. It didn't have a return address, so I opened it."

Gingerly, she set the dandelion square on my charcoal pant-leg, the color brightening all of the monochrome around it. My chest heaved while I stared down, unable to move to pick it up. I knew it might contain the answer I'd been so desperate for so long, but now I wondered… did I *really* want to know?

"What does it say?" I demanded, hoarse. "Does it say *why…*"

"No. It doesn't say a thing about what went on between the two of you. It's an apology. To me. She felt she owed me one after ruining my plans." Mom paused, her expression softening further. "And for hurting you. She knew it would devastate me to see you in so much pain. She apologized for that, as well."

A quiver shot through my hand as I reached for the envelope. My fingers brushed over the loops of her letters, remembering.

"It's a lovely apology," my mother went on, her voice clogged with emotion. "Beautiful, even. When it arrived, I wanted to tell you right away… But you'd just started coming around the house again. Your grades were beginning to recover. You agreed to return to the office. You were so miserable for so long, *mi amor…* Your father and I were scared that reading this would pull you back under."

I remembered that time in my life with surreal horror. The months I spent clawing my way from one day to the next, hanging on to stability by my fingernails.

"If I had known she sent this, I would have gone after her," I realized out loud. "I tried to, at first. I went to her school, her old student housing unit, her friends. They all told me she was gone, out of the city. Then I realized she had blocked my phone number. I thought she hated me; but if I knew she wrote to you, I would have thought there was hope for us."

Mom's frown deepened. "Perhaps there was. Maybe if I'd given it to you…" She shook her head. "I'm sorry, Grayson. I only wanted to protect you from being hurt again."

I turned my face away from her and the letter, peering out at the crush of traffic around us. "It doesn't matter now," I decided. "I can't spend the rest of my life in love with someone who runs from me every time she gets freaked out."

Mom shifted, her air awkward once more. "Did she run away again last night?"

"No." *I did.*

I felt her hand land on the sleeve of my suit. "Then maybe there is hope, after all."

The rest of our ride passed in silence. A few blocks from the office, my mother tapped on the partition and asked Marco to drop her off, pressing a kiss to my cheek before she slid from the car without another word.

By the time we made it into the Stryker & Sons garage, I felt ill. Before Amir got out of the driver's seat, I stopped him. "Marco."

He stilled but did not look at me. "Sir?"

I felt my cheekbones darken. "The cameras on the executive floor. I need the recording from last night wiped."

My head of security raised his hard stare to the rearview mirror. "Already done. After I saw Miss Callahan get into the service elevator with her dress ripped, I deleted all of the footage for the hour preceding her departure."

Ah. That explained all the glaring.

A hot stab of shame poked at me again. "Thank you. Did Ella—I mean, did *Miss Callahan* get to the garage without incident?"

Marco didn't so much as blink. "She was distraught. I had one of our cars take her home."

His intense regard thickened the guilt lodged in my throat, turning my voice into a rasp. "I never should have sent her off like that. I hate myself for it. I'm sorry you had to intervene."

"I returned her other belongings to your apartment, as I'm sure you saw." He finally cast his gaze down. "And I collected her personal effects after the gala. She left in a hurry and didn't want to go upstairs with her dress ripped, so her coat, purse, and cell phone were left behind."

Dear God. A burst of panic gripped me. If Marco hadn't spotted her, she would have been alone, on the streets, without any money or means of contacting anyone.

Because of me.

"I need to take them to her," I determined. "I'll cancel my morning."

Without hesitation, Marco threw the car in gear. "She'll be at her office by now."

I'd figured as much, though I'd never allowed myself to look through the schedule he assembled for me. "Let's go."

Ella

"You're late, Ella."

I hung my head, hiding from Marjorie's shrewd gaze. "I'm sorry, I—"

"None of that," she snapped. "No excuses."

None of that, little princess. The horrible memory of my reoccurring nightmare rose inside of me, along with a blast of bile. I barely slept all night, but, when I did, my dreams took me back to that cursed frat house mattress.

I stood shaking in the middle of Marjorie's office, hugging my arms around my torso to hold myself together. "I think I should go home," I whispered. "I don't feel well."

Marjorie sighed, exasperated. "I just said, no excuses. We're *all* hungover. And I need you here today to answer my calls while I work on this Stryker project."

The thought of cheerfully answering calls all day brought tears to my eyes. "Marjorie, really, I can't be here today. I should have just called in."

Between confronting my biggest fear by attending the gala, seeing the one person who could destroy me, running from him, being caught, and then having sex on Grayson's desk only to have him dismiss me the second he could… I was fully triggered. My past trauma took control of my subconscious all night… and now it had taken over my conscious mind, too.

Every man on the subway gave me a stab of panic. Every sudden movement or loud sound startled me. The concept of facing Parker or Marco or *anyone*, really, vaporized the breath in my lungs.

"I need to go home," I insisted again, fighting to inhale. "Please."

Marjorie's stony gaze narrowed for a long moment. Finally, she held up her hands, relenting. "Fine. Go home. But you might want to stop in the conference room first. Someone has all the stuff you left behind last night. Oh, and, I'd avoid Parker's area if I were you. He was pretty pissed when you disappeared on him. Said you went to get him a drink and never came back…?"

I swallowed down some more regret. "Yeah… I started to feel sick and decided it was best to leave without making a scene. I didn't want to embarrass… anyone."

It wasn't entirely a lie. I did feel sick to my core after what happened with Gray. And I would have sooner died than humiliate him or my boss on their big nights.

But Marjorie's squint tightened. "Just go, Elle. We can discuss this Monday."

I didn't know how my body could possibly produce any more tears, but they dripped off of my chin as I made my way back into the elevators. Without a coat or a phone, I came in with only a little cash and Maggie's spare keys, both stuffed into a small knit pouch. The same coin purse I handed to Grayson on the subway platform so long ago. My fist tightened around it protectively and I dashed the tears from my face, sniffling. I didn't want Marco to think he needed to rescue me again when he saw me.

I scuttled out of the cart and over to the conference room, keeping my head down so no one would see my make-up-less face and the blotches covering it. I wished I had some way to also keep them from seeing my outfit—which consisted of the first items my hands collided with in my dresser that morning; an orange cable-knit sweater with a corduroy skirt I belated realized had a hole along the seam—but that was a lost cause.

The lights were off inside the conference room, leaving the space dark aside from the sunlight filtering in through a window at the far end. I stepped inside and turned, expecting to find Marco or some other henchman dressed all in black.

Instead, Grayson stood just a few yards away, with his head bent and his hands in the pockets of his fitted charcoal suit. Natural light reflected off of his glossy black hair and his olive complexion, glowing warmly despite appearing paler than usual.

The sound of my gasp, his head snapped up. Bright shocks of green paralyzed me. "Ellie."

He moved toward me, but I fell back as fear streaked through my body. My eyes flew around the room, ensuring we were alone. My adrenaline spiked before draining off too quickly. As my heartbeat started to slow back down, I swayed on my feet.

Grayson caught my upper arm in an iron grip, steadying me before I fell face-first into the carpet. Part of me expected him to haul me into his arms; the other thought he'd thrust me away. Instead, he stilled for an endless moment, his solemn gaze absorbing the look on my face.

"We're going home," he announced, holding me hard but guiding me gently to the door. "Now."

Grayson

"Here we are."

I stepped into the Hallway to Nowhere with Ella at my side. My coat hung off of her frame, hiding the orange sweater dress underneath. Her blue gaze remained wary as she hugged her arms around her body.

"I shouldn't be here," she muttered, more to herself than me.

I replied anyway. "Yeah, well. I think we're well past what we should being doing at this point."

She shrank back from the bitterness in my voice. Fresh guilt pricked my stomach before rising up to join the thick, thundering apprehension swirling in my chest. *She's probably right... what the hell am I thinking?*

Back at her office, I'd taken one look at her splotchy nose and watery eyes before bundling her in both of our coats and all but carrying her out of the building. She seemed too exhausted to put up any sort of fight. She let me hold her up by the arm all the way down to the street, where she silently got into my car and scooted all the way over, leaving as much space between us as she could for the duration of our trip back uptown.

That was fine. I didn't trust myself, anyway. The fact that I was currently blowing off all manner of important work shit to take her home with me at 10AM on a Friday morning seemed like a pretty obvious indication that I'd lost the last of my sanity.

All the way up to the top floor, I watched her fidget and chew her lips, bouncing in place. I realized she didn't have her knitting with her to channel her anxiety and wished I could reach over to hold her restless hands.

Being so close to her, alone, after years of longing for her, was its own form of torture. I'd imagined what would happen if I ever had her back within reach so many times… but none of those fantasies could happen. She was a mess and so was I.

Outside my door, Ella glanced around the useless strip of hall and bit the inside of her cheek, considering. "Does someone else live on this floor?"

She clearly saw the needlessness of the whole arrangement. I smirked, "Just me."

I ushered her into my penthouse and let the metal slab fall closed behind us. It suddenly dawned on me how completely alone we were… and I paced away before I could reach for her and tug her body into mine.

"I'll makes us some coffee," I muttered, striding to the kitchen area. "Or do you want something else? I can send out for anything."

Ella didn't reply. She stood just inside the door, like she wasn't sure she should venture any further. Even huddled in both coats, I could see her body shake. Just like back at her office, she seemed weaker after her initial anxiety bled off. The vacant expression on her face stopped me in my tracks.

"Ella?" A bolt of fear struck me. I moved back toward her instinctively. "Did you sleep at all?"

"Sleep," she repeated, still staring into space. "Not really, no. Not much all week. I keep having—" She cut herself off as I reached her.

Concern overrode my pride, the reflex to protect myself. I reached for her face, cupping my palm around her jaw until she finally looked at me. "What? You keep having…?"

Shadows danced through her eyes. "Nightmares."

Before she shuddered through another breath, I snapped her up, bending to put one arm under her knees and balancing the other under her shoulder blades. She gasped, but didn't argue when I said, "You need to sleep, Ellie. I'm putting you to bed. I can work from here while you rest."

She folded herself closer to me, clasping my lapels in her small hands while I made for my bedroom. Depositing her on the end of the mattress, I turned to my dresser and pulled out a sweat suit. "Use these, if you'd like. Your phone is dead, so I'll plug it in while you sleep. It'll be out there if you need it… and so will I."

She accepted my clothes with a meek nod. I stepped into my closet to shuck my jacket, tie, and shoes. I also used the room controls to lower the bedroom's black-out shades and turn on the fan. By the time I came back out, Ella had donned my large hoodie and gotten under the covers. The neat stack of clothing she left at the foot of the bed told me she'd forgone my joggers.

My cock twitched at the idea of having her in my bed, half-dressed. I tamped down a startling surge of raw lust and cleared my throat. "Come get me if you need me."

Out in my living room, I paused to figure out what the hell I needed to do. Lunch sounded like a good idea. And I knew Beth probably had a thousand things to rail at me about. I shot off a message to Marco before calling my office.

Predictably, my assistant ranted about the schedule changes. Her outrage always managed to toe the line between prim professionalism and motherly disappointment. It had quite the effect.

"The head of the legal department needed two hours of your time, today, Mr. Stryker," Beth barked. "*Two hours.* Have you any notion how difficult it will be to rearrange that? Not to mention; Daniel asked to speak with you first thing this morning and so did the new employee in acquisitions, Miss… B-something. I don't recall. But HR also needed a word—some issue with an intern? And so did Milton, in accounting, and—"

My head spinning, I cut her off. "Alright, I see your point. Just tell them all…" I didn't know what. Truth was, since beginning my CEO role in earnest, I'd never missed a single day of work.

Thankfully, her stern voice interrupted me. "I *told* them that you had multiple meetings scheduled out of the office today and alluded to a large international project of great secrecy and import. I may have also implied that it was above each of their pay grades and they would do well not to presume that they are entitled to your time. You are the true CEO, now, after all. These people cannot expect you to bend to their whims."

A wry smile tugged at my mouth while her brilliance sank in. "But you can?" I asked.

"Yes, sir," she replied crisply. "I most certainly can and I do."

Well, she had every right to. Clearly, I'd be a lost cause without her. "Fine, then," I acquiesced. "I accept those terms. Now, while I'm out of the office working on this 'large international project of great secrecy and import,' who do I actually *need* to get back to?"

"Milton," she said immediately. "And you may want to at least begin email correspondence with the legal department. Whatever Mr. Carter needed two hours for sounded intensely detailed and getting a jump on it this weekend could only help." She paused, then belatedly added a hasty, "Sir."

Thanking her, I hung up and made my way over to far corner of my great room. Tucked behind the kitchen, I had a desk and a work area I seldom ever used. I fired up the iMac there, hoping to least find my email setting pre-loaded on the device. But, of course, Beth had provided an exact replica of my office desktop, complete with a single file labeled with the day's date, which contained an ordered list for me to work from.

First thing's first.

I started with Milton, as she suggested, and asked him to give Beth a raise. Two-thousand extra per month sounded reasonable. He wrote back confirming the pay boost and fired off a series of questions for me. He used bullet points, which I liked; and didn't seem interested in kissing my ass over my promotion, which I loved.

Carter, the head of the legal department, wasn't as shrewd. He sent two whole paragraphs' worth of adulation before turning around and condescending to me for the remainder of his message. I'd just started to craft a reply when I heard a sound from my bedroom.

A wail. Haunting and full of anguish.

I threw myself to my feet and crossed the room before I drew another breath, bolting through the shaded glass walls, into the master suite. There, curled into a ball under my covers, Ella's entire frame pulsed as she panted in her sleep. Another sound escaped her slack lips—this time, a fearful squeak.

Fuck.

For the world's longest minute, I felt frozen. Undecided. The cruelest part of me—wounded and full of spite—wanted to leave her to whatever horrors she never deemed me worthy of knowing. The rest of me loved her so desperately, every tweak in her expression felt like a blade between my ribs.

The next whimper that escaped her hit me like an arrow to the heart, making my decision instantly. I left my shirt where I stood, not bothering to take time to remove my pants, and barreled under the comforter.

"Ella," I murmured, bending over her shoulder to speak into her ear. "Ellie?"

She groaned, but didn't fully rouse. I stretched one arm over her, stroking her hair back from her face, while the other slid around her waist. "Ellie, it's just a dream. Wake up for me."

Instead, her fists opened, then grabbed at the forearm I tucked against her sternum. Her heaving breasts slowed as she stopped sucking in gusts of air.

She was so exhausted, even her horrible dream couldn't wake her. Somehow, though, my presence seemed to chase it off. She gradually relaxed, tension draining from her body as it fell back against mine little by little.

I watched her beautiful features soften. Even in the dark room, I knew the details by heart. The slope of her button nose. The dusting of freckles under her eyes. The peachy glow on her cheeks.

The moment suddenly struck me as miraculous. *She's really here.*

There was a time I would have done anything to have her back in my bed. *Bargaining*, the experts called it. A state of grief where I told myself it didn't matter what she'd done or why… that I would do whatever I had to do, just to have her back in my life.

Unhealthy. I knew that then and I knew it now. No matter how much I longed for her, I couldn't abandon all pride, reason, and whatever else just to hold on to her while she let me. I needed to be able to trust her. Without an explanation, I never could.

…could I?

My eyes roamed over her face, adjusting to darkness. Despite all my unanswered questions… I felt like I knew her. I felt, in my soul, that she would never hurt someone on purpose.

Especially me.

I believed that.

And I felt like an idiot for it. Because I had absolutely no proof she wouldn't wake up and bolt, save for the thick pulse of faith beating to life in my chest.

What if I could help her feel safe with me, once and for all? What if she's changed?

After our wild interlude on my desk, she didn't run off. I did. Maybe that meant there was hope for us, the way my mother seemed to think.

The scent of honeysuckle warmed my nose while I laid my head on the pillow behind hers. The length of her back melded into my bare chest.

God, she was so warm and sweet.

The longer I lingered, the less I wanted to leave. I felt my muscles go slack, pressing into and around her while drowsiness dulled the edges of my mind. My forehead fell forward, resting against her crown.

I said a silent prayer that she would still be there when I reopened my eyes.

Ella

I woke up feeling like I'd slept for a year.

Delicious heat radiated into my back, warming me from the nape of my neck to the backs of my thighs. When Grayson's nose brushed over the place just below my hairline, I realized why.

The muscled arm hooked around my middle tightened, drawing me further into his hardness. I barely dared to breathe, afraid he would wake up and push me away like he did the night before. I worked to keep my movements undetectable while I traced my fingertips up his forearm, lingering over the veins roped up over his muscles.

I saw him shirtless the weekend before, in my bed. Touching him was different, though. His well-honed strength, his smooth tan skin… it all felt so wonderfully familiar wrapped around me.

He shifted, moving closer and pressing his groin into my backside. A muffled groan escaped him as his erection met the curve of my ass.

Unable to help myself, I chuckled. Gray grunted, hugging me harder and turning his face into my hair. His cock only grew while he huddled closer. When he unwittingly started to grind into me, I couldn't hold my laughter any longer. At the sound of my giggles, his entire frame stiffened.

All at once, he ripped himself away with an exasperated growl. "Damn it."

Something about his sleepy embarrassment struck me as hilarious. Laughter shook my body while I hid the lower half of my face inside his hoodie, doing my best not to snort.

Gray's head snapped to the side. He frowned, flushing, but levity gilded the green of his irises. "You think this is funny?"

His stern tone only brought me to the edge of true hysterics. I rolled onto my back as peals of laughter escaped, echoing off of his high, square ceiling.

Reluctant amusement pulled at his sculpted pout, tugging it into a half-grin. "You couldn't have let me sleep another five minutes?" he asked wryly. "I was almost done."

His rueful joke surprised and delighted me. Where was the wary businessman who tore my skirt and taunted me? The impassive, imposing titan of industry who walked away from me without a second look?

I sobered at the memory. My arm stretched across the space between us, reaching for his cheek. While my fingers grazed the square angle of his jaw, I opened my mouth to apologize once again.

The glow in his gaze smoldered, darkening. "Don't," he murmured, suddenly serious. I flinched away but he snatched my hand and pressed it back into his cheek. "No, I mean, let's not fight. Let's just... Why don't we just pretend nothing is wrong? For a little bit. The evening, at least." Without waiting for a reply, he turned and kissed my palm tenderly, letting his mouth linger against my skin. "It's probably dinnertime," he said, taking a different tact. "What sounds good?"

My heart ached, wishing I could ask him for dessert before our dinner. Since I couldn't, I chose something I could eat without embarrassing myself or making a mess. "How about pizza? I have a coupon in my wallet if we order it from the right place."

Grayson slid into my side. His large hand floated up to hold my cheek. "A coupon, huh?"

I rolled my eyes at him. "Well we don't *have* to use the coupon, I'm just *saying—*"

Gray's lips interrupted me, slanting over mine in a slow, insistent kiss. I opened for him without thought, forgetting all of the reasons why I ought to push him away. He said he wanted to pretend. And I was too weak to resist such an enticing offer.

You're safe here, with Gray, a small voice inside my heart tempted. *Stay with him while you still can.*

A moan leapt up my throat while I surrendered, hugging him closer. My hands skimmed down his naked back, re-learning the solid planes of his body, luxuriating in the warm softness of his hair. When my fingers tangled in it and pulled softly, a soft sound rumbled through Grayson's chest.

He broke away far too soon, breathing hard. "I'm being forceful with you. I was too rough last night, too. I didn't keep your boundaries in mind. When I woke up this morning, I hated myself for all the ways I could have scared you off again."

The genuine remorse softening his features undid me. I held his face in my hands, debating how best to comfort him. "I'm a lot better now," I ventured. "I've been seeing a therapist for two years and she's helped me a lot with my anxiety stuff."

Memories from my panic attack on Grayson's office floor whirred through my mind. "Well," I added, grimacing. "She tries to help, anyway."

But the truth was, the events of the night before were a rarity. Before Grayson Stryker reappeared in my world, I hadn't dealt with a full-blown episode in months. The fact that he handled me so fiercely in his office and I didn't get triggered was a testament to all of Dr. Laura's hard work. And mine, too, I supposed.

His steady gaze didn't betray even a hint of disapproval. "I think that's really brave."

"Telling you?" I asked. "Or going in the first place?"

He stared for a long moment, eyes flickering. "Both."

Before I replied, he lowered his face back down to mine, kissing me softly at first, then deeper. His tongue moved against mine with aching slowness, savoring me as if we had all the time in the world to stay in that one magic moment. I gripped the broad blades of his shoulders, leveraging myself closer, surrendering to his seduction.

His cock twitched against my hip. The sensation reminded me of his unconscious antics and I smiled against his mouth, breaking the seal of his lips.

Gray pulled back, regarding me with a heady mix of affection and accusation. One of his dark brows arched. "Something funny?"

"You are!" I told him, grinning for what felt like the first time in ages. "You object to a coupon but you'll press that rod into my leg? Some gentleman."

"*Rod*?" A chortle burst out of him. Then another. And another. Until he threw his head back to laugh the same way I had.

I loved the rich, masculine sound. The way his eyes squinted and the dazzling smile stretching his handsome features. It was impossible to decide which I loved more—his boyish grin or his intense gazes. Really, it didn't matter. Regardless of his mood or his expression, he was always the most beautiful man I'd ever seen.

At that thought, a pang rebounded through my breast, leaving me winded. Grayson caught on to my mood, his face clouding over with a tumult of emotion. The air between us changed, growing thick with some unnamed force. His emerald eyes flashed.

"We're playing with fire. I'm never going to be a gentleman if we stay in this bed," he mumbled. In the next breath, he once more scooped me up into his arms, pausing to snatch the sweatpants off the foot of the massive bed before charging out of the room. He dropped them on top of me. "And you should probably put these on. Right now, I can feel how wet your panties are."

I longed to press my throbbing center against the forearm banded around it, but rejected the urge. With a slight nod, I clutched the joggers. As soon as he placed me on his sofa, I shimmied them on and rolled the waistband.

Wanting to return us to our good spirits, I shot his naked chest a pointed look. "And you should probably put on a shirt."

With a huff, he went back to his bedroom. A few moments later, he emerged in a pair of grey pajama bottoms and—*dear Lord*—my very favorite of all his shirts… the muscle tank with torn arm-holes that left the sides of his mouthwatering torso exposed.

"Better?" he smirked, casting me another arch look.

I narrowed my eyes. "Oh *loads*."

My sarcasm earned another warm burst of laughter. His fond regard filled me with a buzz of joy. "I'm glad some sleep has you back to normal."

I *felt* normal. More like myself than I had in ages. Not wanting to read into the reason why, I shrugged and made one last jest. "Maybe it was the rod."

Grayson and I bantered and bickered while we ordered our pizza. In the end, he relented and let me use my coupon, shaking his head at me all the while. During the thirty-minute wait for our delivery, he excused himself to make a couple of hushed phone calls and sat at the desk in the farthest corner of the great room for ten minutes, tapping out a series of emails with remarkable efficiency.

I used the time to retrieved my re-charged phone and send Maggie a message. It turned out to be earlier than we thought—just a bit before five—so I let her know not to expect me home until after dinnertime, possibly later. She responded with a donkey and a question mark.

Setting the phone aside, I took a moment to look around. The penthouse was… spotless. And *cold.* White oak, gray furnishings, steel countertops. It reminded me of a hospital.

When Gray retrieved our food from the concierge and brought it to the island, I couldn't resist teasing him. "So what kinds of surgery do you do here?"

Unamused, he glowered at me. "It's minimalist."

"It's an operating table," I returned, smoothing my hands over the cool metal.

He cracked a smile and winced at once. "I know it's a bit… stark. I designed it that way on purpose."

My mind stuttered to a halt. "*You* designed this? The penthouse?"

Gray ripped a bite off of his first slice and shrugged. He kept his gaze low as he admitted, "The building, actually."

I dropped my piece of pizza without tasting it. My mouth hung open. "The *whole* building? So you did this one *and* the one I was in last night? Gray, that's amazing!"

He rubbed his hand over the back of his neck in a familiar gesture that made my insides quiver every bit as much as the rueful look on his face. "Yeah, well. As you saw from the useless hallway I put outside the elevator for literally no reason—I'm not exactly a savant."

I rolled my eyes and reached across the stainless island, wrapping my hands over one of his. "Gray," I said, waiting for him to meet my eyes. "You're too hard on yourself. One tiny strip of hallway doesn't undo all of the things you got right."

I turned to the great room behind me, scanning for examples. "Look at the way you positioned this room! Look at this light at sunset! And the bedroom was so cool, too. Three walls of glass? It's like a peninsula, only with light instead of water. The inverse of what you did with your office at Stryker & Sons. And both rooms have the most incredible angles and views; they don't even need art or décor."

When I turned back, Grayson swallowed hard, his eyes burning into my face. "Thanks, Ellie," he murmured. "That's… thank you. For saying that."

I drew my hands back, suddenly feeling awkward. "You're welcome."

A poignant silence descended, banishing my appetite. I twisted my fingers in the hem of his hoodie and spoke through my teeth while I worried my lower lip. "Gray… I know we called a truce, but… what is this? I mean, I know you're so angry with me… so why did you bring me here? Why are you being so nice to me?"

His face froze over. "Am I? I can't tell anymore." He sighed, shifting on his feet. "Everything inside of me is so muddled up… I can't get a grip on how I'm supposed to handle this."

That made sense. "You must hate me," I thought out loud.

He didn't so much as flinch. "Sometimes I think I do. But that's more of a habit at this point. I spent a long time teaching myself to loathe you for what you did. But when I'm alone with you… I know that was all a lie I told myself. I'm starting to believe I never truly hated you."

A painful pulse of hope throbbed through my chest. "Why not?"

He stared at me for so long, my cheeks started to flame. Finally, he dropped his eyes to his plate. "I don't think I ever quite convinced myself you left for no reason," he muttered. "I just… know you. Or, I *knew* you, I guess."

It pained me that he had to make that distinction. "Do you want to know me, now?" I asked.

Gray's mouth lifted into a grim half-smile. "You don't seem that much different, actually. You're still appallingly beautiful. And funny.

Considerate, hard-working, humble. Compassionate. Genuine. As far as I can tell, the only major change is your shoes."

A blush blazed over my face at his begrudging praise. "My *shoes*?"

He lifted his pizza back to his mouth and looked away again. "Yeah. The clogs. I looked for them in your room and didn't see them."

Something about his admission warmed me. "You liked those? Maggie always told me they were the most hideous shoes ever conceived. I suspect she burned them when we moved back in together."

Finished with his first slice, Gray grabbed a second. He seemed to be working hard not to look directly at me. "So when did you, uh, move back?"

I felt my eyes go wide. I had no idea he knew that I ever left. "I only went home for one semester," I told him. "I didn't have anywhere to live in the city or any savings for a down payment. Student housing was full by the holidays. So I had to defer my courses."

The naked pain in Gray's eyes nearly undid me, especially when he smiled softly. "The prospect of living with me was *that* bad, huh?"

I thought his cold fury the night before ruined me… but witnessing the agony smoldering in his emerald depths was a hundred times worse.

What could I say, though? Not much. Nothing about why I left that day or why I couldn't explain… But I simply couldn't bear to lie to him. Instead, I settled for a different, somewhat-relevant truth.

"I tried to," I whispered, hanging my head. "A couple weeks after I left…. I came back to the city after break and went to the apartment you rented on the date we were supposed to move in… hoping you'd be there…"

My mind drifted back to that terrible day—the day I realized that he'd given up on me completely in just a matter of weeks. I already knew he didn't want to talk to me when all of my messages and calls went unanswered… but when I saw that he'd relinquished our apartment to another couple rather than live somewhere I may be able to find him, I knew he'd decided he could never forgive me.

Grayson must have rounded the island while I was locked in my reverie, because the next thing I knew, his hands were on my shoulders, holding just a bit too hard. Turbulence roiled in his eyes while they stared hard into mine.

"You went to that apartment?" he demanded. "You showed up that day?"

It remained the single most desperate, selfish thing I'd ever done. I nodded as tears clogged my throat.

"Yes," I whispered, equally ashamed and relieved to finally tell someone. "I did."

Before I could consider the repercussions of my confession, his lips sealed over mine with surprising force. He pinned me to his chest, kissing me with frantic abandon. His hands clutched at my waist, lifting me onto the cool metal island, pulling me as close as he could get me while plunging his tongue into my mouth, the kisses almost violent.

He broke away just as suddenly, panting as he moved to frame my face. "*Why*, Ella?" he asked, agonized. "*Why* did you show up that day after ignoring me for *weeks*? I must have called you a thousand times."

His mouth crushed mine before I could answer. I let him kiss me, fisting my hands in his hair and wrapping my legs around his torso, holding on for dear life while he ravaged me to his heart's content. My lips started to feel bruised before he broke off again, moving to my neck, leaving a series of punishing bites in his wake.

"*I* called *you*!" I cried, whimpering as he licked away the sting of his roughness. "So many times… I wrote messages…"

Gray's hands held fast to the sides of my face. "No, you didn't," he insisted, almost glaring.

"I did!" I promised, "Almost as soon as I left, I regretted it."

He snatched me back up against him, once again kissing me so hard it hurt. "No," he growled, adamant. "I know that has to be a lie. If that were true, why did Maggie tell me you left the city for good? She told me you never wanted to see me again!"

My heart stopped. "*Maggie*? You talked to Maggie? Back then?"

"You didn't *know*?" he roared. "I thought she would tell you right away. I thought you probably thanked her for telling me to fuck off and refusing to give me your address."

A dizzy rush of betrayal and anger choked me. My mind boggled, unable to imagine why my best friend would ever say such a thing.

"No!" I wailed, stroking my fingers over his cheeks. "No. She *never* told me she talked to you and I *never* told her I didn't want to see you again. I just said we broke up! I didn't—I couldn't—she still doesn't know—"

When I couldn't finish any of my thoughts, he groaned, the sound tormented. "Ella. You're killing me. You mean… that whole time… you were… waiting for me? Trying to contact me? Trying to come back?"

Two of those things were true. But I didn't have it in me to tell him that I could never truly "come back" to him the way I longed to. I certainly couldn't say so while he looked like his soul had left his body.

"Yes," I whispered, hoarse. Tears splattered down my face as I focused on the one vow I could honestly offer. "I never stopped waiting for you. For three years, there hasn't been anyone else, Grayson. No one."

Disbelief melded with his tortured expression. "Last night, when I kissed you… you almost seemed like you didn't remember how," he told me, his voice low. "Are you telling me you really haven't been with any other men? Not even that guy from your office?"

I brushed my fingers over his lips and stared hard into his eyes, not caring if he saw mine spill over. "No one, Gray. Only you. Just… you. For always."

His face broke. My name came as a cracked whisper. "Ellie."

"I meant what I wrote," I whispered, pressing my lips to his cheek. "I will always be yours."

Grayson

I will always be yours.

The words sank into my center. To the very heart of me. Slicing deep. Cutting open old wounds, inflicting new ones. But healing me, too, somehow. Filling dead places with searing light.

She looked so beautiful, tear-stained and fervent. Her sapphire eyes begging me to believe her. To believe *in* her.

And, God help me, I did.

A desperate sound sloughed out of me as I ripped her off of the counter and turned back for the bedroom. "I need you," I spat, unable to form any other coherent thought. "Please."

She hugged her arms around my neck. "Like I said," she whispered. "I'm yours…"

I lowered her onto my mattress, not even able to part from her long enough to turn on a light. We stripped each other's clothes off with quick, graceless movements, both too eager.

Once we were nude, she reached, stretching both hands up toward me. "I love you, Grayson," she murmured in the twilight, cupping my jaw. "I always have."

I felt my features crack, my lips pulling into a pained grimace. "Ellie. God. Don't *say* that."

"It's true," she replied, her smile sad and soft. "I knew it then and I know it now."

"Then, why—"

She halted me, brushing her fingertips over my mouth in a caress that made my throbbing cock twitch. "I know this is an impossible thing for me to ask," she whispered, her dark blue depths glowing urgently. "But… trust me. Please. I can't tell you why I left. But you have to believe me when I say that it wasn't because I didn't love you, Gray."

All too easily, I gave in. Let myself have her, her love, her promises. Everything I'd lost, laid out for me to take back.

I took it, knowing it was wasn't real. Knowing it was dust, slipping through my fingers with every passing second.

It didn't matter. Falling into her arms felt like finally deciding to set down a boulder. The relief was instant. Heady. And the feel of her underneath me was so exquisite, I forgot to hold myself up for a moment.

Instead of freezing in fear, though, Ella held me. Her hands smoothed down my spine while she nuzzled sweetly against my temple. More relief broke over me, along with a rush of gratitude.

My throat knotted, turning my voice thick. "I don't have to be on top."

"I want you just like this," she assured me, rearing back to lock gazes with me. "I want you every way."

Emotion flooded my eyes for the first time in as long as I could remember. Lost, I dropped my forehead to hers, surrendering to the riot inside of me. She cried, too, the tears sliding down to wet her golden hair.

Bracing on my forearms, I ran my hands over the sides of her head, holding her still as I sealed my mouth over hers. Without words, I told her all of the things I never got to say. I made amends for the night before, gently bringing her to climax twice before carefully pushing into her. We moved together, making love; so slow and sweet, I thought it would kill me to stop.

Ella

I woke around dawn, wrapped tightly into Grayson's side. He continued his deep sleep, the sculpted planes of his chest barely rising and falling under my cheek even when I shimmied up to go to the bathroom.

While I was up, I realized I never answered Maggie. Even though I was angry with her for what Gray told me, I knew I needed to at least tell her I was okay. Grumbling internally, I put my borrowed hoodie and joggers back on to go in search of my abandoned phone.

When I found it on the island, only one message waited for me. And it wasn't from my roommate. Or any other number I had saved.

But, somehow, I *knew.*

A dizzy wave of terror rushed over me as I swiped it open.

I know where you are, it said. *You better run.*

CHAPTER TWENTY

December 2013

Grayson

I found it incredibly endearing that Ella still got nervous about garnering my parents' approval.

While Marco sped across Long Island, she sat pressed against my side, looping yarn around her knitting needles at warp-speed while her sapphire gaze peered out the Mercedes' window.

Dressed in a simple traveling outfit of grey leggings and her NYU hoodie, she looked beautiful, but tired. The care she took with her hair and makeup couldn't hide the remnants of her nightmare. She woke up crying sometime before dawn and I spent thirty minutes singing her back to sleep. While I slept in, though, she got up early and spent the morning anxiously cleaning my spotless apartment.

I knew her dreams usually resurfaced when she felt especially nervous. The tidying and speed-knitting were also telling.

Maybe, when we get there, I'll take her straight into the jetted tub. Then we can take a nap…

Cupping my hand around her chin, I turned to press a kiss against her brow. "This trip will be great."

A weak smile played at her lips. "I think so, too. I'm sorry we have to leave on Christmas day, though."

She kept apologizing. I grunted, annoyed. "You have to stop feeling bad. You have a family, too. I'm looking forward to meeting them. Though, I'm not sure sleeping on the couch will be my favorite."

Instead of gracing me with her warm little laugh, Ellie's frown deepened. Her hands didn't even pause. "You can have my bed. I'll take the couch."

I kissed her again. "I'm only joking, of course."

It wasn't really the couch that bothered me, anyway—it was the thought of spending three nights without her curled up next to me. Although, my dick hardened every time I imagined sneaking into her bedroom.

We'll have to be very *quiet...*

Volume wouldn't be an issue at the Hamptons House. Mom prepared the largest of all the guest suites for us... conveniently located in a wing opposite theirs. Classy to the last, neither of my parents mentioned the need for privacy. Theirs or ours.

I wasn't sure where they planned to stick my uncle and my cousin, though. After years of pretending they didn't exist, I couldn't picture them casually sitting through family dinners.

My father insisted that the holiday posed a perfect opportunity for all of us to reconnect. He believed we needed them in order to make our revised succession plan work. And I decided to go along with it, if only because—between Ellie and designing the new Stryker & Sons headquarters—I was the happiest I'd ever been.

"Tell me more about them," Ella whispered, reading my mind. "All I know is that Ted is your father's younger brother and your cousin is older than us."

It was kind of her not to mention the sordid details she surely read online. My lips pressed together while I tried to condense the story.

"My grandfather and his brother took over the company from their father and *his* brother. But my great-uncle never had children, so Stryker passed directly to my dad and Uncle Ted. They figured it was perfect, since each of them had a son—me and Daniel. They planned to run the place together and eventually pass it down to the two of us.

"But, a few years after my grandad passed, my father started to notice that Ted's spending didn't make sense. He caught him in a few lies... Long story short, Uncle Ted had a plan to embezzle money into his pension account. He was jealous that my father had taken his trust and invested it successfully—Ted felt that since their wealth started out the same, that they should remain equal.

"He thought he deserved more money from the company to make up for the wealth he squandered. And, apparently, there was also some bullshit about my dad working fewer hours, because he was still married and spent more time at home than Ted, who got a divorce and sent Daniel to live with his ex-wife most of the time."

I shrugged off my embarrassment. "Obviously none of that mattered. Once my dad figured it out, he gave Ted a choice between stepping down or being prosecuted. He did it fairly—gave Ted his pension, cashed out his investments, doubled Daniel's trust so he wouldn't face any consequences for what his dad did."

God, that was chaos.

For months reporters hounded our family for the "real" story, refusing to accept that anyone would willingly step down from running the city's most lucrative company. I spent my sophomore year of high school with hired security, a paranoid father, and Mom threatening to move us all to Lake Como indefinitely.

Remembering, I shook my head. "It wasn't enough for Ted, though. He made a scene, refused to see us ever again. Pulled Daniel out of prep school and made it seem like he no longer had the funds for his education—which wasn't true at all. He just wanted to play the victim and using my cousin to guilt-trip my parents seemed like the best option."

Ella's hands finally stilled. "So that's how they left it?" she asked, melding her deep blue eyes into mine.

"Not really. We paid for Daniel to go to Columbia and Dad granted him access to his trust early. After he graduated, he took a gap year that turned into a lifestyle choice. I think he mostly wanted to avoid his parents. It's actually sort of a big deal that he's coming back at all, now. I don't know what my dad told him, but he must have been convincing."

She nodded, thoughtful. "Hmm. Well, I'm glad he'll be around to help you. That's the way it was always supposed to be, right? Two Strykers running things?"

I shrugged again, noncommittal. "Dad says Daniel wants to run the acquisition side of things. Finding properties on the cheap, getting people to sell below market value, muscling people out of their places so we can assemble parcels. All of which I detest. So."

Even exhausted and anxious, Ellie turned her attention to comforting me. She brushed my hair back and combed her fingers into it. "So, it's perfect. You both get to do what you want. And Ted can act as an advisor when your dad… needs a break."

Sweetheart.

I nuzzled into the crown of her head, twirling her braid in my fingers. "I'm grateful," I admitted quietly. "They may not be my first choice but they're really the *only* choice. If they weren't willing to come back, I'd have to scrap my project. Dad wouldn't have any peace of mind about me taking over."

Blowing out a breath, I turned her face to mine. "I'm also grateful to you," I murmured. "None of this would have happened if you didn't show him that sketch."

She fought for me when I wouldn't even fight for myself. I still didn't fully comprehend how much that meant to me. Hopefully, I'd have her entire life to figure it out and show her my appreciation.

Thinking through my plans, I cuddled her close while she resumed her knitting.

The rest of the ride blurred by—Southampton to Sagaponack, East Hampton. Then, finally, we turned onto our sandy, winding road.

Ella stashed her knitting in one of her bags and scooted up to the window, peering out at the canopy of trees overhead the way a child might. "Wow," she breathed.

God. We weren't even at the house yet and she already sounded overwhelmed. I wondered what she'd make of the ten-thousand-square-foot estate my parents casually called "the beach house."

In their defense, it *was* a house on the beach. Set about an acre back from the water...

It had spectacular views, though. I knew Ellie would love the one from our guest suite, with its wall of windows. When the sun set, it felt like sitting in a panoramic bow of light.

When our car stopped in the gravel driveway, I gave Ella a moment to absorb the cobblestone manse and the sprawling grounds.

My mother went all out, it seemed, trimming every column and eave in Christmas lights and greenery. She even had a fake Santa sitting in one of the rocking chairs on the front porch.

Ella turned to offer a shy smile. "It's funny… I know your parents are insanely wealthy and this house is basically a dream-come-true… but there's just something so relatable about a mom over-decorating to an embarrassing degree."

I laughed, then grimaced. "There really is, isn't there?"

I couldn't tell if she was truly acclimating to the way my family lived or just playing it cool, but she didn't turn white or chew on her lip the whole way through the house tour. She even met the main living room's three-story stone fireplace and two-story Christmas tree with a calm smile.

But I did catch her eyes widening a bit when she caught sight of all the gifts. There had to be at least fifty, all wrapped perfectly and arranged in artful piles. On top of one heap toward the back, I spied the small red-wrapped box I specifically asked my mother to place on top of Ellie's stack.

While I tamped down a bracing bolt of exhilaration, Ella fingered the nearest ornament on the tree. Her sapphire eyes glinted at me. "So… where are your parents?"

I checked my watch. *3:12. Plenty of time.*

I stepped up against her softly curved frame, sliding my hands over her hips. "They're meeting us for dinner in few hours at Nick & Toni's."

Ellie blinked adorably. "Who are Nick and Tony?"

I grinned so hard, my cheeks hurt. "It's the name of an Italian restaurant on Main Street. Very quaint. Good wine. You'll like it."

Completely deadpan, she looked down at her sweatshirt and then back up at me. "I'm assuming Nick and Tony won't approve of my leisurewear. They sound like snooty bastards."

God, I love her.

Chuckling, I bent to brush a kiss against her lips. "Then I'll help you take it off."

Peals of squealing laughter echoed off the stairwell as I threw Ella over my shoulder and carted her upstairs. "Grayson!" she giggle-screamed. "Put me down!"

"You know," I replied conversationally, turning for our hallway. "I've never had a girl in this house. I wonder if all the rooms echo like this. That could be fun."

"Gray!" she laughed. "What if someone hears us?"

There were probably a few housekeepers wandering around, but no one who would dare interrupt us. In front of the double doors to our suite, I slid her down my body, growling, "You think I'd let anyone else hear you come?"

She nipped her lower lip. "Well, *no…*"

I pressed her into the second door. "And you trust me?"

Any trace of hesitation cleared. "More than anyone."

That was all I needed to be a happy man. *But stripping her clothes off certainly won't hurt.*

We shoved into our room, pulling off garments as we went. Her slender fingers worked over the muscles of my back. My hands traced the outline of her breasts until she trembled.

On a moan, she slipped her tongue against mine. My cock hardened, pressing out from my button fly until I reached down and ripped it open. I let her push her leggings off; but, when I found her naked underneath her sweatshirt, it was all I could do to slide her thong down instead of ripping it from her hips.

Gloriously nude, my Ellie fell onto the cream-covered duvet. Clear afternoon sunshine cast her peachy skin and golden hair in a hazy halo. Deep ocean eyes blinked up at me while her kiss-swollen lips curved in a bemused smile.

"Gray?"

She wondered why I suddenly stopped. Tracing her perfect body with my gaze, I swallowed hard, forcing down another wash of emotion. My voice sounded thick. "I want to make sure I never forget this."

Adoration softened her expression. She held both hands out to me. "Come here."

I still approached her with caution whenever I wanted to be on top. It didn't seem traumatic for her anymore, but I always tried to be careful. Her trust was my most prized possession.

Settling over her silken warmth, I bent to kiss her long and slow, working my palms over her plush softness. She stroked her hands over my back, lingering on my shoulders. When I shifted my weight, flexing the muscles, she moaned again.

"Gray. You're so strong. It makes me so wet." Her words vibrated against my throat as she sucked lightly on my neck.

I loved that she finally felt comfortable enough to talk dirty to me. Her thoughts always came as whispered confessions, but I cherished each one. More evidence that she trusted me with every part of her.

I wanted to grind against her, so I shifted my weight again, dropping my hips down. And she froze.

Shit.

Not every *part of her.*

I hated that she wouldn't tell me why some things clearly frightened her. And why those things only scared her sometimes, not others. By keeping me in the dark, she forced me to tiptoe around her boundaries without any context.

Helpless frustration seethed in my center. My cock throbbed, impatient for a whole different reason. I started to push off of her, but she held fast, bringing my hips back to hers.

"I'm sorry," she mumbled, hiding against my shoulder. "Ignore me."

I almost smirked. Ignore her? I was about to be *inside* of her. I smoothed my palm over her hair, positioning her face so I could look into her eyes. "Can't. I never could. The moment I saw you, I knew I'd never be able to."

Her trepidation melted as her chin wobbled. "Gray."

I thrummed my lips over her cheek. "Tell me what I can do, baby. What do you need?"

She lifted her hips. "Touch me? Please?"

The feel of her soaking sex grazing my shaft was indescribable. I groaned before sealing my mouth over hers, slanting at an angle as I reached between our bodies.

Her wet heat coated my fingers. My dick pulsed, desperate for her. "Fuck, Ellie."

She reached for me, too. Gripping me with both hands, she pushed one up to the base while the other stroked down to my head.

Pre-cum slicked her palm when she moved it back to meet the other in the middle.

My body jerked into her hands, wanting more. She ground into my touch, too, crying my name louder each time I pinched the swollen bud at the top of her folds and plucked her nipples.

I felt her getting ready to come. Each time I slipped down to tease her opening, she gasped and bucked. Finally, I slid two fingers into her while my thumb rubbed circles on her clit. She let go with a beautiful, breathless keen that echoed through the white, sun-washed room.

I was too close to the edge to go slow and control myself. Instead, I flipped us, settling her legs on either side of my thighs and yanking her down onto my raging erection.

Holy. Fuck.

The exquisite sensation of her snug heat enveloping my cock ripped all the air from my lungs. Chest heaving, I leaned back to watch her move on top of me. Tossing back her unraveling braid, she glided up and down, tipping her face up.

The glow around us made the whole thing feel ethereal. Like a dream. Or some type of heaven. For a moment, I reveled in the way the light hit the arch of her neck; the color of her coppery nipples, furled tight while her breasts bounced in front of my face.

Her fingers tangled in the hair at the back of my neck, pulling hard. My balls drew up while tingles streaked over my spine. A broken groan tore out of me. "Yes, *Ella*. Fuck. You make me come so hard."

She ground down with renewed dedication, moving her hips in a delicious circle that completely undid me. Three more swivels sent me sailing over the edge. I pressed my cheek into her chest, clutching her hips down onto mine, spurting into her with an animal roar.

Ellie hugged me close, caressing my back while we caught our breath. Holding her tight, I sank into her, relishing her sweet, guileless touch. Always giving, even when I thought she couldn't possibly have any more love for me.

After a moment, she straightened and looked around, as if realizing where we were. When her gaze snagged on the view, she gave an impish smirk. "Huh. You'd think I would have noticed that before…"

The swooping, sinking sensation swelled. Now that I knew it was love, I couldn't believe I didn't recognize it the very first time I felt it, back on the first morning we ever woke up together.

Grinning like fool, I tucked her loose hair behind her ear and guided her head down to the crook of my shoulder. Contentment settled over me when she folded herself into my chest, letting my arms envelope her.

While she snuggled closer, a sound drew my eyes across the room. *Oh. Fuck.*

I realized, way too late, that I didn't check to make sure the double doors closed all the way after we barreled into our suite. One of them hung ajar, revealing a strip of the hallway and what looked like a shadow.

Shit. I narrowed my eyes, trying to see into the unlit stretch.

Nothing. Thank God.

You have to be smarter than this, I told myself. *You're going to be running a company. A housekeeper or landscaper could take a video or a photo of you. Or Ellie, God forbid. They could extort you. Or just publish it for clout.*

A prickle of unease rose the hairs on the back of my neck. My hold on Ella tightened protectively, covering as much of her bare body as I could.

"Let's take a bath," I suggested gruffly, wanting to get her out of sight. "The tub has jets and I think there's a wine fridge in there, too."

Her adoring blue eyes beamed at me as she framed my face with her palms. "And, knowing you, there's a bottle of Dom in there for me?"

Just like that, she chased my dread away.

I smiled back at her and clutched her closer, surging to my feet. "Very possible."

Ella glowed all through our bottle of Dom and dinner with my parents.

Her enthusiasm kept everyone in good spirits. She giggled over all my parent's silly Christmas stories from my childhood and asked them about their own holiday traditions growing up.

I kept my touch on her at all times, unable to resist the allure of her exposed neck and shoulders under her slouchy red sweater. My fingers strummed against her nape as my father summoned the server for the check. She cast a sideways glance at me and I grinned, unabashed.

Once he handed off the black card, Dad grunted and extracted his cell phone. "Damn," he grumbled, scowling. "Ted texted. Daniel's flights were delayed. Nothing got out of Dublin, today. Some sort of storm. Now their whole system is backlogged. Ted wants to know if he should come out alone or wait for Dan."

My mother's brows folded. "When will Danny get here?"

"Not until Tuesday," Dad huffed. "Apparently."

The day before Christmas Eve. Flying commercial would be hell.

I recalled our conversation about gratitude on the car ride over and forced down a begrudging flare of irritation, rubbing my hand over my neck. "Tell Ted to come tomorrow. And tell Daniel there's a Stryker & Sons jet on a tarmac in Paris. If he can get there by train, I'll call and have it prepped."

Pride glimmered in my mother's eyes. She turned to Dad. "That's a good plan."

I shrugged. "Eh. It's a plan, at least. A seventeen-hour train ride isn't ideal, but if he can get to France by tomorrow afternoon, the jet will get him here a day sooner."

We set the plan in motion with a few quick calls and a flurry of texts. When Daniel personally messaged me to thank me for hooking him up, I found Ella gazing over, approval clear in her eyes.

"That was nice of you."

I kissed her palm. "You know, I'm in a good mood for some reason…"

Her cheeks—already sweetly pink from champagne and wine—blazed. The nervous look she slanted at my parents doubled my teasing grin.

Baby, they know we sleep together. They put us in the same room.

Months of letting me take her body every way I could imagine hadn't stolen her innocence. In some ways, she was still the shy girl who hid in a pile of yarn on the subway.

My heart throbbed in my chest, aching, until I pulled her side into mine and nuzzled my face into hers, letting her peachy blush warmed my cheek. When I pulled back, startled blue eyes widened with mock-solemnity. "Grayson Stryker, get ahold of yourself. What will Nick and Tony think?"

When I burst into a loud laugh, both of my parents turned to me. Dad gave me an unfathomable look while my mother practically bounced in her chair, barely able to suppress her delight.

As Ella dropped her gaze to her lap, I shot Mom a pointed look. Honestly, I figured it would be a miracle if we made it to Christmas Eve without her blowing my proposal with her obvious excitement. She'd already asked one-too-many telling questions over our meal. Luckily, Ellie didn't seem to take any to heart.

Even so, once we were all back at the beach house, I caught up with Mom in the kitchen while Ella went upstairs to call home.

"Listen," I groused, glowering at her. "You *have* to take it down a notch. Or six."

She flashed her teeth in a grimace. "*Sí, amorcito*, I know. Your father lectured me in the car."

I could picture that. "He's like me—nothing is a done deal until she says yes, so there's nothing to get all excited about."

Mom guffawed. "*Of course* she'll say yes! Though, I did want to ask—you got her another Christmas gift, right? Something else to throw off suspicion? That way the ring at the end will truly be a surprise."

I thought the same thing. "Yes. I got her a telescope. I had it wrapped and delivered here so she wouldn't see it. It's already under the tree."

"A *telescope*?"

Her expression brought a smile to my face. "Yeah. Ella used to stargaze with her dad before he passed. She misses the stars in the city. I got a telescope strong enough to use from a rooftop in Manhattan, but I figured I'd set it up for her after she opens it on Christmas Eve. The view from the beach is probably incredible. Maybe it will be our first holiday tradition."

Tears glossed my mom's eyes. "Oh, Grayson. That's a beautiful gift. I'm just so ecstatic for you, darling. Both of you. I haven't seen two people so in love since—"

She choked on her own words, flinging her focus from my face out the nearest window. She made a watery chuckling sound. "Goodness. I'm all over the place."

Without a thought, I folded her into my arms. Consternation pressed into my middle. "Mom?"

She sniffled, but didn't pull back. "It's only that you two remind me of your father and I, back when we first fell in love. It's a wonderful thing to remember, of course, but..."

But now he's dying.

I did everything I could not to think about it. But, when I did, I got the distinct feeling we might be embarking on our last Christmas as a complete family.

And, yes, I would lose my dad. But Mom would lose her everything.

How would I feel if I knew my days with Ella were numbered? If I had to face the possibility that any given moment could be the last time I ever saw her?

"I can't even imagine," I admitted. "I'm so sorry, Mom."

"Me too," she mumbled, sniffing again and stepping back, using her cashmere shawl to swipe at her face. "I'm just grateful that this is shaping up to be such a special holiday. Between your plans and your father reconciling with your uncle, everything feels just right."

I wanted to stay, but Mom lightly pushed me toward the stairs. "Now, get upstairs to that beautiful girl." She reached up to touch my cheek. "You don't want to waste any time; it all goes by too fast. Believe me."

Ella

I woke up with Grayson's face nestled against my left breast and his snores feathering my nipple.

Did I fall asleep naked*? In my boyfriend's* parents' *house?*

Lord. I couldn't decide if his nudity made mine better or worse.

"Gray," I hissed, shaking the thick ridge of his shoulder. "Wake up."

But he only burrowed closer, pouting drowsily. "No. You're soft and warm. And these floors are always fucking freezing. Plus, it's early. The sun isn't even all the way up."

"How do you know?" I demanded. "You haven't opened your eyes."

The veins along his forearms bulged as he gripped me tighter. "I know because I know *you*, Ellie. You're always up at the crack of dawn when you're anxious… no matter how thoroughly I wear you out before bed."

He had a point. Rather than debate a fact, I gave a resigned sigh. "I'm not wearing any clothes. I have to put something on."

His biceps flexed. "In that case, you're *really* not getting up."

He liked to claim that I always cracked him up, but his dry wit and rueful expressions constantly wrung giggles out of me, too. My titter sparked into true laughter when he flashed a roguish grin and cocked one eye open, giving me a pirate smile.

A second later, he relented, rolling off of me with a grunt. "Alright, alright," he yawned. "Get up. But I'm sleeping in and so is everyone else. We're all on a vacation."

I never excelled at being on vacation, even when I was a child. I always felt unsettled in new places… Even when my surroundings rivaled every Architectural Digest and Martha Stewart Home magazine.

"I'm a bad relaxer," I owned. "I'll be downstairs making coffee and possibly cinnamon rolls. Do you think your mom has yeast?"

Grayson huffed into his pillow. "I guarantee she does not."

I kissed the back of his neck. "Then I'll be downstairs making *sub-par* cinnamon rolls."

While being naked practically gave me hives, dressing presented its own dilemma. *Should I put on a whole outfit? Proper pajamas so I'm not over-dressed and weird? But what if I wear nice pajamas and they're robe people? Will my pajamas make them feel weird about their robes? Or I could put on sweats. But I only packed a few sets and I don't know what activities we have planned….*

I finally settled on a pair of Christmas-red pajama pants and a matching camisole, topping it off with a long, thick sweater I knitted a couple weeks before. I figured I could close the sweater up if I needed to. Satisfied, I added socks and crept out of the room, browsing recipes on Pinterest while I made my way downstairs.

Just like their townhome, the Hamptons kitchen was a culinary dream. I found the cabinets stocked with every appliance, gadget, product, and practical tool imaginable. Even yeast.

Within twenty minutes, I slapped some dough together and covered it to let it rise while I made coffee. The espresso machine was a temperamental Italian beast, but I put my barista training to good use. Eventually, I emerged the victor with a latte for myself and piping hot water for the French press. I decided to bring Grayson a carafe of fresh coffee to drink when he woke up.

As I finished soaking the coffee grounds, I heard a thump behind me. Whirling, I found myself face-to-face with a completely unfamiliar man. He stood on the threshold to the enormous kitchen, wearing a black leisure suit and holding a newspaper under his arm.

I started to panic until I recognized a few small similarities between the stranger and Mr. Stryker. They had the same tawny eyes and comparable bone structures. Otherwise, the man standing before me sort of resembled a blond, balding emperor penguin. Squat, with rounded features. Nothing like Grayson and Mr. Stryker's imposing heights and builds.

"Theodore Stryker, dear girl."

His voice gave me a chill. Anxiety snaked down into my stomach and coiled there, seething.

He didn't notice. He smiled, revealing a row of falsely white teeth. "My brother usually doesn't employ such young, attractive staff; but I see, in his old age, he's learned the error of his ways. Are you our chef for the weekend, sweetheart?"

Yikes. When Gray described his uncle as "smarmy," I somehow thought he had to be exaggerating. *Apparently not.*

I smoothed my hands over my messy bun, then forced myself forward to shake his hand. "No, sir. I'm Ella Callahan. Grayson's girlfriend."

He eyed me in a new, shrewd way I didn't care for. As if sizing up his competition. "Ah, yes. The famous Ella. I've heard a lot about you."

I was tempted to tell him I'd also heard a lot about *him*… none of it good. Instead I discreetly pulled the edges of my sweater together, hiding my cleavage from his overzealous appraisal.

"It's so good to meet you," I fibbed, pasting on a smile. I glanced behind me at the messy kitchen. "I apologize for just helping myself. Grayson told me his parents would still be sleeping for a while yet and we weren't expecting you until this afternoon…"

Theodore's sharp smile reappeared. "As soon as we got my son's travel arrangements worked out, I came right over. Got in late last night." A wholly inappropriate gleam lit his gaze. "Very late… Although, I don't believe I was the only one awake. The guest wing was far from quiet."

He capped his observation off with an exaggerated wink. Shock stabbed right into my throat, rendering me speechless.

Did he seriously just imply that he heard Gray and I when he got to the house?

Much to my mounting mortification, his insinuation made sense. When Gray joined me in our suite after dinner, he came straight at me. The fierce lines of his face betrayed a wealth of emotion—pain, longing, adoration. I didn't know why, but I knew he needed me. And I fell right into his arms, all too happy to spend the rest of the night making love until we both drifted off.

Still… even if Ted overheard us… wasn't it unspeakably rude to mention it to me?

"Ellie?"

Gray's voice filled me with relief. I cleared my throat, hoping to sound somewhat normal. "In here! With your uncle!"

He appeared behind Ted, wearing only a pair of navy sweats and some socks. The second his gaze touched me, his face folded into a frown. When he noted the shame blazing on my neck and chest, his eyes hardened into emeralds.

Ignoring his uncle, he sailed over and stepped between us, giving Ted his back. His hands flew up to frame my face. "What's the matter?"

I paused for a beat, debating the wisdom of lying to him. I hated to be dishonest, but I didn't want us to get off on the wrong foot. We had a lot riding on mending fences with his uncle.

"Nothing!" My voice sounded too bright. "We were just getting acquainted!"

Gray didn't buy it for a second. His eyes narrowed in suspicion. I widened mine slightly, shooting a fretful look around his arm and giving him a glare.

Be. Nice.

With a quiet sigh, Grayson pivoted, positioning himself to stand beside me. He reached across my back to grip my hip and dropped his face into my hair, nuzzling me instead of meeting his uncle's expectant eyes.

"Good morning, Ted," he rumbled to my crown, veiling disdain with a tissue-thin layer of apathy. "Nice to see you."

Either Theodore didn't take the hint, or he wanted to push Gray's buttons. "Grayson, my boy!" he crowed, surging forward to clap my boyfriend's bare shoulder. "Last time I saw you, you were scrawny as all hell. Good to see you finally filled out."

He waved at the mess behind us, adding, "And you put your little woman to work, I see."

Gray's fingers dug into my side, his expression darkening like a thundercloud. For some reason, the moment suddenly struck me as hilariously hopeless. I had to swallow the incorrigible urge to laugh in Ted's face.

A squeak slipped out before I could squelch it. Gray caught my gaze, reading the amusement there. We had a silent moment where we agreed not to let some casual sexism ruin our morning. Or our vacation.

His lips turned up at the corners. "Ella is wonderful and we're lucky to have her," he said, still gazing at me. "Though, we weren't expecting you until later in the day."

When he finally met Ted's eyes, Gray's stance altered. He drifted partially in front of me. Shirtless, with his hands all over me and his shoulders rolled back, he presented the very picture of confidence. Making it clear that I was his. That their house was his. And, I suspected, Stryker & Sons, as well.

Ted seemed to sense the same thing. He drew himself up to his full big-boy-penguin height.

"I wanted to wake up here," he replied. "The city is so hectic this time of year." He turned his sneer on me. "I bet my dear nephew didn't mention that I live so close by."

He hadn't, actually. But I was Gray's teammate; I wouldn't give his uncle the satisfaction of my agreement.

"Oh, he did," I insisted, then canted my head at Ted. "Isn't it so generous of Mason and Jacqueline to get us all out of town for a bit? They mentioned you used to have a home up here, too, but wound up selling it for some reason…"

Ted visibly quailed. "Yes. Well."

He snatched the French press off of the counter, along with the mug I laid out for Gray. "If you'll excuse me, I think I'll read my paper on the deck."

After he walked off, I turned to my boyfriend. "Well, there goes your coffee. Out into the cold. Whatever. I can make some more."

He cupped my face again, bending to lay a warm, chaste kiss against my lips. "No. I will make my own coffee. And then I'll help you with whatever you're doing in here because—once again—you are not a caterer, Ellie."

I kissed his chin and squirmed away. "Fine, make your coffee. But then you need to sit at the island and let me look at you while

I work because: A—you're handsome as hell, and B—you cannot cook."

Gray raised a sardonic brow. "Yes, ma'am."

Grayson

I spent most of Sunday vying for Ella's attention. My competition—our three-hundred-square foot cottage-style kitchen, and one powder-blue Kitchenaid mixer, in particular—won most of those stand-offs.

Though, after insisting on preparing cinnamon buns and coffee for the whole house, she did let me take her down to the beach. Turned out she loved the water, even in the thirty-degree weather. I sat in the sand and watched her twirl along the shore, laughing in the weak winter sunshine.

She splashed and squealed about the cold, but kept going back for more, rolling her jeans up and wading to her ankles until her feet took on a bluish cast. I wound up carrying her back up to the house, then warming both of us in front of the fireplace until lunchtime.

Once again, I lost her to the lure of the kitchen. She and Mom giggled and clucked while they assembled trays of sandwiches. I awkwardly watched while my father and Ted attempted not to antagonize each other.

By the middle of the afternoon, I gave up on trying to get Ellie to relax and gave in to her chaos. She was determined to make Christmas cookies—"For Santa," she claimed—and I couldn't resist the genuine joy the whole thing gave her.

Ted ducked out to do some last-minute errands and my parents disappeared, leaving Ellie and I on our own when the cookies finished baking. We took a plate of them into the TV room on the second floor and watched both of our favorite holiday films—*Home Alone* for me and *The Family Stone* for her.

An entire movie about a family engagement ring and a Christmas proposal… I had to concentrate on the feel of her hand in mine just to keep from breaking into a nervous sweat.

Mom managed to head Ellie off at the pass and ordered in pizza from Serafina's. During dinner, the ladies once again proved themselves the superior gender by keeping the conversation afloat, flitting from one easy topic to the next without ever touching on anything to do with the company or old grudges.

Everything was going perfectly to plan.

Except I *hated* Ted.

I didn't know why. The last time I saw the man, I was fifteen and completely oblivious; so, perhaps, he'd always been odious and I just never noticed it before. Maybe he was always mildly bitter and completely slimy. Or, maybe, years of exile from the Stryker legacy changed him for the worse.

Either way, as Dad, Ted, and I settled in the informal sitting room with glasses of brandy, it was all I could do to keep from downing half of my snifter in one gulp.

"…who knew Katie Couric's tits weren't real, right?" he cackled.

My mouth pulled into a grimace I tried to hide behind the rim of my glass. Dad's gaze snagged on mine, part amusement and part exasperation. He also took a healthy draught of liquor.

"So, Teddy."

I recognized his tone immediately. He wanted to get down to brass-tacks.

We shared another look, this one more loaded than the last. I understood immediately—he thought talking to Ted without Daniel would give us an advantage. Two-against-one, instead of a level playing field.

As far as I was concerned, any negotiation on our part was simply a show of good-faith. Dad owned the entire company. He didn't owe his brother a thing. In fact, he bought Ted's shares out instead of resigning his brother to prison and getting full control of the company for free. Ted had been living off of my father's goodwill for years, even though he didn't deserve it.

I didn't have any siblings, though, so I owned that I might not fully understand their relationship. From what I gleaned listening to Ella nag Darcy over the phone, brothers and sisters seemed to share a special bond that transcended most petty squabbles.

This hardly seemed trivial, but I knew my dad didn't feel right being high-handed with a company that my grandfather always meant to share between the two of them.

We'd discussed our goals ahead of time. He wanted to hire Ted as a consultant and pay him an executive consultant's salary—so, a lot of money. He also wanted to hire Daniel to begin learning the parts of the business that didn't interest me; namely, acquisitions, holdings, and sales.

But my father was a brilliant man. He didn't plan to give either of the Other Strykers (as Ellie jokingly called them) control over one single penny of company funds. For the time being, Dad planned to maintain financial and operational control. While I continued to learn those ropes, I'd also take creative control on our new headquarters.

Ted listened as we outlined our plan. His expression remained neutral, but glimmers of avarice sparked in his eyes. "So you two would like to *hire* me, to consult for *my own company*?"

My hackles rose. I sat forward, about to speak, but Dad's hand fell on my arm. He took a sip of brandy and rolled it around before calmly replying, "No. We would like to give you an opportunity to come back to *our* company, in a senior advisory position. With proper compensation, naturally."

Ted stared him down. "I want my shares back."

"Absolutely not."

The words fell from my lips before I could stop them. I didn't feel angry or rash. My voice stayed dead even.

"You tried to steal money from my father and he saved you from rotting in a cell. Your shares are being transferred to me; [illegible] my father and I will retain control of the entire company, until his shares inevitably pass to me as well."

I cast my father a sideways glance—a warning, before I pulled my trump card. At his slight nod, I finished, "Of course, I'm not heartless. Daniel is my cousin and my father's nephew. If he proves he can do the work and you manage to stay out of trouble, I'll consider transferring some of those shares to your son."

Ted glared at me. "So I'm supposed to sit at your side like some sort of vizier while you play at being king? All so you *might* throw Danny your scraps?"

His objections were exactly what I expected. I peered down into my glass, doing my best not to appear smug. "No one is playing. When my father steps down, I will be the CEO. And I will need advisors. As for the shares… I don't think many would classify a thirty-percent stake in a twenty-billion-dollar company as 'scraps.' It's certainly a hell of a lot more than whatever's left of his trust."

Ted ground his jaw, considering. I had him on the ropes much sooner than I expected. He must have been more desperate than I realized.

While I still had the upper hand, I finished my drink and set the snifter aside, rising. "The thing is Ted," I went on, staring steadily. "I don't give a goddamn what you do."

A lie. But he didn't know that my professional happiness hinged on this deal.

I continued, "My father wants to make amends due to his illness. I want someone who knows about what we do to advise me while he undergoes treatments. But neither of us need you. If you think you an aniel can do better, feel free to turn me down. No hard feeli As for your relationship with your brother…" I nodded at .d. "That's not my business. I'll leave you two to sort it out. If m .d excuse me?"

I propelled myself out of the sitting room, exhilarated. It felt good to tell Ted off. But, more so, I actually felt like I did well. Of course, it was easy to bet when you held all the chips.

Riding my high, I strode toward the guest wing. I couldn't wait to tell Ella and watch the way her face softened when she told me she was proud of me. If there was any better feeling in the world than earning admiration from the woman I loved, I'd yet to find it.

"Grayson."

My mother's whispered voice caught me as I passed the east wing. She waved her arms, beckoning me over to her shadowy stretch of hallway.

"Thank goodness I caught you," she mumbled, eyes wide. "It's about the proposal. While Ella and I were in the kitchen after dinner, I caught her eyeing this."

Mom flashed the aquamarine ring on her right hand. "So I let her try it on, of course," she went on, "and it's too small!"

Fuck. We used my mother's fingers to choose the right ring size for Ellie. If Mom's ring didn't fit her…. "I need to get it resized right away," I muttered, reaching for my phone. "Is there a jeweler in town?"

My mother quirked a sardonic brow. "This is the Hamptons, *mi amor*. Of course there is. I've been a customer at Marinelli's on Main for many years. They know me. We'll head down there first thing tomorrow morning."

Reeling, I tried to think through a plan. "I suppose we can probably slip out while Ella's in the kitchen. God knows what she's planning on making tomorrow."

The thought made both of us smile. "She's so lovely," Mom whispered. "You chose very well, Grayson."

I couldn't agree more.

Sometime just before dawn, I felt Ellie's cool hands against my face.

"Gray?"

I didn't know if I was awake or dreaming. "Mmm?"

She traced my eyebrow. "Grayson?"

Gradually, reality sank in. I felt the chill creeping in from the windows across the room, the slight dampness of being near the sea, her heart thrumming against my chest. Quick, staccato beats. Unusually so…

My eyes flew open. I searched for her face. "Ellie? Another nightmare?"

Peering at her through the darkness, I realized she wasn't upset at all. She looked… elated. A dazzling smile filled her sweet features.

"No. Gray, it's *snowing*."

Still drowsy, I let my eyes slip closed as I groaned and tried to pull her back on top of me. "It's also the middle of the night."

"No, Gray," she said again, shaking me lightly. "*It's snowing*. At the beach. The day before Christmas Eve!" She bounced on her knees, vibrating with excitement. "We have to go outside, come on!"

Grumbling, I scrubbed at my face. "Outside? In the dark? In the cold?"

Luminous sapphire eyes glowed down at me, beseeching. "Please?"

She looked so hopeful and happy. A fresh swell of love surged through me, pushing me up onto my elbows. I pressed a soft kiss between her brows. "Alright. Lead the way."

We wandered outside, dressed haphazardly in sweats, unlaced shoes, and open coats. Bracing blusters rolled up from the ocean, banishing my grogginess. By the time we made it to the sand, I felt wide awake. But I could have sworn I was still in a dream.

With snowflakes studding her eyelashes and melting on her peachy cheeks, Ella looked like an angel. She held her palms up to the sky as she turned in fluid circles along the shore. Her laugh floated through the wind.

"See?" she called. "It's like magic!"

And it was. *She* was.

Every bright, beautiful thing about the world. Everything right about *my* world.

I did see. I saw that I was the single most fortunate man on the whole damn planet, to have this woman love me. I saw that my entire life would be worth more than I ever imagined. Because of her.

God. I didn't know that I could love anything so much that it would become a physical ache inside of me. Covering the place where my heart threatened to pound out of my chest, I rubbed at it while I watched her dance in the snowy sand.

Her delighted hums and giggles put a wide grin on my face. When she caught me staring, she charged right at me, leaping up into my arms. I caught her with a grunt, holding her body with one arm while my palm cupped her face.

Our gazes connected, sending me back to the very first time she ever looked at me. Just like that day on the subway, something in my soul simply clicked.

Ella felt it, too. Her delight softened into adoration.

"Grayson," she whispered, leaning her forehead into mine. "I love you so much."

Fuck. My throat burned, longing to return her precious words back to her. I'd already made her wait for weeks, saving them for my proposal, determined to give her the romantic moment she deserved. I couldn't give it all up mere hours before I popped the question.

Disappointing her was hell. Like an oil spill spreading over an ocean, hurt bled into her irises. I clutched her tighter, praying she wouldn't try to pull away from me.

She didn't at all. Instead of retreating to protect herself, she surrendered even more, brushing a tender kiss over my cheek.

Sometimes, in my darker moments, I almost hated how much she loved me. How could I ever deserve it? I didn't know. But, in that second, I felt like a failure.

"Ella—"

She pressed her frozen fingers into my mouth, hushing me. "No. Don't. This is all too beautiful. We should just… enjoy it."

I nestled her closer, hiding my face in her damp hair. "Ellie…"

Wrapping her arms around my neck, she hugged me. "Can we sit?"

Without any other recourse, I blew out all the air trapped in my lungs and lowered us to the ground. Ella rearranged herself, turning to drape her legs across my lap and lean her head back into my shoulder.

She gazed up at the swirling sky, her expression taking on a wistful note that matched her voice. "I only wish we could see the stars."

I thought of my gifts for her—the telescope, the ring—and folded her closer. *Soon baby,* I vowed silently. *I'm going to give you everything.*

Ella

After Grayson and I stripped out of our wet clothes and got back in bed, I spent the last few hours of darkness struggling to find sleep.

Every time I closed my eyes, I saw his face when I told him I loved him. The way panic flared in his eyes. The rigid set of his jaw.

What if he really doesn't love me?

My stomach cramped, twisting in pain. I rolled away from Gray and pressed my palms into my abdomen until the nausea died down long enough for me to drift into a shallow slumber.

It only felt like a few seconds passed before I started to sink into my well-worn nightmare. Before it could pull me under, I snapped my burning gaze open and scooted back into my spot at Grayson's side. I focused on his warmth to steady my breathing, then let myself imagine him singing to me.

Next time I opened my eyes, light glowed on the horizon. Feeling forlorn, I wrapped my arms around my knees and stared out at the water.

I had to face the possibility that Grayson may not have the same feelings for me that I had for him. At first, I convinced myself he was just working up his nerve to tell me. But weeks had passed.

Maybe, with everything he's going through, he needs someone in his life for support and I just happened to be the closest one to that position at the time. It's possible to need someone without loving them. Maybe he would have gotten attached to any girl he happened to be dating when he found out about his dad.

The thought left me cold. But the fact remained—no matter how he felt about me, *I* loved *him*. And we were hardly in the proper setting for a potentially-catastrophic conversation.

I'll feel better after a cup of coffee. And I should call my mom. Hearing her voice will help.

I had to shake off my funk before I faced the Strykers. Whatever issues Gray and I had… I wouldn't let them ruin what might have been his father's last Christmas.

I dressed in another pajama-sweater combo, then stuffed on socks. The impulse to bolt blurred through me. I held still and stared over at my clogs, remembering the way I used to flee whenever my anxiety surged. All the times I almost lost Gray before we even began.

If I'd allowed those instincts to rule my life, I would have missed out on so much. Even if he didn't love me… even if he never would…

I got to fall in love with him, for however long it might last.

On my way down the stairs, I did my best to extinguish my dread. There really wasn't a need for it, anyway. Nothing had changed.

Emotionally, our relationship remained right where we left it at Thanksgiving. And, practically, we were making huge strides. A new apartment, his upcoming graduation and promotion. We both seemed happy and motivated.

So why did I feel low-grade panic buzzing beneath my diaphragm?

The overcast morning didn't help my mood. The snow melted off, leaving the ground muddy and the sky a sunless, pale grey. The gloom even turned the ocean from its usual aqua to anemic blue.

I frowned out at view, ignoring the sparkling Christmas tree and its array of presents en route to the kitchen.

While I flipped on the lights and set to work with the espresso machine, I wondered if I was using cooking and kitchen work to mask my apprehension about being part of the Strykers' lifestyle. Their fifty-million-dollar townhome and country estate felt massively overwhelming to me. Every fixture and furnishing seemed a reminder of just how little I had to offer.

But the kitchens, by virtue of their practical purpose, were less opulent than other spaces. I could count on them to have all of the familiar, mundane things I grew up with—trash cans, garbage disposals, paper towels.

They also offered a way for me to contribute. I couldn't buy fancy gifts or pay for extravagant meals… but I could bake cookies and make waffles and wash dishes.

I couldn't decide if the whole thing was a healthy coping mechanism or toxic self-deprecation… even as I went about organizing the ingredients I needed to whip up pancakes.

My hands shook while I lined everything up on the island in the center of the room. I glanced over my shoulder at every small sound, expecting something ominous each time.

Why did I feel so unglued? I was fine for nearly two full days and *now* the entire situation suddenly triggered me?

Ridiculous, I told myself, blowing out a trembling breath. *You're being silly. There's no reason to be this upset.*

I heard another noise, one more distinct than the others. Whirling with my hand clutched over my heart, I came face-to-face with yet another strange man.

Only… he wasn't so unfamiliar.

For a moment, I thought it must have been the way he also resembled Mr. Stryker. Light hair, a strap of blond facial hair. Rounded features and sharp ocher eyes.

Then he smiled—a pointed grin just like Ted's.

It's Gray's cousin Daniel, you lunatic, my brain jeered. *Get ahold of yourself.*

Unfreezing my lips and forming a fake smile was the best I could do. "Oh," I tittered, sounding squeaky. "Hello…"

He didn't move, but his eyes flicked down my body, then back up. Silence stretched over us for a beat too long. My heart hammered at my ribs, urging me to *run away right now.*

But I ignored the impulse again, fighting panic with everything I had in me. "You must be, um, Daniel. Or Danny? I'm Ella, Grayson's girlfriend."

Our eyes met. The force of his loathing sent me back a step.

"You know," he said, "I didn't believe it was really you until right now."

The second I heard his voice, I *knew*. My lungs splintered. Terror curdled my guts. A wave of dizziness swirled my thoughts into soup.

Seeing my distress only widened his smile. "So we meet again, little princess."

***

Chapter Twenty-One

October 2016

Ella

Getting out of Grayson's building and back to Brooklyn felt like a horror movie. One where a menacing psychopath nipped at my heels, brandishing a blade.

I took a cab, hoping to blend into the crush of city traffic. My eyes flew from one window to the other, constantly looking to be sure I wasn't followed. When we rolled up to my apartment, I tossed all the money I had at the driver and streaked upstairs, dying to get to Maggie as quickly as possible.

I knew I had to tell her everything. I needed help. The police, probably. And, whatever I did, I had to keep it all away from Grayson and his company.

Bouncing in place, I undid all three locks on our door and burst into the living room, spinning to re-latch them all immediately, including the chain we usually didn't close. As soon as I realized I was home safe, my adrenaline rush receded. For the third time in as many days, my legs turned to water. I fell to my knees.

Behind me, Maggie's door creaked open. Or maybe it was mine? *Maggie's door doesn't usually squeak like—*

I spun on my knees. The edges of my vision faded to black.

"So glad you could join me, little princess." Daniel's steps ate up the distance between us. "I've been waiting for you."

Grayson

She was gone.

Again.

After everything she told me. After insisting she tried to come back the last time. After swearing Maggie never told her that I tried to find her. After explaining how she went to therapy and demonstrating how much she'd worked on her anxiety triggers…

She still ran.

I hovered on the threshold between my bedroom and the great room for an eternity, unable to process her absence. Not believing it.

Because that was just it: I *didn't* believe it. I refused.

I no longer felt angry or numb or spiteful. Instead, completely certainty solidified into concern. Determination. Something was wrong. I needed to determine what it was. If she wouldn't tell me… I would figure it out without her.

Whipping my phone out, I dialed Marco's number immediately.

"Amir." He sounded unusually alert for so early in the day.

Good. I needed him on his game. "Marco. Where are you? I need you here as soon as possible. There's a situation with Ella."

"Downstairs," he returned. "We had a workout scheduled, sir."

I'd totally forgotten… and probably would have gotten my ass handed to me after spending the better part of the night making love to Ellie. "I need you to come up. And I need the security footage from the penthouse for the last two hours."

While he made his way to my door, I hustled to retrieve the dossier he compiled on Ella, sitting abandoned on my bar. By the time Marco swept in, clad a casual version of his usual all-black, I had it spread out over my coffee table.

"Ella was here overnight," I began without preamble. "She left early this morning. I think within the last hour. We're going to figure out why."

Marco dropped down on the stark white chair perpendicular to my sofa. His focus snapped to the contents of the file immediately. His hand reached into the pocket of his joggers. "Right. I pulled the footage."

Disquiet marred the space around his dark eyes as he set the phone between us. "She didn't just leave," he murmured. "She *ran*. Out of the apartment, out of the building, into a cab. She didn't take anything with her aside from her purse and her phone. Not even shoes."

Fuck. Ellie. I wrapped both hands around the back of my neck, pulling at it. "Well did you see what she was doing before she bolted?"

Marco's finger adjusted the video reel, scrubbing it back. I bent forward, peering down at the image. Ella shuffled out of my bedroom, her gate sluggish. She surveyed the damage from the night before and shook her head a bit before crossing the wide floor to the kitchen area. She picked something up. Froze. And tore out of the room seconds later.

"What did she—"

Marco had his answer ready. "Her phone. I already tapped into the building's Wi-Fi to see if any calls or messages pinged off our service. No dice; she probably didn't have the passcode to link into it, so she was running on cellular data. I could get cell records from nearby towers but that would take a while."

"We don't have time for that," I decided out loud, shaking my head. "What else is there?"

"Well..." Amir trailed off, considering. After a few seconds, I noticed the way his eyes flit to a particular document in the far-right corner of the coffee table. Each time he glanced at it, his mouth tightened.

Without a shred of patience, I reached over and snatched it up. Marco's hand halted me, wrapping around my forearm. "Wait."

I shook him off. "Why?"

A hard edge crept into his features. "Have you read all of this yet?"

"No," I admitted. "It felt like an unnecessary invasion of her privacy. I only glanced at her personal information and her schedule. I didn't even let myself save her number in my phone or I would have called her by now. Or had you call her, since I was blocked years ago."

Marco sighed heavily. He looked back at the pages curled in my fist. "You might not want to look at those right now, Grayson."

He never used my real name. The fact that he did in that moment sent a frisson of panic down my spine. "Why not?"

His eyes burned like coals. "Because it will distract you from the task at hand. Trust me."

My attention snapped to the pages. "What *is* it? Could it explain why she ran? Why she left back then?"

He didn't reply. My mind reeled to the worst case scenario. "Is she… sick? Or a murderer?"

"No." His impassive mask broke as his head fell forward. "It's… When I compiled her information, I used everything NYU had in their system to track her past addresses, her tuition payments, her graduation info. All standard stuff. But there was… an "incident report," they called it. I thought it might have been some type of disciplinary thing, so I pulled it…"

Unable to stand another moment of uncertainty, I brought the pages to my face and scanned them. *Incident Report*, the form read. And there, under her name and a date in spring of 2012, three words: *student alleges rape*.

It made horrible, perfect sense. I always suspected she had some history with sexual assault. Even though she refused to tell me details, her triggers and nightmares gave her away. But I always allowed myself to believe—to *hope*—that it was something less insidious than rape.

My stomach flipped inside out. "No."

Before Amir could stop me, I turned the page. A roar tore from my chest. "*God, no!*"

The second sheet was a supplementary report from the campus police force. Including pictures. Bruises on her neck, deep purple fingerprints smudged over her jaw. A bald patch above her temple where hair had been ripped out at the root. Her small, elegant hands… with dark shadows blooming over her wrists and half her nails ripped from a struggle.

Blood. Bloody stockings. A bloody skirt.

No underwear recovered, the page informed me.

I dropped the papers and doubled over, putting my head between my knees. Visceral pain gored into my guts. My diaphragm heaved. It took everything I had to force air in and out of my body, to keep from vomiting on my feet.

Ella. All of the times she shrank away from me. The fearful way she looked at me the first few times I touched her. The way she used to panic if I settled my weight over her.

She was brutalized. Savagely.

"Who?" I bit out, my wild gaze staring at the white oak floor. "Who did this?"

"She only filed a report with the campus security people and student health. No police, no DNA evidence. From the scant wording of their reports, I got the sense they didn't plan to pursue her attacker in any way."

I'd never felt such outrage. "*What?*"

His bleak eyes looked black. "If she went home and showered, if too much time passed before she came to them, if she was drugged… The campus police would have known they couldn't build a case based on her testimony."

"*Drugged?*" The blade wedged into my stomach twisted. "He *drugged* her?"

Marco looked at his folded hands and squeezed them, clearly repressing his own fury. "They didn't even test her, Grayson. She couldn't answer any of their questions about who did it or how she knew him. She told them she was at a frat party and had some drinks… they took that to mean she was an unreliable witness and didn't do any follow-ups, aside from charging the fraternity in question some sort of administrative fee. Six weeks later, Ella was sent to the dean of her college for issues with her grades slipping and they added her name to an endless list of students who warranted 'psychological screening.' I never found any record of her seeing anyone, though."

Sweetheart. My heart shattered, thinking of her suffering alone. Scared. Not even knowing who violated her or how to keep herself safe from them.

"She sees a therapist now," I mumbled, hoarse from horror. "She probably couldn't afford to, before she got her full-time job."

I hated myself so much in that moment, I wanted to pitch myself off the balcony. *I could have paid for her to go to therapy. I should have seen that she needed that. I should have asked if she wanted me to go with her.*

Jesus. No wonder she ran from me. How could anyone go through what she went through and not have massive panic issues around sex and intimacy?

Issues she did her damnedest to overcome. For me.

The need to hold her ripped through me. I had to know she was safe. "I need to go to her place," I said. "I need to see her."

Ever practical, Marco made no move to leave. "We don't even know if that's where she went. Or why she left this morning. If there's a threat that requires some sort of back-up, we need to know."

"Then call back up," I demanded, stalking to my room. "I don't care what it takes. We're going to find her."

I sat in the front seat next to Marco, too keyed up to drive myself or sit in the back. We used his phone to call hers several times before giving up. Each attempt went straight to her voicemail without ringing, which only heightened my dread, since I knew her cell wasn't dead.

Halfway through the Lower East Side, without moving his eyes off the road, Amir asked, "Did you ever…? You never told me what happened, in the Hamptons, did you?"

No. I never spoke about it to anyone. Apart from the family members who bore witness and, eventually, Graham.

"I'm thinking," he went on, "I get that she had the urge to run from trauma. But… why run *when* she did? Today it was a text message that set her off. But what was it that day? What changed from the day before—or even the night before—when she was totally fine?"

I'd asked myself the same question a million times. There was only one answer. And it made absolutely no sense. "Danny got there, after we were all asleep. Aside from that, nothing was different. I guess she spoke to him before she left, because he was in the kitchen when I came down that morning and he told me Ellie had gone for a walk to call her mom. I never saw her again."

Marco's head snapped to the side, pinning me with an urgent look. "Daniel?"

"Yes." I blinked at the vehemence in his features. A chill moved through me. "What about him?"

He shook his head, as if dismissing the thoughts inside of it before they could take hold. "I'm sure I'm mistaken."

I didn't have the fucking patience for him to tip-toe around my feelings. "About *what*?" I growled.

He shrugged, but the motion was tight. "You know I have security files on everyone at Stryker & Sons. Your father requested extra detail for the one I compiled on your uncle, after what happened with the company funds and his pension account… So I did that and I also took the liberty of using the same broad scope for Daniel. He'd been out of the country for a while, so I pulled international records, domestic records. There was nothing of note, obviously, or I would have told your dad."

"But…?"

His fists blanched against the wheel. "*But…* there was a sealed juvenile record. From his time in prep school. I couldn't access it, because of the seal. From what I gleaned from school records, he had some sort of incident with another student and was subsequently charged, then expelled. He transferred schools. His father paid to have the record sealed and then expunged."

I remembered him changing schools during his junior year. Uncle Ted made it seem like it was a financial decision; the result of my father's move to dissolve Ted's interests in our company following his misconduct. I heard some rumors about Danny getting in trouble, but no one ever implied anything sinister.

"Did you tell my father?"

Amir nodded, his jaw clenching. "He told me that Ted had spoken with him about it and they decided amongst themselves that the issue didn't merit any further action. It was a 'youthful indiscretion,' he said. A fight, or some other immature shit. Standard stuff. Which is why courts allow juvenile records to be sealed in the first place. I figured he knew the details and trusted his judgment on the matter. Only, one thing about the school incident report did give me pause."

We hit the Brooklyn Bridge as I stared at him, too dismayed to ask.

He answered anyway. "It was a girl," he muttered. "The student who reported him to their school… it was a female classmate two years younger than him."

Chapter Twenty-Two

December 2013

Grayson

I wondered if finding Ella's place in bed empty would always bother me.

After our mid-night journey to the shore, we agreed to sleep late; but the clock on my phone said *8:24*. Hardly a luxurious lie-in.

I also had a text from my mother, telling me to message her when I woke up because we needed to try to get to the jewelry store the second they opened, at nine. She hoped if we arrived before any other customers, the jeweler might agree to size the ring on the spot instead of making me come back for it later... which would involve coming up with another excuse to sneak away from Ellie. Either way, I knew it would cost me.

After exchanging a handful of texts, we agreed to meet downstairs in ten minutes. She also informed me that my travel plan went off without a hitch and Daniel had already arrived. I rushed through dressing, throwing on the first sweater and pair of jeans I could find, nearly tripping over Ella's clogs on my way out.

My parents were waiting in the kitchen, chatting up a scruffy, world-worn version of my cousin that I barely recognized.

"Grayson, my brother!" he hooted, greeting me with a hard slap to the back. "How the fuck are ya?"

He'd never been known for his polish. Briefly, I wondered if that unorthodox edge would work in our favor once he ran our real estate holdings.

"I'm well," I told him, meaning it. "Very well."

He nodded, smiling. "I met your new girl. She was in here when I woke up." He slapped me again. "And damn, she's *fine*. Good work, cuz."

I glanced around, looking for traces of my girlfriend. The neatly ordered ingredients on the island seemed to suggest she'd only stepped away for a moment.

"Did you see where she ran off to?" I asked, reaching for the French press she left out for me. "She snuck away from me this morning and I didn't get a chance to tell her that we're going into town for some last-minute shopping."

Daniel leaned into the counter, sipping from his mug. "She said she was going to go for a walk on the beach," he told me, shrugging. "Then she mentioned something about making waffles?"

Dad chuckled fondly. "That sounds like Ella, alright."

Mom laughed. "It's just as well. Gives us the perfect opportunity to slip out before she sees what we're up to."

I found a thermos for my coffee and started pouring. "I'll text her from the car and let her know when we'll be back."

Daniel unwound, loping over. "Speaking of, do you mind if I borrow your cell for a second? Mine died in the car on the way in from the tarmac and I only have a European charger. I just need to check the market real quick."

Impressed that he had investments to track, I handed the iPhone to him. "Yeah, no worries. Code is 0924. I'm just going to go grab something…"

With a meaningful look to my parents, I slipped out to the great room and plucked Ella's ring out from under the tree. When I returned, they both had their coats on.

Danny handed me back my phone. With a nod and a salute, he waved us out. "Godspeed, bro."

Ella

It took every scrap of courage I could muster to return to the Strykers' house.

After dramatically running out of the place as if the flames of hell licked at my (shoeless) heels, I ran as far up the shore as my frozen feet would carry me, fighting to breathe the entire way. Only after I collapsed in a heap on the ground did I realize I left everything behind, including my cell phone.

For a long time, I didn't care. *Couldn't* care.

I was too concerned with the notion of Daniel following me. Even though I knew it made no sense—if he wanted to attack me, he could have done it right there in the kitchen. Or snuck up on me some other time.

Still, I folded into a ball and hid in the tall grasses lining the sand, hoping to be still enough to make myself invisible.

Eventually, I felt certain he wasn't after me and tried to get my body back under control. Watching the waves roll up the sand and fall back helped quiet my mind.

With the benefit of distance, I started to review our encounter objectively.

And, the fact remained; I didn't *know* it was him. To claim something with absolute certainty based off of a handful of words would be… irresponsible. After all, lots of men called women misogynistic pet names. And it was possible Daniel and I *had* met before… just not on a damp frat house mattress.

I was already anxious when I came downstairs. Maybe I overreacted. Or got triggered enough to spiral and start imagining things. I mean, realistically, what are the odds? Zero, probably.

Sometime later, I noticed the waves creeping further up the beach. The tide changing. That meant I'd been gone awhile…

And I had to go back.

It's fine, I coached myself. *You'll go back, go straight upstairs to your room, wake Gray up, tell him everything, and tell him you have to leave so you don't ruin the holiday. He'll be upset, but he'll understand. And at least you won't be running out on him without a word.*

The house felt eerily quiet when I stepped inside. I left my wet socks on the deck and tiptoed to the second story, choking back bile.

Breathe. Everything will be okay once you find Gray. He won't let anyone hurt you.

But the moment I burst into our guest suite, I knew he wasn't there.

The door fell closed behind me and I jumped, turning to find Daniel with his hand on the handle, locking it in place.

"Hi, princess," he drawled, cocking his head at me. "We've been waiting for you."

Ted appeared at my elbow, gripping my forearm. I flailed and shrieked, but he only snapped up my other wrist.

"Now, now," he admonished, his voice oddly serene. "There's no need for that. I'm here to make sure my son behaves himself this time. I understand he wasn't a gentleman at your first meeting."

I barely heard him through the sound of my panicked panting. I tried to scream again, but the sound died in my dry throat. Daniel lunged, cupping one hand around my skull and smashing the other over my mouth.

The horribly familiar gesture sent black spots blooming over my vision. I swayed, nearly fainting as my legs went limp.

Oh my God. This is real. It's actually him.

My literal worst nightmare… all over again.

Daniel's face loomed right in front of mine. "Are you going to be a good girl and listen to what we have to say? Or do I need to take you my room and tie you up?"

From behind me, Ted pulled my arms tighter. His tone sounded resigned. "Probably better to tie her up in mine. No one would think to look in there."

A sick gleam lit Daniel's eyes as they leered at me, considering. "I'll have to gag her, of course."

Hot tears spilled down my cheeks. "No," I begged, muffled by my mashed lips. "Please. I can listen. I'll do whatever you want."

"Oh, don't tell me *that*, princess. You know what you do to me."

Ted's hand released my left arm and flew up to strike the side of his son's head. "*Daniel.* That's enough. Focus."

Reluctantly, he took his hands off of me and stepped back, glaring as he rubbed his hand over his skull. "She's still a stuck-up little bitch," he muttered, eyeing me. "Even though she's clearly a slut. You should have seen how hot for it she was the other day."

Ted walked around to stand beside his son, casting me an appraising look. "Yes," he agreed dryly, smirking, "I got an earful of it later that night."

I didn't even have it in me to be disgusted or ashamed. I only felt terrified. So scared that I thought every particle of my body might just vibrate apart.

Daniel's leer looped back up to my face. "She was riding him, desperate as all hell. I'd probably just be doing her a favor…"

Ted's face furrowed into a frown. "There's no time for that. They've already been gone over an hour. We have to make this quick."

My mind worked feverishly, trying to piece together everything they said. The Strykers were out somewhere, along with Grayson. There was no time to violate me… but then what were they doing in our room? Were they going to hurt me… or kill me?

Dear God, *why*?

Because they know that you'll tell Grayson what Daniel did… and then he'll kill Daniel. And everything else will fall apart.

Confusion crowded behind the panic. *When did Daniel* see *us? He said something like that this morning, too… how he didn't really believe it was me when he* first *saw me… But Gray and I didn't have sex last night… or yesterday. Not since Saturday night, when he was at me until morning… The same night we found out Daniel was stranded in Dublin.*

"What are you talking about?" I squeaked hoarsely. "You just got here."

His grin took on a crooked quality. "I've been here since Saturday afternoon, princess. Arrived right after you, apparently, because when I came upstairs, I caught the little show you two put on."

None of it made any sense. My first instinct was denial. *He's lying.*

"Why would you claim to be stuck overseas?" I demanded, shrill from fright. "I heard Gray call the jet for you."

His eyes hardened. "'Gray,' is it? Christ. I don't know whether to laugh or vomit."

Ted sighed deeply. "I told you they were sickening."

My nails dug half-moons into my palms, drawing blood. "Someone answer me!" I begged.

With a scoff, Daniel once again regarded me with scorn. "Try to keep up, princess. I got here on Saturday, saw you fucking my baby cousin, and realized I *knew* you. But, because of the *way* I knew you, I couldn't very well risk you recognizing me on the spot. Not if I ever wanted to cash another check from Stryker in my lifetime. No one ever saw me come in, so I just left. Got a room in town to regroup."

My thoughts spun through the implications. "So you only pretended to be delayed?"

"Mm hmm," he replied with an indolent shrug. "Figured I'd sit out until my father could get over here and assess the situation. Once he saw that you had *Gray* wrapped *all around* your little fingers, we decided I had to check and make absolutely sure it was you. Then, after our run-in this morning, we knew we had to take drastic action."

Oh God. They really were going to kill me. I tripped over my own feet, shuffling backward.

"Please," I pleaded. "Please don't hurt me. I—I'll—"

...what?

I couldn't promise not to tell Grayson. Of course I had to tell him... Even if I somehow lived with this horrible discovery and didn't automatically spiral into a blind panic every time he even mentioned his family... I couldn't let someone so treacherous stay in his life. Right?

Ted made a clucking sound. "Now, dear, don't make a liar of yourself. You'll go running to your boyfriend the second he walked in the door, if we let you. We can't have that. Last night, we hammered out a deal for our company. An extremely lucrative deal. I won't have anything get in the way of it. Least of all you."

Daniel's sneer brought a prickle of fresh tears to my eyes. "I never did catch your name, back then," he said. "*Ella*. Perfect for a little princess."

Grayson once told me the same thing. Remembering, my stomach churned and heaved. "Please," I begged, still not sure what to ask for. "Please just... leave us alone."

Ted actually looked remorseful for a second. "Poor, sweet thing. I wish that was an option. But I'm afraid there's really no other solution—you're going to have to leave. Now."

"*Leave*?" The word snapped out of me, escaping before a rush of bile sprang up my throat. I choked it down, holding my hands over my face while I shook my head.

"We've already packed you up," Ted went on. "And drafted a message for you to send Grayson before you go. We thought you ought to add your own spin to it, though. For authenticity."

A flash of anger shocked me. "What makes you think I would ever let you do this?" I yelled. "I won't leave him! The second I tell him what you did to me—what you're trying to do *now*—he's going to make sure I never have to see either of you ever again. So…" I faltered, losing steam. "Tie me up, I guess. He'll be back eventually and he'll find me."

All traces of compassion vanished from Ted's face. "We thought you might feel that way. So I took it upon myself to make some calls…"

He reached into the inside pocket of his jacket and pulled out a sheaf of papers, tossing them at me. I sifted through the first page, but couldn't understand any of it.

"That's a loan document, dear, from your mother's bank. Did you know she took out a second mortgage on her house to help you pay for school? Very touching."

He grimaced and spread his palms in a chagrinned gesture. "Unfortunately for both of you, my good friend *owns* that bank. And your mom missed her second payment this month. For the last *three* months, actually. A common problem, around the holidays… it usually goes unnoticed by the bank, as long as one makes the payments up quickly. The thing is, I had my friend pull her records so now they're *aware*… and if I don't call in a favor, your family's house will go into foreclosure. Tomorrow."

Oh my God. I was going to pass out. Or throw up. Or scream.

But if I did any of those things, this man would call up his buddy and leave my family without a home. Without the home where all the memories of my father lived, too.

Daniel's smile took on a predatory air. "You have a sister, right? Darcy? She a little cock-tease like you?"

Another desperate rush of rage and denial assailed me. "I don't—I can't understand any of this! Grayson told me you went to Columbia! You didn't even go to NYU—what were you doing at that party?"

"Eh, I prefer not to shit where I eat. Learned that lesson in high school. Lots of socialites and future colleagues at an Ivy League university—too many people to risk developing an unsavory reputation. No risk of that in the slums though." He gave another shrug. "You get it."

Ted took a step toward me. "So, you know your options now, Ella. You can break up with Grayson, leave now, and disappear from his life. Or I can call my friend and have your family turned out on the street. In fact, even if she made all her payments on time, I could still get her mortgage revoked with a single phone call. And I will, if you ever come sniffing around our family again.

"I've read your mother's accounts, Ella. The process of foreclosure would probably bankrupt her. I'm guessing that would mean no more college for you and no college in the future for your sister, either. No credit for your mom to get a new home, finance a car, get a credit card… It would be a shame if you made a selfish choice to destroy their futures. After all, there are other fish in the sea."

"Ones who won't ever find out that you're… you know," Daniel added, gesturing at me. "*Ruined.*"

I didn't even have it in me to object. In that moment, I *felt* ruined. Utterly decimated. Permanently wrecked. Stained, scarred, burned to ash.

How would Gray look at me if I told him what his cousin did to me? How would he ever want to hold me or kiss me again? How would I ever allow him to? I knew I would regress on all the progress I'd made. Possibly to the point of not ever being able to have sex again.

How could Grayson deal with that, on top of everything else in his life? He already had to sacrifice any scrap of free time for me. I couldn't ask for *more.* If I didn't leave, he'd wind up pouring himself into fixing me, my family, our finances. He'd be left with my charred husk in return. And that wasn't even taking into consideration whatever Daniel might do to me if I refused to leave…

Gray needed someone sane and whole. A person who would help him, not drag him into a bottomless mess.

Victory lit Daniel's amber eyes. "There is one other thing, of course." This time, he reached into his pocket and flung a folded blueprint at me.

I recognized the writing immediately. *Gray's building.*

"We all know it's no coincidence that I'm being called back into the fold after years of exile just as my little cousin decides he wants to pursue a creative interest in Stryker & Sons. I'm guessing that if I walk away—or get *sent* away—the Great Grayson Stryker won't get to design his big-boy building. Which has always been his dream, right?"

That was it. The final shot.

Bullseye.

My legs went out, sending me to the cold wood floor. Frantic, my blurry vision swam while I hyperventilated on my hands and knees.

If I try to run or refuse to go, Daniel will hurt me...again. If I don't leave, Ted will have Mom and Darcy bankrupted by Christmas. Even if I go... and then find a way to somehow tell Grayson any of this, he'll lose everything he's working toward. Because of me.

Sobs began to wrack my body. "Please," I cried. "I'll do anything you say, but don't make me leave him like this. At least let me say goodbye." My voice broke. "I have to say goodbye to him."

My control collapsed as I gave in to my hopeless anguish. Above me, they had a whispered conversation.

"What do you think?" Ted asked. "If she breaks up with him in person it would mean less questions for us... He might doubt the text message and go after her."

"Hmm," Daniel considered. "No. We can't risk it. All it would take is her blurting out something ambiguous about any of this and we'd be screwed. Better to just have her send the text and let me deal with Grayson. I'll convince him not to go after her. Besides, I already called her a cab."

"Well done," his father praised. "No need for us to abandon all chivalry just because we've gotten our hands a bit dirty."

My phone clattered to the floor between my hands. "Here," Daniel said, louder. "Go ahead and add your two cents, but don't change any of the details. Or your mother and sister will be homeless by lunch."

He nudged the phone with his toe. "Go on. Be quick. You know the consequences if all of this blows up in our faces."

But I couldn't move. I cried so hard, I honestly believed I'd vomit any minute. With a sigh, Daniel went to his knees. My entire body recoiled from his proximity, sending me back, onto my butt. I curled into a tight ball.

"Oh, princess," he said, feigning regret. "For what it's worth, I never would have taken you that night if I knew how much trouble you'd be. You weren't nearly worth it."

"Just pick her up," Ted chipped, exasperated. "We don't have time for this."

Daniel's hands grazed my shoulders before I let out a deafening, primal screech. "*Don't touch me!*" I jerked back, scrambling to my feet. "I'll go now. I'll leave and I won't come back. I won't try to call him or text him. Just… don't touch me ever again."

My attacker rose and very deliberately snatched my hand, pressing his palm into it before handing me my phone. His eyes turned flat and hard. "Add. Something. Authentic."

I ran my eyes over the screen, trying to read each agonizing word.

Grayson, I'm so sorry to do this to you, but I had to leave. I've decided that I don't want this life or this relationship anymore. It's all too much for me. I hope you'll understand and respect my choices. Please don't make this any more difficult by trying to follow me.

With shaking thumbs, I swapped "Grayson" for "Gray," and added one final piece. *I know I said I wouldn't run anymore… but I failed. At least, this way, I won't ever fail you again.*

Before I could think better of it, I signed the text. *Yours for Always, Ellie.*

***

Chapter Twenty-Three

October 2016

Ella

I hoped, when someone eventually found my body, they wouldn't let Maggie see it.

That one thought plagued me as I sat in the corner Daniel designated for me and watching him pace my living room.

"I told my father we should have killed you when we had the chance," he snapped. "Little bitch. You know, after two years passed and I never saw any messages from you on his phone, I assumed you wised up. Imagine my surprise when I checked out a hot piece at the gala and she turned out to be *you*."

Manic, he kept on. "And then *he followed you out of there*. So *he* knew you were there, too. I've got to admit, that one tripped me up. I almost ran after you both, but then I realized bitch boy probably had his body guard lurking somewhere. And I couldn't get caught on camera, of course. So I had to let you both go. But, then, when my baby cousin didn't show up for work the next morning, I knew *exactly* why. You wear him out little princess?"

I never replied, but he didn't let up. Taunting me, going on rants about what a tease I was. How I was lucky his father was on his way over or I would be right back where he had me before...

I tuned him out. Chose a spot on the dusty wood floor and stared at it while Dr. Laura's trigger management tips ran through my mind on a loop.

I could tell he wanted to terrify me. Just like that day in the Hamptons, my fear seemed to gratify him, somehow. But, unfortunately for Daniel, I'd had three years to think about what happened and ponder what I wished I would have done differently when he and his father confronted me.

Processing what they did took months of therapy. Dr. Laura gently walked me through the day from every angle, helping me come to terms with the enormity of what I lived through, as well as little things that made my skin crawl later. Like the fact that he once again helped himself to a pair of my underwear when he packed my bags. The look of victory in his eyes when he saw he had me in his clutches. How he dared to mention my teenage sister, just to make me sick.

In the end, Dr. Laura helped me decide that he didn't deserve the satisfaction of terrifying me for the rest of my life. Anytime I thought of him and felt fear, I reminded myself that he *liked* my fear. He *wanted* it.

And I could refuse to give it to him.

It worked for a long time. Years. Until Grayson Stryker reappeared and all of the threats Ted and Daniel made became possibilities again. Until I saw Daniel at the Stryker & Sons gala, looming just beyond Gray, watching me.

I still didn't know how he tracked me to Gray's apartment. Or how he got into mine. In all of his monologuing, he never explained that part. Instead, he listed all of the ways he could hurt me. All of the sick ways he'd dreamed of "putting me in my place."

All the while, I refused to cower for him. It was one thing to run away from evil. But another to feed it once it caught you.

Every few moments, my gaze slid to the gun lying on the end table beside the couch. I couldn't get to it… not that I even knew how to use the thing if I somehow got ahold of it.

Part of me was grateful. If he planned on killing me, there were a lot worse ways than a gunshot. That would be quick.

The other part of me, though, suspected the weapon was just a prop. He used it to get me backed into a corner and then set it down where he knew I wouldn't be able to reach it without going through him. If he *really* wanted to shoot me… why wait?

A dizzying wave of nausea rolled over me as I thought that, probably, he didn't want to shoot me. Yet. He probably wanted something *else*, first.

While he kept on rambling, I determined that I wouldn't fight him. If he wanted to violate me one more time before he killed me, I wouldn't give him the satisfaction of showing my fear like I did the first time. And I didn't want to have defensive wounds all over my body when Maggie eventually found it. That would just make the whole horrid ordeal even more traumatic for her.

Assuming they didn't hide me somewhere. *Maybe, if I asked nicely… Ted seemed to possess some twisted notion of chivalry…*

After what felt like an eternity, there was a knock at the door. Ted's voice came through it, muffled. "Daniel? It's me." He grunted. "Open the door, son."

"Fucking finally," Daniel muttered. "You're lucky he's here, little princess. I didn't know how much longer I could restrain myself." With one final sneer, he picked up his gun and stalked to the door, disengaging the chain and locks.

The next ten seconds passed in a blur of motion. The door swung in. Ted fell forward, going to his knees as someone rolled over him. Another figure, clad entirely in black, rushed over the threshold. The gun rang out. Someone shouted. Blood splattered across the room, landing in a fine mist over my bare feet.

The room tilted on its side. Then swirled. And then, all at once, it wasn't there anymore.

Or I wasn't.

Grayson

11:06, my watch said.

"And you had no prior knowledge of Mr. Stryker's activities?"

My mind moved sluggishly. I blinked at the detective standing opposite me, on the other side of Ellie's blue Formica counter.

"No," I finally replied. "I didn't."

My voice sounded like a stranger's. Thick and halting. I'd cleared my throat a hundred times, but it didn't help.

"Not even—"

My eyes snapped to the officer's, quelling his question. "None of it. If I knew what he'd done," I said slowly, "I would have killed him."

The full extent of his crimes remained elusive, though. Now I knew what he did to Ella… and that poor girl from his prep school… but how many other women did he turn into victims?

"Grayson!"

My father's voice lashed across the room. He darkened the doorway for a moment before crossing to stand between me and the detective, cutting the officer a dismissive glance.

"My son and I will confer with our legal counsel before anyone answers any further questions," he stated, then turned his back to the other man, facing me. "Son, were you hurt? There's an ambulance downstairs."

"It's for Ella," I murmured, sick to my core. "She was unconscious. I don't know what he did to her before we got here."

I held her the entire time we waited for paramedics and police to arrive, huddling in the corner of her living room while Marco single-handedly restrained Ted and Daniel. Danny didn't pose much of a threat, though, considering he shot himself in the leg the moment we charged him.

Marco's idea to use Ted as a Trojan Horse worked brilliantly. Right as we got off the Brooklyn Bridge, Barnes called to inform us that he was on his way to provide the back-up we requested. When we told him the address, he paused for a long moment before informing us that Ted Stryker had also requested a ride to that address moments before.

Barnes picked up my uncle and drove him to Ella's borough, where Marco and I intercepted him. Unable to offer another explanation for why he was there, Ted eventually admitted that Daniel called him to tell him to come. We forced him up the stairs and made him knock before rushing Daniel and knocking him out.

The second the gun went off, Ellie collapsed.

"They took her down on a stretcher… They won't let me go to her," I rasped, "I'm not supposed to leave the scene until they clear it. They've threatened obstruction of justice."

"It won't be long now. They have Ted in a squad car. Daniel's on his way to the hospital, but I've sent Barnes down there to be sure he doesn't evade the police, somehow. Marco is speaking with the lead investigator downstairs," Dad reported. "He knows him; they worked together. I'm sure he'll convince him to clear the scene shortly."

He slanted a pointed glare the detective hovering near us. "Perhaps you could help with that?" he suggested.

The officer made for the door, leaving us alone in the cozy apartment. Everything about it made me ill, now—the little pieces of Ellie I would normally adore, all the glaring evidence of our struggle. The blood on the floor. Her yarn on her desk. Yellow, like the first day we ever locked eyes. Like the crocheted Big Bird purse I used to tease her about. It looked like she was knitting something larger, now.

Will she ever finish it?

"He drugged her once before," I whispered, voicing my greatest fear. "What if he gave her something again and it was too much? She wouldn't wake up."

My father was a serious man, but I'd never seen him so solemn. "I'll go down and check on her."

Just as he turned, though, Marco sailed back into the room. With Ella right behind him.

I didn't think. I just reacted. A second later, she was in my arms.

"Gray!" she cried, clinging to my neck while I fought for breath. "Are you hurt? The gun went off! There was *blood*!"

I couldn't get my lungs to stop shuddering long enough to reply. *Sobs*, I realized. I was sobbing.

I took her to the only piece of furniture not covered in a fine mist of blood—the tangerine armchair—and sank both of us into it, tucking her against my body before pulling back to examine her face. My fingers followed my feverish gaze, searching for any hint of injury.

"Did he touch you?" I asked tightly. "Did he harm you?"

"Just my arm. He grabbed it and drug me across the floor pretty hard, but I'm okay." Her hands ran over my face in a similar fashion. "What about you? Where did this bruise come from?"

I didn't know I had one. There were a lot of fists flying in the heat of the moment. I had no idea who landed a punch on me. But I knew my uncle and cousin both looked like hamburger meat before Marco finished with them.

"I'm fine," I insisted, gruff. The longer I looked at her beautiful, ashen face, the harder it got to breathe. Everything I could have lost beamed back at me—her wide sapphire eyes, reflecting the depths of her emotions, the heart beating so hard against me.

I clutched her closer and she hugged me back, smoothing her hands over my head until my chest stopped heaving. "Shhh," she whispered, "It's okay. We're okay."

The absurdity of her comforting me in that moment finally broke through my dread. I turned to inhale the beloved scent of her hair, soaking it into my lungs. Once, twice; by the third breath I felt more settled.

The hapless detective who questioned me wandered back into the apartment. "Miss Callahan?"

She shrank back slightly as a shiver moved through her. My arms flexed protectively, pulling her further into the overstuffed recliner. Her fingers curled into my blood-spattered tee shirt.

"Yes?"

"I need your account of each of your interactions with Mr. Stryker." His eyes slid over to my face, then back to hers. "Uh, the, um, *other* Mr. Stryker."

"So she can relive all of the shit he put her through," I snarled. "For what? Your fucking paperwork?"

He liked me better when I was traumatized. His features furrowed into a frown. "If Miss Callahan wishes to press charges, we'll need her statement. From all three attacks."

Three attacks. Dear God. He really did attack her three separate times. Because of me. Because I let him back into her life.

"I want to press charges," she told him. Then she turned to me, speaking softer. "I always regretted not doing it the very first time; but I didn't know who he was or how to find him. And the second time… he threatened my family and you… so I missed that opportunity, too. And I promised myself I would report him, if he ever… if I ever got another chance."

One of the crime scene techs who processed the room left thin white tarps behind. We used them to cover the sofa before Ella and I moved onto it while the lead investigator sat in Ellie's desk chair. Marco hovered behind us, lingering by the kitchen area to listen along with my father.

"Do you want them to go?" I asked her, desperate to make what she had to do easier for her, somehow.

She shook her head, whispering, "They all need to know the details, I suppose. If you want to make sure you can keep your company safe from Daniel."

Stryker & Sons was the furthest thing from my mind. I hadn't even considered what we would have to do to take Daniel's shares back, dissolve Ted's interests. Replace them both.

In the end, everyone stayed where they were and Ella began talking. Listening to her confusion as she recounted the initial attack was heartbreaking; but the facts she did remember were worse. There were moments when I wanted leap up and walk away. Times when I thought I'd surely wind up vomiting after all. Details that shattered me. Filled me with a molten rage. Made my eyes sting.

Marco interrupted quietly a couple of times, letting her know that he had evidence to corroborate her claims. That seemed to bolster her confidence. By the end of the first story, as she relayed the student resources available to her at the time and how each one failed her completely, her tone took on a bit of an edge.

That anger bled into the next account. She told us all about the day she came downstairs at the beach house only to come face-to-face with the man who raped her. How she ran. How she came back to find me and tell me she needed to leave but instead wound up trapped in a room with Ted and Daniel.

Marco started typing into his phone as she recounted Daniel's story about seeing us in bed together and recognizing her—including the way he fled, hid out in town, and lied about his whereabouts. I knew my head of security was making notes of leads to chance down later, again to help validate Ella's narrative.

I heard my father's knuckles pop as she recalled the threats they made against me and her family in order to force her to leave me. Our eyes met across the room and I read the lines of his face, knowing mine reflected the same abhorrence. The surreal dismay of realizing that our own flesh and blood could have so much malice running through their veins.

The memories drifted through Ella's eyes like ghosts. I rubbed at my burning eyes, trying to dispel the sickening images her story conjured as she finished recounting it.

"And when I came back from town, you were gone," I said.

With a nod, she stuttered through a deep breath. Tears fell down onto her folded hands as she bowed her head. "They paid the cabbie to drive me to the airport and gave me a stack of cash for a flight home, probably in hopes that getting me out of town would help make the break-up stick. But I only made it halfway to JFK before I called you…"

She swallowed hard, turning to look at me. "I called you a lot, for a long time. I'm sorry about that. Again."

Like a reflex, my old bitterness sprang up. "You *didn't call me*, Ellie. I never got any calls from you."

Ella swiped at her cheeks, nodding some more. "Yes, I did. I called you for weeks and weeks. Every morning, every night. I sent texts. Probably a hundred. Eventually, sometime after the New Year, I got a message back telling me that I had the wrong number, asking me to please stop."

Everything inside of me seized. "You did?"

"Yeah," she whispered. "I thought you changed your number because you were angry and didn't want to hear from me anymore. That's why I came back to the city for the day I thought you'd be moving in the apartment in midtown. I wanted to apologize. But you weren't there… and when I went to your old place, you had already moved out."

A boulder sank into the pit of my stomach. "How did you get a wrong number? I tried to call you a million times, too. Did—"

Memories from the morning she disappeared streaked through my mind. Including one of me handing Daniel my phone… telling him my passcode. *That son of bitch.* He could have looked at anything on there and I wouldn't have known. Could have been slipping it off my desk or whatever bar we chose for happy hour, and checking it, for years.

"Give me your phone," I whispered.

Her trembling hand extended the iPhone to me. I swiped it right open—she never used a passcode, even back then. In a few taps, I found my contact. Unlike me, she never deleted the number. Even when she believed it was no longer mine.

But, it *wasn't* mine. The number saved under my name was incorrect. Off by one number.

"He changed it," I realized aloud. "He made you send that text to me, deleted the thread, and then he changed the number saved in your phone by one digit so any messages you tried to send later didn't go to me."

Her voice quivered. "W-what? He… I knew he deleted the text thread but I didn't…" An agonized whimper slipped from her lips. "So all that time, I really wasn't calling you? You weren't ignoring my messages?"

Again, my instincts spurred me. "Never." I reached for her free hand, grasping it between both of mine, bringing it up to my mouth. "I didn't believe you," I rasped, distraught. "You told me you tried to call me multiple times and I just wanted to fight like a jackass."

Ella glared at her phone as fresh tears spilled over her cheeks. "I thought you knew I was trying to get in touch with you and you just hated me too much to pick up. If I knew you were waiting for me, I would have found some way to track you down at school or your parent's house or your work… I only stayed away because you seemed hell-bent on avoiding me and I couldn't blame you."

I shook my head, refusing to accept any of it. "This still doesn't explain why you didn't get any of *my* calls. Why was my real number blocked?"

Ella's wide eyes blinked at me. "I purged my contact info a couple years ago, after graduation… but there was only one blocked contact I didn't recognize. Saved as, like, Insurance Scam. I didn't remember adding the contact or blocking them, so I just deleted it altogether…"

Because who would ever assume some sick fuck had saved their ex-boyfriend's *real* phone number under a bogus contact just so he could also block said ex-boyfriend?

No one sane.

"What?" she fretted, reading my black expression. "Do you think he did the same thing to you? Did he block me?"

"No."

He didn't need to. All he had to do was make sure she didn't answer any of my attempts to reach out. And I did the rest with my stupid anger and my wounded pride.

"After I couldn't get ahold of you over a few months," I rumbled, sick. "I deleted you."

I dropped my face into my hands, reeling. *God.* This was entirely my fault. Because I believed that text message. Even when everything inside of me railed against it, I believed. In her fear. In her doubt. In her past mistakes.

I believed the worst in her.

There were hundreds of moments when she proved her love. And I chose to accept the one instant I thought she let me down.

After Maggie told me Ella left the city, I never looked for her. I never hired someone to find her. I spent years driving myself to hate her. The beautiful girl with the radiant soul. I forced myself to replay all of her flaws, just to protect myself from everything I lost.

I gave up on her.

The thought echoed through me as I stared into her luminous sapphire eyes. And something inside of me broke.

Ella

"Please," Mr. Stryker said, lingering in my doorway and staring hard into my eyes. "Contact me with anything you need, Ella. I can't adequately express how sorry I am for the pain my family has caused you. I would like to make up for it."

I'd seen Grayson's dad from afar at the gala. Now, up close, I saw the wear of his illness in his sallow skin, his baldness, the deep grooves carving his features.

"Mr. Stryker," I mumbled, "It's really—"

"Entirely unacceptable," he finished, still as intimidating as ever. His thin white brow lifted in an arch expression Grayson often mimicked. "I've left an envelope of cash to get you started on refurnishing this room, but you will, *of course*, send me the bills for any additional things you require. And your therapy sessions, Ella. On that I must insist." Sadness touched his ocher eyes. "I know you have our home address."

Oh Lord. My letter to Jacqueline. Just thinking about the tear-stained apology I mailed her brought another wave of sorrow. "I do," I agreed softly. "Thank you, sir. Will you please give Mrs. Stryker a hug for me? And assure her there's nothing she could have done? I know how she worries."

Brusque emotion filled his face and his voice. "I will, Ella. I promise you."

He left. And—after muttering with Grayson in the kitchen for a few moments—Marco followed him out, looking pissed off. When I turned back to Gray, I knew why instantly.

"You aren't staying."

The words burst out of me, but they sounded quiet. My utter shock echoed in the silence between us. Because, honestly, in all the horrors I imagined might befall me when I saw Daniel in my apartment, Grayson leaving me when it was all over never occurred to me.

Even his blood-stained tee shirt couldn't detract from how beautiful he looked in the midday sun slanting through the kitchen skylight. It gilded his black hair, lit the golden flecks in his green eyes. filled all of the grief-stricken creases drawn in his features.

"I have to go," he confirmed. "I need to speak with the police, the attorneys, HR. I need to make sure Daniel pays for everything he did. It's the only way for me to even begin to make amends for all of the ways I failed you."

I floated toward him automatically, but he took a step back, maintaining his distance. "Gray," I whispered, his name a mournful sigh. "None of this is your fault."

His jaw hardened. Loathing simmered in his eyes, but his voice sounded totally even. Despondent. "It is all my fault. I didn't press you for details on what happened to you before we met, even though I knew there was something you hadn't told me. I was too cowardly to tell my father what I wanted to do before it was too late; then I allowed my desire for creative control of Stryker & Sons to cloud my judgement and encouraged my father to let Ted and Daniel back into our company despite my misgivings. I didn't even look into their backgrounds myself."

His hands fisted at his side. "I thought the worst of you the day you disappeared, and believed you'd really left by choice. I gave up our apartment because I was too weak to live there with all the reminders of what might have been. I let my pride and my anger rule me to the point of deleting your information and throwing myself into fucking every random woman who wanted me."

He'd mentioned the other women before, the night he showed up outside my building. And I saw him at the gala with that girl, Olivia. Now, after the night we shared, the thought of others stung like a hard slap to the face. I clutched my hands over my stomach, holding myself together as my breathing sped.

Gray wasn't finished. Fervor brightened his turbulent eyes. "I treated you like *shit* over the last week—showing up drunk when I thought you didn't want to see me, mocking your book, deleting it without even reading it, taking your bed and letting you sleep on the couch, showing up at your job without warning, inserting myself into your work. And—God—the way I acted Thursday night will haunt me until the day I die. I can't believe I sent you off like that. I can't believe I walked away. Even last night, when you swore you tried to contact me after you left me… I didn't really believe you. And I'll never be able to undo any of it. Right now, I'm not sure how I'll live with myself."

"Grayson," I started, desperate for him to understand, "I forgave you for all of this so long ago—"

"Well, you shouldn't have!" His voice whipped between us, lashing me. "You should never forgive any of us. By God, Ella, when I think of what we put you through… what *I have put you through*. Do you *get* that?"

"You didn't do any of this!" I cried. "It was Daniel!"

"Even if that were true," he shouted back, "*how* could you ever be with me knowing what my own blood is capable of? How could you let me *inside of you*, knowing *my cousin* was the one who *violated* you? Doesn't that *disgust* you?"

Dr. Laura once asked me the same question—albeit in a much kinder fashion. Truly, when she posed the notion to me, I realized I'd never even considered it. Even though, of course, such a reaction would be natural. What victim would willingly choose a partner who was related to their attacker?

But I knew Grayson, down to his soul. There wasn't even one tiny fraction of me that believed he had any sort of evil or viciousness inside of him. And I loved him; so completely that my feelings would never be deterred by whoever happened to share his family tree.

There was part of me, though, that worried and wondered… if I ever found myself with Grayson again… and he ever found out the truth… would *he* reject *me*?

As Daniel was so fond of pointing out, he thoroughly ruined me. Physically, at first, then mentally and emotionally. Now that Gray knew what I'd been through… would *he* be disgusted? By me?

I tried to swallow the knot in my throat but only managed to send a fresh round of grief to my eyes. "No," I whimpered through tears. "Does it disgust you?"

"Of course it does!" he yelled. "I have never been more repulsed than I am right now. By him, by myself, by my family. Christ. I'd die before I hurt you. But look what I've done! And I will only hurt you over and over again every time you have to look at me and remember what my family's done to you!"

In that moment, I'd officially faced my two worst fears in one morning. Daniel—the threat of what would happen if I ever had to face him again, what he would try to do to Grayson and my other loved ones. And, now, Grayson—confirming my deep-seated fear that he would never be able to love me after finding out the truth about my brokenness.

"Gray," I sobbed, trying to move toward him again. "I love you."

His face twisted into a mask of agony. "God, *how*? How can you even *say* that, Ella? How do not see how fucked up and twisted this shit is?"

"I see it," I shrieked, "But I still love you. I said 'yours for always' and I meant those words with everything I have in me, even in that horrible moment. Knowing who Daniel is and what he's done can't make me stop loving *you*, Grayson. *Nothing ever could.*"

A sheen of tears covered his face. I watched him absorb what I said, his entire frame heaving while he fought to breathe. He moved all at once, stalking past, moving too quickly for me to reach for him.

"Maybe it should, Ella," he muttered, already to the door.

And then Grayson was gone.

Chapter Twenty-Four

October 2016

Ella

Maybe I shouldn't have been surprised when Dr. Laura called me Saturday evening.

After all, even if Grayson was sickened by me... he was still Grayson. Thoughtful and thorough in his trademark take-charge way. He apparently got my therapist's information and called her personally, relaying what occurred and informing her that he would foot the bill for any treatment I required. Indefinitely. She immediately called to schedule an emergency session for me the following day.

I probably also should not have been surprised to find Marco waiting for me outside my building on Sunday morning, when I emerged for the first time since Grayson left. He took one look at my swollen, splotchy face and wordlessly produced a coffee cup from behind his back, along with a pastry.

"My Abuelita baked this," he told me. "I thought you might be hungry."

I'd spent the entire day and night locked in my bedroom, refusing to answer any of the thousand knocks Maggie pounded into the hollow slab. And Marco was right—I certainly hadn't had the stomach for food of any sort.

In truth, I still didn't. Every time I recalled the way revulsion twisted Gray's gorgeous face, the vitriol in his voice—*"I've never been more repulsed than I am right now"*—my insides swirled and heaved.

I took Marco's kind offering anyway, ducking my head to hide my puffy eyes. His tone took on a sympathetic note. "Mr. Stryker asked me to drive you to your appointment. He's… unwell. Or he would have been here himself."

"How do you not see how fucked up and twisted this shit is?"

"Oh, I sincerely doubt that," I mumbled. "But thank you for coming."

I didn't bother to ask if Gray was okay. I knew him well enough to know he would continue to blame himself for everything and steep in his guilt for as long as his loved ones allowed. Instead, I inquired, "Is he with his parents, at least? He shouldn't be alone."

"His mother has been to see him," Marco reported quietly, turning the car into traffic. "I don't believe she stayed long, though."

He was isolating himself, then. The same way he did after he found out his father was terminally ill. "Please make sure he doesn't drink too much," I murmured, sighing out the window. "It only makes him feel worse."

Marco's dark eyes met mine in the rearview, brimming with empathy. "I'll see to it, Ella."

Well, if nothing else, at least the guy finally calls me by my actual name. With a nod, I leaned my head against the cool glass and closed my eyes. "Thank you, Marco."

Dr. Laura passed me a new box of tissues after I finished off the one she originally offered me.

"What I'm hearing," she intoned, watching me with her calm, solemn gaze. "Is that your largest source of grief in all of this isn't what happened to you because of Daniel—or even the way Gray treated you last week—but the aftermath of all of it when Grayson left you."

A humorless snort of laughter combined with a sniffle. "I suppose that's truly pathetic, huh?"

Dr. Laura sat back in her seat. "I'm not judging your feelings, Ella. And I would argue that there is no 'normal' or 'healthy' way to feel after a deranged man holds you at gun point. Particularly one who's harmed you in the past the way Daniel did."

I nodded into my tissue. "I just… I've spent years trying to get over Gray to protect everyone. Yesterday, when Daniel attacked me, I kept thinking; *at least now Grayson will know everything. He'll know I loved him and never wanted to hurt him. Maybe he can forgive me.*"

Dr. Laura's brow pinched. "Those things may still be possible, though," she pointed out. "It's only been a day, Ella. You've had years to process what Daniel did to you. Grayson's only had hours."

The simple truth of her words sank down into my chest, finally halting my tears. When she saw me listening, she went on. "What he went through yesterday—seeing you on the floor, passed out. Hearing excruciating details about your attacks. Learning his entire family life and company structure were based on malicious people who set out to harm and control him from the jump… All of that would be very traumatic. It's possible he didn't mean a lot of the things he said—or that, once he has time to process the trauma, his feelings will change."

Of course, she was right.

I wanted to fall in his arms and finally let him comfort me after years of longing to hear him tell me everything would be alright. I wanted him to vow to fix what Daniel broke between us. When he left, it crushed me. I didn't ever stop to consider that his entire world had imploded moments before he rejected me.

"Am I stupid if I hope he comes back?" I croaked. "Again?"

"Hope is never stupid," she replied. "I would argue, in this instance, hope is an act of great courage."

It was a lovely sentiment. One I probably should have found reassuring. But I'd been in therapy long enough to hear the double meaning in her words.

Hoping Gray would come back to me was courageous. Because there was a chance he never would.

Grayson

Marco and my mother got me dried out by dinner time on Sunday.

After taking Ella to her appointment, Amir showed up at my penthouse and proceeded to take every last drop of alcohol out of the place. Since I was passed out on my sofa—unable to confront the bed that smelled like Ellie and me and the love we made—I didn't get a chance to object.

Next my mother arrived. In full dudgeon. She spent about twenty minutes ranting at me in Spitalian before switching to English. Her yelling cleared what little buzz remained, launching me head-first into a midday hangover from hell. Without a drop of sympathy, she forced several glasses of water down my throat and all but marched me to the bathroom, demanding I shower and dress for dinner.

When I emerged an hour later, she silently handed me coffee in a travel mug—Ella's travel mug. Refusing to give explanation, she simply said, "Let's go."

By the time Barnes delivered us to my parents' townhome, I felt like an empty shell. Hollowed out. With the occasional throb of pain where my heart should have been.

We ate a meal in complete silence. I didn't even know what. Some meat, potatoes. A salad course. Some other thing. I ate it all, stuffing food down my throat to keep a lump from forming there, hoping it would smother the seethe in my stomach.

Plates were cleared, Mom went to make even more coffee.

"Son."

I knew it was coming. I'd studiously ignored his heavy stares since I arrived; I figured he wouldn't be able to hold his tongue all evening.

"I have nothing to say to you right now."

It was the most diplomatic thing I could come up with. And true. I didn't have a single idea of what to say to him. He'd helped my uncle cover up Daniel's "youthful indiscretion"… and encouraged Mom to hide Ella's apology letter from me.

"You need to listen to me," he argued. "That girl from his prep school—"

"Save it."

The lash in my voice surprised me. In all the years my father and I spent going around in endless disagreements, neither of us were ever cruel.

He seemed to have aged years in a day. Weariness saturated his eyes as they met mine. "I only meant to say—there's no excuse for disregarding allegations like the ones that were leveled against your cousin. I hold myself personally responsible for every woman he harmed thereafter. And doubly so for anyone he's attacked since he's been in our employ."

A new sort of guilt invaded. I hadn't known there could be another type. I thought I'd felt them all. But, sitting there, listening to my father take full responsibility for the depraved actions of a monster—all because of me—lent a new sort of chagrin.

"You're not *personally* responsible," I muttered, deflating slightly.

He dropped his gaze to the table between us. “I feel as though I am. I should have asked more questions. Gotten more involved. Had him followed or monitored or…”

Jesus. He sounded like me. Or I sounded like him.

Graham often told me I was too hard on myself. He claimed I always took responsibility for things that weren’t my doing. Seemed I came by it honestly.

While that realization sank in, the last of the fight drained out of me. There wasn’t much left, after all. With everything I once loved lying in waste, I didn’t know if I’d ever summon the strength to move forward.

“What do we do now?” I asked.

My father straightened in his chair, his expression hardening. “We will find a way to disqualify him as an heir to our business interests. And see him locked up for the rest of his life.”

I already had Marco working on both of those goals. “Amir says the hospital discharged him for the bullet wound late last night and the investigator took him into custody. He’ll be held until he’s arraigned.”

Fury and determination clenched my jaw. “I will use every resource at our disposal to make sure he never gets out. I have to know he won’t ever come after her again or I won’t be able to live with myself.”

Something dark moved through Dad’s eyes. “Neither will I.” He paused. “Have you… spoken to her? Your mother is quite concerned about her. So am I, actually.”

But neither of them could possibly be as worried as I was.

The nauseous disquiet roared back to life within me. I reached for a leftover basket of bread and swallowed half a roll in one bite, piling more food on top of it.

“No.”

I couldn't. I'd picked up the phone to call her so many times, I lost count. And every single time I realized I had no idea how to adequately express just how much I hated myself for everything I'd done. And all the things I failed to do.

I felt like I had a new regret to languish over every hour. Why did I believe she had run when in my heart I always knew better? Why did I let my pride take over and stop me from trying to find her? Why didn't I ever question how Daniel got so many women to go home with him, why he always insisted on purchasing and delivering their drinks for them? Why the fuck did I go around chasing girls to drown out my loneliness instead of waiting for Ellie the way she waited for me?

Sitting in the opulent dining room, immersed in grief, one of my most poignant regrets rose to the surface. "I never even told her I loved her."

"Yesterday, you mean?"

"No," I murmured. "Ever."

I'd spent years under his tutelage. As his son. As his heir. As the future of our family and our company, both. I'd fucked up more times than either of us cared to remember. But never, in twenty-six years, had my father looked at me like I was a failure.

Until that moment.

"Grayson." He blew out a sigh and shook his head in dismay, unfolding from his seat as he returned my earlier words to him. "If that's true, I have nothing to say to you right now."

The crushing weight on my soul bore down harder, pulverizing the shards into dust. Prickling, heated self-loathing streaked down to join the smolder in my stomach. Longing was a fearsome thing, burning through my blood.

What the fuck am I doing?

I didn't stay long enough to think about it.

Ella

After a three-hour session with Dr. Laura, I left Marco idling at the curb outside her office and took the subway home. Maggie was out—presumably using the money Mr. Stryker left us to replace her couch—so I went straight to my room and closed the shade, hoping a nap would cure my exhaustion and the stinging in my eyelids.

When I woke up, my rumbling stomach told me it was dinner time. But I couldn't bring myself to go out to the living room and face my roommate.

Turned out, I didn't have a choice.

Maggie opened my door, but, for the first time ever, didn't immediately barge over the threshold. She lingered halfway in the hall. "Elle? Can I come in?"

I wasn't ready for our reckoning. I knew I had to employ Dr. Laura's advice and tell her that I wasn't ready to forgive her yet, after finding out Grayson came to her and she sent him away without informing me. Honestly, though, the thought of placing space between me and my best friend in the midst of my bleakest days only made everything seem darker.

It was strange for her to wait in the doorway. It was also weird to see her in plain black yoga pants and a grey sweater. She didn't have on any make-up, either.

"I just woke up," I told her instead of agreeing. "I was about to make dinner."

She held up a bag I hadn't noticed in her right hand. "I got you some stuff from your favorite Italian place up the block. Pasta and bread and chocolate cake. Carbs, basically. I got you a shitload of carbs."

Belatedly, it hit me—she was nervous. Rambling, the way I ordinarily did. A swift gasp of guilt sank into the bottom of my lungs; but I did my best to quell it, reminding myself that I had every reason to be angry with her and she, therefore, had every reason to be anxious.

"Thanks," I replied, sighing.

She edged into the room, bending her left arm behind her back and placing the takeout bag on my vanity. Her dark eyes remained wary. "How was therapy?"

"Long. And I sort of don't want to talk right now, so…"

With a nervous huff, she looked down at her feet. "Listen, Elle… I'm really, really sorry for how I handled the whole Grayson thing. If I had any idea what was actually going on, I obviously wouldn't have sent him away."

I didn't know if I believed that. "You've never liked him," I pointed out, pressing my lips together. "You were always mentioning the possibility that he would ghost me or cheat on me. I think part of you didn't understand why he liked someone like me."

Maggie's head snapped up as indignation filled her features. "I never said that!"

"It makes sense," I went on, my voice flat. "Why would a handsome billionaire want to be with someone poor and damaged and weird like me?"

"Ella!" she yelled, truly angry, now. "I literally never said or thought any of that shit! I love you like a sister. Anything I said about Stryker wasn't about *you*. I don't trust men in general and most guys in the city are playboys. I just didn't want you to get your hopes up and have your heart crushed! Which is exactly what happened!"

"Because of Daniel!" I shouted back. "Not Gray! None of it was ever his fault. He was so good to me, always. You *knew* that, Mags. Why would you send him away and refuse to tell him where I went?"

"He hurt you!" she replied. "You should have seen how you looked when you came back from the apartment that day and realized he'd given it up. You were devastated! *You dropped out of school*, Ella. *You moved back to Maryland.* Why would I give the man who did that to you the time of day? What would you have done if you were me?"

I didn't know, but I still retorted, "I like to think I would have let you make up your own mind! But maybe that's because I respect you and your ability to think for yourself while you think of me as some sort of hapless, pathetic weakling."

"Maybe that's how you think of yourself," she cried. "Ever consider that? Maybe you're just projecting all of your inadequacies onto me! After all, you could have gone after him any time you wanted in the last three years and you were too afraid!"

"See? You do think I'm weak! That's why you didn't tell me back then! Anyway, I know you know how messed up it was to keep it all from me this whole time. The fact that you never told me—even after I started therapy and improved—just shows you felt too guilty about it."

"Of course I do!" she admitted, still shouting. "I feel *awful.* How can I fix it?"

I didn't have a clue. Not one single idea.

Defeated, I sank back down under my covers and turned away. "You can leave me alone."

Night came earlier than usual, another sure sign that my most-dreaded season was upon us.

I stayed in my bed, leaning my head back to peer out the dark window. Overhead, the starless sky glowed, an unnatural shade of orange from all the city's light pollution.

I wished, more than anything, that I could see the night sky just this once. Then, I wondered what my dad would think if he somehow watched the events of the weekend unfold. Wincing, I huddled down further under my covers just as another knock sounded at my door.

"Please go away!" I wailed. "Maggie, just… stop, okay?"

"It isn't Maggie."

I bolted upright. "Gray?"

The door cracked open just a smidge. Half of Grayson's haggard, handsome face appeared in the crack. "Do you want me to leave?"

For a second, I was completely shocked to find that I *did.* After more than twenty-four hours of wishing for him to come back… now, I was angry with him for ever leaving in the first place.

I pulled my knees up to my chest, curling into a ball. "Come in, I guess," I mumbled mulishly.

The second he stepped inside, the room's energy changed. Charged. Even beat-up, in casual clothes, with a bruise fading under his right cheek bone… Grayson Stryker truly had grown into a force. A pulse seemed to beat in the air around him while he stood on the threshold, staring intensely.

Unlike Maggie, Gray eventually came all the way into my room and slowly lowered himself onto the end of my mattress. I felt his eyes on my face for a long moment before he bent forward to rest his forearms on his knees and heaved out a deep breath.

"I came to apologize, again. More. I'm sorry I walked out like that yesterday. I'd say I should have come back as soon as I got my head on straight but, to be honest, it still isn't. On straight."

A pang hit my heart. "It hurt when you didn't come back, but I understood. I hoped you would forgive me, finally. And maybe we could move on together. But I know it must be hard to be around me now that you know… everything he did. I'm sure it changes the way you feel about me."

He lifted his face to meet my eyes, his gaze a blazing emerald ocean of remorse. "Ella, what are you talking about?"

My voice cracked. "You said I repulsed you."

His sculpted mouth hung ajar for one long second. "I never said that," he murmured, hoarse. "I would never say that because it isn't true, Ellie. It's impossible for you to repulse me."

Bone-deep sorrow pierced me as I realized I didn't even want to let myself believe him. The words he spat in anger were so devastating—the epitome of everything I feared the most—that I barely lived through them the first time. To let myself believe they were false, only for him to prove later on that he actually meant what he said… would kill me.

"You said, 'I have never been more repulsed than I am right now.' And you told me you thought that it was disgusting for me to sleep with you, knowing who was related to you," I reminded him. "You said it was fucked up and twisted."

Grayson's jaw clenched while he worked on a swallow. "I—That's not what I meant." He shook his head. "I meant that *I* repulsed *myself.* And that what happened to you was fucked up and twisted. I wasn't thinking about how it sounded when I spoke, I was just… spiraling. I'm sorry, Ella. I was out of my mind, but that isn't an excuse for yelling at you and spitting all of my feelings out without filtering them."

I still couldn't let myself believe he'd come back for me. "So you just came to apologize? Again? More?"

He turned to face me, drawing his bent leg up onto the bed. "I came to see you. To check on you." His hand reached over, settling on top of my comforter a few inches from my foot. He turned it palm-up—an offering.

But he hadn't said anything about staying, and I noticed. My body shrank back. "Well, you saw me," I murmured softly. "In all my ruined, repulsive glory."

Gray's intense gaze darkened while he glared at me. "You are *not* ruined. Or repulsive. You never could be, Ella. It isn't possible."

I felt my chin wobble. "Could have fooled me."

His eyes flashed. He swayed forward, hands raised as if to touch my face. He remembered himself just as quickly and fell back into his original spot. His fists dropped to his sides.

"I'm afraid to touch you," he confessed, his voice low and strained, matching the turbulent swirl of his gaze. "I don't want to scare you or hurt you. Every time I try to reach for you, some alarm goes off in my brain, telling me I should stop."

Oh. Another of my deepest fears, realized. Grayson didn't want to touch me.

It hurt so badly. Worse than anything else Daniel ever did to me. For a moment, the pain stunned me into stillness. Then my face crumpled.

"Ellie, no," Gray rasped. He lurched toward me again, hauling me into a strangled embrace with my legs folded between our chests. His hands landed on the center of my spine and the back of my head, his fingers kneading.

"Baby, I'm sorry," his low voice murmured into my hair. "I'm saying all the wrong things when I really just came to tell you…"

My entire frame went rigid, bracing for impact. *He's going to say goodbye. Tell me he can't handle this and doesn't want to.*

He pulled back to stare into my eyes. A wince marred his brow.

"God, this is all wrong," he muttered to himself. "I wanted to tell you way before the moment you first said it to me. But I waited too long and then I thought I had to make it up to you, so I made this whole elaborate plan to tell you when I proposed—"

His face froze. His fingers tensed, curling into me.

"Pr-proposed?" The word sounded somewhere between a shriek and sputter. "When were you *ever* planning to *propose*?"

Grayson

Surely, I'd eventually get used to being a fucking fool.

But I wasn't, yet, because the second the word "propose" left my mouth, I felt my soul leave my body. *Wasn't it bad enough that she was forced to leave you? Why make her feel even worse about the timing of it all?*

Too late for that, though. Ella gaped at me. Her complexion paled while a burst of blush crept up her chest.

Defeated, I sighed heavily and offered a wistful smile I hoped would help. "On Christmas Eve, actually. I was in town having your ring re-sized the morning you left."

"Y-you—" The pretty flush finally made it to her face, warming the smooth skin of her cheeks. It would have been beautiful if she didn't look so stricken. "You never said anything."

"It was a surprise," I said softly, unable to resist running my hand over her hair and then caressing the peachy pink along her cheekbone.

God, even devastated and wary, Ella was the loveliest woman I'd ever seen. My body ached while I touched her, demanding to have her closer. A surge of desire joined the adoration swirling through me, pushing another admission to the surface. "I wanted a special occasion to tell you that I loved you."

Her plush lips fell open on a quiet gasp, then promptly shut. Her front teeth sank into the full curve, worrying it. "So, you were going to propose because you wanted to tell me you loved me?"

"No," I told her, locking our gazes. "I was going to propose because I woke up one day and you were everything. The center of my whole world. I never wanted to live without you again."

Tears glittered in her eyes, blurring the deep blue. "I would have said yes," she whispered, her voice hitching.

A stab of self-loathing hit me in square in the gut. I didn't mean to upset her more.

"I guess this just makes everything worse," I muttered, looking down at her rumpled sheets. "I shouldn't have told you."

Feather-light, her touch grazed along my jawline, bringing my face back to hers. "I'm glad you did," she sniffed. "It helps me understand why you were so angry, back then. And last week…"

A hot flood of shame suffused my center every time I thought about the events of the gala, and everything leading up to it. Some sound between a groan and grunt slid through my teeth. "I was such a *dick*. I don't know how to even—"

The fingertips on my chin flitted up to press over my mouth. "I know," she said, "That's how I felt when I left you. How I still feel. I'm so sorry, too, Gray. I never should have left. I should have stayed in that room with them and let them..." She tried to swallow. "Anyway. I could have stuck it out until you got home and caught them."

"*No*." Panic sealed my throat at the very thought. I moved instinctively, hugging her close again. "God, *no*."

Her defenses collapsed all at once. Her legs finally parted, her arms wound around my neck. I pulled her straight into my lap, holding her firmly against the length of my torso and settling her face against my shoulder.

Ella started to cry. Hard, soundless sobs that spoke of the deepest depths of despair and regret. They broke down all of my resistance, until I found myself dribbling tears onto the crown of her head.

We stayed that way for a long time, both of us grieving all of the mistakes we made, all of the time we lost. The proposal that never was. The apartment we both wanted to make into our home. Years of birthdays, holidays, vacations, and quiet Sundays in Central Park. All of the love and support and fulfillment we could have found with each other.

My eyes eventually ran dry, but hers didn't. I simply held her closer, humming all of the songs I used to sing to her after her nightmares. They slowly lulled her from sobs to sniffles.

Finally, she pulled back, revealing her red button nose. The splotches around her eyes made them look them unfathomably blue. I stared for a long moment, memorizing the color.

"What is that song called?" she asked. "I looked for it... after... I couldn't ever find it."

The old Spanish lullaby happened to be one of my mother's favorites. Its name put a hoarse scratch in my throat. "Remember Me."

Her lips trembled on a shaky breath. "Oh, Gray," she cried quietly, fresh tears brimming in her gaze. "What's going to happen to us?"

I pressed kisses to the corners of her eyes, tasting the salt of her sadness. "I don't know," I confessed. "I keep trying to figure out how we could ever move forward with all of this trauma between us… it feels impossible."

Ella held herself still for an endless moment. Then, all too soon, she slipped out of my lap and stood. In her navy camisole and grey leggings, I could admire every dip and curve of her gorgeous body. My blood roared… which sent a new torrent of shame through me.

It felt wrong to ogle her… to think about her in a purely carnal fashion. *Is this what he thought when he looked at her? Am I a monster like him?*

The muddle of lust and guilt only underscored my point. I loved her; I *wanted* her. But I didn't know *how* to want her. I certainly didn't know how to approach the concept of sex.

And how could I move us forward if I couldn't rebuild our physical relationship? Would she even want to try?

Ellie shifted on her feet, swaying with her trademark oblivious grace. Her fingers knotting together over her abdomen. "I think you should go," she murmured. "I…if you don't know what you want, you should take time to figure that out."

Looking at her, my answer was crystal clear. "I know what I *want*," I muttered back, my eyes sliding up her hips, over the fullness of her breasts, to her heartbreakingly lovely face. "I want you the same way I always have. It's what to *do* about it that's eluding me."

She bit her lower lip again. "I'm the same person I always was, Gray. I haven't changed."

That was true. But I had.

And I had no idea how to process that.

"I should talk to someone," I realized, snapping into CEO mode. If there was ever a situation where I felt out of my depth, there was always an expert to weigh in. "How would you feel about that?"

"You could talk to Dr. Laura," she offered, still not meeting my gaze. "She could help you understand where I'm coming from. She already knows our entire situation, our history. It would be easier than starting over with a new therapist. I can give her permission to speak with you, if you'd like. She's excellent."

I trusted her judgement completely. "Then that's what I'll do."

She nodded, the gesture absent. "Alright," she said around her lip. "I'll call her now. But I think… I think you should go, okay?"

I couldn't blame her. She had a hundred reasons to send me away. "If that's what you want…"

"I just can't let myself hope this will work out until we know for sure," she admitted, finally piercing me with her sapphire stare. "I've lived through losing you so many times… If I have to do it again, I need to know before I let myself get any more attached."

Agony squeezed my lungs. I wanted more than anything to fall to my knees and vow never to leave her side again. But I couldn't do that until I knew we would be whole again. She didn't deserve anything less.

She stepped back, leaving an open path to the door. "Just go," she said softly, without even a hint of judgement. "But, please, Gray… stay away until you're sure."

CHAPTER TWENTY-FIVE

October 2016

Grayson

Unable to sleep or drink or live through one more second of the constant litany of mistakes looping through my thoughts, I went into the office at five A.M. on Monday morning.

By the time the sun started to rise, I'd managed to lose myself in making up for all of the work I missed on Friday. Each time I paused, a memory from our day together rose to my mind's surface. Ella giggling on my bed. Ella making fun of my apartment. Her coupon. Her beaming enthusiasm and pride when I told her I designed the place.

Christ.

As I breathed through a searing burst of yearning, the door to my office flew open. Marco strode inside, holding up a handful of files. "We've got him."

I shoved all my other shit aside. "Show me."

He laid out the first document. "Flight logs," he explained. "They show the Stryker & Sons jet Daniel claimed to be on leaving France and landing in New York on the day before Christmas Eve. Our jets are always piloted by professionals we get from a flight contractor. I tracked down the pilot they sent for us that day and interviewed him. Asked him who was on the plane, since the register shows one passenger, listed as Daniel Stryker.

"He testified that there were no passengers, though. The flight was empty. He told me that someone named Ted contacted him and offered him five grand to fake the report. Since he wasn't transporting anyone dangerous into the country by doing so, he didn't see the harm in taking the deal. When I told him what happened, he immediately agreed to give a sworn statement on our behalf."

Marco produced a signed affidavit. I glanced over it, blowing out a deep breath. "This might be enough to get Ted. It's bribery, obviously. Misuse of company resources. Since he's not a voting partner and only acts as a figure-head, something like this is probably sufficient."

"Especially in combination with Ella's testimony against him," Amir agreed grimly.

"But he's not the problem," I went on. "I mean, I want Ted to fry; but I *need* Daniel dead in the water. With this… he could argue his father acted independently without his knowledge."

Marco gave a brusque nod and swapped the pages in front of me for a new set. "I had the same thought. So I went with another approach. I drove back down to Ella's building last night and interviewed her super. It bothered me that we couldn't figure out how Daniel got into her place Saturday morning. When I asked the landlord, he told me he'd never interacted with anyone named Daniel Stryker, but he *had* met with *Grayson* Stryker, the new CEO of the company building the parcel across the street."

"I never met with him," I put in.

Marco nodded again. "Exactly. I knew that, so I showed him a picture of you and he didn't know you. Then I showed him a picture of Daniel…"

"That fucker pretended to be me?" I yelled. "*That's* how he got her keys? When? How?"

Another paper appeared in front of me—a photocopy of a real estate sale. "Friday. He forged this contract and told the super that

Stryker & Sons had purchased the building, to add it to the existing parcel. He literally showed up like he owned the place and demanded his set of keys for the building. He figured the guy wouldn't be savvy enough to know better and he was right."

I turned the papers over, hunting for my signature. It was an obvious forgery—though there was no way some random landlord would have known that. They were also dated for Friday—a day when multiple witnesses knew I was out of the office.

"He must have gotten desperate when he saw her at the gala," I whispered. "He knew he had to act fast."

I held up the fake contract. "This is it, though," I told him. "Misconduct. He used the company to commit a crime. He used my name and signature. This should allow us to terminate him and liquidate his shares."

"I thought so," Amir said, not skipping a beat. "I'll take it all down to the precinct so they can use it as evidence. The DA as well."

I was impressed. "How did you know what you needed to look for?"

He looked a bit sheepish as he straightened, once again holding the files at his side. "I have a cousin who's a lawyer. I used to help her study sometimes."

How many times had I barked at Marco? Or just totally taken him for granted? Yet another new type of guilt assailed me.

A grim, self-deprecating smile twisted my lips. "Your cousin—does she work as hard as you?"

Amir cleared his throat. "Harder, actually."

"Get me her resume," I told him. "And you should probably change yours, too. If you're amenable, you'll no longer be my head of security. I'd like to promote you. Make you the director of security for the entire company. In addition to my personal security, you'll be tasked with implementing security systems and protocols for us to place in all of our residential projects. I never want what happened to Ella to happen to anyone living in one of my properties."

Marco inclined his head in a humble gesture. "Sir, I'm sure I'm not qualified for that task. And it's such a noble one. I'd hate to screw it up."

The briefest hint of a smile crossed my face. This was the first time in days I knew I was making the right call.

"Then don't," I said simply, shrugging. "You were in the military, Marco. You have special forces training. Then you spent two years working for the NYPD. You've revolutionized my family's security in your time with us. And the way you handled the crisis this weekend… I couldn't have asked for more."

He nodded at his feet. "Thank you. If you think I'm up to the job, then of course I accept the position."

Thank God. "You should probably ask me to give you a raise before you formally accept," I suggested. "I was thinking double your current salary, with a housing allowance so you can relocate from Queens into the city. They've finally finished the garage renovations under the lobby so it's time to move our fleet into Manhattan on a permanent basis. Naturally, you'll need to come with it."

I stood up to extend my hand. "An even million should get you a decent place nearby. But we can always renegotiate if necessary. You'll have the standard executive signing bonus as well."

Gratitude and disbelief vied for space in Amir's dark features. Finally, he grasped my hand and shook it. "Yes, sir. Thank you."

"Grayson," I corrected.

"Grayson."

The boost from making one good decision gave me the energy to get back to my other work. By the time the rest of the office arrived, I was more-than caught up. Beth even popped into my office to remark on my progress—with an obvious note of surprise and a stern reminder to stay on schedule, of course.

Naturally, that promptly got shot to hell.

My intercom buzzed sometime around mid-morning. "I have a Maggie Danvers here for you? She's down at reception demanding to be let up."

Fuck.

All of my self-loathing bubbled up, easily dissolving the thin veneer that business placed over it for a few hours. My mouth went dry as I buzzed Beth back. "That's… fine. Send her in."

My hand twitched toward my cell phone, automatically wanting to text Ella. The last time I spoke to Maggie alone, everything got twisted and Ellie never even heard about it. But it seemed wrong to reach out to her for the first time after our heavy conversation the night before, just to talk about her roommate.

Before I could make up my mind, Maggie sailed into the room. Her posture was formidable, but her clothes dampened the effect—a pink muumuu with clear acrylic heels. Though her frown was ferocious.

"You *complete idiot*," she started.

I didn't stop her. Instead, I stood behind my desk and let her rail at me. For several minutes.

And it felt… *good*. Because I deserved it. Everyone else kept trying to convince me it wasn't my fault. That I wasn't in the wrong.

Maggie disagreed. Whole-heartedly. She berated me for every single thing I'd mentally castigated myself over since Saturday. And some things I didn't even know about.

I had no idea Ella hadn't celebrated the holidays once since we broke up. Or that she had to live in low-income student housing the semester she returned to school because she had to cut her work hours in order to catch up on courses. Or that she hadn't even kissed another man in three years.

She also told me about the look on Ella's face that morning when she opened her laptop and saw a picture from the gala on her newsfeed. The snap of me with Olivia Watts—who I abandoned to fuck Ella on my desk—made us look very much like a couple. And, apparently, it had sent Ellie shuffling back to her bed before she could even attempt to go to work.

My shame mounted with every stinging reprimand. The pressure of it all pushed at the base my throat, rendering my eventual reply rough. "You're completely correct."

"About what?" she snapped, her eyes bugging behind her glasses.

"All of it," I owned. "I did every last single fucking thing wrong."

That seemed to throw her off. She clearly expected some sort of defense. I had none. Didn't want to make one.

Maggie stilled. "I didn't say *every*thing."

"Well, I am," I told her. "I failed. Miserably. Many times. I can never make up for what I did and all of the things I failed to do. And I will never be worthy of Ella."

She stared hard for a long minute. Sniffed. Brushed her hands down over her hips. "Well. Never thought you and I would actually *agree* on something."

I might have laughed, ordinarily. But nothing felt funny to me anymore. Nothing except for Ella's goddamn coupons and her sweet little laugh and her Big Bird purse and her—

Green clogs.

Maggie pulled them out of her tote bag, eyeing the offending footwear with total disdain and a bit of bemusement. "I should have known there was something seriously wrong with you when you told me you actually *like* these hideous things," she muttered, setting the shoes on the center of my desk. "I stole them when we moved, hoping she'd replace them with something palatable."

Slowly, I picked the clogs up. My throat and eyes burned. "I know she wants them back. Why bring them to me?"

Maggie rolled her big eyes. "So *you* have to give them back to her. Obviously. Idiot."

"But she doesn't want to see me. She told me last night to stay away until I knew what—until I knew how—" I sighed. "You just said it all, Maggie. I don't deserve her. I ruined everything."

"No," she cracked. "You *are* ruining it. Right now. Sitting here, scared. Backing down instead of moving forward."

She turned her back as quickly as she'd charged in. Making for the door, she issued one last parting sting. "Don't be the man I thought you were, Grayson. He doesn't deserve Ella. But you could."

After Maggie left, Beth appeared in my doorway. She spent a long moment looking at me, holding Ella's shoes, adrift, before turning on her heel and disappearing. When she returned half an hour later, she had a bag of food and Graham Everett in tow.

My best friend unpacked our meal and laid it out for us before sinking into one of my Eames chairs. In a red velvet jacket and pinstriped pants, he looked like he had some sort of costume party to attend later.

Neither of us spoke as I dug into the sandwich and salad Beth ordered for me. Graham sat with his own lunch untouched. When I finished piling a fresh round of food on top of the throbbing ache under my diaphragm, I pushed back from my desk and blew out a sigh.

"Who told you?"

Graham's brows lowered over his black eyes. "You father called me. Saturday. I'm sorry I didn't come sooner. I just had no idea what the fuck to say. I still don't." He shook his head. "All those nights we went out together and he took girls home..."

I'd done the same math. "I know."

"I feel sick," Graham confessed. "I haven't eaten in days."

I snorted at myself. "I can't *stop*. It's the only thing that helps me not want to vomit for five minutes."

"Fuck it." He huffed, picked up his pastrami on rye and bit. With a shudder, he set the sandwich back down. "Nope. Can't do it."

We sat in our heavy silence, with our heavy consciences. Finally, he spoke. Picking at his sleeve, examining it for lint as he said, "You know what I can't stop thinking about?"

I held my breath, almost afraid to ask. "What?"

He looked right at me. "She went back, man. After she saw Daniel at your parents' beach house and she ran away… Ella knew the man who attacked her was in there… and she still went back into that house. For you."

In all my self-loathing and all of my internal scourging, I'd never framed it that way. For a brief second, the pain that ripped through me felt life-ending. I was sure I'd look down at the floor beside my feet and see all of my organs lying in a bloody puddle, gutted.

But he was right.

She didn't run away that day. Not at all. She did the opposite; faced everything she was afraid of just to avoid abandoning me without an explanation. She was willing to confront a man who raped her before she left me. And she only went after he forced her to—by threating her family. And me. And her.

Now that I knew Daniel threatened to violate her again if she stayed and waited for me to return that morning… did I really wish she'd stayed?

No. I was glad she left when she did and got the hell away from him. And it obviously wasn't her fault that he corrupted my contact in her phone so she couldn't call once she was safe.

Graham watched everything click together in my mind. "You were never happier than when you were with her," he told me. "You know I hate this shit to the bottom of my soul, but… she's the one for you, Grayson. Which means this is *it*."

I didn't know how to organize the riot inside of me. But it pushed me to my feet in a rush. I stood there, breathing hard, trying to figure out what to do.

"I'll talk to Beth," Graham said, his voice taking on a note of urgency. "Now get the hell out of here."

As much as I wanted to go charging out to Brooklyn, I knew I needed to make good on my word first.

So I found myself sitting in Dr. Laura Dawn's office. I stayed through two other sessions with scheduled patients before she had a short break to speak with me. Instead of going into her office, I hovered in the small waiting room, feeling completely adrift.

After we briefly introduced ourselves, I rushed on. "I know you have a busy schedule. I appreciate you carving out this window for me."

Even standing still, she had the soft, swaying quality of a weeping willow. Her kimono and long skirt moved as she nodded. "I know you're dealing with something time-sensitive. If you'd like to make an appointment to come back, I can provide much more in-depth advice. But, for now, how can I help?"

I'd had two hours to decide exactly what I would say. What I needed to know in order to move forward with Ellie and never look back.

And it surprised me.

Because I didn't want to know if I'd ever be able to have sex with her again. Or if I'd ever forgive myself. I didn't need any reassurance that we would find our way through anything. Or that she would make me the happiest man on earth.

I realized, I already knew all of that.

I realized, as long as I had Ellie, I would always have everything I needed. We would find a way. Together.

Which left only one question.

"Do you think," I said, staring at doctor down, "if Ella and I were together, that being with me would make her happy?"

Dr. Laura smiled softly. "I think Ella is a bright, lovely, kind woman, gifted with wonderful resilience. I think she will be happy as long as she decides to be."

Huh. A sardonic smile flickered over my face. "Is that a yes?"

"Well, one could argue that whether or not you make her happy is really up to *you*," she returned, her brows arching.

Oh, I would. I felt my features tighten. "If it was safe for me to have Ellie, I would spend the rest of my life making her as happy as I possibly could."

"Well, then." Dr. Laura's face didn't register a modicum of doubt. "It sounds like the only piece of the puzzle you need to figure out is how Ella feels about that. You should ask her for herself."

It couldn't possibly be that simple… could it? "But it wouldn't hurt her, to be with me?" I verified. "Or traumatize her more? In your opinion?"

Kindness and compassion saturated her expression. "No, Grayson. Not at all. In fact, it's my professional opinion that you and Ella would thrive with a little bit of guidance and therapy. You've both been through so much. If you're able to process it together, it should help reestablish your bond. I'd be happy to help you both if Ella agrees."

Inside of me, the rumble of hope built to a deafening roar. My mind raced, looking for any other reason to hold myself back. "She said she loved me," I found myself sharing. "And she—"

Dr. Laura waited patiently. "She?"

I swallowed through my thick throat. "She went back. That day… at my parents' beach house. Even though she knew he was in there… she went back. For me."

The enormity of that humbled me. Ella's goodness was staggering and wonderful. And, maybe… mine. It didn't seem possible.

But Dr. Laura simply met my gaze. "I haven't met very many people who are that brave."

"To face their attackers?"

"No." She smiled softly again. "To love that hard."

Ella

I hated our new couch.

For one, it was *grey*.

But, moreover, it was an ultra-modern piece with almost no padding. Maggie must have picked it out and had it delivered same-day. As I frowned down at it, I wondered, idly, exactly *how much* money Mr. Stryker left for us. I just handed her the stack without counting it.

Mags also picked out a new rug, in a matching shade of charcoal. I scowled at that, too.

My latest knitting project sat abandoned on my orange armchair. I'd been using it as a crutch for the better part of the morning.... Now that I was no longer employed.

After calling out of work, I received a brusque email from Marjorie forty-five minutes later. The missive basically said she couldn't afford to have an assistant who called out "without compunction" and, therefore, she would be asking HR to process my "separation" from Idealogue with two weeks' notice.

At first, I was crushed; but as the morning wore on, I started to feel angry. I'd worked there for almost two years and never called out unless I was desperately ill. Firing me after two missed days seemed cruel. And short-sighted.

Maggie paced all around the new rug. She'd come home and immediately launched into another apology. I was ready to ask her to try again another time, but then she told me she went to Gray's office.

"You told him you were sorry?" I couldn't picture it. In all the years I'd known her, I'd only received a handful of apologies. And she didn't even like Grayson.

"Yeah," she huffed, still moving. "Well, actually, no. Technically not. But. I sort of didn't need to. He got it."

My eyebrows folded together. "You two reached some sort of understanding…?"

"Goddess, I *hope* so! He was infuriatingly contrite. But I think I made my point. If I were you, I'd expect to see him again soon."

My battered heart stirred in my chest. Bruised, the thrill only managed to make it ache. "I don't know, Maggie."

"Well I do!" she proclaimed. "That boy is in love with you, Ella Callahan."

"I don't know," I repeated, afraid to believe. "He's never said he still loves me."

It was true. After he left, I parsed all of his words carefully, hoping he said it and I missed it, somehow. Then, I woke up to five different tabloid stories—pictures of Gray and Olivia Watts splashed over every corner of the web. They looked so right together, both dark and aristocratic. I bet she even had a coat from a department store.

With an agitated motion, Maggie ripped her phone out of her bag and read it before pounding a text with her thumbs. She turned her eyes on me, then the pile of knitting next to me.

"That thing is twice as big as it was this morning," she pointed out, a touch suspicious. "Are you spiral-knitting because Gray hasn't called yet?"

I knew I had to tell her about my job… but I dreaded it. Anxiety pinched my lungs while she focused on her phone once more, then finally turned to me again.

"No," I admitted, wincing. "I got fired, actually. Because I called out Friday and today."

Mags froze mid-stride, her face torn between murderous and calculating. "You know what we need?" she finally asked.

I ran my hand under my nose. "Money? The 'want' ads? A LinkedIn profile?"

She reached her hand out to me. "Margaritas."

I only agreed to go for drinks if I got to bring my knitting.

Between the tote bag stuffed full of mustard yarn, my over-sized purple sweater dress, and my general status as Forever Alone, I was officially The Crazy Woman On The Subway.

Maggie refused to tell me where we were going for our "Welfare Margaritas." She babbled while we rode uptown, uncharacteristically chatting about meaningless topics designed to distract me from all of my misery.

Our train bumped along while she talked and I knit. Somewhere around downtown, she got a call and excused herself to go to the other side of the car to take it.

"Is it a blanket?"

I made a face, irritated that some stranger would try chatting me up. *Today of all days? Seriously?* With my nose scrunched and wary eyes, I chanced a peek at the figure suddenly standing over me.

Grayson Stryker loomed a foot away, imposing and handsome as ever. Gazing down at me with an unfathomable look in his eyes and a small smile playing at his sculpted lips.

For a second, the moment transported me back in time. To the day I first glanced up from my lap-full of yarn and fell into his intense green gaze. In a way, I'd never climbed back out.

"Gray." His name came as a breathy sigh. My mouth hung open for a long second before I remembered to close it. "What are you—how did you—"

His face transformed into my very favorite grin. He nodded slightly to the other side of the car. "I had an accomplice." Raw feeling shifted in his depths. "But, to be honest, even if Maggie hadn't helped… I would ride this train every single day until I found you, Ellie. It's not like I haven't done it before."

I felt myself smirk for the first time in days. "I remember."

As we stared at each other, all traces of levity dissipated. His eyes burned, brilliant smoldering vats of emerald. I couldn't help but fall into them all over again while I asked, "What are you doing here?"

Right there, in full view of a subway full of strangers, Grayson Stryker, business titan, lowered into a crouch, putting our faces on the same level. His warm hands fell to my knees, kneading gently. "I'm here for you. You told me not to come back until I was sure about our future. Well, I thought about it. And I've never been more sure about anything in my life."

He reached up to hold my face in his palm. The spark in his gaze ignited. "I love you, Ellie. You are the bravest, most beautiful woman I've ever met. And I want us to be together. Always."

Just when I felt certain I would embarrass myself by bursting into tears on the train, his free hand reached under my seat and produced a shoebox. It had a few different things in the bottom... but one very familiar pair of shoes on top of it all.

He glanced down at the green clogs. "I realized, I've known you were the One from the first moment I saw these."

The One. And he loved me? He'd planned this out, within a couple of hours, for me?

"You brought me my lost shoes?" A watery, delighted giggle tripped up my throat. "I always said you were Prince Charming."

His brows rose while his grin widened. "I think it was a glass slipper, not a rubber clog." He shrugged and pulled off my ballet flats. "But I'll take it."

For a moment, Gray focused on gracing my stockinged feet with my favorite shoes. When he turned his face back up to mine, unfettered adoration saturated his features.

"There's my girl," he murmured, framing my face with his hands.

Unable to resist the warmth brimming in his depths and the happy hum in my heart, I launched myself at him. He caught me, enveloping my body in his arms while I planted my lips directly onto his.

Our mouths brushed in a hard, sweet kiss... until Maggie cheered and started a round of applause that quickly spread throughout the car. We both leaned back, smiling while we locked eyes.

"What do we do now?" I whispered through the din, suddenly shy.

Gray guided both of us to our feet, wrapping one solid arm around my waist to hold me against him. "Actually," he said. "I had an idea."

Grayson

Ella caught on as soon as we stepped into the St. Regis's elevator and the attendant once again knew my name.

Her luminous blue eyes slanted a look at me. "Grayson. You didn't."

I couldn't stop smiling at her like an idiot. "It was a gesture of wild optimism," I quipped. "Which isn't my usual style, I know..."

But the prospect of a whole, wide-open future with Ella made me feel punch-drunk. As soon as I left Dr. Laura's office—imbued with the knowledge that we could make our relationship work as long as we did—I called and booked the suite.

Hard work, therapy, making amends. None of that scared me.

The thought of making my grand romantic gesture and then taking her home to my sterile penthouse—where she last fled in terror—or her blood-splattered apartment *had* shaken me, though. I wanted us to spend our free time together in an untainted space where we could catch our breath and focus on our horizons.

I still had my shoebox tucked under my arm. The one with all of the bits and pieces of Ellie I kept for years. Including the engagement ring.

Some voice in my head stopped me every time I wanted to reach for it, hissing that it was too soon. We needed the one thing we'd missed out on for all those years: time.

We would have that, now. All the time we wanted. A dizzy thrill of exhilaration swooped through me whenever I realized that this was *it*. We never had to be apart again.

I would work to make sure we never were. I promised her always, the same way she promised me three years before. And, just like her, I meant it.

"Here you are Mr. Stryker, Miss…" The attendant cleared his throat.

"Callahan," I said pointedly. I wanted everyone in the hotel to treat Ella with the same deference they showed me. "Please inform the staff we aren't to be disturbed, as a rule. If we have any requirements, I will call down personally."

He nodded, chastened. "Mr. Stryker. Of course."

I led Ella out into the hallway. Her glances took on a curious, skittish quality. "You're different," she whispered, smiling a little. "More… in control. I've noticed it all week."

I couldn't deny that. I knew I'd gotten less patient and more demanding. When I started working as Stryker & Son's CEO, I learned quickly that time was my most valuable resource. Anything that threatened to waste it became the enemy. Though, I hated the idea of Ellie finding me different from the man she originally fell in love with. Especially since she was so wonderfully unchanged.

I repressed a cringe. "Guess it's an occupational hazard."

Her fingers glided up my chest, tracing my lapel as her sapphire eyes darkened. "I don't know if I *should*, but I like it," she whispered, as if confessing to some dark secret. "It's… *ridiculously* sexy."

My face split into a grin. "I'm relieved. I don't want you to think of me as… what was it Maggie called me? A dickhead on a donkey?"

She shrugged one shoulder with put-on nonchalance. "I have no idea what you're talking about."

I waved our key card over the creamy double doors at the end of the hallway. They gave way to the suite's charming blue-and-gilt foyer. Ella stepped inside and turned in a half-circle, all casual pretense draining from her face.

"It's the Tiffany Suite," she whispered. Her expression softened with awe. "You booked this for me again?"

I set the shoebox on the foyer table and reached for her waist, finding the gentle curves under her slouchy sweater dress. The feel of her sent a lick of fire through my blood.

"I got it for both of us," I told her, staring down into her face. "For two weeks."

"Two *weeks*?" she squeaked, her voice weedy.

I blew out a breath. "Well, they only allow patrons to book it in two-week blocks. I can always extend our stay."

"You want me to stay here *with* you?" she repeated, disbelieving. "Y-you want me around all the time? Are you sure, Grayson? You don't have to rush. I know what I did to you was unforgivable and everything that happened after has to be hard to process…"

I cut her off by running my thumb over her lower lip, carefully freeing it from her front teeth. "Yes. I want nothing more than to have you around all the time," I answered simply.

When she still looked incredulous, I went on, "And it's not unforgivable because I *have* forgiven you. There was nothing to forgive, really. You were in an impossible situation and you tried to protect everyone. Including yourself. I wouldn't have wanted you to respond any differently, had I been given the choice. Everything that happened after was their doing. And mine. My idiotic pride and anger took over and I let them. I'm the one who isn't worthy of forgiveness, Ella."

"That's not true," she insisted softly, reaching up to caress my cheek. "But I forgive you nonetheless." She drew closer. "You didn't have to do this for me, Gray. We can just go back to your place or mine…"

Our hands seemed to have minds of their own. While our gazes meshed, fully engaged in our conversation, her touch slid over my shoulders, down my arms, back up to my nape. Mine roamed down hips, over the sexy dip above her ass, up the elegant curve of her spine.

"I know this is… a lot," I rasped, forcing myself to focus. "But you know it isn't a burden for me. And I want us to have a neutral place to stay while we reconnect. That's really important to me. Dr. Laura liked the suggestion, too."

Ella seemed touched. "You've already seen her?"

"This afternoon," I confirmed. "She'll see us both as a couple as early as tomorrow evening, if you'd like. I'll have Beth clear my day by five. We can go see Dr. Laura and then I'll take you out to dinner."

She blinked tears out of her eyes. "That sounds like a dream."

Joy combusted inside of me. All I wanted was to make her happy. The pleasure it gave me was unparalleled.

Well, I thought, my fingers gliding over the outline of her breasts, *not* completely *unparalleled.*

She shivered, but I forced myself to move my hands back to her face. We needed to approach anything physical between us with caution. I didn't want to frighten or rush her. And I needed to make sure I never accidentally gave her the impression that her history repulsed me ever again.

"It's unorthodox," I continued, once again refocusing. "But I knew you liked this place. We have good memories here. Plus, the location is practical. Close to our offices, right off the Park."

Ella mashed her lips together. Color ebbed from her expression. "Gray… about my office…"

By the time she finished telling me how Marjorie fired her that morning, I barely had a handle on my fury. My hands crumpled fists of her dress over her shoulder blades.

"Well," I said, my voice much smoother than I felt. "If they don't have you anymore, then they no longer have my business, either."

"No!" she cried. "Please don't fire them. Oh, I was afraid of this. I don't want anyone to get in any more trouble over me."

My Ellie. Always defending people who didn't deserve loyalty and employing empathy for anyone who scorned her. Always too bright and beautiful for all the darkness around her.

I sighed, glowering at her. "Well, *I* don't want to work with people who would fire an employee going through a crisis because of a few absences."

Her mouth pulled into a grimace. "You got me there," she muttered. "Could you just… be nice?" She didn't sound optimistic. "They're good people, Gray, and—"

"Good people would not treat you as disposable," I argued. "And I will tell them that. You're my life, now, Ellie. I will protect you and defend you, always. Anyone who wants to fuck with you or cast you aside will quickly learn their lesson."

Her eyes dilated while her thighs pressed together. An answering jolt twitched through my cock, tightening my hold on her dress. I breathed through the lust, forcing myself not to rip the damned sweater over her head.

The dynamic was new for us. Three years before, we were both still kids, in some ways. Both of us were trying to figure out who we would be, what our relationship would look like. Back then, I didn't have the power to protect her this way, the ability to shape our world. She fell in love with me anyway. She adored me, for *me*—not my potential. Ella loved the person beneath all of the wealth and influence and fame.

But, now, I had all of those things. Directly. They weren't just a mantle I borrowed from my parents. They were mine. Me. And it seemed to turn her on.

In return, the way she softened and surrendered, trusting me so completely without a single doubt, made my blood roar. I wanted to make her *mine*. She wanted to let me. And I *would* take care of what was mine.

"We have a lot to figure out," she breathed, reading my mind. "This is all so…"

My hands resumed their roaming, sketching over every part of her, longing to relearn each precious piece. "Foreign?" I tried. "Nerve-wracking? Ellie, if I'm making you nervous, I can—"

Her mouth collided with mine, silencing me. I could tell, once again, that it had been a long time since she regularly kissed anyone. She seemed eager, but hesitant, like she wasn't sure she remembered how to do it.

Tamping down a rush of shame—because I'd never really given myself a chance to fall out of practice—I decided to focus on my gratitude. She waited for me. That notion still filled me with amazement and appreciation.

And raw, scorching hunger.

I wanted to make up for all the pleasure she denied herself. Give it all back to her tenfold.

Cupping her sweet face in my hands, I tilted her head and sealed my lips over hers the way she liked, licking into her mouth slowly, until she moaned and pressed her breasts into my chest.

Ella held fast to my jacket, her desperate clutches betraying her urgency. I broke away, already a little short of breath. "Do you need me, baby?" I murmured, brushing my lips over hers once more. "I know I have a lot of time to make up for…"

Her fingers tightened while worry split her expression. "I—I don't know. I was alone for so long… And then Thursday and Friday were such a blur… Honestly, it feels like I have no idea what I'm doing or what I want. I thought I'd completely lost touch with all of this…"

Her sexuality, she meant. The thought of such lush, glorious beauty wilting on the vine sent a pang to my heart.

"I'll find it," I vowed, kissing her again.

She melted and came to life simultaneously. Letting me support her weight while arching into every caress and every kiss. She pushed my suit jacket to the floor, untied my tie, and unbuttoned my shirt. Her hands touched my bare skin with reverence, lovingly gliding up the planes of my abdomen, turning my cock to stone. It pressed insistently into the fall of my trousers, spurring me on.

With a reluctant grumble in my throat, I unsealed my lips from hers. I was determined to seduce her properly and we hadn't even made it past the foyer.

"We should take this slow," I panted quietly. "I want this to be right."

Her fingers moved nimbly over the back of my neck, massaging knots from the corded muscles she traced. God, how I'd missed her touches. Always so giving and guileless.

"Gray," she said, an adoring smirk playing at her lips. "Don't take this the wrong way, but you think too much."

A laugh stuttered out of me. She had a point. Taking her out on our first proper date. Telling her I loved her. My thwarted proposal. All of it could have happened much sooner and much easier if I went with my gut. I had a tendency to over-think where she was concerned, because every decision I made felt monumentally important to me.

Her sapphire eyes glowed up at me, luminous and full of love. "I want you to do exactly what you want to me," she murmured, "without thinking about it."

White hot desire bolted down my back. "I don't think you know what you're asking for," I bit back, doing everything I could to rein myself in.

Her hands slipped down my abs, over my waistband, and finally met the throbbing erection begging for her touch. "Please," she breathed, licking her lips. "Make me yours again."

Ella

Grayson swept my feet off the floor without another second of hesitation.

He carried me in his arms, striding from the foyer, past the opulent lacquered dining table and its pearl chandelier. Through the beautifully-appointed living room, with its gilt-leaf ceiling and silver velvet furnishings. Into the grey marble bathroom, with all of its sparkling mirrored surfaces and Tiffany-blue accents.

He bent slightly to turn on the bathtub's tap and promptly spun us, setting me on my feet just in time to press me into the wall. His mouth devoured mine, sending delicious tingles through my breasts. His groan vibrated in my core.

"I want to see you," he told me, lifting the hem of my dress. "All of you. Up close."

I wasn't sure I understood, but I started to tug my tights off anyway. His large, warm palms followed the movement, smoothing over the exposed skin of my hips while his tongue glided over mine. Liquid heat pooled low in my belly, right where his erection pressed through his pants. When I undid his fly, he shucked them, along with his boxers, socks, and shoes.

I had an ugly lavender sports bra on, but he didn't give me a moment to feel self-conscious. With a growl, he lifted me off my feet and set me in the tub. His emerald eyes glowed hotly while he stared down at me. "Sit on the edge."

My legs were quivering, anyway. I rushed to follow his command, riding a thrill of anticipation. The warm water felt delicious as it rose up my calves… especially a moment later when Grayson unceremoniously flipped on the tub's jets and dumped bath oil into the eddies swirling around my legs. Within seconds, a clean burst of eucalyptus filled the air.

My gaze roved over his naked body, cataloging every detail I missed in his dark office and penthouse on Thursday and Friday. He stood beside me for a long moment, breathing hard, affording me the opportunity to take in each pristine part of his perfection.

If anything, he looked even stronger than he used to. His chest seemed wider, more square. The ridges of his abdominals, more defined. Thick muscles bunched over his thighs, his biceps, the broad expanse of his shoulders. Veins roped over his forearms, outlined the brawny strength of his closed fists, and bulged along his glorious package.

Every inch of him—and there *quite* a few inches—gave masculine perfection a new meaning.

A woeful wave of inadequacy washed through me. I folded down, crossing my arms over my grubby bra and closing my legs tightly.

"Hey."

Gray frowned as he stepped into the tub, going to his knees in front of me. His hands immediately flew to my cheeks, bringing my face up to his. "Baby, what's wrong? Am I going too fast?"

I shook my head. The feel of my limp, greasy hair brushing over my back only made me shrink down more. "I'm just… I didn't know I'd be here, with you, and I'm…"

Not groomed. Not good enough.

Grayson ran his hands over my head, burying his fingers in the hair at my nape and bending to rest his forehead on mine. "Are you not ready?" he asked.

It was actually embarrassing how ready my body felt for his. Wetness collected at the apex of my thighs and I squeezed them together again. His glittering green eyes tracked the movement, then moved to the outlines of my nipples, furled tight under my bra.

When his gaze finally snapped back to mine, understanding dawned. "You're self-conscious."

A desperate swell of mortification burst out of me. "I didn't shave or—"

His palms slowly slid up and down my thighs, moving closer to their sensitive inner skin with each pass. "You've forgotten," he murmured, staring intensely into my eyes. "How I feel about you. How your body affects me."

He straightened and took my hands in his, bringing both to his straining erection. He wrapped my palm over his length and moved both of our hands over his shaft. "Do you feel how hard you make me?" he asked, lust tautening his features. He brought my other hand to balance the weight of his full, tight sack. "How I'm ready to come just from thinking about all the things I want to do to you?"

Everything below my waist shuddered. Molten moisture slicked my sex. My fist closed around his cock, stroking harder. "Grayson…"

His intense regard did not waver. "We're in this tub right now because I want to savor every single second of you. And I knew, if I took you straight to bed, I wouldn't be able to restrain myself. Because you *wreck me*, Ella."

He grunted as pre-cum wet my working hand. A second later, he bent back, disengaging from my touch. He braced both his hands on either side of my hips and gazed down at me. "Spread your legs."

Anticipation coursed through me again. My knees wobbled as I parted them. I expected him to touch me, but, instead, Gray just… stared.

His eyes ran over my exposed flesh, smoldering. "I couldn't really see you," he rumbled, "before. At my place. And the office. It was dark." He worked on a swallow before his mouth fell open slightly, as if in awe.

From… *me*? Surely not.

But he kept his eyes on my wet folds. "You are the most beautiful woman," he murmured, utterly sincere. "Ever. Always."

His words sent a blush over my entire body. "Gray…"

"I mean it," he rumbled, his face drawn. "You should see how you look right now. All of your creamy, perfect skin." He kissed my shoulder. "Your gorgeous face." He kissed my cheek and then bent forward. "These long legs." Kissed each of my knees.

"And here," he whispered, planting his lips right above my clit. "You're glistening. Pink and swollen for me. You smell like heaven. And you taste—"

His words cut off as he sealed his mouth over my sex. I gasped, my hips jumping forward to meet him. He gave a deep, masculine groan of satisfaction, pulling me closer while he licked over the bud pulsing between my labia.

I cried out, my hands falling to his head and gripping his hair. He growled, shoving the breadth of his wide shoulders between my legs, tipping me up to expose my entire pussy to his hungry lips and tongue. They sucked, drawing on my clitoris and then my opening. He slipped inside the trembling slit, teasing with slow half-circles until I started to shake and tug at his roots.

"Gray," I keened. "Oh my *God*."

His approval vibrated over my slick, sensitized flesh. "Mmm. That's my good girl."

His hands ghosted up my sides, tracing the outlines of my breasts before finding the tight buds of my nipples. He tweaked both and sucked my swollen nub between his lips, drawing circles over it before finding the sensitive underside and working it with the flat of his tongue.

My body pumped up against him, desperate to relieve the scorching pressure pulled taut through my center. His fingers impatiently bunched the sports bra up, exposing my bare skin, tugging on the taut nipples directly. Rough and unrestrained, exactly the way I wanted him.

His tongue slipped from the bottom of my clit, dipping into my pussy before returning to the sweet spot he loved so well. Two more circuits, and I found myself gasping, crying out his name as euphoria crashed over me, breaking like storm waves on rocks.

Grayson made a feral sound, lapping up all of the cream that seeped from my core as I came. When he'd wrung the last shiver of pleasure from me, he pressed kisses over my belly and hips. His hands gave another tug on my sports bra, silently demanding I remove it.

Once we were both completely stripped, he pulled my chest into his, nuzzling his face into my hair. Holding me. The familiar gesture sent tears to my eyes while I stroked my hands down his back.

I noticed how he held himself stiffly, clearly aroused beyond all reason but trying to hold himself back. Turning my head, I took his mouth, my kiss voracious. He caught on immediately, gripping me with same urgency with which he chased down my release. One of his hands left me for a moment. Then I felt a towel brush over the small of my back.

He tugged me off the edge of the tub and flipped me. In one breath, I found myself on my knees, facing the mirror surrounding the bath, with my elbows balanced on a folded towel Gray pushed up against my ribs.

"Like this," he murmured.

His entire chest pressed into every line of my back, warming me just as much as the whirling jets of heated water spinning around my legs. The rush of it, rising to the place just below the lips of my sex, heightened my arousal. As did Grayson's solid cock, wedged against my backside.

At first, I pressed back, thinking he wanted me bent forward to accommodate him. He repositioned me, though, pressing the slick, blunt head of his erection into my opening as he snaked his arms around my body, pulling me upright. One of his hands sprawled over my hip while the other gently held my neck and jaw, turning my head to the left.

His face loomed beside mine. He nodded at the mirror in front of me. "Look."

My gaze flickered to the image reflected back at us. Grayson's hard, muscled body wrapped around mine, his strength enveloping me. His impossibly gorgeous face nuzzling into the side of mine.

His hips pressed forward, sinking the first thick inch of his member into me. "Watch," he commanded. "Watch me make you mine again."

With that, he buried his face into the curve of my shoulder and bit the tender chords of my throat. I moaned, my eyes snapping forward at the same moment his cock claimed my pussy. A soul-deep cry sloughed out of him, curling my toes as he screwed his body into mine.

I watched his face in the mirror, riveted by the pure vulnerability and ardent emotion that tore through his features. "I love you, Ella" he panted, thrusting a second time. Ecstasy and adoration filled his face. "Do you see it?"

I did see it. *Gray loves me.*

And he always had. The truth of that finally sank down into my middle, sending a new sort of bliss sparkling through my blood.

"Yes," I whispered. "I see it."

His arms constricted. He worked in and out of me, still moving slowly enough for me to feel every bit of him. When I clutched around him, he made a pained noise.

"I love you, too," I told him, reaching up to tangle my fingers into his hair. "I'm yours now. I always was."

Another desperate sound tore from his throat as he lifted his head and looked at my face. His hips pumped faster. "Never leave me again."

"Never."

I turned and sealed my lips with his, kissing him with wild abandon. It broke his grasp on control. His thrusts picked up speed and lost finesse. The hand at my hip slipped down to my clit while the one around my neck found the curve of my breast, kneading it.

Our open mouths moved together, sloppy and unrestrained. The edge of the water had risen, just barely sloshing up to bathe the place where we connected. The warmth felt indescribable as it melded with soft circles he drew on my throbbing bud. Unable to help it, I moaned again, my pussy sucking him deeper. He groaned into our kiss, his fingers picking up speed while he bucked his hips harder.

"Jesus, Ella, I'm going to come."

His pained confession sent me over the edge. I tugged on the roots of his hair, clenching down on the heavy length of his cock while another climax spiraled through my core. Grayson followed me, calling my name into my nape while he slammed into me one last time and spilled deep.

Without wasting a single second, Gray pulled out of me and fell back. He brought my body into his arms, tucking my face into the hollow under his throat. His hands smoothed my hair back as the jets pushed pulses of water over my sensitized skin. Along with the glow pulsing through me from my climax, it felt like paradise.

Gray seemed to agree. He hummed, the deep sound vibrating under my ear while he cut the tap off. The jets continued, bubbling quietly around us as silence fell.

I was already in heaven, but Gray had other ideas. He slipped his wet fingers up my back and massaged the tension in my spine, holding me closer as I burrowed into his hard chest. His lips grazed my forehead every few moments.

"Gray?"

"Hmm?"

I tilted my head back to look up at him, despite feeling shy. "Would you sing to me?"

A small smile played at his sculpted lips before he pressed them into mine gently. "Of course," he agreed. "Which song?"

I swallowed past a lump of gratitude. "Remember Me?"

Unfathomable love flared in his emerald depths. "Always, Ellie," he vowed. "Always."

***

Three Months Later

December 2016, New Year's Eve

Ella

"It's almost time."

Grayson's deep, sexy voice rumbled as he skimmed his lips over my shoulder. "Are you ready?"

I reached up to pat the side of his black hair with one hand while the other adjusted the fall of my favorite necklace. Ever since restoring the entwined circles to their rightful place at the hollow of my throat, I'd only taken them off for very special occasions.

Like the night Grayson brought me a gorgeous strand of pearls as a surprise when he returned from a business trip to Japan. The luminous white stones were so beautiful, it almost made up for three nights without him next to me. They didn't really match my jeans, though. Or my red bell-sleeved blouse.

Gray's emerald eyes met mine in the wide mirror. Grinning, he fingered the hem of the top, skirting his touch over my navel. "You look ready," he insisted, dipping his fingers lower, into my waistband. "Let's see how you *feel*, though…"

I swatted at his hands, laughing. "Here I thought we were in some big hurry! You've been checking your watch every twenty seconds and asking if I'm ready twice as often."

It was only a slight exaggeration. So slight, he smirked at himself. "We *do* need to go," he agreed. "Are you ready?"

I huffed, waving him out of the master bath. *Geez.* When we decided to keep New Year's Eve private and quiet—after a jam-packed Christmas season full of countless philanthropic events, business galas, and holiday parties—I assumed there wouldn't be a schedule. I should have known better. My beloved titan of industry loved a good plan.

With an eye roll, I cast one last look at my loose hair and basic makeup before turning for his bedroom. *Our bedroom*, he called it. I supposed, practically, it *was* ours. For three months, we'd both slept there every single night. We shared the closet and the attached bathroom. And I woke up there, next to Grayson, every single morning.

Unless he had a business trip. It had only happened a handful of times since I moved in, but I always missed him terribly. Though he called me every night without fail, regardless of time zones, and stayed on the phone with me until I started to drift off. I tried to keep myself busy; but being alone in the penthouse left me with so much nervous energy, he usually came home to piles of baked goods and some new knitting creations, to boot.

I didn't know if I'd ever really feel at home the lavish, minimalist apartment, with all of its clinical metal accents, chilly glass, and endlessly blank expanses of white. It hardly mattered, anyway, though, as Grayson insisted that he wanted to sell the place and choose a new one together.

Though I wouldn't miss feeling out of place, I had to admit, part of me was sad for us to move on. We'd grown together so much over the past few months… I would always feel nostalgic for all of the memories we made after coming home to the penthouse following our two week stay-cation in the St. Regis.

It may not have been homey, but his apartment had seen a lot. Tearful conversations after particularly intense therapy sessions, sweet mid-night reunions when he'd wake me kisses, joy-filled preparations for all the holidays I could finally allow myself to enjoy again. And, of course, Gray's general insatiability. Matched only by own attraction to him.

The thought put a bounce in my step while I sauntered out to the great room. I supposed, if I was being fair, the apartment had changed a bit. There were knit throw blankets of various shades over some of the furniture. A vase of flowers on the island that I refilled twice a week. The sunny yellow Kitchenaid mixer Maggie got us as a "moving-in-together/I-told-you-so" gift. And of course, my orange recliner, jammed into the far corner beside Grayson's work area. Whenever he had to work into the night, I curled up there with my latest book or project and shared space with him.

Now, Grayson stood across the expansive room, beside the door, bent over his Christmas gift to me. He adjusted the straps securing the folded telescope, offering a perfect view of his broad back and tight backside, encased in a black cashmere sweater and grey slacks. The ensemble suddenly struck me as odd.

"Why are you so dressed up?" I teased, floating to his side. "Aren't we just going up to the roof and coming right back down?"

"Yeah." He straightened, frowning down at his outfit. "I was in a hurry. This was just the first thing I touched."

Again, his haste made no sense to me. We were just going upstairs to stargaze. Usually, we wandered up there at our leisure, dressed in whatever clothes we happened to have on. We'd done the same thing most nights since we returned from our Christmas trip to Maryland earlier that week.

Even with the trip behind us, I still felt guilty about it. Our holiday plans created a lot of tension between us—I wanted us to try to re-create the Christmas we all lost, while Grayson insisted we go visit my family and let the painful memories lie. In the end, he'd admitted he didn't know if he could handle reliving it all and

I relented; but I still felt bad that he'd missed out on one of his father's last Christmases because of me.

"Hey," I said, brushing my hand up his arm. "Thank you again. For going home for the holiday with me. And sleeping on the couch."

It was one of Dr. Laura's practices—instead of endlessly apologizing, she suggested I express gratitude for whatever sacrifice Gray made for me. The re-frame helped a lot, even if Gray always knew what I was up to.

His gaze softened as he lifted my hand to his mouth, pressing a kiss to my palm. "It was a great Christmas, Ellie. I loved meeting your family, seeing your old high school, your yearbooks, your room…"

He smiled into my skin, clearly recalling all of the ways he defiled the small white bed in my childhood bedroom with me. "That was fun," I agreed, giggling. "Except the one time we almost got caught."

"Oh God." Gray groaned, cringing as he stepped toward the coat rack. "I had no idea little siblings could be so exasperating."

"I tried to warn you!" I crowed. "You didn't believe me!"

When we made our plans, I attempted to describe how Darcy's exuberance and tendency to miss social cues made her a bit… much.

Grayson steadfastly insisted he would love having a little sister, regardless. After growing up without any siblings of his own, he seemed genuinely amused every time my baby sister inserted herself into our plans or thwarted our attempts to be alone.

For her part, Darcy accepted my boyfriend as her pseudo-brother right away. She talked Gray's ear off about her college-level computer programming courses and asked tons of questions about the technology they used at Stryker & Sons. It was rare for any adult to follow her techno-babble—when he kept pace with her, Darcy was thrilled. And I loved watching them forge a bond.

Gray's grin dazzled me as he returned with our outerwear. "I still don't think she's annoying, really. Darcy is sweet and bright. And

I thought it was nice that she wanted to spend all of her time with you. It's hardly her fault you can't keep your hands off of me."

"Um, excuse me," I replied. "If I recall, I wasn't the one on my knees that night."

He held open my second-favorite Christmas gift—the coat his mother carefully sourced to replace my worn one. She'd gone to the trouble of hunting down a pristine version of the vintage, thrifted poppy coat instead of simply buying something from a department store. Gray pressed another kiss to the side of my neck while he slid the garment over my shoulders.

"Mmm," he hummed, chuckling. "So very worth the risk."

He patted down his pockets, checking for his phone and key card before sliding on his peacoat and gathering the telescope under his arm. Within minutes we emerged from the elevator, stepping into the freezing air hovering over the rooftop. Gray guided me to the spot he'd set up for us—two stools, two screens to block blustering wind, and a propane space heater.

Tonight, though, I noticed the flicker of some candles, along with a lump on each of our seats. As we drew closer, I saw that one shadow was actually a bottle of champagne and some glasses. The other was the mustard yellow blanket I knit. It was my first colorful addition to his pristine apartment—and it usually lived on his otherwise-blank couch.

"Gray!" I turned to him, beaming. "This is so romantic! Is this why you were so hell-bent on getting me up here?"

He set the telescope in its place of pride, then turned and gathered me in his arms, flashing a playful, boyish smile. "Could be. I know you just wanted a quiet night in, but I figured it just isn't New Year's Eve without champagne. Which happens to be my girl's favorite."

I melted every time he called me that. "I love being your girl," I told him, whispering.

He brushed his fingers into my hair, holding me and slanting his lips over mine, kissing me so deeply, I forgot where we were until the cold crept through my coat. As I shivered, he pulled back and stretched to the side, clicking on our space heater.

"There's a meteor shower," he murmured, pressing our foreheads together while warmth pervaded the air. "The Quadrantids. I think we'll find it in the northeast. Want to look?"

My heart ached, so full it hurt. Every day, he showed me how much he loved me in a hundred tiny ways—keeping track of shifting celestial events was only one of them. He'd effortlessly taken to the pastime I shared with my father, snapping the telescope together and navigating the dark sky like a pro. I suspected he snuck away a few times to learn what he was doing before ever giving me my gift or bringing me along.

Within minutes, he had the scope settled, pointed in the proper direction. He wrapped my blanket around me and popped the Dom to pour out two glasses.

"To you, Ellie," he said, his gaze turning intense while we clinked.

A blush blazed over my face. "To us," I corrected.

We huddled over the telescope, each of us taking turns keeping vigil for streaks of light. While we waited, we talked. Somehow, the time we spent together in the evenings—whether we were cuddled on his couch, up on the roof, or lying in bed—always lent itself to deeper conversations.

Tonight, he surprised me. "Ellie?"

I peered into the lens. "Mm hmm?"

"If he were here with us, how do you think your father would feel about me?"

It didn't feel like a casual question. I could tell he'd spent a long time pondering it, wondering if he could ask me. And, as I faced him, I saw that my answer meant a lot to him. His eyes glowed, swirling wistfully.

I reached over and ran my fingertips over the edge of his square jaw. A small smile pulled at my lips while I considered the man I loved meeting the man who raised me. "He'd probably think you were too flashy, at first. I know you're not, really, but the suits and the cars and whatnot sort of lend that air."

Gray's mouth flattened into a line. "Hmmm." He tucked a strand of my hair behind my ear, following the movement with his gaze. "You said, 'at first'?"

"Yes, at first," I confirmed. "But, then, once he got to know you… I imagine he'd see what's undeniable."

His lips quirked into a soft curve. "That I love you? More than life?"

A warm rush flared in my chest. "Yes, but there's more than that. I think he'd see how brilliant you are—always capable and informed. And how thoughtful you are—the way you weigh your words before you speak, the things you remember, how you always keep your promises. He'd see that you're kind and generous; and that I love you. Very much."

Gray held himself still, reading every line of my face. "Do you think he would approve?"

I couldn't stand the uncertainty creasing his expression. I moved to sit in his lap, wrapping my arms around his neck. "Of course he would," I assured him. "Especially now that you have me out here hunting meteors."

That earned me a grin. Grayson leaned around me to look down into the scope. "I think I see something," he murmured. "Here, look."

We both stood, hovering over the lens while I closed one eye and stared with the other. Sure enough, bands of light zipped through the sky. I bounced in place. "*Wow.* This is amazing! Look at how many there are!"

He did, bending to peer into the telescope while wrapping his arm around my waist, keeping me close. "It's incredible," he agreed. "There are tons."

Ever a gentleman, he relinquished the device to me indefinitely, happy to stand by while I enjoyed my gift. "I just love this," I told him, running my hand over it. "What made you think to get me one?"

Grayson waited for me turn to him before folding me back against his chest. "Do you remember that first night I ever called you? When you were sad because you couldn't see the moon?"

It was the first time I ever mentioned my father to him. The first time I ever felt the inexplicable soul-deep connection stirring between us. I'd never forget it.

"Yes, of course."

He blew out a deep breath. "Before you," he murmured, his gaze achingly intense. "That's what my life was like. I knew there was more, out there, but I couldn't see it. I couldn't feel it. The lights and the city and the noise just sort of… drowned out everything. But then you came along. And I could *see*. All the color and wonder and light that I'd been missing… I saw it all." He brushed his lips over my temple, nuzzling. "You're my telescope, Ellie."

Tears stuck in my throat. I opened my mouth to speak, but, then, he moved, taking both of my hands in his and stepping back to go to one knee. I gasped, my eyes overflowing.

Gray smiled slightly, beaming up at me from his place on the floor. "You showed me how brilliant my life could be," he went on. "All I needed was you; and you are all I will ever need, Ella Jane Callahan. It would truly be the greatest honor of my life if you would be my wife."

He pulled a red box from his coat, holding it up to me. "Will you marry me?"

Grayson

I had no idea what time it was and I didn't give a damn.

"Yes."

Ella's breathy acceptance echoed through my mind the entire time I held her, kissing her until both of us were panting, sending clouds of elated disbelief swirling through the chilled air. I sealed my mouth over hers again and again—rough, hard, slow, soft, fast. I kissed her any way I possibly could, pouring all of the joy and adoration she gave me back into her.

Warm tears ran over her cool cheeks, melting into my hands, our lips. When I pulled back to meet her eyes, she giggled. The sweet sound reverberated through my chest, piercing my heart with a pulsing ache.

"We're getting married," she whispered, dazed and elated.

"We are getting married," I vowed. With those words, victory swooped through me. The feeling was so strong, I found myself lifting her body into mine and spinning us both, laughing.

In a dizzy rush, we collapsed between the stools and the space heater. Ella straddled my lap, her luminous sapphire eyes glowing down at me. A tiny smirk played at her kiss-swollen lips.

"Okay, Stryker," she teased, holding out her palm. "Let me see the merchandise."

Love for her burst through me all over again while I chuckled, bringing the ring box in my fist to her waiting hand. I set the red leather cube there, flipping the lid back as I retreated.

"Oh my—" Her reply drifted into stunned silence while she stared at the oval diamond.

"It's engraved," I told her, resting my forehead against her shoulder, kissing the curve of her collarbone.

She slid the ring from its velvet perch, turning the soft gold band to see the inscription I added weeks earlier. "For Ella," she read aloud, "For always."

A riff on her book's dedication. The four words that brought me back to her. Now, she'd have them on her finger forever, the same way I carried them in my soul.

Radiant happiness glittered in her eyes, spilling over her face. "Oh, Grayson." She burrowed closer to me, turning to press a kiss to my face. "It's *perfect*."

My pride swelled. I reached for her slender fingers, plucking the ring up and holding her left hand aloft, sliding the engagement ring onto her third finger, where it fit seamlessly. I turned her wrist gently, watching the city lights play off the sparkling stone.

"I've had it for three years," I confessed. "I could never get rid of it. I knew, deep down, it would be yours someday."

Ella kissed me, her full lips coaxing mine open so she could slip her tongue against mine. I responded in kind, relishing the feel of her on top of me, all around me. Off in the distance, fireworks started up. The salvo reminded me of my other plans.

Reluctantly, I glanced at my watch. *11:47*.

We were cutting it pretty damn close.

"I have another surprise for you," I mumbled against her lips, unable to stop kissing her. "Downstairs. But, now, I'm thinking maybe we should just run away together. Or stay here forever."

She made a pained sound of exasperation. "*Another* surprise? Gray, this is already so wonderful. I'm getting *you*. Forever. You never need to give me anything else."

She meant those words. Her guileless sincerity soaked down into my soul, sending a steady pulse of warmth through me. "I know," I murmured back. "But I wanted us to celebrate with all of our closest friends and family. They're all down in our apartment, hoping you said yes."

A dazzling smile stretched over her face. "Otherwise it would be a pretty depressing New Year's party, huh?"

"Yes," I laughed, hauling us both to our feet. "So we better get down there, Mrs. Stryker."

When the elevator spat us into the Hallway to Nowhere, Ella paused, holding me back. "Wait," she whispered, gently pushing me into the wall. "Just one more."

I knew her game. Ever since moving in with me, she took any and every opportunity to make out with me in the useless space outside our door. It took me a few weeks to realize… she wanted to fill the small strip with happy memories, turning the hallway I hated into a place I enjoyed.

And damn if it didn't work.

My body pressed along the length of hers, grinding into her softness for a moment while I braced my arms over her head. Just when I started to wish we'd run off alone, Ellie broke away and tossed me an impish smile. "Okay," she said, biting her lip and casting a teasing look to the semi encased in my pants. "I'm ready to go in now."

Minx. I'd have to get her back for that later. And every part of me looked forward to it. Grinning, I pulled my coat closed and turned to swipe the doors open.

"*Congratulations!*"

The penthouse erupted in cheers and camera flashes, capturing the moment we walked in with Ella's hand held up between us. My final surprise—her mother and sister, both flown in that morning via private jet—barreled out of the crowd first. Ella squealed, embracing them both and bouncing in a cluster while they all spoke at once.

My mother and father came toward us, as well. Mom gushed as she dabbed at her eyes, snapping me into a hug. Dad clapped his hand on my shoulder, grinning. Our eyes met over Mom's head.

"I'm proud of you, son."

Gratitude put a lump in my throat. "Thanks, Dad."

Mom turned to Ellie next, both of them shrieking their excitement. In the months since our reunion, they'd grown extremely close. Normally, they spent at least a couple mornings each week in each other's company—shopping trips, yoga classes, excursions to source the best pastries on the island. Giving my mother the daughter she always wanted was just one of the endless facets of joy Ella brought to my life.

While they fussed over Ella's ring, I turned to her mother. A slight woman with Ella's light hair and tight, anxious features, I'd found that Matilda Callahan only smiled where her daughters were concerned. Though, when I moved to embrace her, a genuine grin softened the lines of apprehension around her pale hazel eyes.

"Grayson," she said warmly. "This is a lovely surprise you put together for Ella. Thank you."

Like her daughter, she had a habit of thanking me constantly for no reason. "Thank *you*," I corrected. "I know you had to rearrange things to be here on such short notice. I wish I could have asked for your permission sooner than last week, but I felt it was important for us to meet in person beforehand."

"It was no trouble," she insisted, though I could see that wasn't true. Matilda worked nights and double-shifts to pay for her daughters' educations, their home. Well, she *did*, anyway. As of the following day, January first, she'd no longer have a mortgage payment. Or any other outstanding debt. None of the Callahans knew that, yet, though.

I knew Ella would put up a fuss, but it was important to me. As far as I was concerned, we were all family, now. I could never watch her mother struggle while I sat on untouched millions.

We had the same argument about Ella's job. After Idealogue fired her, she insisted on looking for a replacement position immediately. I, on the other hand, insisted she use her newfound freedom to work on another book.

After finally reading her first one in its entirety, I saw that I was initially correct—her writing was brilliant. It seemed others agreed—by the time we moved from the St. Regis back to my penthouse, her sales amounted to a sizable portion of her previous monthly income.

I still refused to allow her to cover any expenses, but the money she made from her writing was enough to give her financial independence, otherwise. By the end of October, she stopped mentioning looking for a new job and started spending her days holed up in her ugly orange chair or at the coffee shop up the block, typing away, hell bent on finishing the next installment of her series before spring.

Watching her work became one of my favorite pastimes. She strictly prohibited reading over her shoulder, but I could mostly tell what sort of scene she was working on from her posture and her facial expressions.

Slumped and scowling—intense drama. Thoughtfully chewing her lips and sitting up straight—something philosophical. Casting me surreptitious glances when she thought I wouldn't notice—sex scene.

I dismissed the thought, clearing my throat while her mother stepped aside. A second later, Darcy practically tackled me. I caught her slight, gangly frame by the elbows, holding her upright while she burst, "OhmyGod! I can't believe I'm actually going to have a brother! A brother with *his own plane*. OhmyGod, Gray, it was so cool in that thing. Did you know you have satellite internet on there? *Insane*."

She was the only other person who ever dared to call me Gray; because, I suspected, it never even occurred to her not to. Ella found it annoying, but I secretly loved it.

"And I get an irritating little sister," I quipped, slinging my arm around her shoulders. "You'll have to help me sell Ellie on the jet. She worries about the carbon footprint."

Darcy rolled the hazel-blue eyes hidden behind heavy tortoiseshell glasses. "Oh *please*, she's marrying a cajillionaire. She can deal. Tell her to plant a forest or something."

Like her big sister, Darcy made me laugh. Her complete and utter obliviousness, mixed with her refreshing tendency to over-share, got me every time. I was still snickering when Ella rejoined us, pinning her little sister with an arch, reproachful big-sister look that somehow turned me on all over again.

"Darcy," she scolded, "are you minding your manners?"

Darcy huffed. "Um, duh."

All traces of mulishness vanished from her slender face as her eyes went wide. I turned, tracking her gaze to Graham as he approached us, holding a drink in each hand.

Oh God.

With a textbook teen-girl squeak, Darcy slunk away. We both watched her go, bemused, before Ellie shook her head. "She thinks Graham is gorgeous," she whispered. "She saw a picture of the three of us online and she's been asking about him ever since."

Over my dead body. I guffawed. "Let's not tell him. His ego doesn't need the boost."

With a nod and a dazzling grin, Ella spun to embrace my best friend. "Shithead!"

Graham chuckled fondly, handing each of us a flute of champagne. "The Little Woman," he clucked back at her. "For some reason, Beth assigned me the duty of delivering your drinks."

"She plays to all of our strengths," I deadpanned, sipping my champagne.

Graham narrowed his dark eyes at me, even as his grin widened. "Tell me," he said to Ella, "when you're married, will Grayson wear a bell? Or will a regular collar suffice?"

While my fiancée laughed, delighted, I feigned annoyance. Glowering, I cast my eyes over his ridiculous party outfit—a pair of black trousers with fine silver pinstripes and a matching sport coat trimmed with flashy silver sequins. "You look like a disco ball."

Graham shrugged, unbothered. "And you look like an undertaker on Casual Friday," he returned. "At least I'm *festive*." His eyes flashed over to my big screen, where a muted program displayed the famous Big Times Square New Year's Eve Ball, poised to drop in a matter of moments. "Speaking of which, I believe it's time for me to find the lucky lady I'll be kissing at midnight."

He loped off, heading toward the busty woman tending my penthouse's wet bar. Ella and I both shook our heads. She stared hard at his sparkly back, her gaze contemplative. "Hmm," she said, then lifted her shoulders and sipped from her flute. "I don't buy it. I give him six months, tops."

"Until...?" I prompted.

She aimed a beatific grin at me. "Until he's as hopelessly in love as you are."

I laughed loudly. Though Ella's intuition was second-to-none, there was simply no way my shithead best friend would settle down any time soon.

"You mean as hopelessly in love as *we* are?" I shot back, setting both of our glasses down to draw her into my arms.

All levity vanished from her fathomless blue eyes while she gazed at me. Her hands floated up to my face and I felt the cool touch of her engagement ring against my cheek. "Yes," she murmured, entirely sincere. "That is exactly what I mean."

All around us, our guests began counting down. But I couldn't wait. I bent and sealed our lips together, not caring who saw. In full view of everyone who mattered, I kissed Ellie—my bright, beautiful girl, my future bride—holding her close as we embarked on a new era.

***

A NOTE TO READERS

THANK YOU SO MUCH FOR JOINING ME ON THIS JOURNEY.

IF YOU LOVED GRAYSON AND ELLA,
FOLLOW ME FOR INFO ABOUT THEIR SEQUEL,
ALMOST ALWAYS.
(I MEAN, GRAYSON STRYKER IN A WEDDING TUX? PLEASE.)

AND… IF YOU FOUND YOURSELF INTRIGUED
BY A CERTAIN HANDSOME, WELL-DRESSED SHITHEAD,
GRAHAM EVERETT'S STAND-ALONE NOVEL
FOR EVER
IS NOW AVAILABLE!

HERE'S A SNEAK PEEK INSIDE THE MIND
OF OUR FAVORITE MANHATTAN PLAYBOY…

Sneak Peek of For ever, The second instant always stand-alone novel

January 20, 2017

Graham

It was hard to tell exactly how fucked I was.

But the fact remained, I definitely should not have been there.

That didn't stop me from lying about having an appointment with a dentist. It didn't stop me from hailing a cab and taking it up to midtown instead of over to Wall Street. It didn't stop me from throwing a $50 at the driver and striding up to the building like I owned the place.

I figured—Grayson was my best friend and *he* owned the place, so close enough.

The lobby of Stryker & Sons brought elegant minimalism into this century. The base of the twisting cylindrical building sprawled for fifty yards in any direction. Snowy marble covered the expanse, gleaming in the weak January sunshine.

The pure white stone reflected enough light to burn my eyes. Instead, I focused on the one focal point of the monochromatic scape—a wide, obsidian vein that started in the center of the room and stretched toward the elevators, into a gaping yawn of onyx.

And there, amidst all the black, I saw her.

A bolt of heat snaked down my spine, stopping me mid-stride. My hands fisted in my pockets while my eyes followed the blatantly sensual sway of her hips.

Hot damn.

Had I ever seen such a dirty girl before? My cock told me no—but he was a notoriously fickle bastard. *Surely*, she wasn't the sexiest thing I'd ever seen. I dated famous super models. Visited brothels in Thailand, Amsterdam's famed Red-Light District.

Why, then, did this random woman stop me in my tracks?

Was it the red dress? I had to admit, no matter how pedestrian the proclivity, the color appealed to me. Like a bull reacting to the crimson flash of a matador's cape.

But I refused to believe I was that easy.

No, it must have been the way the cut followed every line of her dangerous curves. *Lethal* curves. At least from the back…

Deep red fabric skimmed over her thighs and covered an absolutely stunning ass. Up higher, it nipped into a tight, thick waist before flaring a bit up top to accommodate two ripe, round breasts. The slit in the back offered a tantalizing glimpse of her thighs. Bare—which was curious, considering the 20-degree weather outside. Almost as intriguing as the gold coat draped over her arm, a shimmering "notice-me" signal.

All signs pointing to girl who wanted it. Bad.

My body moved of its own volition, clipping across the marble floor with too much haste to maintain my usual air of detachment. I couldn't stop, though.

The elevator opened and I guess I stepped on. All I knew was, I was there and so was she. The matte black doors slid closed at my back. My gaze rolled over the front of her. My mouth watered.

Jesus.

The square neckline of that godforsaken dress might as well have been a frame for the perfect caramel swells of her cleavage—outlined by the dark crimson fabric on three sides and the thick gold chain clasped around the base of her throat.

And what a picture they made. Art, plain and simple.

I stared. Gaped, really.

And she noticed. Of course. Because I was the only other person on the damn elevator and I hadn't even bothered to pick a floor.

"Excuse me?"

Ah shit.

Without a word, I turned and hit the top button—Stryker & Sons executive floor—before shoving my hand back into my pocket, fisting it around my phone again.

The air grew awkward, but I decided not to address her indignant remark. It was one elevator ride. A minute at most. A stranger I'd never have to see again. I slipped my phone out of my pocket and moved to swipe it open.

"*Excuse me.*"

That time, the sharp edge of her voice instantly turned my head. Her breasts leapt out at me again, drawing my focus before I even had a chance to glance at her face.

They really were exceptional.

It was rare to get to ogle a random woman so completely, too. Most of them spun away or covered themselves up on instinct. But this woman did neither. Instead, she stood taller, sticking her tits out even more.

Fuck me.

A husky, humorless laugh sliced through the confined space. "You *wish*, asshole."

Christ. I said that out loud?

Irritated with myself for my exaggerated attraction—and her for picking such an insanely hot dress—I scoffed. "Baby, if you don't want to be fucked, maybe you shouldn't dress like you do."

WHAP

Her palm connected with the side of my face, backed by stinging force. The shock of it finally jolted me from my gawking. Automatically, my eyes flew to her flushed, furious face.

That *gorgeous*, flushed, furious face.

Arresting gold eyes snapped with fire, lending her lush frown true ferocity. A dark blush stained her high, wide cheekbones, highlighting the diamond shape of her face and the way it tapered to a pointed, defiant chin.

Her gaze bored into mine, unrelenting. So fiercely revolted, I felt it scrape at my insides. If I ever wondered what true hatred looked like, now I knew.

It was a fearsome, beautiful sight to behold.

While I stared, the heat blazing in her golden depths cooled into disdain. She reached up as if to deliver another blow.

And—*goddamn it*—I flinched.

Victory lit her gaze and played at the corners of her full, wide lips. Instead of striking me, she merely reached for the control panel and hit a button somewhere in the forties. It didn't even occur to me to look at the directory and check which business she visited. I was too busy fuming.

"Are you aware," I hissed, "that you just assaulted me?"

But she simply tossed her dark, glossy hair back as the elevator glided to a halt. Cocking a single brow, she shot me a derisive look over her shoulder. "Sue me."

Get **For ever** free on Kindle Unlimited now!

ACKNOWLEDGMENTS

First and foremost, I owe all the gratitude in the world to my incredible friend. Kelly, none of this would have happened without you. I wrote my whole life and never had anyone show as much encouragement and commitment toward my dream as you have. Thank you so much for all of the support. You are the very best editor, beta-reader, social media advisor, Basic Bitch music consultant, and kick-in-the-ass I could ever hope for and I thank the Lord every day for you! As our favorite girl would say, "I love you so much!"

To G, who has been with me on this journey since we were sitting next to each other in middle school—thank you for always being in my corner and cheering me on. There have been so many times I would have given up if not for your encouragement. I love you like a sister.

And to Katie, who does not read, but assures me I am talented despite not having any proof. Your friendship, enthusiasm, and the memories we've shared are inked into every story I write. As always, it's you and me forever, babe.

To my loving and supportive family—thank you for giving me all the tools I needed to get here. From my education to the conscience that guides my heart, I would truly have and be nothing without you. Every story you told, every life lesson you shared, and every value you instilled goes into the worlds and characters I create. I am so proud of that.

To my third grade teacher and middle school English teacher. I will not name them in the interest of their privacy, but I must mention them here because they taught me how to write, how to edit, and—most importantly—how to love reading. I will always be eternally grateful to them both.

Last and most importantly: Matthew. Thank you for supporting me endlessly on this journey. Thank you for your incredible patience as I spent hours and days and weeks and months bringing my stories to life. Thank you for pretending to like them when you read them, even though they're not sci-fi novels or history books. Thank you for making time and space for me to grow this part of my soul. I could not "have it all" without you. You are the best choice I ever made and I love you so much.

About Ari

Ari Wright resides in a sun-soaked corner of the United States, where she spends her days raising littles, cooking, reading, consuming massive amounts of music, and doing entirely too much daydreaming.

Ari began writing novels at the age of twelve. A passionate book-lover all her life, her mother once joked that she had to start writing her own stories because she had read everyone else's. After fifteen years of writing, Ari finally set out to author her debut contemporary romance novel. It has been her lifelong dream to share the worlds inhabiting her mind with others. Welcome to her dream come true!

Made in the USA
Middletown, DE
15 October 2023